Daughter of the Rose

Rick Lee

2QT Limited (Publishing)

First Edition 2012

2QT Limited (Publishing)
Burton In Kendal
Cumbria LA6 1NJ
www.2qt.co.uk

Cover design by Martyn Davis
www.marengo.cc

Typesetting by Dale Rennard

Printed in Great Britain by Lightning Source UK Ltd

This is a work of fiction and any resemblance to any person living or dead is purely coincidental.
The place names mentioned are real but have no connection with the events in this book

A CIP catalogue record for this title will be available from the National Library
ISBN 978-1-908098-47-4

To Rob + Lois

long time no see!

Rick

April 2012

Dedication

To Dorothy — both of them!

Acknowledgements

I'd like to thank my friends Carola Makowitz, Aline Rideau and Neil Taylor for their continuing enthusiasm, constructive criticism, encouragement and support.

Karen Holmes for being both a wise and straight talking editor.

CHAPTER 1

Fern Robinson didn't become a serial killer until after her mother died.

Her mother had not lingered, slipping away unaccompanied in her sleep as the sun set on her eightieth birthday on Sunday, February 29th 1976. Fern had been the previous evening. Her mother was asleep most of the time when she visited. Fern knew that it wasn't the drugs; her mother wasn't ill, didn't complain of any pain, but the nurses sedated her as a matter of course. Afterwards Fern found a stash of pills in a hidden pocket of her mother's handbag. She showed the staff nurse, who pulled a face. Fern had smiled at her. She'd enjoyed that – stuck-up cow.

Her mother had only opened her eyes once during that last visit. Fern was reading and had looked up instinctively to find the clear blue eyes gazing straight at her.

'One white rose, my dear. Only the one.'

Fern was about to speak, but her mother gave a contented smile and closed her eyes. She knew then that her mother was going to die the next day. She knew why, and a long unacknowledged sense of injustice stirred within her.

Ursula Robinson was buried in Shap graveyard on the 3rd of March 1976, alongside her mother Annie. She'd outlived many of the folk who'd been evacuated from Mardale, but there were nearly twenty people at the funeral – many of whom Fern didn't know. Folk like them didn't say much, but Annie's niece Elizabeth was there. She didn't walk so well and was helped to the graveside by her son, John. She looked down at the single white rose, which Fern had obediently placed on the coffin.

'Ay, well,' the old lady said. 'There's a strange tale goes wi' yon flower, lassie.'

Fern looked at the old lady, who was just a bit older than her mother. She might be crippled with arthritis, but her hazel eyes beamed intelligently.

'I know,' said Fern quietly.

She could feel Elizabeth's gaze on her but wouldn't meet it. Eventually she heard the old lady sigh.

'Some things are best forgotten. No point in digging up old bones, eh, lass?'

Fern looked at her. Old bones? What did she know? Did she know her mother's real name – Rose-Marie de Blanche – or why Annie Robinson had brought her up as one of her own? She decided it was best not to ask.

'I'll not forget,' she said and turned away. She walked out of the graveyard without another word. She knew where she was going.

The old path through Swindale to Haweswater would take her a couple of hours at least, but she knew this was what her mother would have wanted. Hopefully she'd be able to cadge a lift back to Penrith from someone. She'd spent a lot of time on these fells when she was younger. Even after they'd been evacuated from Mardale, her Robinson cousins regarded the wild black horses as theirs, though truth to tell they were free spirits. She'd managed to ride one or two herself and still remembered the fear and the excitement as she hung on as fiercely as she could, with the high white clouds billowing over the tops.

Fern saw the distinctive black shapes high on Selside as she reached the col. She looked down at the lake. The reservoir was full. She could see a few of the field walls climbing up into Riggindale, but little else to show where her mother had grown up. All now under water. A drowned village. A lost childhood. Dreadful memories. Her mother had come to terms with her demons long ago. Her nightmares had faded. She had made peace with her past. Only the rose remained.

Fern closed her eyes.

A once familiar call woke her. She must have slept where she'd sat down and it was now late afternoon. She looked up into the blue sky and focused on the slow, sweeping glide of a Riggindale eagle. It called again and there was her mate floating over Harter Fell. She watched them as they effortlessly surveyed their domain and wished she was as free.

It only took half an hour to reach the road and, minutes later, she was in a car with two young lads driving back to Penrith after a long day on the fells. She bought them a drink in the pub and they were gone. She'd stayed on and drunk too much; went home with Jimmy Mack and hated herself even more in the morning.

* * * *

She didn't choose her first victim; the woman pushed herself into the frame. In fact, it had never occurred to Fern that a vengeful act might bring her some comfort. She'd never hurt any

3

living creature before. She was the one who scolded the boys for torturing frogs and spiders.

After that first night, when she'd lapsed into a drunken coma while Jimmy tried his best, she'd not had a decent sleep without alcohol – although she'd generally been able to avoid the other part of the treatment. In her experience, sex had always been something to be endured; even the one time it had created something beautiful. In her innocence and despair she'd thought that working as a nurse in a children's home might be a way of making up for losing her own child – an event she kept locked away – and her mother's story was the stuff of nightmares.

The children who ended up in the home had their own horrors to keep them awake at night. Fern came to look forward to the night shifts, because that was when they most needed someone. Most of them came from what she'd learned to call 'deprived homes', although she had her own views about what that might mean. Her own mother had lived in a two-room flat owned by the pub she worked in, where she'd ended up after being evacuated from Mardale. They had very few possessions. Her father, John Tirril, had died in 1936 during the Spanish Civil War shortly after Fern was born. It was only when she was old enough to earn some money as well that she and her mother were able to find a small house to rent. One of her mother's friends had a hairdresser's shop and Fern had started on evenings and Saturdays, brushing the floor. Slowly she'd learnt the trade and was surprised and proud when people started asking for her. Her skill had come in handy later, when she'd had to leave the children's home.

But there was a young girl who arrived one bright spring morning in late March 1976, only weeks after Fern's mother's funeral, who changed everything. Fortune had decided that Fern

4

should be the senior person on duty when the police car arrived and a WPC helped the girl into the reception area. She wasn't crying – that was to come later – just numb with fear and despair. The WPC was visibly relieved to have completed her part of the rescue and hurried out, saying she would be in touch.

Fern could see immediately that this was no ordinary case. The girl was well dressed, her hair was fashionably cut and she was clean. The only signs of the trauma she'd been through were her swollen face and glazed expression. Fern took her to the duty doctor who quickly ascertained that although her face didn't look pretty, the girl's injuries didn't merit a visit to the hospital. Her mental condition was another matter.

Fern took her to a single room. She knew better than to try questioning her about what had happened yet.

'What's your name?' she asked.

The girl looked at Fern as though she'd hit her.

'I'm called Fern. I work here. I'm here to look after you. You don't need to be frightened.'

The girl looked around the room as though she was checking for escape routes. Fern sat on the bed, leaving the way to the open door available. The girl considered this for a moment and then reluctantly sat on the chair. Fern waited, didn't stare at her, but looked out of the window. She gave the girl chance to look at her, size her up.

'We've got a big garden here. The other children like to play out as often as they can.'

The girl paused, still not looking at her.

'Many of them have never had their own garden. What about you?'

Now Fern allowed herself a sideways glance. The girl was staring out at the trees.

'We've got a big garden, too,' she said. 'My mother loved her flowers.'

It was the moment when the seed was sown. Fern didn't question her any more that morning. The girl's words disturbed her. She decided to leave her be for a while.

Surprisingly, the WPC was true to her word; more often than not they were glad to get the kids off their hands. It was always difficult with domestic cases, but children made it ten times worse. She reappeared two days later and asked for Fern.

'What has Dawn told you?' she asked.

'Not a lot, but that's fairly normal.'

'I know that, but she's not your normal sort of case.'

'What makes you say that?'

'Well, I'm sure you realised she doesn't come from a poor background,' said the police woman.

'Yes and the other children were quick to spot that as well! She's not found it easy.'

The police woman paused, then she said, 'My name's Yvonne, by the way.'

Fern smiled. 'It's not often we get return visits from the same officer,' she said.

Yvonne returned the smile.

'Well, it's not often we get a case like this. Not that the other kids deserve less attention,' she was quick to add.

'You don't have to explain yourself to me,' countered Fern.

Yvonne gave her another thin smile. 'It's just that I find it difficult to believe,' she said.

Fern sighed. 'I think I've probably lost any ability to be surprised by what some people do to their children.'

'But this family is seriously well off!' exclaimed Yvonne.

'So . . .?' asked Fern, with a frown.

Yvonne gave her an uncertain look and launched into the story. And that's when the seed began to grow.

*   *   *   *

Dawn Courtney was just sixteen when Fern met her in March 1976. It was only when the woman doctor insisted on a full examination that they began to understand what was going on. Dawn was covered in old bruises. The doctor reckoned she'd probably suffered from broken ribs and later X-rays confirmed this. She was thin, like many teenage girls, but her weight was verging on anorexic. She had no appetite when she arrived and seemed very lethargic, more so when she stopped flinching every time a door opened or someone approached her unexpectedly. For more than a week she wouldn't say anything about what had happened. WPC Yvonne Dodds had warned that the parents would cause trouble and they did. Fern's boss had to speak to the Director of Social Services and get a court order before they backed off, but not before threatening legal action. Yvonne said her inspector reckoned they had only a couple of weeks to come up with some hard evidence or they'd lose Dawn.

It was early one morning towards the end of a night shift when Fern found her. She couldn't see her at first, but was reluctant to switch the light on. The whimpering sound she heard in the quietness of the sleeping house was more than she could bear. She'd dealt with lots of very distressed children, but this sound was piercing. She moved slowly towards the corner of the bed.

Dawn was huddled as far into the corner as she could get. Her hands were over her head and her eyes were staring into a nightmare. Fern stayed very still. It reminded her of the day she found an abandoned fawn in the woods. It turned out that the mother had been caught in a trap and had died a long slow death. Fern had taken the trembling creature to a vet. It had survived and he'd invited her along the day he released it back into the woods.

She knelt down and waited.

Eventually Dawn's eyes focused on her. A look of terror was slowly replaced by a harder gaze. Fern stayed where she was. The girl rubbed her eyes and lay on the floor.

'If you tell me what's been happening to you, I can make it stop.'

Dawn stared at her for a long time. Fern's knees were aching. She was about to change position when the girl spoke.

'She's not my real mother. My real mother died when I was six. I remember my dad crying. Day after day. I looked after him.'

Fern managed to stretch her legs out and leant against the bed.

'We were fine for a bit. We looked after each other. He stopped crying. I stopped crying. But we both missed Mum.'

She looked sternly at Fern. 'I'm not a baby. I can look after myself,' she said.

Fern nodded.

'I never thought that he'd meet someone else. I was too young. I think I understand now, but when she arrived two years ago I couldn't believe it.'

She began to cry. Fern wanted to hold her, but knew that wouldn't work. Through the tears Dawn told her terrible story.

'She was kind at first: bought me presents, took me shopping, lots of lovely clothes, all the things I never got to do with my real mother.'

The tears became angry.

'But then she changed: started to whisper horrible things, told lies to my father, made him angry with me. She broke a vase that he gave to my mother. I saw her do it deliberately. I told him. They had a row, but she convinced him that I'd broken the vase and was blaming her because I hated her. And he listened to her. I couldn't believe it.'

'She was jealous,' offered Fern.

Dawn gave her a fierce look.

'That's what she said was wrong with me. That I was the jealous one.'

'So when did she start hitting you?'

Dawn huddled back into the corner and began to shake. Fern worried that she'd pushed too quickly, but it all came tumbling out.

'She's evil. She punches me, pinches me, waits till I'm asleep and puts a pillow over my face. Last week she tried to strangle me. Look!' She opened her nightdress and showed Fern the marks.

'I showed my father the bruises. She denied it – said I must have got them at school. He went to the school, made me show my bruises to the headmistress. She said she'd find out who was bullying me. She had all my friends in one by one and demanded to know who was hurting me. They were upset and angry with me. They thought I'd been telling lies to get them into trouble. It didn't matter what I said. No-one believed me.'

She broke down and cried pitifully. Still Fern held back, afraid to interrupt.

Eventually, Dawn sobbed herself to a standstill.

'I tried to run away but she caught me and tied me up. Put me in the cellar, in the dark. My father was away for a week. Each day she came down and tortured me. She didn't need to do very much. Just an occasional slap. It was what she said she was going to do that was the worst. Needles and knives and poking my eyes out. She's a monster.'

Fern reached out and offered her hand.

'My father came back, but she told me that she'd kill me if I said anything. So I didn't say a word. I was too frightened.'

Dawn put her hand in Fern's. It was cold. Icy. Fern held it hard.

'But the worst thing was what she did to my father. She knew I could hear.'

Fern held her breath.

'I could hear them arguing and I crept out of my room. She was screaming at him. He was saying he was sorry. I could hear her slapping him, hitting him. He was begging her to forgive him. It went quiet. I could hear her voice. It was sarcastic. I couldn't hear what she was saying, but I knew it was unpleasant. He was whimpering like a puppy. I couldn't bear it, I put my hands over my ears and tried to shut it out, but then I saw him.'

She couldn't go on; couldn't, wouldn't say what she'd seen, shook her head as though she was trying to shake the images away. She shuddered and looked Fern in the face.

'I ran back to my room. It went on and on. It was terrible.'

Fern held her close and felt the poor girl sob till there was no breath left. Afraid to interrupt, until the morning light slid into the room and Dawn completed the story.

'When the noises stopped, she came for me. I knew she would. She had the stick in her hand. She didn't use it. She told me that now both of us would do as we were told – for good.'

Fern hugged her until she stopped shuddering.

'The next day I ran away. The police found me. They tried to take me home, but I made them bring me here.'

'It's alright,' said Fern. 'You're safe now. She'll never harm you again.'

Even then she'd no idea how she was going to ensure that safety – but the terrifying resemblance to her own mother's story was what kept Fern awake all night.

CHAPTER 2

Friday 29th February 1980

Detective Inspector Mick Fletcher was trying hard not to sulk. Not that hard. He hated being taken off whatever he was doing and sent on an errand for some rich bastard who had some personal problem coupled with the power to ensure the police responded immediately.

It didn't help that he was doing naff all anyway. He'd ended up being sent even further north to Penrith following his unacceptable behaviour in Rochdale. Never mind that he'd got a commendation for bravery. He'd upset too many toffee-nosed public schoolboys and superior officers to be allowed to stay – and he'd not even received the bloody commendation. The case had been deemed too politically sensitive for public consumption and he'd had to sign several state documents forbidding him to say a word. He knew there were very few further transfers left – he was nearly in Scotty land for God's sake. Next stop Iceland. So here he was, sitting in a car, summoning up as much of a sympathetic persona as he could muster, whilst his sergeant was his usual expressionless self.

Fletcher had worked with a lot of different sergeants: male and female, sarcastic and clever, big-heads and vicious bastards, but DS Harold Strickland was something else. Nothing got him going. He was efficient; he did everything you asked him to do without so much as a raised eyebrow. Even took the initiative on occasions. He knew his territory and everyone in it going back twenty years or more.

Fletcher had tried winding him up, tried upsetting him, but nothing. Not bright as a button every day – more like a well-polished boot. Not raring to go, just . . . there.

'So what do you know about this lot, Harry?'

Harry looked across at the house gates. They were electronically operated, which wasn't as unusual in the countryside round Penrith as one might expect.

'Do you want the Debrett's version or the police records, sir?' he replied.

'Both.'

'Local family, originally farmers. Sold up in the late sixties, but kept the house and gardens. Mr Charles Soulby, ex-gentleman farmer, now an academic researching the history of local Border families. First wife Liliane, from another local family, died ten years ago. One daughter, Diane, sixteen, at a private school in Windermere. The second wife, Caroline, is from London, I think. She went missing two days ago.'

'Have we been in touch with her family?' asked Fletcher.

'Coming to that, sir,' continued Strickland.

Fletcher kept his mouth shut and listened.

'The wife is the only one to figure in police records, sir. Numerous parking and speeding fines locally and elsewhere, including those in her previous married names and her maiden name Grenville. Many of these infringements were combined with both verbal and physical abuse of investigating officers and traffic wardens. She's been officially warned at least three times, but always hires expensive briefs who bombard the judges with doctors' notes regarding her highly-strung nature and artistic temperament, which they seem to accept . . . sir. She comes from a very wealthy family, but has apparently fallen out with them. Some disagreement over her father's will, I'm told . . .'

'So what do we think?' asked Fletcher.

There was a long pause as Strickland considered this question. Fletcher had taken some time to get used to this, but had come to understand that there was no point in rushing him. It was as if he needed the time to search all his files – no doubt mentally tucking them spine-side right-way-up back into their allotted places after he'd perused them.

'Probably in London sleeping off a hangover.'

'Is that your general opinion of the upper classes, Harry?'

'I don't have an opinion about anyone, sir. Only experience . . . sir,' he replied. Harry didn't do irony, so Fletcher let it go.

'Okay. Let's get on with it. You'll no doubt tell me what your experience informs you after we've spoken to the husband.'

Strickland didn't seem to think this worth commenting on, but indicated right and selected first gear.

A few minutes later they were sitting in Soulby's study accepting the offer of a cup of tea from a Mrs Langdale, who seemed to be some kind of housekeeper although Fletcher suspected she was well past her retirement date.

He let Strickland lead the interrogation. He'd already met Soulby, so it seemed a good idea to let the husband have a soft ride to start with. Fletcher was of the firm belief that husbands should be treated as number one suspects when anything happened to the wife. He didn't think anyone had got round to collating the statistics, but he was confident that it would be nearer eight out of ten than four out of ten husbands who were responsible for the violent deaths of their wives. Mind you, this one looked like he'd buck the trend. He couldn't see this bloke killing anything, never mind a person.

Charles Soulby was slightly built, with thin blond hair. He spoke with a detached Radio Three accent, had a dry handshake and seemed on the verge of tears. Fletcher told his inner homophobe to shut up, but couldn't help thinking that if the wife was half the troublemaker her police record claimed, then she'd drown this poor slice of manhood in her first G&T before lunch.

'So the last time you saw her was on Wednesday?' asked Strickland.

'Well . . . I didn't exactly see her . . . she shouted to me from the hall.'

The two police officers affected polite interest.

'I was in here all day – apart from a stroll round the garden after lunch. I'd been up since about six o'clock. I don't sleep very well . . . and . . . Caroline is a bit of a night bird really so . . . we can go for days without meeting . . .'

His voice tailed off and, as Fletcher feared, he pulled a handkerchief from his pocket and began to sniff.

'Did she say where she was going?' asked Fletcher, hoping to staunch the tears.

He wished he hadn't asked, because this was the question that produced some not unexpected but rather feeble sobs. Eventually Soulby controlled himself and apologised.

'I'm sorry. I'm pathetic. It's just . . . I know that you think we're an odd couple, but–'

He pulled himself together and replaced his thin-rimmed glasses. Fletcher had a fleeting, yet confusing, image of Heinrich

Himmler and was so startled he was lost for words. Strickland glanced at his open-mouthed inspector and pressed on.

'We're not marriage guidance councillors, Mr Soulby. We're just trying to find your wife. So what time was this on Wednesday?'

'I think it must have been late afternoon. It was getting dark.'

'Can anyone else verify this, Mr Soulby?'

Soulby looked at Fletcher like a frightened rabbit caught in the lights of his wife's speeding car. The image of Himmler was dismissed out of hand.

'Er . . . No . . . I don't think so. Mrs Langdale wouldn't have been here at that time of day.'

The woman in question entered with a tray of tea and scones. She agreed with her employer that she hadn't been present on Wednesday evening.

'Mrs Soulby is not a lady one could set one's watch by,' she added.

Mr Soulby nodded with monk-like meekness.

Strickland asked him to provide a recent photograph and a list of names and contact numbers for his wife's friends and relatives. Soulby went and fetched her address book, which was stuffed with lots of letters and notes. Strickland tightened his lips at the prospect of wading through such an untidy collection of documents; he knew that would be his next task. It would have been more useful to see her diary, but Soulby had asserted that she kept it in her handbag. He spent a few agonising seconds staring at the photograph he'd chosen before handing it over.

They were back in the car driving towards Penrith before Fletcher spoke.

'So what do you think now, Sergeant?'

Strickland answered immediately. 'Nothing to make me

change my original assessment,' he said, without even a shrug of his shoulders.

Fletcher wasn't so sure. The local historian had unsettled him. Something he'd said hadn't sounded right – not exactly a lie, but not the whole truth. He looked at the photograph he'd given them. That didn't fit either. This was no Cruella De Vil. She was smiling at the camera. She was attractive in demure sort of way: dark hair blowing in the wind, red and white spotted dress – not what Fletcher had been expecting.

* * * *

They knew the minute they got back to the station that something had happened from the looks on people's faces and the lack of welcoming smiles. They didn't even get to the main office before Sergeant Hornby stopped them.

'We've found a body, sir, near the motorway.'

Fletcher held up the photograph of Soulby's wife. Hornby flinched and nodded.

'I think so, sir.'

They got back in the car and set off. Strickland didn't race anywhere so, by the time they got there, the scene of crime officers were busy. Fletcher had been disconcerted when Strickland had turned off the ring road and driven down the A6 instead of going on to the motorway roundabout. He didn't ask.

He'd been this way with Laura, when they'd taken Grace for a day out. It hadn't gone well. Teenagers weren't interested in historic buildings or walking around gardens.

Strickland went over the bridge and turned right at the end of the houses. A small lane on the right was blocked off and police vehicles were parked everywhere. Blue and white tapes were flapping in the wind.

Fletcher got out of the car and was immediately aware of the motorway traffic. The little lane ran parallel to it and they'd parked near a bridge. Someone had been careful to preserve any tyre or shoe marks by placing a line of planks down the middle of the lane. Two white-coated officers were examining some car treads at the junction. Fletcher and Strickland kept to the planks until they were level with the tapes. Opposite there was a steep embankment with a ring of large trees. A green footpath sign declared it to be Mayburgh Henge.

The body was down the motorway embankment. The traffic police had closed the nearest lane, which slowed the motorists down so they could take a proper look. The sooner they got this sorted the better, thought Fletcher. It was going to cause an accident.

He and Strickland climbed over the fence and made their way down to the blue tarpaulin covering the body. The photographer had just arrived and was nearly ready. One of the SOCOs pulled the covering away. Red and white spotted dress. Dark hair. But definitely not Caroline Soulby.

The pathologist had followed them along the planks and was now kneeling down beside the body. The girl's dress was torn and pushed up round her waist. Fletcher didn't need to ask what had happened to her. The doctor glanced back at him as she pulled back the white cardigan to reveal the woman's face and neck. Fletcher had had enough. He climbed back up to the road and stood looking at the ancient mound. Strickland came up beside him and waited.

'Tell me what you know,' said Fletcher.

'I don't recognise the woman, but when I was young this was a courting spot. Young couples used to come up here on warm summer nights. Old folk would tell you tales about it being a magic place.'

He sniffed and leant over the fence.

'And now?' asked Fletcher, sensing that his sergeant had more to say.

'It's different now. Not the sort of place to bring your girlfriend, especially on a cold night like last night. That's not to say people don't use it, but not young lovers, if you understand what I mean.'

Fletcher had spotted the withered condoms amongst the other rubbish and knew exactly what he meant. The doctor vaulted the fence with ease and came across the road.

'That's just showing off,' said Fletcher, without looking at her.

He'd been told Jane Sykes was a keen fell-runner, the sort of person who hurdled five-bar gates for pleasure. She had that slim, muscle-toned look about her; short blonde hair and no-nonsense blue eyes. She looked at her watch.

'I don't think there's much doubt about cause of death, Inspector, or when. I think we'll find that the poor lass was raped and strangled with her own belt last night round about ten-thirty.'

'I can see the cause, but what makes you so sure about time of death?'

'Chucking-out time, Inspector. I reckon you'll have caught the killer before I've time to do the autopsy.'

'Thanks for the confidence in our investigative prowess, Doctor.'

She gave him a severe look.

'It's not a compliment, Inspector. I'm hoping that you'll find him before her husband or brother finds out – or he'll end up on the next slab in the mortuary by this afternoon. This is Penrith,

19

remember. The sort of family she comes from won't wait for you to carry out your enquiries; they'll find out quick enough and act upon it faster. Am I right, Sergeant?'

Strickland looked at Fletcher and nodded. 'She's right, sir. We'd better get to it.'

Fletcher looked from one to the other, wondering whether he belonged up here in the wild North West. Jane Sykes set off back to her car at a brisk pace.

'Have they found any ID yet?'

'Nothing, sir. I've suggested they widen the search to include the circle.'

Fletcher looked across at the trees.

'Pub to pub enquiries, Sergeant?'

'Already started, sir.'

'Photos?'

'He's promised us them within the hour. He's already on his way back to the lab.'

Fletcher looked at the trees. Their bare branches swayed in the cold wind. 'You carry on, Harry,' he said. 'I'm just going to see if I can feel the magic. Maybe find a handbag while I'm at it.'

He made his way through the sheep gate and set off up the slope. Strickland watched him climb to the ridge of the earthwork, shook his head and went back to the car. When he looked again Fletcher had disappeared.

CHAPTER 3

That same morning, in a small cottage on the edge of Helton a few miles outside Penrith, Octavia Hutton was in a fine temper because she'd broken a mirror. She wasn't superstitious about such things but there was glass everywhere. It was at the last minute, so trying to clear it up made her even later. The mirror was on the wall in the entrance to her little cottage. She'd stopped to take a quick look as she opened the front door. Her hair was a mess; it always was. Unruly curls. Medusa. She made a gruesome face. Then the mirror fell off the wall, hit the metal statue on her great aunt's table and broke into hundreds of pieces. Octavia stood and looked at it in disbelief.

She tried to pick up the bigger pieces too quickly and cut her finger. She decided it would have to wait, went back to shut the door into the corridor so the cat couldn't get through, and crunched her way out into the pale sunrise. She cursed to herself as she unlocked the car door and threw her briefcase onto the passenger seat. The windscreen was covered with a thin layer of pebbled ice. She got out and attacked it with the plastic scraper. It wasn't much good. Back in the car she turned on the engine, put the blowers on full and peered through the small hole she'd managed to make. Another car went slowly past.

A few minutes later, she was making her way out of the village street onto the main road. She was supposed to be in Penrith by nine thirty. It was already twenty-five past and the journey took a good quarter of an hour at the best of times, but it was wiser to take the higher level road than cutting down by the river. She was glad she had the Land Rover her father had bought her when she got the job, but it wasn't the fastest of vehicles.

She was about a mile out of the village when a huge stag leapt out in front of her. Its eyes glowed red in the headlights and she swerved across the road. The creature jumped over the fence from a standing start and charged off into the wood. The back of the Land Rover slewed round as she braked and fought with the wheel. She very nearly kept it on the road but, as it came to a stop, it slowly toppled sideways into the ditch.

As the engine stalled and died, she realised that the deafening noise was coming out of her mouth. She stopped in mid-scream, looked at her trembling hands and burst into tears. A woman's face appeared at the window. She wrenched open the passenger door and reached in towards Octavia.

'Are you alright?'

Octavia managed a nod.

'I . . . I . . . think so!'

'Can you move your legs?'

She found she could. With the woman's help she was able to scramble out through the passenger door. The woman insisted she got into her car and found a blanket to put round her shuddering body. Another car turned up and the woman sent the driver for help.

'I think you're going to be okay,' she said. 'What's your name?'

'Octavia,' she said.

'Good. I'm called Rose; I used to be a nurse. You're probably suffering from shock, but the ambulance will be here soon. Don't worry.'

Octavia nodded helplessly. She was still shivering.

'It was a stag. I don't know how I missed it. It just came out of nowhere.'

The woman nodded and held her hand.

*   *   *   *

Later at the hospital, Octavia couldn't remember much about her Good Samaritan: tall, with short, dark, spiky hair and a stern face. The paramedics had helped her out of the woman's car and put her in the back of the ambulance. The last she'd seen, the woman was getting back into her own car. She couldn't even remember her name and the woman had gone before the police arrived, so there was no way of getting in touch with her to thank her.

Octavia was released from hospital in the late afternoon. Her father arrived and insisted on taking her to his home. By early evening she was tucked up in her old bed, after surrendering to a bowl of soup and a sandwich.

The next day she woke early. Apart from a slight headache and the cut finger, she seemed to have come away largely unscathed from the two accidents. She crept downstairs and made herself a cup of tea. She was standing in the lounge looking out at the familiar view, when her father appeared in the doorway.

'Are you sure you should be out and about, young lady?' he asked in his booming voice.

'I'm fine, Dad. Don't fuss. Nothing broken . . . apart from the car,' she added.

'No. It's just a scrape. Farmer friend of mine pulled it out in a trice. It's out by the stables. Ken's giving it the once over as we speak. Says it'll be as right as rain. A few scratches and a broken wing mirror is nothing to a Land Rover. He says it means you've joined the club now. Proper driver!'

She laughed. He walked over and hugged her. 'It's good to see you standing there. I miss you, you know.'

'Dad, stop it. If you're going to get all soppy, I'll be driving that jalopy out of here in my dressing gown!'

'Sorry, old thing,' he said, biting his lip as the tears welled up.

Octavia held him close until he'd composed himself. Despite his gruff exterior, she knew her mother's death still cut deep like it was yesterday, even though it was nearly twenty years ago.

'Your boss was on the phone last night, wanting to know how you are.'

'Goodness! I forgot all about the solicitor's. What did he say?'

'Not to worry. Everything went to plan . . . and you've got lots of hard work to look forward to.'

'Oh. Great! That means we've got it.'

'I assume so. He didn't give me any further details, but he sounded very pleased with himself.'

'I'd better go and see him,' she said, setting off towards the door.

'Not until you've had one of Mrs. Hesket's breakfasts, you're not.'

Octavia's nostrils told her stomach that this was true. She sighed in mock surrender and went to put some clothes on. She was halfway up the stairs when his voice echoed off the walls.

'And you forgot to say "rabbits"!'

She giggled all the way to her bedroom, but stopped to look out at the bare trees against the glorious morning sunshine. Her father was right; today was the first of March.

*   *   *   *

Over breakfast, her father asked about the 'hard work' she was about to embark upon. She'd not told him anything so far. The team had all been sworn to secrecy while they were awaiting the Court of Probate's decision. She'd had a quick conversation with Martin when she went back to her room. He'd spared her the legalistic jargon and cut straight to: 'We could start today if we wanted to!' She could hear the suppressed jubilation in his voice. It was, after all, a tremendous coup for the local National Trust to acquire such a huge property in such an accessible place.

'I bet you've already worked it out anyway!' she said, cutting herself a chunk of home-reared sausage.

Her father looked at her in surprise.

'Well. I think you overrate my powers of deduction. Especially as there've been bugger-all clues. Although . . .'

'What?'

'It's just something old Jack Harper said after he'd pulled your Land Rover out of the ditch yesterday.'

'Uhuh,' said Octavia through a mouthful of bacon and egg.

'He was just getting up into the tractor, when he turned and gave me one of his looks.'

'And?'

'Strange. He said "Tell't yon lassie o'yors tu mind how she gaas wi big ouse."'

Octavia looked at her father to see if he was winding her up, but his blue eyes were gazing steadily at her. She finished her meal and wiped her mouth.

'Well that's intriguing. How would Jack Harper know about it?'

'Which big house?'

'It's Blanchard House.'

Her father's look told her this was a genuine surprise.

'Martin's been working on this for nearly three years. Yesterday the Probate Office finally decided that it could become the property of the National Trust. It's been abandoned for over sixty years. There is lots of conjecture about what happened, but there are no surviving relatives and previous attempts to claim it have been unsuccessful – until the will turned up.'

'The will? Whose will?'

'Duke Edward de Blanche's will. He was killed in the First World War.'

'So what did it say?'

'Well, he left everything to his daughter, but if she and his wife died before him the property should pass to the National Trust.'

George Hutton stared out of the dining-room window. Octavia waited.

'So what do you know?' she asked.

He looked at her as though he was surprised to see her sitting next to him.

'Sorry. I was miles away.'

'I could tell . . . and a long time back as well, I shouldn't wonder.'

He gave her a quizzical glare.

'Don't get too clever, young lady. Just because you think I'm an old fogey, doesn't mean I didn't have a few adventures in days gone by.'

She grinned and laughed. 'Alright. Tell me what you know and I'll see you're acknowledged in the brochures as a local historian of repute!'

'There's no need to take the mickey. In any case, I don't know very much.'

'Come on, Dad. Cough up.'

He went and poured himself a cup of coffee and stood looking out at the distant fells.

'Once upon a time . . . long before you were born . . . before I'd even met your mother, when I was just a lad . . .'

'Dad, please! Spare me the melodrama! It's excruciating!' she laughed, joining him at the window. 'Just tell me the facts.'

'Ah . . . facts? That's the problem. Stories told on winter's evenings by the fireside to frighten little girls and boys. What I know is only a long-forgotten memory.'

'OK, Dad. Tell it your own way, but I'm going in five minutes.'

He didn't look round, but continued to stare at the skyline.

'It's said that it's haunted. That it's an evil place. A house of dark deeds and terrible secrets.'

Octavia folded her arms and waited, suppressing her cynicism.

'I only went the once. Me and Billy Harper, Jack's brother. It was a dare. The other lads said we were too scared to climb over the wall and go into the house – so we said we'd go one night.'

He looked round to see how she was reacting. She was looking at him with her head to one side, a smile on her face.

'It's true,' he insisted. 'We went one warm summer's night. It was moonlit – not a full moon, but bright enough.'

'So what did you find?'

He hesitated.

'Nothing.'

'Why? Didn't you get into the house?'

'Well, sort of. It wasn't that simple. The walls are over nine feet high and the gates are spiked. We got over the wall, but that was the easy bit. The grounds were almost impossible to get through. It was a forest and no-one had looked after it for . . . must have been well over twenty years, but that wasn't the worst. Once we got closer to the house there was thick undergrowth: nettles, briars – taller than us. We were scratched and stung something terrible. If we hadn't found this little path, we'd have turned round there and then.'

'So did the path take you to the house?'

'Not all the way. It led to a shed; it must have been the gardeners'. There were old tools and mowers, cobwebs and rustling creatures. Rats probably.'

'But did you get to the house?'

'At first we couldn't see a way. The path had finished. We could see the dark outline of the building. A tower. But the briars were even thicker and higher. Then Billy pointed at the wall. The shed was built against it. It went in a straight line towards the house.'

He took a swig of coffee. His eyes were alive with the story; he was there as though it were happening to him right now. Octavia had never seen him so animated and she was spellbound.

'Billy went first. It was tricky. The wall was thick, but it had a rounded crest, so we could crawl along it. Either side we could see the mass of briars reaching up to catch us and pull us down.'

He paused again, thinking, remembering. Then he shivered.

'It must have taken us only five minutes to get right along, but it seemed a lot longer. At the far end there was an archway. We scrambled down to a ledge which ran along the wall of the house just below the windows. We got to the first window. Fortunately one of the panes was broken and Billy was able to reach in and turn the handle.'

He looked down at his hand and then showed it to Octavia. 'Look, there's the scar. I cut my hand on the broken glass.'

She could see the pale smooth mark on the palm of his hand.

'So you went in?'

'Yes . . . but . . .'

'But what?'

'That's as far as we got.'

'Why?'

He looked up from his hand and stared at her.

'It's difficult to explain. You'd think we'd got so far that we should have carried on, but . . .'

'What was it?'

He looked back out the window. 'Nothing. There wasn't anything.'

Octavia reached out and grabbed his arm. He flinched and shivered.

'That was it. There was nothing. No sounds. No little creatures scuttling off into their holes. No cobwebs. Even the air seemed to be empty. I could make out the shapes of furniture covered in sheets. There were big pictures on the walls, but you couldn't see what they were. Just dark rectangles. We couldn't move. Billy started to shiver. It was cold. Freezing.'

He was shivering now. Octavia put her arms round him. He was staring into the past. She shook him. He looked at her without seeing her.

'Dad! Stop it. You're frightening me!' She shook him again.

He sat down on the window ledge and put his hands to his face.

'We got out. I don't know how. We went back along the wall and followed the path. It took us a different way than we'd come, deeper into the forest. We seemed to run for miles.'

He stopped and looked at her. 'I've never told anybody this, you know.'

She nodded and held his hands in hers.

'Not even your mother.'

'It's alright, dad. It's a scary story. I'm glad you didn't tell me when I was younger. It would have given me nightmares for ages.'

He gave her a little smile. 'It's not the end. There was one other thing. It wasn't scary, just odd.'

'What happened?'

He looked back into the past.

'Billy was in front. He was always quicker than me. He suddenly stopped dead in his tracks and I ran straight into him. We both ended up in a heap on the ground. I cursed him, but he wasn't listening or looking at me. He was pointing to the middle of this clearing in the trees. The moon was right above us and a beam of light shone down into the open space . . . and in the middle was one single white rose. Around it the ground was clear. No other roses. No grass or weeds, just earth.'

Octavia held her breath. Then she said, 'So what did you do?'

'Billy wanted to pick it, to prove that we'd been there, but I said not to. I don't know why. Didn't feel right.'

'Did he pick it?'

'No . . . for once in his life, he did what I told him. We made our way round the edge of the clearing, picked up the path on the other side and carried on.'

'Where did it lead?'

'Miles and miles out of our way. Halfway up the fells. The moon went behind some clouds and it started to rain. We found a clump of trees to shelter in and fell asleep. It was after dinnertime before we got home and your granddad gave me the thrashing of my life. My mother didn't speak to me for a week. Billy got the same.'

The two of them sat in silence for a while.

'I hardly ever saw Billy again. We both signed up. He died in the desert, burnt to death in his tank.'

Octavia stared at her father, who looked exhausted. 'Dad, can you write that story down?'

'What? Are you serious?'

'Of course. The kids will love it!'

He looked at her and smiled. Suddenly he stood up and set off towards the door. 'I know you're in a hurry, but just wait there one minute. I'll be back with the proof.'

She stared at the empty doorway and listened as her father ran up the stairs to his room. Two minutes later he reappeared with a triumphant grin on his face. He looked like he was twelve years old again. In his hand he held up a wooden stick.

'Look. What did I tell you? Proof!'

He held it out to her and she took it in her hand. It was a plant marker but not any old bit of stick. It was hard, polished wood, about eight inches long, flat, with a pointed end. She turned it sideways so that she could read the elegant handwriting, saying the words out loud.

'Boule de Neige . . . April 17th 1895.'

Her father took it back and held it up to the light. 'It's a white rose that flowers midsummer and has a strong scent – but look at this.' He showed her the top of the stick which glistened in the sunlight. 'What do you think that is?'

She held it again and angled it so the light caught the embossed initials.

'U . . . de . . . B . . .'

'I'm only guessing, but I suspect the "de B" is de Blanche. I don't know what the "U" stands for, but I'd suggest it's his wife's name.'

Octavia's eyes sparkled and she hugged her father. 'What a treasure! Can I take it to show Martin?'

'Only if I get it back. I gave it to your mother.'

'Oh! Of course – but he'll be dead impressed. He'll have been thinking I need bringing up to speed and here I am – way ahead!'

She danced about the room and after giving him another big hug, waltzed out of the room and into the courtyard. Five minutes later a bemused Ken and a beaming father watched as her Land Rover trundled down the hill towards the main road.

George Hutton walked back into the house and spent the rest of the morning looking at old photographs, some of which he'd forgotten he had. He made a small collection for his daughter to look at, before having a spot of lunch. That afternoon he set off to go for a walk on the fells. Somewhere he hadn't been for over forty years.

* * * *

Octavia had done a fair few jobs in her young life: waitressing, barmaid, typist, even outdoor activities leader. She'd enjoyed that the most: canoeing, climbing, bivouacking and camping – she'd gone back to her childhood, which she had spent outside as much as she could.

Her father could have afforded to send her to a public school but he was adamant that she attend the local grammar school. She went to university to study her first love, biology, but got sidetracked into architecture in the second year. She remembered the moment very clearly, listening to Nikolaus Pevsner telling his stories, the slight middle-European accent making the tales sound even more Gothic. She'd always loved drawing, which she'd regarded as a useful gift for recording specimens, but he made her look at man-made structures in an entirely different way.

She'd grown up in a Victorian house with long corridors to chase around and had adored it as a child, but she'd only thought of it as an adventure playground, full of old stuff. Now she appreciated how fortunate she was. Her father had inherited the house and spent his life looking after it, but she knew that he was tiring. The constant care and attention an old building and a huge garden needed was draining both his energy and his finances. He'd told her long ago that she was unlikely to be able to afford to keep it on when he died. Sometimes this made her sad but she had too pragmatic a nature to dwell on it for long.

Martin Winter was by far the best boss she'd ever worked for – not that he was easy. He had a mercurial energy that could send him off in all sorts of unexpected directions – not all of which were worth the time or effort. He could get obsessive, tetchy even, and this could be frustrating, but he was a man of passion and principle. The one thing you could be certain of was that life was never boring when you were in his company.

She arrived at their office at about ten thirty. The local National Trust was housed in an old village school, which provided them with four large, high-ceiling rooms to work in. She found Martin with the rest of the team in the old school hall. They'd pushed together six of the old tables and were examining a large-scale map.

'Aha. Her ladyship graces us with her presence,' announced Dave Ransome. He was the Trust's education officer, a fierce socialist and historian, who was quick to inform you that he had worked in some of the toughest schools in Manchester and other deprived areas in the north-west. He could never resist having a dig at Octavia's aristocratic background, but was constantly thwarted by her ability to rise above his jibes.

'Aha, indeed, Dr Ransome, but look what she brings.'

She held aloft the plant marker, making sure it glinted in the sunlight pouring through the high windows.

'An artefact. A primary source, sir. What make you of that?'

They all looked up at that point. She walked over and offered it to Dave, who inspected it with growing interest. As she'd hoped, her father's treasure more than made up for her absence yesterday and when they all trooped across the road to the pub for lunch, she felt she'd been fully repatriated into the close-knit team she liked so much.

They'd spent the time before lunch planning a visit to their newly-acquired property that very afternoon. Martin had managed to get hold of both the 1901 and 1911 census documents, plus a large-scale map from 1893. Ransome had unearthed some of the original designs and sketches of the house and even some old photographs. Although there seemed to have been quite a few different hands at work, the chief architect appeared to have been Thomas Rickman, who had designed and renovated numerous buildings across Cumberland in the latter part of the nineteenth century. There was, however, little information as yet about the extensive gardens, which were Octavia's main interest. All of this already promised a rich treasure house, preserved intact since before the Great War. They could hardly contain their excitement.

At this point Octavia hadn't told them her father's story; she thought she'd wait until he'd written it down. But, as they waited for their lunch to arrive, she was reminded of his description of the dark rectangles on the walls as Rivka waxed lyrical about Burne-Jones and speculated excitedly that they might find an example of his work. She was recounting all the known work in the immediate vicinity and was halfway to convincing herself at least that she was going to make the find of the century. Rivka was rarely so animated, being of an age and background that led her to affect a decorous and unexcitable manner towards most things. She was a German Jew, the only member of her family to escape the Holocaust. It was only since she'd started to feel safe in England that she'd reverted to her original name – Weill. Her father had been a Professor of Art History at Dresden University. Her passion was for the Pre-Raphaelite Brotherhood and their followers, and the English Lake District was her heaven on earth.

The final member of the team was the one an outsider would have least expected to find in this company. Octavia glanced across at Lex, who was standing next to Martin at the bar. As usual she wasn't saying much; Martin was in full flow. The word that always came into Octavia's head when she looked at Lex was *sinuous*. It was as if she swam through the air, her body sliding between the molecules like mercury running across a plate. She only answered to Lex. Anyone attempting to call her Lauren would probably find her looking over her shoulder to see who they were talking to. She wore her hair short like a man; only a brave or foolhardy person might wonder aloud if her hairstyle would change if David Bowie's did. She was the team's archivist. Although she had an immaculately maintained, if eccentric, filing system, most of the team thought she had it all in her head anyway.

Octavia tuned back into Rivka's monologue to find she'd moved back in time to Rossetti. They ate their food far too quickly and were all in the minibus by half past one. Lex was driving, so they arrived outside the main gates of Blanchard House before two o'clock. Their attempts to gain entry were to become symbolic of the weeks of frustration ahead. The secrets of the de Blanche inheritance were not given up easily and the wisdom of even trying would be severely questioned.

CHAPTER 4

Fletcher didn't find a handbag or feel any magic, though he did think that on a moonlit night the place might be atmospheric. In the centre of the circle of trees there was a single standing stone but he wasn't sure it was original. He was cynical about ancient monuments. He'd read somewhere that the Victorians had created more Neolithic monuments than the old stone shifters had managed themselves.

For no good reason he paced round the raised embankment and was unsurprised to find that it was exactly a year's worth of strides. Victorians! The last pace brought him back to where he could look down and see the crime scene officers beavering away. A line of uniformed men was making its way along the motorway embankment from the junction towards the north, poking amongst the uncut grass and roadside rubbish. The circle behind him wasn't that tidy either. The Victorians would be outraged. They'd moved tons of earth to create a memorial to their ancient forebears and now it was a picnic site cum outdoor brothel.

Fletcher made his way back down to the hard-working officers, who showed him a shoe they'd found. He cadged a lift back into town and went for some lunch. Staring into his pint of Jennings, he wondered why he was so disinterested. After all, one woman was dead and another was probably lying somewhere else, going cold as well. Despite what the pathologist had said, Penrith was hardly the murder capital of the north.

The woman on the slab was only the second murder victim since Fletcher had arrived last May and the other had been the result of a pub fight. There had been no need for an investigation. Poor sod had owned up next morning after being dragged in by his mother, and was sent down a couple of months later for manslaughter. He'd be out in three years time. Fletcher suspected it would be the same with the woman next to the motorway, although he was less sure about the other one. What was it that Soulby had said? An odd couple? Why did he say that?

Fletcher finished his drink and wandered back to the station. Jane Sykes had been wrong about the woman they'd found this morning; his officers had come up against a blank wall.

DS Hornby was collating all the information they'd received so far on the boards in the incident room. Fletcher stood and looked at the pictures of the murdered woman.

'Nothing definite yet, sir,' said the sergeant.

'Um,' said Fletcher.

He moved over to the smaller collection of items connected to Caroline Soulby. He looked back over at the other boards.

'They're both wearing red and white spotted dresses.'

Hornby looked up. 'Yes, sir. But it's probably just a coincidence.'

'And they're not the same quality,' added DC Garner.

Fletcher continued to look back and forth at the two pictures.

'And they have the same colour hair,' he offered.

'I think statistically there are more brunettes than blondes in

England, sir,' said Garner.

Fletcher checked this against the people present. Brunettes seven. Blondes one. Redheads one. He pulled a face at her, but she looked away. He continued to look at the boards.

'Do we know how old Caroline Soulby is?' he asked.

Hornby checked his records. 'Thirty-four, sir.'

'DC Garner, do you think that this picture was taken recently?'

She came over and considered the girl in the spotted dress. 'No, sir. She looks mid-twenties to me.'

'Thank you.' He turned away. 'Does anyone know where DS Strickland is right now?'

'I think he's doing the pubs, sir.'

'Tell him I've gone to see Mr Soulby again, will you.'

Fletcher made for the door, but had another thought. 'DC Garner, would you accompany me? I think I need a woman's point of view.'

'Certainly, sir,' she replied and gathered her bag and coat.

The rest of the team waited until they were out of earshot.

'"Certainly, sir!"' mimicked DC Lonsdale. 'He'd better watch out. "Good night Irene" is on the prowl!'

The others laughed at him.

'Just 'cos she turned you down, Alan.'

'Who said she did!' Lonsdale growled.

'Cos she's a prick-teaser and you're a ginger cake, that's why!'

'Shut it, you lot,' said Hornby, but he knew the rumours would spread. He'd seen Fletcher's girlfriend, Laura. She was a good-looking woman, but he had to admit that Irene Garner was a man hunter. She'd even had a go at him and he couldn't deny he'd been tempted. He sighed and got back to his cross-checking. He hadn't found a single thing about the dead woman. He hoped forensics would come up with something or the Chief Super was going to be on their backs.

* * * *

Fletcher was no fool, not where women were concerned. He'd a pretty accurate idea of what would have been said after they'd left the incident room. No-one had said anything about Irene Garner, but then it didn't need saying. She was a flirt. He'd seen her operating. Strickland despised her; he didn't think she should have got through the selection process.

He had asked her to collect a car from the pool and now they were heading out of town towards the Soulby house. Neither of them spoke for the first few minutes.

It was Irene who broke the silence. 'Do you miss it?'

Fletcher looked across at her. She was wearing a short, tight-fitting skirt, but she'd pulled it up higher so she could drive. He glanced at her exposed thighs.

'Miss what?'

'London?'

He stared back out at the countryside flashing by. 'Not really,' he found himself saying, not sure any more.

She flashed him a smile. Despite regulations, she was wearing lipstick and eye-shadow. Her blonde hair was cut in the latest fashion. He knew this because Grace had come back with a more extreme version last Saturday. It had provoked yet another row between her and her mother. Fletcher was always in two minds about intervening. More often than not they both turned on him instead. He thought the new style didn't flatter Grace at all. She had naturally wavy brown hair like her mother and she'd come back with a bleached blonde quiff, scraped back over both ears and held in place by rock-hard glue. It resembled the androgynous looks of her favourite band. He'd asked her about them one day and got the succinct reply – 'Japan' – her look telling him that it wasn't open for discussion with *old* people. This hair was accompanied by heavy white make-up and panda eyes.

Irene hadn't gone that far – well not for work, anyway – plus he suspected she'd qualify as *old* as well in Grace's estimation. He also thought she wouldn't have counted as the only blonde present in his statistical survey without the use of chemicals. Despite all this he had to admit she was very attractive – 'in a tarty sort of way,' sneered Laura's voice in his head.

They'd pulled up outside Soulby's house. Irene turned off the engine and gave Fletcher a smile.

'So what am I looking for, sir?'

He stared past her at the house. 'I'm not sure. It's just something he said.'

'Telling lies was he?'

'Not exactly – more like letting the truth slip out without meaning to. . .'

'A Freudian slip?'

Fletcher couldn't help but look surprised at her use of the term. She responded with a fierce look. 'Just because all them chauvinist pigs think I'm a tart doesn't mean I'm thick,' she said.

Fletcher waited to see if there was any more where that came from. There was.

'I know what they think of me, especially Harry Strickland. They'll have to change their tune when I make inspector – and don't raise your eyebrows at me. I sailed through my last review and I'm taking my sergeant's exams next month.'

He waited to see if she'd run out of steam. She looked him in the eyes.

'I'm not apologising. I just thought you ought to know.'

He held her gaze. Then he said, 'And I can tell you that the previous sergeant I worked with is now an inspector in the Met – and she deserves it. So don't include me in the pigsty.'

She grinned. 'I hadn't. You're not that sort of animal at all.'

He looked away.

'Let's go and see what we can find under Mr Soulby's slip, shall we, Irene?'

She laughed – and it was a laugh which contained both malice and pleasure.

They got out of the car and approached the house. A figure was silhouetted in the front window. It disappeared as they walked up to the front door. Irene glanced across at Fletcher, who smiled back.

A few minutes later they were sitting in that front room facing a nervous interviewee. Fletcher was struck by the difference in the man's behaviour. The worried academic had been replaced by an anxious sixth former. There was no offer of tea and scones, so Fletcher assumed that they hadn't arrived during Mrs Langdale's daily visit. He ought to find out when she was on duty.

'Have you got any news, Inspector?'

Fletcher replied that they had no new information but a few more questions might help. He introduced Irene and that was when the awkwardness began. He noticed that the promotion hunter needed no encouragement to increase the suspect's anxiety by displaying her thighs to his evasive glance.

Soulby adjusted himself to face Fletcher and folded his arms.

'We were wondering, sir, if you had a more recent picture of your wife as I think this one was taken some time ago.'

Fletcher offered him the photograph. Soulby took it in his hand and gave it a cursory glance.

'Why yes. I'll go and find one straightaway.'

He left the room and was gone for some time. Irene gave their surroundings the once over before getting up to examine a painting which Fletcher hadn't noticed as he'd got his back to it. He twisted in his seat to look. It was a very striking portrait of a woman, undoubtedly Caroline Soulby, but nothing like the photograph they'd been given. The spotty dress was replaced by a far more sophisticated affair which, whilst covering a lot more of her body, was far more alluring. However, it was the look of arrogance on her face which gave a completely different impression. This was a woman who demanded attention and would certainly get it if she walked round looking like this. The loose hair blowing in the wind was tightly tied back from her forehead into a high black chignon. Her head was turned to the side to reveal a long neck and sharp cheekbones that you'd expect to see at a fashion show. Her dark eyes fixed the viewer with a chilling glance. Much more Cruella De Vil than the pretty girl of yesteryear.

DC Garner turned and looked at Fletcher. 'Now that's a picture of a woman in her thirties,' she announced.

Fletcher nodded.

'Your sort of woman, I imagine?' she added, as she moved round the room.

'Why do you say that?'

'I think you like strong women.'

'I seem to attract them,' he said, not sure whether he should be playing this game.

'Anyway, I think I'm inclined to agree with Harry on this one,' she said. 'She'll turn up in her own good time. Maybe they've had a row?'

Fletcher nodded and looked at the clock. Irene checked her watch.

'Shall I go and see what's keeping him?' she asked.

It suddenly occurred to Fletcher that Soulby might have done a runner. He got to his feet and saw that Garner had had the same thought. They were both making towards the door when it opened and a fair-haired girl stood in front of them. The two police officers stopped in their tracks. The girl looked at them without expression. She was obviously Soulby's daughter. She had the same fine, almost colourless hair tied back in a loose ponytail with a fringe in her eyes. She stood her ground.

'Hello, I'm Inspector Fletcher and this is DC Garner. We're here to see your father.'

The girl didn't acknowledge the introduction, as though it was self-evident who they were, and retreated without a word. Before either of them could say anything, Soulby reappeared from another door, making Fletcher feel like he was on the set of an amateur farce.

'I'm sorry to keep you waiting. It's not a shortage of photos; it's just finding a recent one. Here, this was taken last Christmas.'

Fletcher took the picture and saw the woman posing with three other people. They were all dressed in regulation green 'huntin' and shootin'' outfits. Two of the women were wearing flat caps, whilst the other wore a headscarf. Caroline Soulby was one of the two with a cap. The other was Louisa Cunninghame.

Fletcher looked at the photograph in disbelief. Was that woman going to stalk him wherever he went? He realised that Soulby and Garner were both staring at him, one with anxious anticipation and the other with growing interest. He handed it to Irene who studied it and then glanced at Fletcher.

'Is that any good?' Soulby asked. 'I'm sure you could enlarge it and cut out the other people. It's the best I can do, I'm afraid.'

'No. This is fine, sir. We'll get it back to you as soon as we've made a copy.'

The three of them stood waiting for the next move. Fletcher was hesitating because of Louisa, Garner because she knew there was something in the photo which had startled him and Soulby because he was worrying if they were going to ask any more questions. Finally, Fletcher took the initiative and set off for the door. Garner hesitated, but decided to take a chance.

'Would that be your daughter who just looked in a minute ago, sir?'

Now it was Soulby's turn to be startled. 'Is she here? She isn't due back until this evening. Did she say anything?'

'Not a word,' she said.

He couldn't hide the look of relief that flitted across his face. Fletcher took the opportunity to ask his question. 'There was one other thing I wanted to ask you, sir.'

Soulby was one of those unfortunate people whose every emotion was written in headlines across his face from one second to the next. This time his expression verged on the fearful.

'It was just something you said to me earlier.'

'What was that, Inspector?'

'You said that you and your wife were an "odd couple" – what did you mean by that?'

Soulby removed his glasses and gave them a quick wipe on his handkerchief.

'Well . . . we're a bit chalk and cheese really. She loves company, being at parties and hunt balls, that sort of thing, while I'm . . . more . . . well, happier in my study with my books . . . that's all I meant, Inspector.'

He replaced his glasses and looked at them both. Fletcher

smiled at him.

'I was just wondering, sir, that's all.'

He signalled to Garner and turned towards the door. Soulby followed them to the front door. At the last moment, Fletcher held up the photograph and pointed at it.

'Would you mind telling me who these other people are, sir?'

Without needing to look, Soulby replied. 'The lady next to Caroline is a school friend, Louisa Cunninghame, but I'm surprised you don't know the gentleman, Inspector. He's your Chief Constable and the other woman is his wife.' The slightest of smiles played across his lips.

Fletcher smiled back and said, 'Well, there you are. I've been here nearly a year and he's not invited me to dinner yet!'

All three of them laughed and the two officers made their way back to the car. As Irene looked back, she caught sight of the pale face at the upstairs window but it was quickly withdrawn. She got into the car and started the engine. Fletcher's face was grim.

'I'm sorry, sir. I thought you'd recognise him,' she said.

He didn't look at her. 'Not a problem, DC Garner. I'm not the one looking for promotion.'

As he didn't say anything else, she drove them both back to the station. When they arrived, he handed her the photograph, got out of the car and walked off towards the town. Not knowing whether she'd done something wrong or not, she entered the station and went in search of the photographer.

* * * *

When Irene got back to the main office, DS Strickland beckoned her over. She put on her best good girl behaviour and offered him the cropped picture, which the photographer had blown up for her. He looked at it briefly before asking where she'd lost Fletcher.

'I haven't lost him, Sergeant, he's gone off in a huff to the pub, I think.'

'Which pub?' demanded Strickland.

'He didn't say,' she replied, dropping the good girl pose. It wasn't working on Harry Strickland.

'Well that's no bloody use, is it, DC Garner?'

Before she could answer, and before she fell into the trap and resorted to kneeing the old bastard in the balls, DS Hornby came to her aid.

'I think he frequents The Old Fox, Harry.'

Strickland glared at the woman officer. 'Typical. Where else would he go?'

With that he stomped out of the office and disappeared.

'Thanks, Sarge,' Irene said.

'He won't be here for ever,' replied Hornby.

'No. It just feels like it,' added Lonsdale. 'Anyway, Irene, how d'you get on?'

This was said in front of the assembled audience who were already sniggering like a bunch of teenagers.

'I shagged him in the back of the car on the way there and then we had another quickie in the ladies loo just now. Piss off, you lot!' she shouted and marched out, followed by hoots of laughter and lots of oohs and aahs.

At the back door of the station she hesitated for a few seconds, then made her mind up and set off in pursuit of Strickland. He'd been detained by the chief superintendent in the car park, so was in an even worse mood when he came in a few minutes later, by which time Fletcher had ordered her a half of Jennings to go with his own second pint. They'd not had time for a conversation, but Fletcher reckoned the drink made up for his leaving her like that.

Strickland appeared at her side, gave Irene a stern look and asked if could have a word with Fletcher.

'Fire away, Sergeant. What have I missed?'

Strickland didn't like having to report in front of a junior officer, but the information couldn't wait.

'We've got a fingerprint match for the dead woman.'

'Aha – local girl gone bad, eh?'

''Fraid not, sir. More like one you've brought with you.'

'How do you mean – brought with me?'

'She's from Rochdale, works the lorry drivers and reps on the M6. Her name's Linda Eckersley, been inside twice and has a string of convictions for prostitution, drugs and – interestingly – GBH. This lass could look after herself.'

'But not this time.'

'No. Sykes says it was a particularly violent attack but that she was still alive when she was thrown over the fence.'

'How does she figure that out? I thought she'd been strangled.'

'She was, but it was the broken neck that killed her.'

'So we're looking for a big chap, or maybe two? She didn't look the lightest of women.'

'You're right but Sykes is positive it was the fall that did the damage. She was probably unconscious.'

Fletcher took a sip of his beer. 'Have you contacted Rochdale?'

'I thought I'd leave that to you, sir.'

Fletcher sighed. 'Don't assume I'm any more popular back there than I am here, Sergeant, 'cos I'm not. Proverbial bad penny, me. Don't feel bad, it's just your turn.'

Strickland looked at his watch.

'So, shall I assume you're going to follow it up anyway, sir? It's just that I'd promised the wife. My shift finished over an hour ago and I'm already late.'

'No problem, Sergeant. Me and the unattached DC will carry on. You get going.'

That didn't please Strickland but he bit his tongue and turned away. If he'd not remembered the other thing he'd got to say, he wouldn't have caught the expressions on their two stupid faces.

'Something else, sir. Chief Superintendent Ogilvy wants to see you on Monday. I think he's a little disappointed by our lack of progress in finding Caroline Soulby. Apparently she's a friend of the chief constable.'

He'd thought this last piece of information might wipe the smiles of their faces, but it didn't work that way.

'Isn't everyone, Sergeant? Apart from me of course. Like I said – "bad penny". I'll see what I can do.'

Strickland gave up and left them to it. They deserved each other. The tart and the chancer. He hurried off, knowing his excuses were going to fall on a pair of very unforgiving deaf ears.

The chancer and the tart looked at each other and shook their heads in unison.

'You want another, Inspector? I'm off duty myself now.'

'I suppose so. Whatever thin level of respect I've been receiving so far from Sergeant Strickland has just evaporated, I think.'

Irene beckoned to the barman and pointed at their two glasses.

'You mean because he found you consorting with the likes of me?'

Fletcher gave her a look of mock astonishment.

'I wasn't aware we were consorting, Constable. I'd have put on a clean shirt.'

'You know what I mean. The pigsty have already got us shacked up.'

He shook his head and started on the next drink.

'I'm not what you think, you know,' she added.

'That's a shame; I was counting on a dirty weekend.'

She gave him a sharp look. 'Don't take the piss . . . sir.'

'Hey. We're off duty. I'm a fully paid up and utterly subjugated gigolo and stepfather to a sullen New Romantic, so no chance of playing away – even if I was tempted.'

She gave him another sharp look and then let it go. They sat in silence for a time. Irene looked at her watch.

'I know you didn't recognise the chief constable or his wife, but you did see something in that photo, didn't you?' she said.

'Observant *and* perceptive,' he replied.

'So it has to be the other woman.'

'Powers of deduction as well.'

'Louisa Cunninghame?'

'Excellent memory.'

'So who is she?'

'Straight to the point.'

'So . . . ?'

'Aye, there's the rub.'

She looked at him expectantly. She'd examined the photo closely while she waited for 'David Bailey' to come out of the dark room. She knew damn well what sort of photographs he was developing. He'd even had the nerve to ask her to let him take a few 'snaps', as he put it. Louisa Cunninghame, whoever she was, was way out of a detective inspector's league, even one as foxy as Fletcher. She was intrigued.

He was weighing up the odds. He took a chance.

'I know her, but I didn't expect her to crop up in this investigation.'

'How do you know her?'

'It's a long story. My friend Courtney calls her "da Ice Queen".'

Irene raised her eyebrows. 'Meaning she's frigid?'

'Quite the opposite. She has a penchant for the fiery encounter.'

'With you?'

'Unfortunately I don't fit the specifications.'

'Oh no?'

'No. Not as inclined to do as I'm told according to her . . . and too old.'

'Too old?'

Fletcher gave her a look. 'She was involved in the first case I had after I was sent up north. She helped me out here and there and I looked the other way on a certain matter. She just seems to crop up wherever I go. Aristocratic lineage, but likes a bit of rough – if you know what I mean?'

Irene gave him a slow nod. 'Well that's unusual,' she said.

'What?'

'Having a toff for a snout.'

'Comes in handy, now and then,' he smiled.

'So I see. So will you be contacting her about Cruella?'

Fletcher nodded. She waited. He was lost in thought.

'I'll be off then,' she said.

'Bye,' he said, without looking.

She picked up her bag and walked out. He watched her leave in the mirror behind the bar.

The young barman picked up the two glasses and asked, 'You want another?'

Fletcher pointed at the optics and said, 'Double Bushmills, please.'

The barman placed the drink on the bar and took his money. 'No luck there, then?' he asked.

'What?'

'Don't waste your time. She's a tease. Leads you on and leaves you panting.' He smirked and walked away.

Fletcher thought of defending Irene Garner's honour, but knew he'd been tempted and was therefore disbarred. He took his time with the malt. He needed to make two phone calls and he wasn't keen on making either of them. They'd both remind him of where he'd been and why he was now in exile.

In the end he made his way back to the station. The 'pigsty' was empty. He couldn't get used to a police station where people went home so early, like they were office workers. He went into his office and shut the door. He looked at the phone and decided to start with the easier call of the two, which he knew to be cowardice but no-one was watching. He dialled the number, which was still in his head. The familiar voice responded on the third ring.

'DS Simpson, you bald bastard, why aren't you at home shagging yer wife?' he said.

There was the briefest of beats, before the predictable reply came down the line.

'Because, you Cockney git, you know very well, someone else is shagging my wife and he's welcome to the vicious cow.'

'You see, Sergeant. That's why you'll never get away from driving that desk. No respect for your superiors.'

'And you know I don't do respect and you're not my superior any more – more's the pity. It's like a morgue here since you and Sexy Sadie left.'

'Calm down, Sergeant. You know she wouldn't fuck you even if you had tits.'

'Yeh. Well. I can dream.'

'No. Don't go there. I've not had my tea.'

'So what d'you want and will I get paid?'

'Don't be daft. Linda Eckersley?'

Simpson laughed out loud. 'Linda Eckers-like. You are going downmarket. What's she done? Kicked one of your plods in the balls 'cos he wouldn't pay?'

'I'm afraid not, Sergeant. She's the one on the slab and although she put up a fight, it probably made him real mad. She's a mess. Raped. Strangled. Broken neck. Dead.'

'Blimey. Suppose she had it coming. She didn't take any prisoners. Well, only if they paid.'

'This one probably didn't. Any ideas? I imagine she might have had a few enemies.'

'It'll be a long list. Take me some time. I'll ask around, but she didn't just work round here. She's been booked as far afield as Cardiff to my knowledge, only a couple of months ago. You've got yourself a large field of suspects there and it could be just the latest punter. Not on anyone's list. Have you got any blood samples?'

'Yeah. Nothing on record.'

'Needle in a haystack, Inspector.'

'I know, but got to show willing, got to have something for a pork butcher by the name of Ogilvie by Monday morning.'

'Ah. Up to your old tricks upsetting the brass, eh? Leopard. Spots. No change there then.'

'Give Digby Rigby a clip round the ear and get yourself off to the pub.'

'Will do,' said Simpson and the phone clicked in his ear.

The second call was much harder. He went to the loo to put it off for a bit and when he came back thought he'd better ring Laura first to say he'd be home soon.

'Hi, love,' he said.

'Don't you "hi love" me, Mick Fletcher. We're supposed to be at the Todd's by seven thirty and it's half six now. Get a move on.'

So that didn't take long. He picked up the phone again. It rang until he was about to put it down but then it was answered. The voice had a strong Scot's accent and for a moment he thought he'd got the wrong number.

'Hello, can I help ye?'

Fletcher had been half expecting one of Louisa's young men to answer but this was an older voice.

'Can I speak to Louisa please?' he said.

There was a short pause.

'I'm afraid she's not here at the moment. Who's speaking?'

This was both defensive and abrupt.

'Just tell her it's Inspector Mick Fletcher. Ask her to call me back.'

'Has she been speeding again?'

'I expect she has, but it's not about that. I'll give you a number, where she can contact me.'

'Hang on a minute. I'll get a pen.'

Fletcher heard an odd sound at the end of the line and knew immediately that she was there.

'Right. What's the number?'

Fletcher gave him the station number and added: 'Tell her it's fairly urgent. It concerns a friend of hers called Caroline Soulby . . . and say . . . say that the flat cap doesn't suit her, it spoils the cut of her hair.'

He put the phone down before the man could say anything else and made for the exit pronto, laughing to himself all the way home.

CHAPTER 5

The first problem the team encountered was the main gate. It was a huge construction of cast iron railings with lots of swirling designs. The left-hand gate's decoration included an elaborate letter B, whilst the right-hand centred round a fleur-de-lys. The lock was rusted shut and of course they didn't have a key. In any case, there was a thick metal chain threaded through and held by a massive old padlock. Again – no key. They stood like a bunch of hobbits outside the giant's castle gates.

'The thing is,' said Dave Ransome, 'they shouldn't even be here. Find me another metal gate or fence round here from before the war. They were all taken down and turned into tanks.'

'Okay, so anyone got any bright ideas?' asked Martin.

'Simple,' said Lex. 'Large metal cutters or a bulldozer.'

'And destroy such amazing works of art?' said Octavia.

Ransome peered through into the darkness of the trees. 'You can hardly make out the drive anyway. I'd say the bulldozer was a good idea once we can get in.'

Octavia joined him at the gates.

'Untamed nature?' he sighed, with the evident distaste of the urban dweller.

'There must be other gates – big place like this,' said Lex.

Martin had already unrolled one of the smaller-scale maps onto the van bonnet. Sure enough there were three other entrances marked. They agreed to split up. Lex and Martin set off in the van and drove to the furthest 'back' gate, checking out the anti-clockwise side gate on the way, while the other three walked clockwise to the nearest gate to the south.

It was a bright sunny afternoon and the high red sandstone walls radiated the heat back towards them as the trio set off to find their gate. Octavia marvelled at the unbroken nature of the walls. There didn't seem to be any crumbling or collapsing at all. They were in remarkable condition, considering their age and location.

They found the door within a few minutes but yet again they failed to gain access. It wasn't very big, just a one-person entrance, made from heavy wood that was probably seasoned oak. It was held together with large iron hinges and bars across the full width. There was a big keyhole full of moss but it didn't give, even when Ransome gave it a hefty kick.

Lex and Martin had had a similar lack of success and the two groups ended up back at the front gate.

Lex decided that she would go and find the nearest farm and borrow a ladder. They'd brought a chainsaw, axes and other assorted cutting implements. Octavia started putting on the protective gear. She might be a London arts graduate, but she was also a farmer's daughter and had been using all sorts of machinery since she was a kid.

Lex returned with a ladder and pointed back down the road to an approaching tractor.

'I've got some help,' she said.

Two minutes later the powerful machine pulled up and a young farm hand jumped down and introduced himself.

'Hello. I'm Tom Harper. Couldn't let you off-coomers get stuck-in here without some local help,' he laughed, shaking everybody's hands. His grip left no-one in any doubt about the muscle which had just been added to the team.

He walked over to the gates and gave them a pull. Nothing shifted.

'Unless you can find a key, it'll need our big Massey to pull them out. Probably bring t'gateposts out as well though.'

'We'd rather not do that, Tom,' said Octavia.

'Bloody hell, Tavi 'utton! I didn't recognise you in that gear. Last time I seen you was at that sixth form dance.'

Octavia was blushing. She remembered it well – *and* what he'd said to her that night in the garden.

'If you say owt else, I'll be reminding you of one or two things you'd like kept quiet.'

His eyes widened. And then he burst out laughing. 'Okay. It's a deal. I won't mention foxes if you keep quiet about the panther.' This made him laugh even louder.

Octavia couldn't stop a smile coming to her face but glared at the others, who all raised their hands in mock surrender. Tom's rough humour kept them laughing as the ladder was put up and they all climbed over the gate.

It took them over two hours to hack their way through the undergrowth before they caught their first sight of the building. Tom had gone off and brought back a couple of his mates, which increased the speed of progress considerably.

It was late afternoon when Lex yelled above the whining of the chainsaws and pointed at the tower looming up in the distance. Even though they'd come over six hundred yards, the tower was still the same distance again but at least now they were at the edge of the trees.

Octavia gasped as her father's description appeared in front of her. The rest of the approach was a mass of tangled briars and overgrown shrubs. The three farmers' lads stood, machines cooling in their hands and took in the size of the job. Tom spoke into the gathering silence.

'Th'ar'll be nee use aginst them bastards.'

'Ay-ye'd be tangled in 'em in a matta a'seconds,' said his mate Ted.

Octavia put down her saw and took a step towards the wall of barbed tendrils. Even as she moved, a large branch fell towards her, its tip cutting across her face as it fell to the ground. They all gasped. Her hand went to her face as Tom took a step towards her. She looked at her hand and shivered. Tom pulled her to him and looked at her face. She turned and they could all see the scratch and the blood on her hand. As she looked at them staring at her, she knew she was the only first aider present and laughed.

'It's okay. I'll live. It's just a scratch. The first aid box is there.' She pointed to it. Lex opened it and found some disinfectant and a plaster.

Reassured that she was alright, Tom said that he'd get the tractor in tomorrow and be through the briars in no time.

'Not unless we can get through the gates, you won't,' reminded Ransome.

'Ah. I'd forgotten about them.'

'It's too late now. It's going to be dark soon,' added Martin. 'We'll have to leave it till Monday. I'll see if I can get hold of someone who can find a way to get us in.'

'Yer best chance'll be awd Fred Tirrel. He's still fixin't shaes ont' nags. He's t'yan'rll git ya thru't metal geats,' said Ted.

So it was agreed. The group made their way back down the

pathway they'd cut and climbed back over the wall. Octavia was last over, taking one final look at the tower peering over the fierce black wall of briar. She remembered her father's story and the single rose.

Later in the pub in Bampton, as the young lads got more and more raucous, she sat quietly in the corner and wondered. She wasn't sure whether the others had noticed. Just after the noise of the chainsaws had stopped and before Tom had spoken she had heard the silence her father had described. It was not just quiet. It was a complete absence of sound. Nothingness. That was why she'd shivered. A cold nothingness.

*   *   *   *

March 1976

Fern soon discovered that she was going to have real trouble protecting Dawn. As WPC Dodds had told them, the parents were determined to get their daughter back. They'd gone to court and their expensive lawyer had persuaded the judge to let them take the girl home. It was only a last minute effort by the social services lawyer that gained them a week's reprieve by suggesting Dawn should receive some psychiatric counselling. Apparently her stepmother was so furious with this that her husband and their solicitor had to physically remove her from the courtroom.

Both the lawyers noticed the way the judge responded to her outburst. Fern's boss had been in court and she thought they had a good chance of changing the decision, especially as the judge who had witnessed the stepmother's behaviour would be presiding at the next stage of the proceedings.

Fern had the difficult job of explaining what had happened to Dawn, who went white with fear when she heard how her stepmother had behaved.

'She'll find some way of getting me back, I just know it,' she said.

Fern tried to reassure her but Dawn curled up in a ball and wept. She lost all the confidence she'd started to recover over the last couple of weeks and regressed into a dull acceptance of her fate.

Things went from bad to worse when Fern got a phone call at home to tell her that the judge had been reassigned to another case. She knew then that she would have to do something. She lay on her bed racking her brain, trying to think of a way to engineer Dawn's escape.

Eventually Fern must have fallen asleep because it was nearly dark when she woke up. A glance at the clock told her she needed to hurry or she would be late for her shift. She had time for a quick shower and to get into her uniform before catching the bus to the children's home.

She hadn't heard a thing so was shocked when she came out of the bathroom, still drying her hair, to find a man sitting on her sofa. Fortunately she was wearing her dressing gown, but still she felt vulnerable. How had he got in and what did he want? It didn't occur to her that it would be anything to do with Dawn.

Overcoming her immediate fear, she demanded to know what the hell he thought he was doing. He smiled at her. He wasn't a big man, smaller than Fern. Black leather jacket, black gloves. He didn't look particularly strong. She fancied her chances if it came to a struggle but there was something about him that unnerved her.

It was his smile.

'I'm sure you can work it out, if you give it some thought,' he said.

'There's nothing of any value here. There's maybe twenty quid in my purse. The telly. I've nothing else.'

'I can see that, Fern. Yours isn't exactly the best remunerated occupation in the world, after all.'

Fern felt a cold fist tighten round her insides.

'I see you're beginning to put two and two together, Fern. Let me help you out, so that you get the right answer.'

'How do you know my name? What do you want?' she demanded.

'Nothing, Fern. The answer is nothing. We want you to do nothing.'

'What d'you mean – nothing?'

'To be clear. Right now I want you to pick up the phone and ring your boss. You've got terrible stomach pains and you're going to the emergency department at the hospital. It's OK, it won't be anything serious, but tomorrow you'll be able to tell them you've been advised to take a week off work.'

'Why are you doing this?'

'Come on Fern. You know why.'

'You're working for Dawn's stepmother, aren't you?'

'There you are. I knew you'd work it out.'

'No. You can get out. I'm going to call the police.'

'Don't think so,' he said. 'The alternative is that you'll have a more painful and maybe fatal stomach pain.'

The phone was in her hand, but she knew it was no use. He hadn't seemed to move, but a knife had appeared in his gloved hand. Before he could do anything else, she ran from the room and locked the bathroom door behind her. She grabbed the clothes she'd left on the floor and was out through the window as she heard him kicking his way through.

Her flat was on the first floor but, as it was quite new, there was a proper fire escape. She climbed out and was about to rush down the stairs, when something changed inside her. Later she was to think of this as *the* moment. In that instant, she became the predator not the victim. She remembered it as a visceral experience: sharp and vivid in its complex diamond clarity. All that actually happened was that instead of taking the two steps to the top of the metal staircase, she took three back into the darkness to the left of the opening and held her breath.

The noise inside the flat had stopped. She heard the intruder come towards the window. He stuck his head out and cursed. Poor planning, thought Fern; he hadn't taken the time to check out the escape options. In his arrogance he'd assumed she'd be too terrified to think, never mind attempt to escape.

He climbed out of the window and took the two steps to the edge of the fire escape. The back alley was badly lit but his instinct told him she wasn't down there, on the ground beneath him.

Too late, he worked out where she must be but by then she'd pushed him and he was tumbling down the iron steps. The staircase had a small landing halfway down which did a quarter turn towards the ground. It prevented him from falling the whole twelve feet, as the railing brought him to a sudden, crunching halt.

In the silence that followed, Fern waited for him to recover, to groan and stagger to his feet. She was ready for him. He'd dropped his knife and now she had it in her trembling hand.

But no breath of sound was to come from this young man, ever again.

He was dead.

Fern began to take this in as she looked at the unnatural angle of his head against the corner of the railings. She cautiously crept down to where he lay, half expecting him to suddenly leap up and grab her. But he didn't. He couldn't.

She reached out and touched him. His arm flopped through a gap in the railing. In the dull orange light his eyes stared blankly at the wall. She felt for a pulse in his neck but she knew already that it was true. She had killed him.

She knelt there for what seemed an eternity. What should she do? People rarely ventured down this alley. It was a cul-de-sac only used by tenants putting out their rubbish. Even the bin men didn't come down here; the tenants had to drag their bins to the end to the street. The only frequent visitors were the local cats and they'd made themselves scarce just now.

Fern leant back against the cold metal and closed her eyes. She'd only seen Dawn's mother at the end of a corridor, waving her arms about and shouting at the police and the reception staff. She was dressed for a fashion parade rather than for visiting her stepdaughter in a children's home. Huge bouffant hairdo. She'd looked ridiculous. But Fern had heard the viciousness in her voice and the way the woman treated everyone as though they were idiots. The dragon inside Fern had stirred and she had had to turn away to calm herself. It reminded her of her mother's suffering and she'd felt her body stiffening with anger. She'd walked back to Dawn's room but had had to take many deep breaths before opening the door.

And now the woman had sent this thug to threaten her – how dare she do that! With a knife! Fern's eyes blazed as a plan burst into her head. She would show her!

She found herself standing over the man's body. Kneeling down, she felt in his pockets and found a wallet and two sets of keys. It was the latter which prompted the solution. It was madness but, at the time, it seemed just right. She looked at the car keys. According to the details on the fob, they belonged to a Mr Hertz and with admirable German efficiency the make and number of the vehicle were also clearly stated.

Her mind made up, Fern coldly prioritised her actions. She manoeuvred the body round until she could manhandle him down the final flight and sit him next to her neighbour's bin. Next she went back up the stairs and found her uniform. She was shivering with cold and the fear but adrenalin was still surging through her body.

She picked up the phone and told a colleague that she had a problem with her plumbing and would be on her way to work as soon as the plumber arrived. She grabbed the case she'd already packed for the next day. She decided the damage to the bathroom could wait and left by the front door.

It took her only a few minutes to find the brand new Cortina. It had that particular new car smell and she found the brakes a little hard compared with her old Escort, but otherwise the controls were very similar.

Fern drove round the block and backed the car into the entrance to the alley. She opened the boot from inside and went to collect her attacker. He'd not moved. She dragged him down to the back of the car and bundled him in. The whole process took less than ten minutes. There were people returning home and cars going back and forth along the street, but no-one paid any attention to her.

She knew there was little chance of any of her neighbours noticing anything. The old lady on the first floor was housebound and stone deaf. The couple who lived above her were on a beach somewhere in Spain. The other side of the alley was a factory which had closed years ago and had stood empty ever since. She drove away and headed for the next stop on her journey.

Once the idea of using his car had occurred to her, Fern had given some thought to how she was going to dispose of his body. It came to her almost immediately – and it was on the way to work. She lived on a side street near a run-down industrial estate on the edge of the Leicestershire town of Ashby-de-la-Zouche. She'd always assumed before she first arrived here that it would be more genteel than it turned out to be. The main street was wide and edged with red-brick Georgian buildings; there were suburban leafy estates, which were showing their age at this time of year, and a surprisingly large number of council houses. Fern had anticipated a village green and ducks, but the reality was more industrial than she'd expected. Some of this industry had flourished and then lapsed into dereliction, like the factory next to her flat. It was a larger enterprise to which she was now heading.

A few weeks previously, Fern had taken a wrong turning when there was an accident and everyone was looking for alternative routes. She'd followed another driver who she assumed knew the area better than she did. He didn't. They'd both ended up turning round on a concrete wasteland outside an old brick factory, risking their tyres on the broken glass and crumbled bricks. They'd retreated back to the main road. She remembered the other driver winding his window down as they circled round. 'I didn't even know this was here,' he said, in a strong local accent.

She figured that nothing would have changed. The turning was unmarked but she knew where it was.

The new tyres crunched over the gravel and the headlights picked out the expanse in front of the derelict buildings. It was just as she'd remembered it, although nature had made further headway in returning it to its natural state. Weeds and grass sprouted from every crack, whilst elderflower and hawthorn were re-establishing themselves inside the factory walls. Fern made her way across the uneven ground until she reached her goal.

To one side of what she imagined had been the loading bays for the brick lorries, there was a wide ditch. In the headlights she could see that it was still full of water but heavily clogged with shrubs and grasses. She switched off the lights and stepped out of the car. As she waited for her eyes to adjust to the darkness, she could hear the distant swishing of the cars on the main road. People hurrying home from work, indifferent to the magnitude of her actions. People with ordinary little lives, who'd only seen such things on the box in the corner of their living rooms.

It wasn't so dark. The lights from the road and the nearby villages gave the night a pale amber glow. She listened, like she used to listen in the woods of her childhood. She knew there were foxes and deer and rabbits like there were at home, but they didn't bother her. She felt at ease in the thickening night air. She knew what she was doing was wrong in the eyes of the law, but she also knew that what she'd done and what she was going to do was right on some higher plain of justice.

She opened the boot and looked at the man. He lay crumpled and small in his rented hearse. There was a part of her which felt sorry for him but he'd made his own choices. She untangled his legs and tugged them over the edge of the boot, grabbed him by his lapels and pulled him to his incapable feet. Bending beneath his chest she laid him over her shoulder and lifted him up. As part of their training all the staff at the home had done their first aid course with the local fire brigade. Everyone had enjoyed the two days, especially the simulated fire in the kitchen, which had required them to carry firemen a lot heavier than this young man out onto the lawns. She remembered tumbling to the floor with her load and the two of them rolling about in hysterics.

Fern had only a few yards to travel before reaching the edge of the ditch. She'd seen a likely spot in the headlights where the vegetation surrounded a patch of murky water. Without any further ceremony she heaved the man in. At first she thought she'd made a bad choice as he remained stubbornly in view but gradually he started to sink, disappearing into the sludge. A few bubbles reached the surface and the ripples shivered back from the reeds. Everything regained its weary composure and the moon came out from behind a cloud.

She stood transfixed as though spot-lit, centre stage. An owl hooted from the roof of the factory and she saw its effortless flight as it swooped across the arena. The moon disappeared as abruptly as it had appeared. She felt the strange thrill of a performance – but was relieved that the audience was neither human nor concerned with her. She looked again at the water. It was still.

She walked back to the car, got in and drove to the main road. Ten minutes later, she was telling her colleague all about the bathroom disaster and the difficulties of getting a plumber at that time of day.

* * * *

Fletcher was relieved to get out of the house on Saturday morning. The atmosphere was dire.

He and Laura had enjoyed their evening out with the Todds. They'd had a relaxed and pleasant meal; Alice Todd was a traditional cook, but her goulash was superb. Afterwards they'd played bridge. It wasn't the same level of intensity as the evenings at Roger's back in Hebden Bridge. Apart from anything else, Alice and Dougie weren't such aggressive players. Laura had met Alice at the building society where they both worked. Alice had been at the Penrith branch for years, but she and Laura got on straight away. Dougie was an electrician, but his real love was playing in a rock band. It was unusual for him to be available on a Friday night, but he'd been out three nights running and was going to play in Newcastle on the Saturday. Laura and Fletcher generally won but Alice blew them away with six hearts in the last rubber. It was Fletcher's fault. He'd lost concentration and exposed Laura's King of Clubs.

They had a rule that the arguing about cards should finish before they got home. It didn't last that long. Fletcher confessed and remained silent for the last five minutes. Unfortunately this was only a prelude to an almighty row when they got back.

They were a bit earlier than they'd said they'd be. He saw the red sports car parked down the street and his heart sank. Grace had taken up with an older boy; in fact, he was a young man of twenty-six. Laura was very unhappy about this and she and Grace had had a lot of heated exchanges. Tonight was the climax. As soon as they opened the door, they realised the two of them were upstairs in Grace's bedroom. The noises were explicit. Laura was all for going up and catching them at it but Fletcher suggested a more diplomatic approach. He went in the front room and put the telly on. Loud.

Five minutes later the two of them came downstairs. Dekker – that was the man's name – looked a bit wary, if not sheepish. He was a handsome young man, with dark hair flopping over a high cheek-boned face. Slim and fashionable in his long black coat.

Grace was on the attack immediately. 'You said you wouldn't be back until after twelve,' she said with her arms folded.

Laura glared at her daughter and tried to contain her anger. 'Yes. Well I think it's time Derek left, don't you?'

'Just going,' mumbled Dekker.

The two of them went outside. Laura glared at Fletcher. He shrugged his shoulders and set off upstairs to bed.

He didn't get to sleep for another two hours. The row was tempestuous and included the devastating revelation from Grace that although Dekker was married, he was leaving his wife to take up with her and they were going to get a flat and live together.

The rest was predictable: shouting, yelling, crying, accusations and furious argument. Eventually Grace stormed upstairs to her room and slammed the door with such force that a vase of flowers on the landing crashed to the floor, spilling petals and water all over the carpet. Finally, after she'd cleared it up and told Grace she could go to hell for all she cared, Laura came into the bedroom and burst into tears. Fletcher was unable to comfort her and he got a frosty reception when he went down in the morning. Grace was still in her room. Laura was drinking coffee and staring out into the small back garden. He poured himself a cup and stood beside her.

'I'll see what I can find out. Go and talk to him if you like;' he offered.

She didn't look at him. 'Do what you like. I give up.'

He put his hand on her shoulder. She didn't respond. He left her there and went to work.

* * * *

There was only one person in the main office when Fletcher arrived. DC Lonsdale was not the best at keeping up with his paperwork. He'd had a verbal warning from the chief inspector last Thursday and been given a Monday deadline which he would struggle to meet.

Fletcher asked if there was any news on the two cases. Lonsdale shook his head.

'Nothing, sir. The prossie's photo's been displayed in all the service stations and lorry cafés between here and Brazil, but it's not likely to produce a result, is it?'

'What about Caroline Soulby?' asked Fletcher.

'Nothing there either, sir. Although I envy the bastard who's giving her one!' he added.

'I doubt whether he is a bastard, Constable. But if he is, he's likely to be a rich bastard.'

'Typical,' said Lonsdale and turned back to the mountain of files on his desk.

The detective constable's succinct summary concerning Linda Eckersley was confirmed by Simpson when he rang him. Since his messy divorce, he'd been putting in the overtime and looking forward to an expensive holiday.

'Where are you going?' asked Fletcher.

'Australia, and I might not come back.'

'Good for you,' said Fletcher and sighed with a certain amount of envy – although Australia was a bit far and full of Australians.

He put off the next phone call by going for some breakfast in the canteen. His phone was ringing as he got back and Lonsdale had picked it up.

'I'll just see if he's around, madam,' he said and put his hand over the mouthpiece.

'Louisa Cunninghame, sir?'

Fletcher nodded and indicated his office. Lonsdale waited until he'd shut the door, before putting the call through.

'Michael?' The voice hadn't changed: husky, with a trace of a sarcastic laugh. He'd never seen her smoke but the Lauren Bacall impression still worked.

'Mrs Cunninghame,' he said. 'Or is it Miss or Ms, now?'

'For your information, Inspector, it's about to become Knox-Cunninghame. You spoke to John yesterday. We're getting married in June in Scotland and you're not invited.'

Fletcher laughed.

'I should hope not. You wouldn't want anyone offering "objections", I'm sure.'

There was a silence at the other end.

'Not only disinclined to obey; too old, but also cheap, Michael. It doesn't become you.'

'Please accept my congratulations, Louisa. I hope he comes up to the mark.'

Another silence. Then she said, 'What do you want to know about Caroline, Inspector? I have a busy schedule today.'

Fletcher didn't think she'd believe him if he said he envied her that.

'She's gone missing. Last Thursday evening. Not a peep since. Husband is very worried and produced a picture of her which included your good self. A recent picture, which also featured my chief constable and his lady wife. A huntin' you did go.'

'I see. That would be December. She was on the shoot at the Campbells'. I hadn't seen her for years. We were only there for a couple of days. I didn't get to talk to her much. Up to her old tricks.'

'What tricks do you mean?' asked Fletcher, half-knowing what she was going to say.

'I think it's what someone like you would call "shagging around",' she said.

'Oh dear. Anyone in particular?'

'I think you know me and my class better than that, Michael. There are some things we don't discuss with the proletariat.'

'So how do you know her?'

'We were at school together.'

'And?'

'And nothing. We lost touch. I think she's seen off at least two very old dodderers. Must be quite well off by now. Isn't she married to Charles Soulby?'

'Yes. He was the one who gave me the photograph.'

'Well, he wasn't there. Not his scene at all. Bit of a recluse who likes his history books, I believe.'

'So you can't tell me where I might find her.'

'I'm afraid not, Michael. However I suspect her tastes haven't changed. How shall I put it? She enjoys inflicting pain, physical and psychological, on men and women. She was a bully at school; she even had one or two of the teachers under her thumb. I'm not her friend, Michael, and whatever she's up to, someone will be suffering.'

'I see. Nice.'

'No, Michael. Not at all nice.'

There was a further silence.

'Is that all, Michael?'

'I think so, Louisa.'

'Give my love to Laura and tell her I picked up the two of hearts.'

The phone went dead.

Fletcher put the phone down slowly, leant back in his chair and closed his eyes. The two of hearts? He remembered the moment. That bridge night at Roger's when they'd come back into the room to find Laura gathering the cards up. She'd been telling Louisa what the cards meant, like her Aunt Magda had taught her. He hadn't seen the card Louisa had pulled, but he knew on that occasion it had been bad – she was still married to that creep Hetherington – so the two of hearts must be good? He wondered about asking Laura, but knew he wouldn't. Not worth the risk at the moment.

This was how Lonsdale found him. He coughed.

'I'm not asleep, Constable. I'm daydreaming.'

Fletcher put down his feet and sat up. Lonsdale tried to look unconcerned.

'Er . . . I was wondering if you wanted a coffee, sir?'

'You never need to ask, Lonsdale. The answer is always yes.'

The DC sauntered off towards the canteen. Fletcher picked up the phone.

'Hi. How about lunch at Howtown?' he asked.

There was an ominous pause at the other end of the line. Then: 'Are you trying to seduce me, Mick Fletcher?'

'Of course,' he replied, allowing himself a hopeful smile.

'We'll see about that. What time?'

'Half ten? Give us time for a stroll.'

'Don't be late. You can pick me up from the hairdresser's.'

He agreed. Irene Garner appeared in the doorway with a smile on her lips.

'See you later, darling,' he said and put the phone down.

'Lucky girl,' Irene said, lounging against his door.

'I thought you were off duty this weekend,' he said, getting out of his seat.

'I am. Can't you tell?'

She was wearing a black plastic jacket over a red dress which finished about halfway to her knees. Her hair was stuck up with the same glue as Grace seemed to be using and the eye shadow was nearly as dark.

'You'll catch your death in this weather,' he said, brushing past her into the main office just as Lonsdale arrived with the coffee. Irene made no effort to get out of the way and so he got a strong whiff of a musky perfume.

'Shame. I was going to suggest we went to the pub,' she whispered as he went past.

Fletcher ignored her and collected his coffee from the open-mouthed Lonsdale.

'I've got a little job for you, Detective,' he said.

Lonsdale was still gawping at Irene, who was pulling a face at him.

'Derek Wray. Can you run a check on him for me?'

Irene gave an audible intake of breath. 'Wasting your time, sir.'

'Why's that, Constable?'

'Far too sharp to get caught, Dekker Ray.'

His discomfort with her presence shifted to concern about Grace.

'What do you mean?'

'Sex and drugs and rock an' roll,' she offered, leaning against one of the empty desks.

'Can you be more precise, Irene?'

'Well . . . I can't prove it and I doubt whether anyone would grass him up . . . but in one word – pimp.'

'Oh, God,' groaned Fletcher.

'What's the matter, sir? Has he offered you an exciting night out with a young lady?'

'No!' he said with an angry glare. 'It's far worse than that.'

'You mean you accepted?' she said with an expression of mock surprise.

'No, Detective Constable! He's turned his attention to my stepdaughter. Is that clear enough for you?'

The smirk disappeared from Irene's face and was replaced by a look of genuine concern.

'I'm sorry, sir. I didn't mean to . . .' she trailed off.

Fletcher prowled up and down the aisle. Irene adjusted her jacket.

'I know him, sir. We had a brief thing together . . . when we were much younger . . . at his wedding actually. But that's the sort of guy he is. I'll speak to him. Warn him off.'

'You do that, Constable.'

He stood right in front of her. 'And you explain just how bad a bastard I can be. Far worse than you already know. Trust me. Sooner rather than later. You understand?'

Irene was visibly shaken by his display of cold anger. Lonsdale was in danger of getting lockjaw. Fletcher went back into his office, grabbed his coat and made his way to the office door, where he turned and glared at the two of them.

'Lonsdale. Do that search anyway. Anything. A speeding ticket. A library fine. Anything. Bugger the paperwork. You got it?'

Lonsdale nodded.

'And both of you. We did not have this conversation. Right?'

'Yes, sir. No, sir,' they said in unison.

He gave them one last look and left the room.

They waited till they were sure he'd really gone, listening to the doors banging all the way down the stairs. The expulsion of held breath filled the silence. Lonsdale closed his mouth. Irene gave him a sideways glance.

'I've just decided to do some overtime, Lonny. What about you?'

Realising this was the invitation he'd dreamed of, Lonsdale grabbed his coat and followed her out. His only hope was that if they were successful there might be some chance of a reward.

He could have his dreams, but Irene Garner was after bigger fish.

* * * *

It took all of Fletcher's self control not to go looking for Dekker himself. He knew he needed to be careful. Personal involvement with a suspect was never a good idea, especially if it included a member of your family. He had begun to have some confidence in Irene Garner, despite all the come-ons. She was ambitious and she was prepared to cut corners. As his temper cooled he laughed at himself. She may have some of his qualities, but looks weren't one of them.

He was outside the hairdresser's at ten twenty. Laura came out at quarter to eleven. The blonde bob had gradually been replaced by the natural softer brown waves. He said nothing. He enjoyed having a legitimate reason to sit on a wall and watch the world go by. They didn't speak.

His car was parked round the corner on a double yellow line. The warden had missed him out. They got in the car and drove out of town. It wasn't until they'd gone through Pooley Bridge and were driving along the lakeside road that she spoke.

'I'm sorry, Mick. I just can't handle it. She's my only daughter. What can I do?'

He drove in silence, mulling over how much he should tell her.

'I'm on his case. Give me a couple of days.'

She looked out at the lake as it came into view, a gaggle of sailing masts giving it away.

'It'll be alright. It's only a phase.'

'I hope you're right,' she said, fighting back the tears.

'I was far worse. What about you? Miss Goody-two-shoes?'

She laughed. 'Not exactly. My dad and I hardly spoke for years.'

'Why? What did you do?'

'The same as Grace. I went out with an unsuitable young man.'

'What was he like?'

'Handsome. Clever. Funny. A good job. Money and a car.'

'So what was wrong with him?'

'He'd not been to grammar school. Left at sixteen with hardly any qualifications.'

'So he was older than you?'

'Yeah. I was just seventeen and he was twenty-four. He'd already served his apprenticeship, on the way up.'

'So what happened?'

She gave him a severe look and then laughed. 'Reader, I married him!'

'Steve?'

'Grace's father.'

They'd arrived at the hotel car park. Ullswater lay like a dull opaque mirror in front of them. Laura took his hand and they walked down to the jetty. At the end they stopped and watched as the ducks waggled their way from the reed beds to see what they'd got. Disappointed, the birds quarrelled under the pier and continued their search.

Fletcher put his arm round her and they stood, lost in their own thoughts. There were things he knew he should tell her, but he was hoping Irene would sort it out before he needed to. Selfishly, he didn't want to spoil this moment. They left the lake and the ducks and walked back to the hotel.

They had a good meal. There were only two other couples in the dining room. Afterwards they walked up to Martindale church and admired the ancient yew trees. Laura told him that Alice had said they'd provided the arrows which were used at Agincourt.

By the time they'd got back to the car, the late afternoon sun was hovering above the Helvellyn range and some dark clouds were building over High Street. A few heavy drops plopped onto the car roof and by the time they reached Askham the rain was beating off the windscreen so hard that Fletcher had to slow down to see where he was going. He knew that Grace was going to Kendal tonight with a class from school to see a play, so they'd be able to have an evening together without having to worry where she was.

How wrong could you be?

They locked the front door and made love in front of the fire in the sitting room. Grace arrived back on time, mumbled from the stairs that the play had been OK and went straight to bed. They didn't even see her. It was only later the next day that the truth hit them and by then it was too late.

CHAPTER 6

They were up with the eagles. Sunday morning had surprised them. As is often the case in the Lake District, the rain had gone and a newly-washed sun filtered through the curtains. Laura checked the Windermere weather line and declared that it was a Long Stile day.

Fletcher pretended to groan in despair, which only resulted in having the bed clothes ripped off him. They had a good breakfast, packed a lunch and set off south to Haweswater. An hour and a half later they reached the corner above the Rigg and looked down over what was left of Mardale.

Fletcher had been inducted into the Wainright tradition and knew the old man's feelings on the matter. He also knew that although Laura was a couple of years older than him, she hadn't spent half her life smoking and drinking like him, did upwards of two hundred lengths in the local pool every week, so he was going to have a hard job keeping up with her on the ascent up Long Stile. She waited for him at each minor summit until they'd reached the foot of the final steep climb. This involved a bit of scrambling, which he enjoyed, so it went more quickly than slogging up the steady incline.

It was as they lengthened their strides on the last few yards to the summit that they heard the cries. Shielding their eyes against the midday sun, they spotted the elegant aerial acrobatics being performed by a trio of peregrine falcons as they rode the strong thermals being funnelled up the rocky cliffs. For a city boy like Fletcher, this was always a thrill. He stood and gazed at the spectacle until the threesome drifted off across towards Harter Fell – a distance which took them a matter of seconds compared to the hour and a half route-march it would take a couple of walkers. In any case, Fletcher and Laura were headed in the opposite direction, round the head of Riggindale followed by a gentle stroll to the top of Kidsty Pike.

They sat on the summit rocks overlooking the steep precipice dropping away beneath them and ate their lunch. The sky hung like a tent above them; not a single hole in the solid dome of perfect blue. They'd not spoken much during the ascent, but here they were utterly silenced by the still immensity. And that was when they heard a different call. It was not like any other: deeper than the cries of the buzzard or the shrieks of falcons, sweeter than the croak of a raven, a tenor to the corvine bass.

Laura spotted him first, soaring high above them. They were sitting at over two and a half thousand feet, but the eagle was up another thousand again. He was turning in a huge circle, which slowly widened until its centre drifted across the long ridge of the Roman road towards Ullswater. They watched until their necks began to ache. Their eyes met. What use were words? They didn't try.

Later, as they paused at the Roman encampment overlooking the lake, Laura voiced the turmoil going on inside her head.

'Why is she doing this?'

Fletcher stared down at the water and toyed with a dry stalk of fern.

'Is it me?'

He shook his head.

'What can we do?'

'I don't know . . . I've asked a colleague to do a bit of digging. She knows him from school days. There's nothing on file. He's clean.'

'Thanks for looking.'

'It doesn't mean he's never done anything bad. Just that he's not been caught or come to our attention.'

He didn't tell her what Irene had said.

They carried on back to the car, passing across the little bridge over the beck round which the village had grown. The reservoir was full, so there were only a few dry stone walls heading down into the water to give any sign of its existence. They drove home, looking forward to a quiet night in and an early bed.

There was a note on the table. *I've gone to live with Dekker. Don't come looking for me. I'll come and see you Monday night. Grace.*

Laura stared at the paper in her hand and tried to make it say something less desperate, but she couldn't. She didn't cry. She felt numb.

Fletcher picked it up and read it, cursed silently and put his arms round Laura. He held her tight as she sobbed. His head was full of action but he knew he couldn't leave. They talked long into the night. When it grew dark they talked in the shadows.

Eventually they went to bed. Fletcher fell asleep. Laura lay still and went over every moment of her life with Grace, as though she might find the answer to a riddle she couldn't read.

As dawn came she slept.

The next morning was a solemn awakening. Despite Fletcher's pleading with her to stay at home, Laura insisted on getting dressed and going to work. He did the same.

* * * *

The other officers already knew him well enough to realise there was a problem, but no-one had the nerve to tackle him about it.

He asked if anyone knew where Irene was. Lots of headshaking didn't help his mood. He checked the rota; she should be at work. He found her home number. No reply. He asked if anyone knew any other way of contacting her, but this produced nothing. Her parents were both dead. She wasn't married. Despite all her flirting, no-one had ever been to her flat. He had to look up the address in her file.

Ten minutes later, he was knocking on her door. It was on the first floor above a bookmaker's on the high street. There was no reply. He used his keys to get in – the set of keys he'd been given by an old lag the last time he'd put him away. The flat was small: just two rooms and a small kitchen space, very neat and tidy, decorated in simple colours, a few pictures, a top-of-the-range hi-fi system. Clean and empty. No sign of any other person. He was struck by how lonely it felt. There was no address book next to the phone or in the small bureau against the wall. A few photos in chemist's packets, mostly of her with people he didn't recognise on beaches and in bars. Holiday snaps. He left a note asking her to contact him and left.

He returned to the station and asked around until one of the young uniform officers, PC Burke, said he'd been at school with both Irene and Dekker. He thought that Dekker had lived in one of the council houses on the edge of town. Fletcher stuck him in a car and they set off.

It took some time and a lot of patience to get anywhere. There was a collective, dour reluctance amongst these people to talk to the police at all, let alone about one of their own. Fletcher was on the verge of giving up when the young officer beckoned him to the door of a particularly rundown building at the end of a desolate cul-de-sac. Two of the neighbouring houses were boarded up and one of them had blackened marks above the downstairs windows.

The man who opened the door was unshaven and bleary eyed. He stared at Fletcher as though he was looking at an alien.

'Mr Begley says he might know where Dekker lives, but wants an assurance that we didn't find out from him,' said the uniform.

Fletcher gave the man a shrug and growled at him. 'If you don't tell me what I need to know, Mr Begley, I'll be back with a search warrant before you can get out of your pyjamas.'

The man huddled his coat round his thin body.

'There's no need for that. Dekker's probably moved on anyway.' But he did give them a street name and house number.

Fletcher and the young officer headed back to the car with the dubious information they'd received. PC Burke knew the address. It was a semi on new estate on the other side of town.

They parked at the corner and watched for a while. There was a car in front of the house. Fletcher and Burke crossed the road. The constable made his way down to the side gate and nodded back to Fletcher before going through. Fletcher rang the bell.

After a couple of minutes, the door opened a crack and a young woman stared out at him over the safety chain. Before Fletcher could say anything, she slammed the door shut and yelled to someone else back in the house. Fletcher turned to see if he had an audience; nobody in sight. He kicked the door down and found Burke struggling with an older man in the corridor. His efforts were being hampered by the young woman hitting him with a cushion.

In a different situation Fletcher might have found the scene amusing, but not here. He grabbed the woman by the arm, pulled her towards him and slapped her hard across the head. She fell to the floor. Without pausing, Fletcher grabbed the man by his shoulder, pulled him away from Burke and punched him in the face. The force of the blow knocked the man through the doorway behind him and onto the kitchen floor. The woman cowered, holding her head. The man tried to stagger to his feet but Fletcher kicked his knee. He cried out in pain and held his injured leg.

'You may think this is excessive violence for a police officer to use without provocation, so I would advise you not to provoke me. I'm in the mood to do far worse damage. Do you understand?' Fletcher said, leaning against the doorjamb.

The man looked at him with a sullen expression. His left eye was beginning to close and blood was trickling from his nose. But it was PC Burke who was the most shocked. He'd not seen a fellow officer carry out such a brutal attack since he'd joined up.

Fletcher rubbed his knuckles and started to speak. He wasn't interested in what they had to say until he'd made it clear what he wanted. 'Right. Here's what you need to know.'

He looked down at the man who was rubbing his knee, blood dripping onto his shirt.

'None of this happened. You weren't here with this girl. You fell over your own bootlaces or whatever story you want to invent. Otherwise I'll make sure that your wife, children, family, workmates and employers know what you were doing. Am I clear?'

The man nodded and put a handkerchief to his face. He'd only just realised he was bleeding.

'The only other thing you can tell me is if you know the whereabouts of Derek Wray aka Dekker?'

The man shook his head. Fletcher reached out and grabbed

his hair. He raised his fist and asked the question again. He got definite confirmation that the man knew nothing.

'Right. You can go. But if I find out you were lying to me, I'll find you and this will seem like playtime. Now get out.'

The man crawled and staggered his way to the front door, pausing only to take in the savagery inflicted on that inanimate object, before limping down to his car.

Fletcher waited until they heard the car drive away. The half-naked girl was shivering with cold and fear. Burke didn't know what to say or do. Fletcher crouched down beside the girl and put his face close to hers. She cringed against the wall and put her hands in front of her face.

'Please don't hit me,' she whimpered.

Fletcher took her hand and stared into her eyes. She was pretty, in a baby doll sort of way. He wondered just how young she was. He gently pulled her arm straight so that he could see the marks. Her eyes hardened.

'I'm not going to hit you. I'm not even going to arrest you. In fact I'm going to take you to someone who can help you – if you want.'

She stared at him, suspecting a trick.

'You can't prove a thing anyway,' she said with an assertive pout.

Fletcher sighed and sank down against the wall opposite her. She looked towards the younger officer and figured her chances of making a run for it were zero.

Fletcher felt in his pockets, produced a packet of cigarettes and offered her one. She took it and accepted a light. He put everything away and looked at her sadly.

'I'll tell you the truth. I need to know where to find Dekker because my own daughter has gone to stay with him and I don't think she knows what he's really like.'

The girl weighed this up and checked out the uniformed policeman. He was staring at his superior in disbelief.

'I need to find her, before she ends up like you,' Fletcher said.

The girl was recovering some of her resilience. 'Why? Do you think your daughter's better than me?'

Fletcher gave her a long hard stare.

'I don't know anything about you. I wouldn't want any girl your age to end up doing this. You or my daughter.'

The girl dropped her eyes and considered the cigarette.

'How would you get in touch, if you needed him?'

'I've got a number.'

'Ring it. Say you've been beaten up by a punter and need to go to hospital.'

'He won't like that.'

'I know. Tell him you're going to tell the police the name of the punter.'

She laughed. 'He wouldn't believe me.'

'Say you're going to do it anyway and put the phone down.'

'He'll be round here in a flash.'

'Exactly.'

'Then what?' she asked.

'You won't be here. My colleague will take you somewhere safe.'

She looked from one man to the other. 'He's not the main man, you know – and he'll bring some back-up.'

'The more the merrier,' said Fletcher. He got to his feet and fetched the phone. 'Ring him now.'

Reluctantly she took the phone and dialled a number. It was picked up on the third ring.

'Hello. Is Dekker there?' She looked at Fletcher with a puzzled expression. 'When did that happen?'

There was an angry buzz at the other end of the line.

'Alright. I understand . . . yeh . . . .yeh . . .'

She handed the phone back to Fletcher. A smile crept across her face.

'You're too late, copper. One of your lot's nicked him already.'

Fletcher stared at her in disbelief. Then he turned to Burke. 'Constable. Go back to the car and check in. Find out what's going on.'

* * * *

Irene Garner had good reason to be pleased with herself. She was sitting in the canteen washing down a bacon sandwich with a strong cup of tea. DC Lonsdale sat opposite her, tucking into something far more unhealthy. Neither of them could keep the big grins off their faces. Every now and then, they'd look at each other and burst out laughing. Laughing till they cried. They were towards the end of one of these fits when they saw Fletcher standing in the doorway. He was not laughing.

They managed to control themselves with a few coughs and splutters. Fletcher fetched himself a brew and pulled a chair up to their table. They didn't dare look at each other.

'Five arrests, two gentlemen in hospital and a few young ladies filing their nails in the cells. Not bad for a two-man team.'

'Two-person team,' Irene corrected him.

'Is it all written down yet?'

Irene and Lonsdale looked at each other.

'Hang on, sir. Give us a chance. We've not had a break for the best part of two days,' said Lonsdale indignantly.

Fletcher gave him a blank stare. Irene sensed something dangerous.

'What do you want to know, sir?' she asked.

Fletcher continued to look at Lonsdale, who was becoming nervous. He put down the fork full of sausage and waited.

'Give me a list,' said Fletcher.

'Dekker Wray: in hospital with a broken arm, charged with resisting arrest. Ken Drummond: in traction, fell down stairs – a lot of metal stairs, charged with assault. Len Castle: interview room awaiting a top brief from Manchester. Two women – as you say, sir – waiting for the duty solicitor to get them out on bail. One young girl in hospital – in a drugged sleep – suspected sexual assault . . . sir.'

Fletcher's expression didn't change, but his fist tightened round his mug. 'The young girl's name?'

'No idea, sir. Have to wait till she wakes up. The . . . er . . . gentlemen either wouldn't or couldn't say . . . sir.'

Fletcher got to his feet and made for the door. 'General Hospital?'

Irene nodded. 'You want me to come with you, sir?'

'You better had.'

He turned on his heel and strode out. Irene gave Lonsdale a puzzled shrug, grabbed her bag and ran after him.

*　*　*　*

It was the worst moment Fletcher had experienced for a long time. He'd told Irene about the note; she'd asked him to describe Grace.

She shook her head. 'I don't think it's her, sir. This girl's a blonde – like me.'

She saw the look he gave her and concentrated on driving.

When they got out of the car, Fletcher spoke to her quietly as they walked into the hospital. 'Just get me in to see the girl. Don't let anyone stop us. I don't think . . .'

He didn't finish, but punched the door. Irene got him in. Doctors, nurses, visitors and patients all stopped and stared, but she got him through.

A nurse was taking the girl's temperature. Her eyes were closed. She was blonde: bottle blonde. It was Grace. Her eyes opened and widened as they focused on Fletcher. His eyes filled with tears as he crossed to the bedside. Irene shook her head at the nurse.

Fletcher held Grace's hand. She looked at him with a mixture of fear and relief. Irene led the nurse outside and told her to get the doctor. She closed the door, but not before she could hear them competing in the 'sorry' stakes.

The doctor arrived and Irene explained the relationship. The doctor took a deep breath and went into the room. Irene watched the conversation, glad she didn't have to listen to it. The doctor came out and waited. Fletcher spoke to Grace, kissed her and followed him out.

'Tell me the truth,' said Fletcher, leaning against the wall.

'I can't be sure yet,' the doctor replied. 'We need to wait for the test results.'

He paused. 'I won't hide anything from you. The girl has had – was having sex – when it was interrupted. If it's any comfort to you, I don't think she knew anything at the time.'

Fletcher studied the floor.

'The good news is that she's not been . . . hurt . . . I mean there's no tearing or bruising.'

Fletcher stood immobile, clenching and unclenching his fists.

'When will you get the results?'

'Later today.'

'I need to tell her mother – bring her here, okay?'

'Of course, as soon as you can.'

Fletcher set off, walked five yards and turned.

'Thank you, Doctor.' Then he was gone.

Irene chased after him.

* * * *

1976

Fern was well aware that the second part of her plan would be much harder. She knew what she wanted to do, although it didn't turn out the way she'd intended. The first problem was to figure out how to abduct someone when you've not even met them or been to their house.

She knew where she wanted to take the woman and, to some extent, what she was going to do to her. She also had the means of transport. She'd found the man's rental agreement in the glove compartment. He'd booked the car for a week, so she had five days left. She didn't intend to take so long. Fortunately she'd already got the next two days off and she'd told people where she was going. This fitted in perfectly and would give her a solid alibi, if it was needed. The problem was that she needed to carry out the abduction tomorrow morning and get to her destination round about dusk. She knew the journey would take about five hours.

The simplest bit was getting the address. She knew that by the small hours the other two care workers on duty would be dozing in their chairs, so nipping into the office and finding the file would be easy. This was accomplished by half past one.

The address made life a lot easier. Dawn had described the house sufficiently for her to have a good idea what it would look like, but now she knew exactly where it was her task would be less difficult. It was a detached property on the way through the lanes towards Ibstock. If her memory served her right, it was a large house set in extensive grounds on a road alongside similar buildings. Even at this time of year, the large fir hedge would screen the main entrance from the road.

But how to persuade someone to get into the car and not cause any problems en route? Fern knew she could get hold of a range of sedatives, pills and drugs which would put someone to sleep. She spent some time in the dispensary collecting an assortment without knowing which she might use. The problem was one of administering the drugs. It wasn't as if she hadn't done it before, although generally she would have had help from a colleague to restrain anyone who was reluctant. Most people didn't easily accept a needle in their arm or anywhere else for that matter. Also, there was the problem of gaining entry to the house. Fern hadn't met the woman. There might be some advantage in surprise but she sounded like she might be a naturally suspicious person, so that wouldn't last for long.

Fern had all night to work out what to do; she had no desire to go to sleep. It was well past four o'clock when she formulated the plan. It required a short visit to the garage which housed the home's minibus, from where she borrowed a bicycle chain, complete with lock and key, and a piece of thick towing rope that was hanging on the wall. The plan had lots of risks and potential pitfalls, but after last night she felt she could pull off anything. The forces of justice were on her side.

Before dawn, Fern was parked across the road in a lane which went off at right angles to the house. Would the husband go to work this morning? It said in the file that he was a solicitor. She knew the firm; it had offices in an old building on the High Street in Ashby. She hoped it was a busy operation.

Her luck held. At eight thirty-five, a black BMW glided out of the gates and headed towards Ashby. She saw the man's face as it accelerated away. Dawn had said that although her stepmother didn't have a job, she was not inclined to stay in bed all day. She'd stated with some distaste that the woman spent an hour or so applying make-up and arranging her hair before setting off to meet her friends for morning coffee or a shopping expedition.

Fern gave the husband five minutes to get away and then drove the car through the gates and parked outside the front door.

Her heart was beating like a galloping horse as she pressed the doorbell. The woman inside didn't make her wait for long.

The door was flung open and Helen Courtney fixed her visitor with her best finishing-school smile. Fern had only the briefest of moments to take in the spectacle of a woman, six years her junior, dressed for a fashion show, adorned with full make-up in glorious Technicolor and a huge bouffant of shimmering black hair cascading onto her bare shoulders – at quarter to nine in the morning, for heaven's sake! She was smaller than Fern had expected, which was good, but the sheer excessiveness of her appearance completely disarmed her. A waft of expensive perfume billowed out of the warm house.

'Good morning,' said Helen. 'How can I help?'

Fern was equally nonplussed by the confident arrogance with which the woman assumed she would be able to help – whatever the problem.

'Hello. Mrs Courtney? I should have phoned, but I needed to see you today at home.'

The smile began to slip. 'Indeed? And who are you?'

'I'm sorry. My name is Fern Robinson. I work at the children's home. Hasn't Mrs Johnson from Social Services contacted you?'

The smile disappeared altogether. 'No she hasn't and I fail to see why any of you feel you have the right to visit me at home. I would have refused anyway.'

Her dark eyes took on a malevolent glare and she made to shut the door.

'Mrs Courtney. Please. I'm merely here to discuss the arrangements for your daughter's return.'

Fern was right. The woman was immediately suspicious.

'What arrangements? I fail to see why that should require a visit to my home.'

Fern mustered all the humility she could manage, which was difficult, when all she wanted to do was slap the woman's face.

'Mrs Courtney. I've been charged with your daughter's care since she arrived in the home. There are things she wanted me to tell you before she returns. Personal things. It won't take long, but she has pleaded with me to talk to you face to face.'

The look of suspicion didn't soften, but Fern could see that the words had generated some curiosity behind those piercing eyes.

'Well I suppose I can spare you a few minutes but I'm telling you now, I'm not going to be lectured by a social worker no matter what your so-called qualifications claim.'

She stood back from the door and Fern entered the hall.

It was stiflingly warm and, when the woman showed her into an opulent lounge, Fern had an increasing sense of being invited into the ante-room to hell. It wasn't that cold outside for an early spring morning. She could see some eager blossom starting to smother a large cherry tree through the window, which, of course, was firmly shut.

Mrs Courtney indicated a large black leather sofa which would have filled Fern's living room. Fern was burning up.

'You do like to be warm,' she said. 'May I take off my jacket?'

'I do, and you may. But don't get too comfortable. I have an appointment later this morning, which I have no intention of missing. Say what you've got to say and make it quick.'

Fern took off her jacket and folded it next to her bag, which she'd left open for ease of access.

They looked at each other. Helen Courtney had been taught how a lady should sit on a high-backed chair. Her legs were crossed at the knees, revealing well-muscled calves and a pair of expensive high-heeled shoes. Her left hand rested lightly on the arm of the chair to display the gold and diamonds clustering her fingers like barnacles. Her right elbow rested on the other arm so that her right hand could be elegantly held aloft so that the other barnacles would catch the light from the window. The smile had been reassembled, but the red lips glistened with a cruel delight.

And what could Helen Courtney see?

A tall, angular woman wearing inexpensive workman's clothes more appropriate for a stables or a garden. Her trousers were soiled at the knees. Her coat was a hideous brown waterproof; the sort worn by idiot ramblers tramping across grouse moorland. Her hair was unwashed and cut short like a man's. And then there was the smell. Was that something chemical or just animal sweat? Her eyes were an opaque blue and she was staring in a most ill-mannered way as she perched on the edge of the settee. Now she was reaching into her rucksack and looking for something.

A knife.

Fern was pleased to see the astonishment on Helen Courtney's perfect face.

'I don't know whether you know that this was your gentleman friend's choice of visiting card . . . but he has no need of it now.'

The woman had turned into a frozen image of herself.

Fern continued to talk quietly, as she turned the blade over and over in her hand.

'You have two choices. You can submit quietly to a professionally administered sedation . . . or you can put up a fight.'

The woman's dark eyes betrayed the first intimations of fear.

'To be honest with you,' Fern went on, 'I'd prefer the latter, because I think it unlikely that you'd manage any effective resistance . . . and it would give me a great deal of pleasure to make a mess of your beautiful face.'

To her surprise the terrified woman laughed. A high-pitched, hysterical laugh.

Fern produced the syringe from the bag and laid it on the cushion beside her. Helen glanced at the phone on the table beside her. Her abductor shook her head and held up the knife.

'No use. I cut it off at six o'clock this morning.'

Helen's eyes went back to Fern.

'I'm going to count to three, Helen, and then, if you can't make up your mind, I'll assume you're not going to come quietly. . . One . . . '

'You're mad. You're not going to get away with this.'

'Oh, but I am . . . Two.'

Helen uncrossed her legs and gripped the arms of the chair. Fern stood up and came towards her. She'd left the knife and the syringe on the settee. Helen vainly thought this increased her chances of escape. She got to her feet and made to run towards the door. She didn't get two steps.

Fern reached out, grabbed her by her hair and dragged her

back. Helen screamed. Fern took hold of her left wrist, forced her arm up behind her back and put her hand over the woman's scarlet mouth. The screaming became a muffled gargle. Fern forced her onto her knees and then face down on the floor. Pinning her there with her knee and one hand, she picked up the syringe with her free hand and popped off the cap with a deft and practised move. One squirt to break the vacuum and a cruel push with her knee in the middle of the woman's back. Helen gasped for breath. Fern stabbed the needle through the green dress and into the muscle of her victim's upper arm. She listened to her muffled screams until they faltered and her body went limp. Fern held her for another twenty seconds or so before standing up. The woman lay awkwardly; her dress rucked up beneath her waist. Her tights were torn and one of her heels was broken. She began to snore.

Fern moved with care and deliberation. First, she retrieved a pair of plastic gloves from her bag and put them on. She found the cap on the floor; put it and the syringe back into her bag with the knife. Next she picked up the broken shoe and took its companion from the woman's limp foot. She walked calmly to the front door and out to the car. She opened the boot and threw in the shoes. She picked up the bicycle chain and the rope, opened the passenger door and placed her bag on the seat. Going back into the house, she glanced towards the road. It was empty.

It didn't take long to tie the rope round Helen Courtney's legs and put the bicycle chain round her wrists. The sedated woman wasn't heavy; she was no fireman. It took only a few seconds to take her out and place her in the boot. Fern went back to check the lounge one last time, came out, shut the front door and looked at her watch. It had taken her only twenty-three minutes since she'd pulled onto the drive.

Five minutes later, she turned left onto the Burton road in the middle of Ashby and headed west. She would need to stop twice during the journey to ensure the woman remained asleep, but that was already planned. She knew the route well.

As she rumbled over the railway crossing on the way out of Tutbury, she realised that her body was consumed by exhilaration. She made herself slow down and smiled at the sign for the Salt Box. She was heading home. She was still not exactly sure what she was going to do when she got there, but she'd plenty of time to contemplate her plans.

Even at this point, Fern couldn't have admitted that she was going to kill the woman. It was the thought of how Helen Courtney had treated her daughter that had driven her anger, but she didn't know where the coldness which allowed her to carry through the plan had come from. The exhilaration was on the surface; deep inside was something else – some stronger urge which she didn't yet understand or want to examine, lying there like a silent dragon, its cold red eyes blinking in the darkness.

CHAPTER 7

By lunchtime on Monday 3rd of March they were in. Following Ted's advice, Martin had contacted Fred Tirril, who'd reluctantly agreed to come and see what he could do about the gates.

'Mind you,' he added in his gravelly voice, 'there's tales me dad telt wa aboot yon geats and t'ouse. And yah naahs t'sodgers kem tu tek em doon in't waahr. The'gev ower in't end. Story gaas that there waar queer gannins on, wan of 'em deed, t'others wadn't keep gaan. Machines wadn't wark.... And other things...'

Martin couldn't think of much to say to this, but passed it on to the others. Most of them smiled or shrugged their shoulders, but he saw a different look on Octavia's face. When he asked her what she thought, she just shook her head and said it was nothing.

In the event nothing strange happened – while Fred was there. He arrived in his old van, eased his wiry body from the battered seat and walked up to the gates. He examined the chain and poked about in the lock. He'd not said anything so far, other than a grunted nod at the assembled group. Then he limped back to his van and produced a giant pair of metal cutters.

Octavia glanced at Tom who was grinning at her. He winked. She put her tongue out at him; they could have been back in the playground. She indicated that he should give Fred a hand but Tom gave her a very definite shake of his head.

They watched as the old blacksmith approached the gates. He pulled the chain through as far as it would come and caught one of the links in the jaw of his cutter. They saw him take a breath before slowly applying pressure with his thin arms. At first it looked as though he was making no impression. He readjusted his grip and tried again. Octavia looked at Tom, who was watching the old fellow intently. She looked back. Fred stepped back and the chain fell apart.

Everyone clapped. Fred ignored them, gave his wrists a shake and trudged back to the van. Next he produced a thin saw and looked across at Tom.

'Git tha self o'er yon an' holt the lock still.'

Tom clambered up the ladder and down the other side. Fred pointed at where he wanted him to hold the lock. Tom steadied himself and watched as the saw slipped through the gap and Fred jiggled it into position over the giant nib. He rested it there, spat on both hands and grasped the worn handle.

It took about eight minutes. Fred didn't rush at it. He moved the saw back and forth at a steady pace, stopping for frequent rests. Octavia could see his lips moving as he counted the strokes. She smiled to herself; she thought he was almost certainly counting in dialect.

'Yan, tan, tetherer . . .' she counted to herself.

The saw cut through the last few slivers of metal and Tom gasped as he took the full weight of the disconnected gates. The left-hand side slowly sank to the ground. It was only a couple of inches, but for one awful moment Tom glanced to his right to see what was happening to the hinges. There was some movement, but they held. Nevertheless he yelled at everyone to stand clear. He waited until Fred backed away before slowly releasing his grip. The gates didn't move. He came back over to the rest of them. This time no-one had clapped, but there had been an audible sigh of relief as Tom took his hands away.

Everyone started to talk at once, except Fred who put his saw back in the van and stumped over to the gates. He checked the lock and then went to study the hinges on both sides. Finally he looked through to the house in the distance. Octavia went to stand beside him.

'Tha'll be Edward 'Utton's granddowter,' he said.

'Yes, I am,' she replied.

He turned and looked at her. His eyes had both been blue; now one of them had a white cast to it and the other was rheumy and bloodshot.

'Tek care, lass. Yon spot . . .' he hesitated. 'Aa's nut yan fur awd wives' tales, but thar'll be good reason fut rowd it's bin left . . .'

He gave her one more look and walked back to his van. Martin caught up with him, wallet in hand. She watched as her boss tried his hardest to give the old man some money. Fred's hands stayed deep in his pockets. He didn't say much, just shook his head. Octavia wanted to tell Martin that he was insulting the old man, but reckoned she'd only make the situation worse. Eventually, Martin admitted defeat and offered his hand. It wasn't 'tekken'. Fred Tirrel said a final few words and climbed back into his van. They all watched as he drove away.

Martin came over. Tom and Ted were already testing the weight of one of the gates and agreeing it would need a tractor.

'I think I got that all wrong,' said Martin.

'I'm afraid so,' said Octavia. 'But don't worry. He has been known to smile occasionally, but I wouldn't play cards for money with him. He just thinks "tha naws nowt".'

Martin shook his head and grinned. 'You know what he said to me?'

100

They were all listening.

'He quoted Shakespeare at me.'

'What?' said Ransome in disbelief.

'He said "Tek care," and then "there's mair things in heaven un earth than we can ken abaat".'

'Horatio!' completed Ransome and laughed. He looked back down the lane. 'The old devil, where did he learn that, I wonder?'

'We're not savages, you know,' said Tom sternly.

Ransome blushed. 'Of course not . . . but . . .'

'And age has not withered him, neither,' added Tom with a grin. 'It would have taken me twice as long and twice as much effort.'

He and Ted went to get the right sort of tractors. Ransome spent the time at the edge of the briars where they'd come to a halt on Saturday. He sketched various views and concentrated on a few of the more interesting features. He wasn't averse to using a camera, but reckoned sketching was more interpretative.

'Cameras neither lie nor tell the truth,' he said to Octavia, as she looked over his shoulder.

'I reckon we'll find that not only have we a prime example of Rickman's work, but that Rivka will be apoplectic when we get inside.'

'Why do you say that?'

'Well, I bet you a fiver that there's at least one Burne-Jones in there.'

'You're on. Unless you're admitting to some inside knowledge. Family secrets?'

'That's for you to worry about,' she laughed, but at the same time wondered whether indeed the dark rectangles her father had told her about would prove to be unseen masterpieces.

Octavia turned as she heard the chugging of two engines coming closer. She and Ransome walked back down to find Tom and his friend attaching thick ropes to the right-hand gate. Using a simple pulley, they took the rope round the side pillar and tied it to the back of the tractor. It didn't shift easily. While Ted kept inching his tractor away, Tom struggled to lift the gate out of the mud. Gradually it got higher and was soon leaning at right angles to the wall. They uncoupled the ropes and Ted got in position to reverse back for the other gate. He was revving his engine, when Lex strolled up and with one hand touched the broken lock. Without a sound, the huge weight of twisted metal gate swung back as though it was newly oiled and perfectly balanced.

Ted took his foot off the throttle and the tractor engine died. They all stared at the gate and at Lex.

'How did you . . . ?' murmured Tom.

'No idea,' said an equally astonished Lex. 'I . . . just . . . thought it might.'

They all laughed.

'I don't suppose you fancy parting the briar waves for your next trick?' said Ransome.

They followed Ted's tractor down to the edge of the briar. He'd fixed a digger bucket to the front, which he now lowered like a rhino about to charge; he'd dealt with briars before.

'No use trying to force your way through,' said Tom. 'He's going to dig the buggers out.'

So it was that Ted dug a six-foot wide path through to the house, depositing each load of debris to one side. At one point he encountered a low wall and everyone had to help clear it before he could continue. They came to a higher wall ten feet from the side of the house and again it was manual labour that got them through. Finally they had to fight their way up a flight of steps to a balustrade in front of what looked like the main doors.

Lex was invited to try the door handle but her powers seemed to have deserted her. The door was locked tight. Martin decided it was time for a break and a discussion about forcing an entry. They retreated to the main gates and ate the lunch that Rivka had brought from the local shop. The debate quickly resolved that they'd have to cut their way in through the doors, trying to make as little damage as possible so they could be repaired afterwards. Once this was decided, the conversation drifted to a series of bets, like Octavia's with Ransome.

Tiring of this, and with an idea niggling inside her head, Octavia wandered back down the path. As she crossed the gap in the briars, she heard someone behind her. It was Tom. He'd ignored the raised eyebrows and suppressed sniggers from the rest of them and followed her down.

'You'll have people talking about us, Tom Harper,' she said with mock severity.

'Well, my lady. What if they do?'

She laughed and then pointed to her left. 'You see that wall?'

He nodded. It was only just visible above the riot of thorns.

'Does it go all the way to the house?'

He looked around. 'Not sure, but I think so. Yeh, there's a sort of arch.'

Octavia's heart leapt. 'Can you get to it?'

He picked up one of the machetes they'd been using and started hacking his way through. She followed him. They reached the wall and cut their way to the house. Tom stopped and looked back at her.

'How did you know that?' he asked.

'What?'

'There's a window. It's broken. I reckon we could get in.'

A few minutes later, he was picking glass out of the window frame.

'It'll have to be you,' he said. 'I'll never get my shoulders through there.'

'Okay!' she said. 'Give us a bunk up.'

He laughed. '"Give us a bunk up!" my lady? What sort of language is that?'

'Git away wi' yerself, lad,' she retorted.

He laughed again, but then became serious. 'I think we ought to wait for the others, Tavi.'

'What, and miss my moment of glory?'

And without a second thought she put her boot on a handy ledge and levered her way up to the window. Before he could say another word she was through. Her head popped out again.

'Go on. Go and get the rest. I'll meet you at the front door.'

He called out, but she'd gone. He hurried back to the others.

Inside, Octavia allowed her eyes to accustom themselves to the gloom. Her father's rectangles appeared on the walls and white shapes stood all around like beached whales. She made her way round the wall from the window until she came to a door. Turning the handle she pulled it towards her.

She stepped into an enormous hallway. Even in the darkness she could sense it must go to the full height of the building. The breeze from outside followed her in, rustling across the floor and tinkling amongst hanging glass. Octavia saw a few sparkles high above. The floor beneath her feet was like ice, she could feel the cold through her boots. She continued her way around the wall to where she knew the front door must be, although there wasn't the slightest chink of light to give it away. Halfway there she encountered a statue. Cold marble. Naked. Male. The artistic possibilities skittered through her head. Definitely Greek, she said to herself.

Near the door she found a large candlestick holder, followed by thick marble pillars and finally, solid carved wood. The doors were huge. She fumbled for the lock. A key! There was a giant key still in the door. She took it in both hands thinking it would be stiff, but Lex's powers seemed to have passed to her. It turned more smoothly than her own cottage key – but the door stayed solidly shut. Bolts? She felt down below, eased one open. She reached up, but couldn't find the one above. She was obviously too small, she needed a chair or something to climb on.

She continued on past the doors. More pillars. Another candle holder. Another statue. Marble. Naked. Female! Her shins banged against something lower down. A quick exploration revealed a chaise longue, smooth wood and satin fabric. She dragged it across the hall to the door, climbed onto it and reached upwards, feeling for the bolt. Found it . . . began to ease it across . . . nearly there. She could feel the door relaxing as though she was opening a jar of Mrs Hesket's jam. If she'd stopped to think, she might have considered the awesomeness of this moment, but she was too excited. She wanted to see the team's astonished faces as she opened the door in front of them.

The noise was horrendous. The fact that it was accompanied by a flash of brilliant light made it even more terrifying. She didn't know whether to put her hands over her ears or her eyes. But then the pain. Unidentifiable at first, but gradually she felt the pinpricks over every part of her body not covered by clothing. Her head, her face, her hands and where her shirt and jumper had risen up to reveal a slice of her back. Glass, she realised. The noise had subsided. The shower of tiny glass particles had stopped. She slowly turned and saw what had happened. On the vast chequered floor of the hall lay the spread-eagled remains of an enormous chandelier. Its peacock's eyes sparkling from every inch of floor, gathered in an icy slush against the walls and sprinkled up the staircase. Her eyes followed the dazzling display upwards towards the hole in the ceiling high above. Sunlight shimmered off the settling cloud of diamond dust.

She could hear the voices of her colleagues shouting through the door as though they were half a mile away, but they were soon rendered soundless as her brain rewound what it had failed to accept on the upward sweep. Now it took her back to the top of the stairs. To the painting she had briefly seen. A woman. In a red dress. Smiling. Her eyes boring into Octavia's. Black, shining eyes. Alive with an intense desire. Alive!

Octavia Hutton had never fainted before in her life.

She fell from the chaise longue and collapsed onto the cold floor, her arm cracking as it crunched into the layer of glass and smacked against the unforgiving marble.

This was how they found her: unconscious, her right arm horribly broken – her ulna sticking up like a chicken's leg. Her whole body was covered in tiny pieces of glass and her face and arms shone like she was coated in oil. Her blood was seeping from a thousand tiny punctures.

It was a sight none of them ever wanted to see again. Tom cradled her in his arms and carried her to the minibus. She regained consciousness for only a few seconds.

He couldn't quite catch what she said, but thought he heard 'woman in bed'.

* * * *

Irene managed to catch up with Fletcher in the car park. She grabbed his arm and brought him to a halt. He stopped, but didn't look at her – just stared into the distance.

'Hey,' she said. 'You mustn't do anything . . .' Words failed her. He glared at her.

'I mean, sir. You can't get involved. Personal interest and all that. Anyway it's not your case. It's mine and Lonsdale's. We had to tell Inspector Fisher. He authorised it and provided the back-up. You were off duty. I tried to contact you, but . . .'

'So how did you find him?'

She grinned. 'I told you. We had a brief fling. Some time ago.'

'At his wedding?'

'Yeh. Well. That didn't last long. That's how I found him – I went to see Trisha. When she'd finished calling him every name under the sun, she told me.'

'So where was he?'

'Saturday night is his busy night. I think he's running about eight or nine girls. He was in Tina's. It's what passes for a night club round here.'

Fletcher had heard of it, but didn't even know where it was.

'He was nervous of me at the beginning, but I was dressed like a tart and I know he still fancies me. I pretended to get drunk . . . got all loud and giggly. We went back to his place and I let him paw me about a bit, before I passed out.'

Fletcher had begun to pace up and down as she told her story. He doubted that it was the whole truth, but it was as much as she was going to tell him or anyone.

'DC Lonsdale was outside all the time,' Irene said.

'So how did this lead to so many arrests?'

'Ah. Well that's the clever bit. When he thought I was out for the count, he set off to check on his girls. Lonsdale followed him . . .'

'Yeah, and then what?' Fletcher was losing patience.

'We went round the next night and caught 'em at it!' she exclaimed.

'On a Sunday night?'

She laughed at him. 'I don't think the oldest profession gets Sundays off, sir. A lot of their punters have had to spend the whole day with wives, parents and children. They're pretty desperate by the time they can get a couple of hours off to go to the pub . . . except, of course, some of them don't go to the pub. They have other needs.'

'So you lay in wait for them?'

'Exactly.'

'So how did you know which one Dekker would be at?'

'We followed him. He's got a rather noticeable car. It's to compensate for the size of his dick . . .'

Fletcher gave her another fierce look.

'I'm sorry, sir,' she said.

'So how did he end up with a broken arm?'

She looked at her shoes. 'I owed it to Trish, sir.'

'And the muscle?'

'He tripped over my leg, sir.'

Fletcher couldn't stop a smile creeping onto his face. 'And the punter?'

Irene looked back at the hospital. 'That's not going to make it so easy, sir.'

'Why?'

'Len Castle. He owns a haulage company. He's loaded; friends in high places, funny handshake. Even on the police committee, as transport advisor . . . sir.'

Fletcher came up close. 'Was he the one, who . . .?'

Irene flinched and took a step back.

'I honestly don't know, sir. By the time we got past Dekker and his mate, Castle was sitting as calm as you please in another room. He claims he'd come to collect unpaid rent, denied any knowledge of what was going on in his property.'

Fletcher reached out for the handle of his car. 'I'm going to get Laura now.'

'Yes, sir. Of course, sir.'

He looked her in the eye. 'But when I get back from the hospital, you're going to arrange for me to spend five minutes with your Mr Castle.'

Irene's eyes went big but before she could speak, he got in the car and wound down the window.

'That's not an order, Irene. It's a threat.' He kept glaring at her as he turned on the engine and started to drive away.

She stood looking after him long after he'd left the car park. She didn't know what to do, but she was more scared of him than any other superior officer. She slowly made her way back to her own car and headed back to the police station.

* * * *

Fetching Laura from work and taking her to see Grace was the hardest thing Fletcher thought he'd ever done. He couldn't bring himself to tell her all he knew, but was relieved that she was more concerned to find Grace alive and apparently unharmed than to start asking awkward questions. He left them hugging each other and went to find the doctor who was in a small consulting room, reading some reports. He didn't make any effort to hide them and passed them across for Fletcher to read. It took him three goes to figure out what the report was saying and even then it didn't make sense. He looked up at the patiently waiting doctor and frowned.

'It's alright; it took me a couple of times to understand what it means.'

Fletcher continued to frown.

'Firstly, as I have already told you, Grace will have only at best a hazy memory of what was going on. She'd taken enough barbiturates to make her incapable of controlling her own movements and would have been virtually unconscious. The good thing about this is that she would have been unable to resist or even be aware of what was happening. She may not remember a thing.'

Fletcher continued to look at him, fearing the worst. The doctor shifted in his seat.

'I can't be sure. I'm not exactly au fait with certain sexual practices . . . but the physical evidence seems to indicate that although there are clear indications that vaginal penetration occurred . . . there is no sign of seminal fluid.'

Fletcher's frown turned to an expression of calculation.

'The most plausible explanation would be that the penetration was not . . .' the doctor hesitated.

'You mean a dildo,' said Fletcher quietly.

The doctor nodded.

'So nothing to prove who it was?'

'Not unless you find it and it's not been cleaned. Even then . . .'

Fletcher gripped the edge of his chair.

'But on a positive note, it also means there's less chance of your stepdaughter contracting a disease. I'd say she's been very lucky and that your colleagues' arrival was timely to say the least.'

The two of them sat considering this and other matters for a few moments. Then Fletcher stood up and shook the young doctor's hand.

'Thank you. For being so prompt and so honest,' he managed to say.

'Well. Hopefully, you'll be able to put these people out of circulation for some time.'

Fletcher shook his head. 'If only it was that simple. You've got two of them in your emergency department, I understand. Resisting arrest. I'm afraid DC Garner was a little over-enthusiastic.'

The doctor stood up and raised his eyebrows. 'Unfortunately my Hippocratic Oath forbids me such laxity, Inspector, or I'd be encouraging my own colleagues down the corridor to take the same approach.'

Fletcher gave him a discerning look, but only received a blank smile.

He went back to Laura and Grace. He talked quickly to Laura and gave her a neutral version of what the doctor had told him. Grace wouldn't meet his eyes. He explained to them that he'd have to go and as far as he knew they'd be home before him. Then he left the hospital and drove back to the station.

*　*　*　*

Irene wasn't doing very well. Both the girls denied everything. They said they'd met Dekker and his pal in a pub and gone back to their place for a bit of fun. They said they didn't know anything about another girl. The police doctor confirmed that they were both too drunk to drive, but not incapable, and that neither of them had had sex in the last few hours. The fact that they were happy to allow this investigation should have set the alarm bells ringing.

Len Castle was the very acme of smugness. He sat with his thick arms crossed over his barrel chest and grinned benignly at every officer, whether they were bringing him a cup of tea or asking him a question. He'd resolutely stuck to his story of the unpaid rent and swore that he'd be kicking the gentlemen out as soon as he was able. His Manchester brief was already driving up the M6, so things were looking a bit bleak when Fletcher got back to the station. Dekker and Drummond were both saying nothing; Drummond was sedated anyway.

Fletcher took Irene to one side and whispered in her ear. 'Where is he?'

She shot him a fearful glance. 'You can't, sir!'

He squeezed her arm hard. 'Which room?'

'Five!' she muttered, her eyes widening as she watched DI Fisher cross the room towards them.

'Ah! Inspector. I believe you know one of the girls arrested last night.'

Fletcher looked him straight in the face. Fisher. Fish-face. Mashed face. Fearing a complete loss of control, he turned on his heel and left the room. Fisher's face changed from smile to puzzlement. He looked at DC Garner.

'Would you care to enlighten me, Constable?'

She did. He frowned and left in search of Chief Inspector Aske.

Irene took a quick look round the room and set off in pursuit of Fletcher.

He hadn't wasted any time. He'd gone straight to interview room five, opened the door and kicked out the young uniform.

He leaned against the door, looking at the back of the man's head. Castle hadn't moved or turned round. A cup of tea was still steaming on the table in front of him. He was wearing a leather jacket two sizes too small and his thick thighs bulged in tight grey trousers. His hair was cut army style; his left ear resembled a cauliflower. As he reached out to pick up the cup, Fletcher saw the thick sausage fingers of a man who'd worked and played hard all his life. He must have heard the shuffling of the exchange of officers behind him, but his self-confidence was such that he didn't deign to look over his shoulder.

Fletcher walked round to face him. As he sat down, Castle smiled at him.

'Ah. A different face. Are you taking it in turns for the practice or do you think you might catch me out by playing these games?'

Fletcher said nothing. He stared intently at the man as though trying to imprint his image indelibly into his brain. The man's face was ruddy – a combination of an outdoor life and plenty of alcohol, Fletcher suspected. His smile was wide, his lively brown eyes laughed gently at the latest fool who'd been sent to entrap him.

'As I told your colleagues, I was only there to collect the rent. I don't expect to see it now of course, if you're going to put the cheeky scoundrels away.'

Fletcher continued to stare. Castle shifted in his chair. Its legs squeaked under his weight.

'Are you going to say anything, officer? Or have you lost your tongue?'

Irene had insinuated her way into the room and was vainly trying to indicate that Fletcher needed to get out.

Suddenly he stood up and kicked the chair behind him so that it cartwheeled over and smashed against the wall. A startled wariness appeared on the fat man's face. Fletcher leant forward on the table and bent towards him.

'The most important thing you need to remember is my face. Whatever happens in this room, I'm going to be coming to find you – wherever you try to hide. So don't forget my face.'

He gave the man one last look and then kicked the table. Not hard, just sufficient to knock the cup over and spill the contents down the front of the man's trousers.

Castle tried to get out of the seat and escape the hot liquid seeping through to his crotch, but in his haste only succeeded in falling backwards onto the floor, breaking the chair as he went. This was accompanied with a yelp of pain as the tea reached its target and again as his shoulder hit the floor and again as his ankle caught the edge of the table. Before he could get some control over his limbs, Fletcher had pushed the dumbstruck Irene out of the way and was through the door and down the corridor. He heard the voices of DI Fisher and Chief Inspector Aske coming from above, took the stairs down three at a time and burst out of the back door.

By the time the two senior officers arrived in the interview room, the young constable was being cuffed about the head by the irate haulage contractor who had his trousers round his ankles. DC Garner was attempting to placate him, but seemed to be in a state of shock herself.

Fletcher broke the speed limit on his way down the road towards Askham. He was intent on not stopping until he got to the car park at the bottom of Haweswater, but just north of Hilton he nearly came to grief when he took a corner too fast and met a green minibus hurrying towards him. Having survived that, he slowed down and continued the rest of the journey more sensibly.

He stepped out of the car and took in the view, looked up to the sharp pyramid of Kidsty Pike and wished he'd stayed there.

An eagle mocked him with a single croak and swerved over into the Kentmere valley.

CHAPTER 8

Lex was driving the green minibus which just avoided Fletcher's car. In the back Octavia was lying across three seats, barely conscious. Tom was watching over her while Rivka tried her best to staunch the worst of the blood, but she wasn't sure whether she was doing more harm than good.

Fortunately Octavia had had her back to the crashing chandelier, so her hair had protected her head and her face was unscathed. The backs of her hands and the middle of her back seemed to be the worst. However, it was the broken arm which had caused them the most distress. Dave Ransome had backed away and been violently sick, while the others stared in horror. Rivka had seen far worse in the war and had some basic first aid training, so she'd managed to immobilise the arm as best she could – but the bleeding was another matter.

Martin, Dave and Ted had stayed at the house, but Lex said she'd come back for her two colleagues as soon as she could.

When they arrived at the hospital the medics quickly took control and whisked Octavia away. Lex set off back to the house, while Tom and Rivka sat in the waiting room. Tom realised he was shaking.

Rivka put her arm around him and gave him a hug. They looked an odd couple: Tom over six feet tall, big shoulders now heaving with suppressed sobs, curly dark hair and a tanned, outdoor face, his head in his big strong hands; Rivka perched like a starveling bird, half his size, with a thin angular arm not long enough to reach across his broad back, pianist's fingers appearing over his shoulder. She wore her dark hair tied back in a loose ponytail, one tendril escaping to fall across her pinched face with its sharp cheekbones. Her eyes flitted to the door every time someone entered.

'She'll be alright, Tom,' she murmured. 'She's got a strong heart and I've seen her stubbornness. Don't you worry.'

Tom wiped an errant tear from his face. 'It's my fault. I shouldn't have let her go in alone.'

'You can't blame yourself. Once she's set her mind on something, she's a very determined young lady.'

'I know,' was all he could reply. Suddenly he got to his feet. 'We've got to tell her father!'

He strode to the reception desk and asked the young woman on duty if he could use her phone. She asked him for the number, but they had to look it up. Two minutes later, Tom came back to sit with Rivka.

'He's on his way.'

*   *   *   *

At the police station Irene Garner's day was going from bad to worse. She and the young constable had been quickly removed from the interview room. She saw DS Strickland hurrying in the opposite direction as the two of them followed Chief Inspector Aske upstairs to his office, where he left them standing to attention while he went back down to deal with Len Castle. It was a good ten minutes before he returned. She'd made her apologies to PC Porritt, who glared at her.

'It's not your fault. It's that bastard Fletcher. What's his problem?'

'It was his stepdaughter who was found at the house.'

Porritt stared at her in disbelief, shook his head. 'Even so. Stupid thing to do . . . and look where it's got us two.'

They couldn't think of anything else to say, so waited in silence.

The chief inspector walked back into his office, went over to the window and controlled his temper. He turned to face the two officers.

'Constable Porritt. Go downstairs immediately and write your report, including an explanation as to why you left a fellow officer alone with a suspect.'

Porritt didn't need any further instructions and left the room as fast as he could.

Aske gave Irene a long, hard look. 'DC Garner. I think your report will take far longer to write. I suggest you begin with what happened after you parted company with Inspector Fletcher on Saturday. You can do it at that table there; when you've finished . . . well . . . stay here, until I tell you otherwise.'

He pointed at the large table which she knew was used for meetings. He produced a stack of report forms and left the room without another word.

Like most police officers, Irene hated paperwork, but she knew that this particular report was possibly the last one she might ever write. It wasn't as if it was simply a matter of writing what had happened. She knew that it would have to be neither the whole truth nor nothing like the truth, but a pack of lies full of gaping holes. She wasn't just trying to save her own career, but Lonsdale's and Fletcher's as well.

'Damn you, Mick Fletcher!' she cursed and picked up her pen. It wasn't easy. Her bag was soon stuffed full of crumpled-up attempts, and what she'd managed to compose by the time the chief inspector returned was pitiful.

He took a cursory look at it and threw it into the bin. She put her head in her hands on the table and gritted her teeth.

He towered above her. 'Perhaps it would be easier if you were interrogated by a couple of your colleagues?'

She lifted her head and looked at him.

'Downstairs now. Interview room three.'

She hurried out of the room. When she opened the door, her heart sank. DI Fisher and DS Strickland sat waiting, their faces managing to be both stony and eager at the same time.

They offered her a seat. She preferred to stand.

It took a long time.

* * * *

George Hutton took only ten minutes to get to the hospital. After a brief conversation with Tom and Rivka, he demanded to see his daughter. He was taken through and they were left to wait again. Hutton returned about half an hour later, looking relieved.

'She's going to be alright. Her arm's been set in plaster and they're busy removing all the glass from her back. They've given her something for the pain. She's conscious and managed a smile. She says she wants to see you, Tom.' He smiled.

Tom looked up at him. 'Are you sure?'

'Quite sure.'

Tom looked at Rivka and back at Hutton.

'Well go on then,' said Rivka.

He went. George Hutton sat down and turned to Rivka. 'Tell me what happened.'

She told him what she knew. Of course, no-one had actually *seen* what happened, but what they'd found behind the doors told the story clear enough.

'So Octavia got in through a window?'

'Yes. It was too small for Tom, so he came to get the rest of us.'

George Hutton looked at her with a pensive expression. Rivka gazed back at him with curiosity.

'I've been through that window,' he said.

Rivka took in his stature. He wasn't as big a man as Tom, but he was tall. He grinned.

'It was many years ago. I was only fourteen. Thin as a weasel. Me and another lad, for a dare. Never been more frightened before or since.'

Rivka had a rare ability to sit absolutely still and silent for long periods of time. She waited.

'But we didn't get any further than that first room. There was something about it. No air. No sound. We scarpered. Got really lost trying to find our way out again. We got a right thrashing when we got home, both of us.'

A faint smile crossed Rivka's face. He was only a few years older than her. He couldn't know that she was thinking of her own mother.

'I'm sure Dr Winter would be pleased to hear your story and let you come and have a look. I only had a few moments to take in what it's like, but the entrance hall is huge.'

George thanked her and said he'd really like that.

'There was a portrait, on the half landing, a woman in a red dress. Any ideas who that might be?' Rivka asked.

George shook his head. 'Probably the Duke's wife, I imagine.'

Rivka nodded. 'I'm hoping there's a lot more paintings in there. It's my speciality.'

Tom reappeared, smiling. 'She's a strong girl, your daughter, Mr Hutton. All she wants to do is get out and back down to the big house!'

George sighed. 'It was ever thus. Did they say when she could come home?'

'They're keeping her in tonight, but tomorrow maybe,' Tom replied.

George stood up and offered his hand. 'Thanks Tom. I'll go back in and try to persuade her to take it easy. It's her second visit in three days, you know.'

The other two looked at him enquiringly.

'Put her Land Rover in a ditch dodging a stag on Friday morning.'

This gave them all pause for thought, but they parted company and went their separate ways.

It was only later that George remembered that Octavia had been rushing because she'd broken a mirror.

* * * *

It was more what Irene *didn't* tell her two superiors than what she was prepared to admit to.

She didn't tell them about spending the night in Dekker's bed. She didn't tell them how she'd deliberately broken his arm, even though he'd stopped struggling. She did say that Drummond had taken a swing at her, but not that she'd kicked him in the balls – at the top of the stairs. She had to admit that she hadn't actually seen Len Castle with any of the girls, but she couldn't stop herself from declaring angrily that they all knew what had been going on. This made their faces go even stonier, so she shut up. She said that the incident with the teacup was just an accident. DS Strickland – trying hard to be bad cop – snorted. She looked at him coldly and repeated it. She read through what they'd written and signed it. She was exhausted.

They let her go with a stern warning not to go near DC Lonsdale, DI Fletcher or any of the suspects and to stay well clear of Len Castle. She nodded her agreement.

Half an hour later, she opened the door to her flat and found Mick Fletcher sitting in her armchair.

'You bastard!' she said quietly.

'Actually, I don't think I am – although I can't be sure. My dad wasn't exactly a monogamous man.'

'That's not what I mean.'

Fletcher had adopted the same look as 'good cop, bad cop' back at the station.

'What is it with you men, that you think a stony face is going to make anyone inclined to tell you a damn thing?'

'So what did you tell them?'

'Less than I told you.'

'What did they say?'

'Nothing.'

Fletcher searched her face. 'So now what?'

She flopped down onto her old settee.

'Dunno. Suspension. Demotion. Uniform. You and me both, probably.'

They looked at each other.

'What about Dekker and Len Castle?'

'Scot free, I imagine,' Irene said. 'Dekker will be claiming police brutality and Castle's brief will be demanding heads should roll.'

Fletcher considered this analysis and sighed in agreement. He got up to go.

'I suppose I'd better go and give myself up. Get it over with.'

'Your choice,' she replied.

'What are you going to do?'

'Sleep.'

He went to the door. Without looking back at her he asked: 'Did you have sex with Dekker?'

She didn't move, but he knew she was grinning.

'I lied about the size of his dick . . .'

He closed the door quietly behind him and headed for the hospital.

He was just in time; Laura and Grace were coming out of the main doors as he got out of his car. He waited for them as they came over. They passed a green minibus as they crossed towards him. He could see the markings on its side from this angle: 'National Trust' it announced, with phone numbers underneath. As he watched, a tall, lithe figure got out of the bus and glared at him. She obviously recognised him as the maniac who had nearly put them all in hospital.

Fletcher looked away and opened the door for Laura. They got in and he drove them home. Not much was said, but Fletcher explained that he would need to go straight back to the police station. He didn't say anything about Irene, or the case, or about the incident with Len Castle. He reckoned there would be plenty of time for explanations later. After all, he'd been suspended before. He knew the drill: head down, keep your mouth shut, take your medicine. Maybe it was time to admit he'd had enough. He thought of the eagle, drifting across a clear blue sky.

* * * *

Only minutes after Lex had set off for the hospital with Octavia, Tom and Rivka, Fern passed the gateway to the house. She couldn't take it in. What had happened? Who could be allowed to do such a thing? She pulled in further along the road then made her way back and peered up the drive. In the distance up near the house she could see a large tractor. Beyond, there were three men on the balustrade in front of the main gates. One of them sat with his legs dangling over the parapet, while the other two stood talking.

She slipped in beside the gatepost as she heard a vehicle approaching. It turned in at the gates and drove on. Edging back out so she could see, she watched as two of the men got into the green minibus, whilst the other hauled himself onto the tractor. She ran back to her car. Through the mirror she saw the minibus come out and park on the verge. The two men and a tall woman got out and went back inside the gates. As she watched, she realised that the tractor was pulling one of the gates back into position. After about half an hour they got back into their vehicles and drove off down the lane.

Fern waited until silence descended. She walked back down to see what they'd done. The gates were pulled together and a large chain with a new padlock was threaded through the ironwork on both sides. She put her face to the cold metal and looked at the house. She'd never seen it from this angle. They must have done this over the last few days, although her usual route didn't take her past here. She'd never been in the house. Never thought of trying, but now?

She strode back to the car and drove to her usual parking spot behind an old farmhouse which had been abandoned long before she first came here. Its roof had fallen in about ten years previously and the ruins were overgrown. Even if a vehicle came along this lane, the driver wouldn't see her car unless they stopped and went round the back of the barn.

It had been a lovely early spring day, but the sun had gone down behind High Street a few minutes earlier and, although there was probably another hour or so of daylight left, the warmth had gone out of the air. The birds chattered noisily in the hedges and the trees on the other side of the estate wall as she made her way to the secret entrance.

Once inside, she made her way to the clearing. She'd only come to check on her recent actions but now her head was full of questions. What were they doing at the house? Who were they? Would they be exploring the gardens as well?

She reached the shed. From the outside, it also looked abandoned. She'd been careful not to cut back any of the undergrowth, some of which had started to creep inside. She'd been able to deal with that, and fortunately the door opened inwards, so the weeds and a small bush appeared to have set up residence in front of it. She was careful to stretch over them and open the door before leaping through. Inside she shut the door and gave the contents a new look.

What might someone think if they came in here? Just an abandoned garden shed? Lots of tools covered with cobwebs and dust, unused for sixty years? The shears were hidden under an old cloth. The new spade was in the boot of her car. The only giveaway was the condition of the old mower; she resolved to cover it with an old curtain or something. She went back out and closed the door, then walked on to the clearing.

She stood at the edge. She remembered the first time she'd stood here, the dark trees towering above to the stars. Her mother had brought her here on her sixteenth birthday, nearly thirty years ago, and told her the story. Back then there had been one rose. Six or seven steps into the middle. The grass grew slowly. A small amount of light and a constant showering of pine needles meant it only needed to be cut two or three times a year. The old mower was sufficient.

Now there were five roses. The new one was only a foot tall with three naked prongs sticking up like knitting needles. She'd got better at removing the turf and replacing it afterwards so this latest rose sprang from a flat green sward. One or two of the others grew from more uneven ground. It might be an odd place to find such a display but nevertheless it was just a rose garden. Why should anyone think anything else?

What could she do now? Was this the end?

She thought of the first one. She hadn't intended it to happen the way it did. Had she?

*   *   *   *

1976

On that day four years ago, Helen Courtney wasn't heavy. Fern put her fire-drill training into practice and threw the woman's sedated body over her left shoulder. She got her to the shed in less than twenty minutes.

She tied the woman to the sturdy gardener's chair and stood looking at her. Even at this point Fern wasn't sure what she was going to do. Helen's head hung forward, her overly-abundant glossy black hair cascading onto her knees. It was this that gave Fern the idea.

She opened her rucksack and found her scissors. While the woman was unable to resist she could do it. It only took a few minutes and she did it expertly. After all, she'd done the same thing plenty of times although she couldn't remember anyone with such a luxurious head of hair coming into the salon and asking for it all to be cut off. She remembered one woman with a long pigtail halfway down her back who'd marched in and asked for a Twiggy cut, but that was different. Helen Courtney would be mortified when she woke up to find she'd lost her pride and joy. And that was why Fern did it and why she waited. It was what had happened to her mother and her friend Fern Rigg. All because her stepmother couldn't bear to see someone with as beautiful hair as her own.

She must have dozed off, but the woman's groans woke her soon enough. Gradually Helen came round and lifted up her head. Her eyes focused on Fern and a look of fear flashed across her face. She felt the tightness of the ropes and struggled vainly against them. She looked around at the abandoned tools and the cobwebs. Fern hadn't thought to gag her; there was no-one to hear.

'Where are we? Why have you brought me here? What are you going to do?'

The questions tumbled out, Helen's eyes looking this way and that, but always coming back to Fern, who crouched against the wall watching her.

'You won't get away with this. You're mad!' she shouted and struggled with the ropes.

Fern did what she'd wanted to do when they first met. She stood up and slapped Helen hard across the face.

Helen gasped in pain and disbelief. She'd never been hit before, not even at school. She'd slapped Dawn several times, but that was because the spoilt brat deserved it. She'd even slapped Philip, but instantly realised that he found it exciting. She'd been surprised, but found she enjoyed it as well. But she'd made him

127

beg. That was an even greater turn-on – for both of them. But this was different, it hurt and when she'd got this mad woman to untie her she'd give her a real beating.

Fern didn't know what was going on inside Helen's head, but she slapped her again to regain her attention.

Helen screamed at her. 'How dare you do this to me? Let me go! Immediately!'

She flinched, thinking she'd get another slap, but something worse happened.

Fern reached above her and lifted something off the wall. She crouched back down in front of Helen again with a rectangular piece of wood in her hand. Before she could figure out what it was, Fern rotated it and held it in front of her.

For a few seconds Helen didn't recognise herself. Before her was a picture of a woman a bit like herself, but with horrible short cropped hair. Terrible make-up. Mascara all down her cheeks and a smudge of lipstick where her mouth ought to be. No! It was a mirror! Cracked and dirty, but . . . the shock of the reality hit her harder than any slap. Her mouth opened. No sound came.

One. Two. She began to wail. A deep-seated cry of anguish, which rose to a scream of bloodcurdling anger. The sinews on her neck tightened like hawsers as she threw back her head and howled to the heavens. In her rage she tried to get up, but only succeeded in falling backwards and rolling about like an upturned beetle.

Fern stood back and watched. This was better than she'd ever imagined. She waited until the howling stuttered into a coughing fit and finally into rasping gasps for breath. She knelt down and looked into her victim's face. Helen's eyes were black with hatred.

'You brought this on yourself,' said Fern.

Helen gasped for breath.

'You're a bully and a wicked ugly bitch.'

'And I'm going to kill you!' said Helen, through gritted teeth.

Fern stood up and looked down at the woman. She'd stopped struggling, but lay glaring up at her.

'You can't keep me like this for ever. Eventually you'll have to let me go. People will be looking for me. You'll pay for this.'

Fern laughed. 'You've no idea where you are and neither has anyone else. I'm going to leave you now to reconsider your position. The only way you're going to get out of here is to learn some humility and start begging for your freedom.'

Before Helen could spit out any sort of a response, Fern stood up and kicked her hard in the stomach. Helen cried out in agony. Fern stepped back and opened the door.

'That was for Dawn. See you in the morning.'

Helen hadn't grasped that the light in the shed was provided by the storm lantern, which Fern took with her, so she suffered the further shock of being plunged into total darkness. She heard her captor walk away and within seconds a silence descended on her the like of which she'd never heard before. She did something she'd never thought she'd ever do. She whimpered.

It was a long night.

* * * *

1980

Fern took one last look at the clearing and set off back to the shed. The light was fading fast now. The total darkness of a pine forest at night is a fearsome thing, yet Fern was comforted by it.

She knew this path well. She'd marked the trees four years ago, so that she could feel her way to safety. It wasn't a comfort to her victims though. She went back into the shed and lit the lantern.

She sat for a long time considering what she was going to do next. She hadn't identified her next one, although there were a few candidates. The hairdresser's seemed to attract them.

Her eyes settled on the handle of the old spade. She relived that first battle. Now it left her cold, but that first time it was different.

*   *   *   *

1976

She'd returned the next morning. She figured a night in the pitch black, with the accompanying investigations by the shed's nocturnal occupants would have had a sobering effect on Helen Courtney and perhaps the promise of further sessions might be sufficient to persuade her of the error of her ways. How wrong could you be?

To her credit, Helen had not panicked and run away. She might have got lost in the woods, but she could have tried to find her way out. Instead she'd waited for her abductor with murder in her heart. Her only mistake was her choice of weapon.

By the time Fern arrived, there was plenty of light. Fern opened the door. A creature burst from the shed knocking her backwards towards the trees. Instinctively Fern dodged behind the nearest trunk. It saved her life; the hammer thudded into the trunk inches from her head. Regaining her balance she zigzagged her way between the pines, putting as much distance as possible between herself and the crazed animal now hunting her down.

How had Helen managed to free herself? There wasn't time

to consider that now. She was blundering her way towards her, screaming her intent. Fern moved to her left and circled round behind the shed. She needed a weapon but anything suitable was inside. She stopped and listened. She'd been brought up in woods like these. She'd tracked the most elusive of creatures: fawns pricking their ears at the sound of a leaf falling, foxes picking their way through the pine needles. Helen was no match for this terrain. Her footfalls were heavy. Twigs snapped and branches rustled.

Fern crept round the side of the shed. She got to the corner.

Suddenly Helen worked out where she must be and came hurtling back through the undergrowth. Fern backed away. She was safe in the trees. Her foot trod on something round and she bent down. A handle. She felt its length; it was entangled in grass and nettles that stung her. Her fingers found the edge of rusted metal. An old spade. Fern dragged it out of the clinging vegetation.

As she grasped it in her hands, an apparition flew round the corner. Spiky dark head, bloodied face, hollow eyes. Consumed with hatred and carnal vengeance, it leapt towards her. The hammer was raised and a war cry erupted from the red mouth.

Fern swung the spade. The mouth widened into a gash. Blood spurted into the cold morning air. White marbles scattered like confetti. The creature faltered, its eyes filled with fear. Its head gurgled; its legs buckled. The hand dropped the hammer. Then the creature fell; poleaxed into the bed of nettles. A brief writhing of reluctant limbs, a couple of desperate spasms and then a gentle settling into the green embrace.

Fern was transfixed. The force of the blow had broken the spade's handle. She couldn't take in that with just one strike she'd managed to disable her attacker. As the stillness gathered round her, it slowly dawned on her that the creature might be dead. She picked up the hammer and carefully approached the body, half-expecting Helen to leap up and continue her savage onslaught. Fern reached out and touched her arm. It slowly dropped into the nettles. No response. Emboldened by this she decided to search for a pulse, but as she reached over to feel the woman's neck she realised that wasn't going to be possible. The lower part of Helen's face was separated from the rest of her head. There was blood everywhere.

Fern knew at once that Helen Courtney was dead. She stood up and looked down at her. The woman's eyes were open, staring sightlessly at a sky she'd never see again. The remaining tufts of black hair glistened with blood. Fern slumped to the ground. It was barely eight o'clock.

Fern attended two burials on that day, four years ago. Her aunt Elizabeth's was attended by over fifty folk. The gathering at the Bampton Inn afterwards numbered well over a hundred and fifty. People had come from as far afield as Australia. There was singing and speeches, tears and laughter, well into the night. Her aunt's relatives and friends reminisced and rekindled lost relationships. A young couple 'plighted their troth' in her honour and were married the same day the following year.

Helen Courtney died alone and was buried alone. Her murderer was her gravedigger. No words were spoken. No tears or laughter.

* * * *

1980

Fern put out the lantern and felt her way back to the entrance. Nowadays she didn't have so far to travel. She knew it increased the risks, but a part of her needed to be where she belonged. She needed time to think what this unexpected invasion of the garden might mean. Part of her wanted to go into that house, despite the fact that her mother had told her never to even think of it.

When she eventually slept, she dreamed of Helen.

CHAPTER 9

Fletcher had been here before, sitting on a chair in an upstairs corridor with a blue carpet. He reckoned you could tell both the level of the superior officer you were waiting for and the depth of the shit you were in by the thickness and quality of the carpet beneath your feet. He reckoned deputy chief constable, and up to his eyebrows.

The secretary had indicated where he should sit. His well-polished shoes made hardly a sound as he crossed to the solitary chair. It reminded him of school. He remembered the moment in *Kes* when a poor unfortunate messenger had been included in a group caning, despite his protestations of innocence. Fletcher had been caned plenty of times. He counted up: four official warnings and three suspensions. The two commendations didn't seem to weigh much in the equation.

He looked back down the corridor at the secretary. She was typing at a measured pace, paying no attention to the condemned man. She was in her late forties, soberly dressed in a dark-blue business suit, blonde perm with a side parting, neat features, hint of lipstick and careful make-up. Fletcher's mind wandered away to Louisa in a rundown old bar, wearing a ridiculously extravagant hat. Getting married to a Jock. He must be loaded.

The door opened and Chief Inspector Roger Aske stepped out. Fletcher got to his feet and made an effort to adopt a stiffened posture.

'Come in, Inspector,' said Aske, and stood to one side.

Fletcher walked into the room.

To his surprise it was empty. Aske followed him in and went to sit behind his desk.

'Sit down,' he said.

Fletcher hesitated. Aske nodded at him. He took the chair indicated, questions battling for a hearing in his head.

Roger Aske looked at him for what seemed an age, before looking down at a slim file. 'You've had an interesting career, Detective Inspector.'

Fletcher shrugged his shoulders. 'I think the word is colourful, sir,' he offered.

Aske didn't smile, but opened the file. Fletcher couldn't imagine that it was thick enough to be a full account of his exploits.

'Five official warnings. Three suspensions. Three commendations. Twenty-seven successful arrests leading to prosecution.'

Fletcher frowned. Aske continued without looking up.

'An endless list of complaints from suspects, witnesses, members of the public and other officers.' Aske closed the file and folded his hands on the desk. 'I wouldn't call that colourful, Inspector.'

Fletcher waited. The two men's eyes met. Two brown. One blue. One green.

'You're a bloody nightmare. Good cop and bad cop all rolled into one fucking kaleidoscope of mayhem.'

Fletcher stared hard at him, trying to keep control of the swirl of colours whirling through his mind.

'I've spent the morning with the chief constable, his deputy and the chairman of the county council police committee.'

Fletcher couldn't help but think that must have been a very glittery affair – all those epaulettes and braid – perhaps a medal or two.

'They decided that I should be the one to explain our rather delicate position to you.'

Fletcher tried to ignore the word 'position' and projected the best attentive face he could muster.

'Local businessman Mr Leonard Castle has made a serious complaint of violent conduct by you against him this morning. His lawyer informs us that he intends to take this all the way to the high court, if necessary, to secure your dismissal from the force and bring a civil case against you for damages. He wants to see you in prison.'

Fletcher waited. His instinct told him something odd was going on. Why was Aske telling him this? By rights he should be in front of the ACC at least. Aske looked away and coughed.

'Unfortunately, Mr Castle has no witnesses to confirm this attack, although he claims there were other officers present. We have questioned these officers and they all deny seeing anything resembling violent conduct. They are prepared to say this under oath in court. We have informed Mr Castle's solicitor and await his response.'

Fletcher was biting the inside of his mouth to prevent anything resembling a smile escaping onto his face.

'Therefore your orders are as follows. You are to take DC Garner and DC Lonsdale to Rochdale to help the investigation into the disappearance of a number of prostitutes from north Manchester, including the woman found on our patch last Friday.'

Fletcher waited.

'Is that clear, Inspector?'

'Yes, sir.'

'Then get out of my sight, you lucky bastard.'

'Yes sir.'

Fletcher stood up, attempted a salute, changed his mind when he saw Aske's face, turned quickly and left the room. Out in the corridor he shut the door behind him carefully and set off towards the stairs. The secretary didn't look up as he passed. He reached the top of the stairs and looked back. She'd got up and was walking smartly back towards the chief inspector's room. As he watched she turned and smiled at him. A strange smile. A smile full of knowingness and collusion. He frowned. She opened the door to the room he'd just left and went in. What was all that about?

* * * *

Despite everyone's protestations, Octavia insisted on being present when they opened the main door for the third time. The rest of the team had been there briefly on the Tuesday to help with sweeping up the chandelier. It had taken longer than they thought. A local antiques dealer had come to offer them some advice. Obviously it was beyond repair, but he was hugely impressed by its size and the volume of glass. He told them it was essential they all wore masks and goggles, as the air was still filled with glass dust. They'd decided that it was best to leave further exploration until the next day – partly because of the glass, but also because they knew Octavia wanted to be there. However, they were unable to stop Rivka climbing up the first flight to inspect the massive painting. She didn't take long, but her face was enough to tell them that it was something special. She shook her head and refused to enlighten them, saying she needed to make some phone calls before she could be sure.

The following morning, as they waited expectantly in the

great entrance hall, she just smiled and walked slowly up to the landing. She stood and admired the picture for a good minute, before turning to them and announcing her findings in a trembling and emotional voice.

'Ladies and gentlemen,' she wavered, her accent strong, 'may I present a previously unknown and unrecorded work by the late nineteenth-century portrait painter, John Singer Sargent.' She paused for effect, before continuing.

'I phoned someone I know in Italy last night and he is already on his way. If I'm right you're looking at a piece of art worth at least four or five million pounds – although as it's never been seen before, it could fetch an absolute fortune.'

The others gasped in collective astonishment.

Martin broke the silence that followed. 'Needless to say, this has to be kept to ourselves. I've been onto head office and they're sending their top specialist, Sylvia Urquhart, straight away. I've to meet her at the train station later this afternoon. She's insisted that we keep all the doors and windows shut and cause as little disturbance as possible. If this is an indication of the quality of art work in the rest of the house, it could turn out to be the find of the century.'

They all looked at each other in wonder. Lex was the first to speak. 'How could such a work of art be unrecorded, Rivka?'

'I'm not sure. That's why I've sent for Guilio. He can't believe it either, although he trusts me enough to miss an important conference in Florence to come here. It's possible that the work was commissioned privately and that it was never displayed. There's no record of the Duke buying or commissioning any artist's work during the period before the war.'

The others gave this some thought. This time Ransome spoke. 'Well, if what I've heard about Sylvia Urquhart is true, I suggest we take a quick tour before she closes up the whole shop. She won't want a bunch of northern upstarts like us fumbling about in an uncivilised manner amongst works of art of that quality.'

'It's ours, David, until head office says otherwise,' said Martin.

'Ay, well. All the same, I think you'll find she's got some very powerful friends in high places. She'll want to take over, that's for certain.'

'Well, I'm not without influence myself,' replied Martin. 'I've been on the phone this morning. There are some very influential people up here, who won't want a Cumbrian inheritance disappearing down south.'

Dave smiled and shrugged his shoulders. 'All power to your elbow, Martin . . . but I still think we ought to take a quick squint.'

Martin grinned. 'As if I could stop you.' He pointed over Ransome's shoulder at Rivka Weill slipping through a door to the right of the hall. They all laughed and trooped after her.

In deference to the approaching Dame Urquhart, but probably more out of reverence for any further Singer Sargents, Rivka had brought a powerful torch, which she was now shining around what appeared to be a huge drawing room. Her light went from one painting to another. Each one brought a sharp intake of breath, her hand becoming more and more unsteady with each discovery until Lex took it from her and followed her round the room.

By late afternoon, Lex had a list of unbelievable artistic wealth. They had opened a treasure trove of extraordinary beauty and historical importance. Octavia felt as if they'd stumbled across a Nazi hoard, except as Rivka enumerated each piece, each painting and statue, she realised the majority was Italian. Much of it was older than the house. Sixteenth- and seventeenth-century furniture beside eighteenth- and late-nineteenth century artwork.

The names kept tumbling from Rivka's disbelieving lips. It was in one of the upstairs rooms that her dream came true. Two Burne-Jones and a Rossetti, one that she knew about, the other two unknown. One was of a woman as beautiful as the lady in red downstairs – except she was a classic Burne-Jones, with piercing blue eyes and an enormous cloud of red golden hair. And this one had a title: 'The Duchess Ursula de Blanche'.

As Martin set off reluctantly to go to the station, Lex informed him of the figure she'd calculated Rivka's estimates had reached. It took his breath away. It was beyond comprehension. How could all this just be sitting here? Unsuspected and unknown.

After he'd gone, the rest of them finally arrived in the room to the left of the main hall. This was where Octavia – and previously her father – had entered through the window. The revelations here in the large dining room affected Rivka in a very different way. She cried.

When she'd dried her eyes, she explained they were probably damaged beyond repair. The open window had allowed the damp and bacteria-carrying Lakeland air to attack everything. All was mould and mildew and rot. They resolved to board up the window and close the door in the faint hope that some of the contents could be saved.

They stepped out onto the balcony and contemplated the view. The late afternoon sky had become overwhelmed as darkening clouds tumbled over the fells. A heavy downpour was inevitable. As the first large drops landed, Martin's car pulled up at the main gates. By the time he'd stumbled up the track with his guest, they were both knee deep in mud. Dave Ransome couldn't keep the grin off his face. As the two sodden figures ascended the steps, he stepped out with his umbrella and offered a few steps worth of protection as they approached the main doors.

'Welcome to Blanchard House, my lady,' he said.

The lady in question took his hand and allowed herself to be led into the great hall, followed by a dripping Dr Winter. She took a couple of steps forward before removing her headscarf and undoing her long raincoat. Her expensive Italian shoes were ruined, but she simply stepped out of them and walked towards the staircase.

At the bottom she stopped and turned to Rivka. 'Rivka, my darling. What a find! It's stunning!'

Even Dave Ransome had to admit later that the woman cut a commanding figure. Wet through, ruined stockings, mud-splattered coat dripping onto the marble, removing her sodden leather gloves, she turned and gave them her most ravishing smile. Her long black hair glistened in the gathering darkness.

'You lucky, lucky people. What treasures you must have uncovered. I must see them now!'

Octavia was not the only person to stare at her and then involuntarily look up at the painting. The resemblance was striking. Uncanny.

Martin was the first to speak. To be honest, he hadn't noticed what everyone else was trying to take in. 'Of course, Sylvia. If you wish . . . although perhaps tomorrow would be better?'

'No. Absolutely not, Martin! I *must* see everything now!!'

She strode up to Rivka and, linking her arm in hers, insisted she lead the way.

And so it was that they didn't get to dinner until after nine o'clock. Sylvia had booked a table at the Sharrow Bay Hotel on the shores of Ullswater and she continued her conversations with Rivka and Lex far into the night.

* * * *

1976

Fern didn't really know how she got through the next few weeks. She was in a recurring nightmare which wouldn't go away.

She'd killed two people.

Not only that, she'd had the resolve to cover her tracks. She'd driven the hired car back to Burton and left it in a supermarket car park; caught the bus back to Ashby and gone to work.

The police took their time. It was a week later before they turned up at the home. Fern wasn't there; she was on night shift. Her boss told her that she'd explained that Fern had been on her way up north the day Helen Courtney had disappeared.

The police didn't want to speak to her. She read about the search for the missing woman in the papers. There had been an emotional appeal by her husband on the television, but she only heard about it from a colleague. The missing hit man didn't even make the papers.

Fern stayed on for a couple of months but her heart had gone out of the job. She gave in her notice in July and applied for a job in a hairdresser's in Newcastle. She'd never been there, she had no relatives there. She couldn't have given a reason for choosing the place; she just had to get away.

She found herself a small flat in Whitley Bay, a couple of streets back from the promenade. She still had the nightmares: kept seeing Helen Courtney flying at her from the shed. But gradually she came to accept that no-one was going to find her or even think she'd been involved. No bodies had been found.

People went missing for all sorts of reasons.

It was a Monday in late September of the same year, when she was sorting through some old papers, payslips and bank statements. Tucked in amongst them was a hospital note – an internal memo.

She recognised it immediately and felt the anger it had aroused at the time. It was an official document from the ward sister to her concerning what she called an 'act of insubordination'. The memo had been also sent to a senior administrator. Fern remembered having to go and see him. She remembered the humiliation. Having to be reprimanded by a little man in a suit – who'd never seen a bedpan never mind emptied one – in front of that smirking cow, Sister Pauline Brett. Having to apologise and promise to show proper respect to her superiors in front of patients. Like some naughty schoolgirl. All this, knowing full well why it was happening.

She and Pauline Brett both worked in the children's ward at the General Hospital in Leicester. Sister Brett 'ran a tight ship', which meant that little children did not whinge or complain. Injections 'didn't hurt' and, in any case, they were necessary to make them better so they could go back home and leave spare beds for people who were 'really ill'. Needless to say, she and Fern didn't get on.

There were numerous incidents before the occasion when Fern told Sister Brett to get out of the ward and leave her to take care of a young girl who had terrible stomach pains. The fact that the girl had a ruptured appendix and was rushed into the operating theatre less than an hour later counted for nothing with Pauline Brett. She wasn't going to let anyone speak to her like that in front of patients and other staff.

Fern resigned a few weeks later after applying for the job at the home in Ashby. On her final day, she was in the linen cupboard looking for some clean sheets. She heard the door shut behind her and turned round to find Pauline facing her. Before she could do or say anything, the woman pushed her back against the shelving. Fern lost her footing on some blankets on the floor and banged her head against the wall as she went down. The next moment, Fern felt a hand round her neck. Pauline Brett wasn't a big woman, in fact she'd probably be described as petite, but she had a strong grip. Her face was up close and her eyes were shining.

'It's a good job you're getting out, Fern Robinson, before I show you who's really in charge round here.'

Fern could hardly breathe but began to push back with her free arm. Pauline let go and stood up.

'You fucking giraffe. If you weren't so damn ugly, I'd fuck you stupid.'

Fern had never heard anyone speak like that before, and was rendered speechless. Pauline opened the door, gave her one last glare and was gone. Fern never saw her again but she remembered how frightened she'd been.

Now she sat on her bed and allowed another seed to grow. The thought blossomed. She knew where Pauline Brett lived; she'd been to a party at her house shortly after she'd started at the hospital. It slowly dawned on her why there'd been so few men there.

Fern had a modus operandi. The next week she hired a car. It went as smoothly as the first time.

She knocked on the door. Pauline opened it and Fern enjoyed the changes in the woman's expression as puzzlement turned to recognition and transformed into fear. She pushed her back in and Pauline fell against the stairs. Fern grabbed her by the neck and rammed the needle into her arm. A few seconds of wriggling and the woman's body relaxed. Two minutes later she was in the boot and Fern was driving out of the cul-de-sac and heading for the motorway.

Six hours later, Pauline Brett groggily focused on the confines of an old shed. Cobwebs meant spiders. Terror reached into every part of her body. In front of her was a picture; in the picture was a small woman tied to a chair. Her dark brown fringe had disappeared. Her hair had been cut off. She looked like a prisoner, she *was* a prisoner. A warder came into view; someone she remembered. It was Fern Robinson. What was she doing here? She was speaking to her. Her mouth was moving. Pauline couldn't make out the words.

'. . . last time, Pauline? Do you remember in the linen cupboard? You said some terrible things.'

As Pauline Brett tried desperately to understand what was happening, Fern suddenly slapped her hard across the face.

'Or perhaps you remember the time in that man's office? Did you enjoy that even more?'

Pauline began to sob. Fern stood up.

'I'm leaving you now. In the morning we'll see if you can put up a fight. I'll give you a chance. But you need some time to yourself. To reflect on how those children you mistreated must have felt when they were in pain and frightened. Let's see how you cope with that.'

Fern stood up and extinguished the light. Pauline heard her closing the door. It was dark and silent. For a while. But soon she could hear things moving. Small creatures. Spiders. She screamed until she was hoarse.

No-one came. No-one heard her.

In the morning Fern came for her. It wasn't much of a fight. A bit of flailing about before Fern's strong hands encircled her thin neck and forced her face down into the nettles. The stinging was unbearable, but it didn't last for long.

Fern rubbed her hands with dock leaves and looked down

at the rag-doll at her feet. It was different than the first time. Satisfying – but without the exhilaration. The dragon had hardly been disturbed.

She picked up the spade and walked into the clearing. When she'd finished and the third rose was planted, she looked up at the stars and smiled. She knew that this wasn't the last. She didn't know who or where or when, but she knew they were out there and she would find them.

CHAPTER 10

Dave Ransome had to admit that Sylvia's reputation didn't match up to the charm offensive they were being subjected to. She flirted with all the men, including Martin, who hadn't the slightest idea how to cope with it. They were all doubled up at his hopeless attempts to deal with 'Martin, darling' and 'Martin, you sweetie'. Dave had to get used to being called her 'last surviving Marxist'. She treated Rivka with deference worthy of the Queen. This respect was magnified ten times by the arrival of Rivka's Italian contact, Count Guilio d'Este. Not only was he a scion of one of the oldest and most noble of Italian aristocracies, but his family and Rivka's had been dealing in fine art for five generations. The three of them spent hours looking at each painting, marvelling at the brushwork and the clarity of the vision.

Octavia felt a little excluded until Sylvia heard someone mention her surname.

'Darling, you're not related to George Hutton are you?'

'He's my father,' she replied.

'Oh, my dear, dear darling. You must be Josephine's daughter?'

Octavia found herself in a fierce embrace and felt tears on her cheek. Sylvia Urquhart was weeping. It turned out that she'd been at school with Octavia's mother but was in South America when she heard that her friend had died.

Sylvia insisted on being taken to see Octavia's father, who was as startled as his daughter. He remembered his wife talking about Sylvia, but they'd never met. He had little choice but to ask her to stay at the house and so it became Sylvia's court. Guilio and Rivka were also invited and soon the old house was as busy and full of laughter and chatter as it had been when George was a young man and his parents entertained the local gentry. The whole commotion of coming and going left his head in a whirl, but he couldn't help but be uplifted by the exuberance around him.

Sylvia suggested, and Martin agreed, that such a treasure trove of art needed protection. The walls and the briars had worked for sixty years, but word was getting around. Martin arranged for a local security firm to come and clear a four-yard gap around the house and erect ten-foot high barbed-wire fences. Security guards patrolled this perimeter day and night, whilst all the team and visitors were provided with passes. However, Martin refused the security firm manager's suggestion that everyone be searched before leaving.

The excitement of the first few days gradually dulled to a cataloguing exercise. The team adjusted to being in the presence of millions of pounds worth of art history, until it seemed nothing to walk down a corridor of Pre-Raphaelite paintings interspersed with eighteenth-century Italian statuary.

After coming out of hospital with a pot on her arm, Octavia retreated to her cottage. Rumours persisted about her and Tom, but it was lambing time. He was working long hours and they saw each other only rarely.

At first nobody noticed the gradual change in Sylvia's

behaviour. She continued to spend a lot of time in Rivka's company after Guilio returned to Italy. She had a cool relationship with Lex, who resented her interference and the adjustment of her archiving systems.

Dave Ransome was abandoned to research the de Blanche family history, which initially turned out to be a frustrating and unrewarding task. Octavia spent her time photographing and drawing the architecture, trying hard to ignore the modern steel fencing. To her irritation, her camera – which was new and state of the art – developed a series of problems demanding expert technical servicing. Many of her photographs were blurred, whilst others were obscured by faint white patches. She was glad of her drawing skill – and the fact she was left handed – because otherwise her records would have been paltry. Her father solved the problem of holding the sketch pad by producing an easel which she'd been given for a birthday present years ago. Lex took on the role of erecting it wherever Octavia wanted to work.

It was Dave Ransome who discovered the next exciting development. He'd easily found birth, marriage and death records for Edward de Blanche. The family was, as expected, originally French. They'd arrived in England in 1849 following the troubles which resulted in the establishment of the Second Republic. Once again the surviving aristocracy decided exile was preferable to persecution; some of them didn't wait for Louis Napoleon's coup because they saw him as an unreliable, shifty character. Edward's family was from the remote hills east of Limoges. His father, Edouard, was rich, even though he'd had to abandon his numerous chateaux and their contents. He had friends in the north of England and eventually found the ruins of the original fifteenth-century house and commissioned architects and garden designers to create an Italianate neo-Gothic villa on the banks of an unremarkable tributary of the River Lowther. Edouard became a noted fell walker and ardent follower of the Lakeland artists and writers, many of whom were later to be guests in his house. This is the background from which Edward emerged, becoming Duc de Blanche at the age of twenty six on the death of his father in 1894. He'd married Ursula Douglas three years earlier but tragically she died giving birth to a daughter, Rose-Marie in 1896. The child had survived.

Here the information dried up. Ransome had found one reference to de Blanche at the signing of the Entente Cordiale in London in 1904. He seemed to operating in the role of minor diplomat, probably helping with the inevitable language problems endemic amongst both the British and French diplomatic officials. Most of them could understand and converse in each other's language, but the 'entente' was certainly not so 'cordiale' that they would admit it.

The only other reference he could establish was the death of de Blanche in one of the earliest battles of the Great War. He was awarded the Legion d'Honneur posthumously for leading a brave, yet foolhardy, cavalry charge against the lethal German Maxim machine guns. He was one of the first to have his horse killed beneath him but, despite his injuries, he insisted on remounting a loose horse and following the rest of his cohort into the hail of bullets. The resulting battle killed thousands of men and horses. His body was never formally identified.

This is where it became interesting. Ransome knew how to lull an audience into a stupor by reciting lengthy factual accounts. He also knew that he had a secret to reveal, one that he reckoned only he was aware of. While the others were revelling in the house's artistic and architectural riches, he had spent his time in Edward de Blanche's study. Rivka and Sylvia had quickly assessed it as being devoid of artistic interest. It contained no outstanding works of art, no statues nestling in corners, just rows and rows of books. Many of them were no doubt first editions, but that wasn't the art experts' field. It was, however, most definitely Ransome's. His particular interest was the diplomatic intricacies and machinations of the late nineteenth century leading up to the outbreak of what he persisted in calling the Great War. He had been intrigued to discover that Edward de Blanche had been present during the protracted, difficult and largely secret negotiations between the French and the British in the face of German aggrandisement. Alone in the study, he set about a systematic search for any evidence of this involvement.

It was the third day of his rooting through and behind all the books on the shelves that he found the letters. With trembling hands he placed them on the mahogany desk. He'd not uncovered some hitherto unknown exchanges between the grand diplomatic game players, but he had found the key to the mystery of Blanchard House. If only he'd been less persistent. Having assembled everyone to admire his find, he held aloft the beribboned collection for them all to see.

'*Eduardo, mi amore . . .*'

He held up one of the letters and, placing his glasses on the end of his nose, read:

'*Il tuo amante adorante, Eleonora.*'

The assembled company waited for further explanation. Ransome enjoyed his moment.

'Eleonora was Duchessa Eleonora Lucretia Chiara di Nerezza; born in 1880 into one of the most ancient of Florentine families, mentioned in numerous letters written by Singer Sargent and his artistic circle. Although noble, her family had fallen on hard times. She became a courtesan, a lover and muse to the artists and musicians of Florence, Milan, Paris and Vienna.'

He paused for effect, holding his audience in the palm of his hand.

'But on the 25th June 1912, she married Duc Edouard de Blanche in the church of the Santa Maria Maggiore in Ravenna.'

Everyone gasped in astonishment.

'So comrades,' he finished. 'You've been salivating over the collection of an Italian aristocratic prostitute rather than a French chevalier – although I suspect he would have paid for most of it. One way or another.'

Everyone was talking all at once. Martin stood up and asked for their attention.

'I'd just like to offer our thanks to David for this revelation, even if his choice of epithets might not be to everyone's taste. This information will greatly help our endeavours and open numerous doorways for research. However, although Professor Ransome may be entitled to make the most of his discovery, I must remind you all that anything found here is technically treasure trove and therefore the property of the Crown.'

He turned to ensure his friend understood the need for this statement. Ransome gave him a gentleman's smile and shrugged his shoulders. 'I'm afraid my Italian isn't that good anyway, Martin . . . and in any case I'm still after the diplomatic secrets. You take them. I'll carry on with my search.'

As the letters were handed over Octavia happened to glance at Rivka; her face was turned away but for one brief moment Octavia was puzzled to see the ghost of a smile on her otherwise placid features. Not a smile Octavia could interpret. Not pleasure but something else. Something colder.

* * * *

1977

Despite her decision, it was nearly a year later before Fern found another woman – or rather before another woman put herself into the spotlight. Fern had got into the habit of spending the occasional weekend in one of the many small seaside villages on the Northumbrian coast, so she could walk the cliffs and the long lonely beaches. She avoided the tourist traps like Lindesfarne, although she'd been there one freezing January Sunday morning.

It was a weekend in late May when she found a bed and breakfast in Seahouses. It wasn't a holiday weekend, so she thought she'd avoid the worst of the Geordie rowdy crowd. The village itself was a bit tacky but she knew she was only a few minutes from Bamburgh and its fabulous beach. She'd spent the whole of Saturday walking and was looking forward to a good dinner.

She'd just finished eating when a man and his teenage daughter entered the bar. Fern didn't take much notice of them. The girl looked miserable; so far, ordinary teenager. But then the woman arrived. She'd obviously delayed her entrance so that people would see her without the family distraction and marvel at her beauty, highlighted by a cascade of thick blonde hair falling over the right side of her face. Bright red lipstick, low-cut, tight-fitting top, short skirt and high heels completed the look, which was intended to attract any bloke within fifty yards and embarrass her husband and daughter. It worked – even though she was obviously already very drunk. All the men in the room stared. One guy, carrying three glasses, bumped into a chair and spilt the lot. Whilst this caused some hilarity, many of the other men were getting sharp looks and kicks under the table.

The woman enjoyed the reaction immensely, but her smile turned to a sneer as she approached the table in the corner where her husband had tried to hide himself. People – men and women – tried hard not to watch, but most of them saw her bend forward, her face close to his and heard her waspish whisper. He blushed and followed her as she weaved her way to a table in the bay window, bumping into various people's chairs on the way. The daughter sullenly trailed after them. From this vantage point the woman could see and be seen by everyone else.

The husband hurried to the bar to get her a drink. The woman paid no attention to the daughter but gave the men in the room a droopy-eyed, yet predatory, once-over. The sneer returned as she quickly assessed the lack of suitable males brave enough to meet her eye. Her husband arrived with her drink. As he tried to correct the angle of the umbrella in her glass, she leaned across and smacked his hand away. Her comment was audible across the room.

'Leave it alone, you stupid prat!'

The drinkers studied the contents of their glasses and glanced at their watches. Five past nine; too early to go to their room or the caravan. They decided to stay. The entertainment may be excruciating, but it looked promising. They were not disappointed. A few minutes later a gang of rowdy Geordie lads tumbled through the door. Already the worse for wear, they were blissfully unaware of the expectant atmosphere in the room. After some argument about whose round it was, they ordered the predictable quota of Newcastle Brown and turned to check out the lasses.

Fern watched as their eyes searched the room. It didn't take long. One of them spotted the woman straight away. This resulted in a lot of elbow nudging and laughter, but despite her responding smirk, they turned back to the bar. They might fancy her, but she was with her husband and daughter. Off-limits.

Fern could see the consternation in the woman's face. Without looking at her husband, she got up and walked unsteadily across the bar towards the toilets. Her route was less than direct so that she could get close to the young men. Crucially, as she went to go past, a man and woman decided it was time to go and stood up. This forced her to squeeze through the narrow space and make physical contact with the men clustered at the bar.

'Excuse me,' she said and giggled.

'Never mind, bonnie lass,' came the reply, followed by lots of laughter and a few glances across at the husband. Both he and his daughter were looking elsewhere.

She went on to the side door, where she stopped, reached into her handbag and pulled out a packet of cigarettes and a lighter. With a long look at the five young men, she backed out of the door. They'd all watched this blatant exhibition and now turned back to their drinks. There was a hushed conversation followed by loud guffaws. One of the gang put down his glass and without more ado made for the door. His exit was accompanied with more laughter and more furtive glances at the husband.

The whole room quietened in tense expectation. Their imaginations were running riot. Couples eyed each other with a variety of looks: envy and lust, disgust and denial. A thousand glances flitted across the space between them and the abandoned husband and his daughter. None of them were returned. The girl stared through the window into the darkness. The husband looked deeper and deeper into his empty glass.

From outside came a sound then the door burst open and the young man stumbled through. He regained his balance and put his hand to his face but it wasn't enough to hide the livid cheek and the blushing face. He rejoined his companions, who demanded an explanation. He spoke, they roared with laughter. The door opened and everyone turned towards it. The woman took in the audience's collective stare and haughtily brushed her dishevelled hair from her face before making her way back to the window seat. The anti-climax was like a tyre deflating. People began talking all at once, although the glances continued to criss-cross the room. Was that it? Was there more?

There was.

There were a few moments lull, the calm before the storm. A few of the crowd could feel the tension building and fidgeted in their seats. When it came, it was cataclysmic.

'You nasty little bitch,' yelled the woman. She was on her feet, round the table and grabbed the girl by her hair. 'What did you call me?'

The girl screamed and tried to escape the woman's grip, but she was too weak. The woman pulled her this way and that, before slapping her hard across the head. Wrenching herself from the woman's grip, the girl escaped and ran from the room. Her father was still sitting at this point, his mouth a desperate vortex. Now he stood and approached his wife. It didn't matter what he said, he got the same treatment. The crowd was silenced by the crack of the slap. He stumbled and nearly fell. The crowd gasped. He regained his balance, gave her a beseeching look and followed his daughter out through the door. The crowd held its breath. She smiled, sat down and surveyed their horror-struck faces. Gradually they all looked away. Conversations stuttered into gear. A few men approached the bar; they all needed a drink after that display.

Only one man kept looking. He wasn't one of the young lads, who'd closed ranks, he was a bit older. He must have come in during the fracas because Fern hadn't noticed him until now. She watched as the woman's gaze was drawn to his. Their eyes met. Two sets of eyebrows were raised. The woman played with her drink, her fingers sliding up and down the stem of the glass. It wasn't empty. She reached into the liquid and brought out one of the ice cubes. She rubbed it against her lips and put it in her mouth.

Fern was transfixed. The woman glanced her way so she looked down at her book. When she looked up again, the woman was halfway across the room and the young man had gone. Fern followed her with her eyes as she went out the side door. Fern made a decision. She put the book in her bag and also made for the door.

Outside it was pitch black beyond the pub lights. She could make out the orange glow of the village half a mile away, hidden behind the intervening trees. It wasn't far to her bed and breakfast.

As Fern got to the car, she heard them. She climbed into the driving seat and switched on the headlights. The man and the woman were leaning against a wall, shielding their eyes from the headlamps. Fern switched to sidelights, started the engine and drove out of the car park.

There was a lay-by a few hundred yards up the road. She pulled in, turned off the engine and got out of the car. She was wearing trainers, so made little sound as she walked back to the car park and peered round the gatepost. She knew where they were and, in any case, she could hear them clearly. They weren't talking; they'd got well past that. As she watched, her eyes adjusted so that she could make out their squirming bodies in the shadows.

A light came on in an upstairs room. It didn't spotlight them but it gave Fern a better view. The woman had her back to the wall and her skirt was round her waist. The man had his hands under her thighs holding her up. His body moved rhythmically as he pushed into her. She had one hand round his waist and the other in his hair. His thrusting increased in speed and force. She pulled back his head. He gasped in exultation and his body spasmed. The woman laughed. A hard, cruel laugh. The man withdrew.

Then the woman pushed him away and he fell backwards. She pushed herself from the wall and stood over him. She laughed again and dropped down onto his chest. Fern winced as she watched the blows. The woman hit him three times; he tried to protect his face, but then lay still.

The woman stood up and looked down at him and again she laughed. Quieter this time, but somehow more cruel. She took a few awkward steps back and pulled down her skirt, bent to pick up a discarded shoe and nearly fell over. She put her hand against the wall as she forced it back onto her foot. She didn't hear Fern coming towards her until it was too late. She caught a glimpse of a pair of jeans and trainers as she looked up.

A fist glanced off the side of the woman's head. She fell back against the wall. A hand was round her throat. She tried to call out. She felt a pain in her arm. The world went black.

She was unaware of being carried, fireman style, along the road to a small white car in a lay-by. She was dimly aware, some hours later, of the sound of a car engine and a face above her.

The next time she woke, she was in an old garden shed. She'd reached the end of her journey. It had been a spectacular show, but the finale had been written by a different hand. Farce was now to become tragedy. She had a splitting headache.

She opened her eyes.

* * * *

Fletcher couldn't have been more miserable. He'd uncovered an uncomfortable truth: he hated going back. Fair enough if that meant Rochdale or Todmorden. After the red stone buildings of Penrith and the surrounding green fells, the pair of them looked like the proverbial 'dark satanic mills' . . . except the fires had gone out.

They'd left the northern Lake District bursting into early springtime, lambs gambolling in the fields and birds chattering in the trees and hedges. In Rochdale it was raining. Heavily. The sort of rain which soaked through your outer layers within minutes, so even a quick sprint from Georgio's café to the police station left them wet through and dripping on the entrance hall floor.

Sergeant Sonley was his usual dour self, regarding Fletcher and his two companions as if he couldn't decide whether to send them back out or put them in a cell. Although he obviously knew it was Fletcher, he made no acknowledgement of their previous working relationship. DC Irene Garner looked round at the distinctive tobacco-stain yellow walls and shuddered, partly from the cold seeping into her bones, but also out of disgust. DC Lonsdale gazed in astonishment at what he knew must be a *Coronation Street* set, waiting expectantly for one of the characters to come through the door. Sonley broke through the collective thoughts of his rain-sodden guests and announced that DS Simpson awaited them in the main office. With that, he returned to his duty rosters like some Victorian clerk.

Garner and Lonsdale followed Fletcher up the gloomy stairs to the first floor and entered a smoke-filled den which reeked of despondency. A few faces turned their way. One or two grinned at Fletcher, but just as quickly looked away when they saw the look on his face. In the middle of the room sat a man at a desk piled high with files and dirty cups. He was bald and wore John Lennon glasses. He was smiling. A big welcoming smile.

'What are you so damn happy about?' said Fletcher.

'I said to this lot. The one thing you can be certain about is that Detective Inspector Fletcher will light up any room, especially because he always brings such delightful female company.'

He leapt out of his seat, pulled a couple of chairs away from nearby desks and offered one of them to Irene. She looked at Fletcher, but he shrugged his shoulders and walked towards a side office.

'I think, as usual, DS Simpson, you've bitten off more than you can chew, but don't let me stop you.'

Irene followed him with her eyes, before accepting the proffered chair. Lonsdale took the other.

Fletcher entered the office without knocking. Irene saw a neatly dressed little man rising from his seat as Fletcher shut the door.

DI Creasey couldn't say he was glad to see Fletcher. They'd never got on, but he'd been told to be polite and helpful, so he thought he'd make an effort. Fletcher didn't sit, but walked over to the window and leant against the radiator. Within a few seconds, to Creasey's consternation, Fletcher's clothes began to steam. Silhouetted against the 'palely loitering sun' as it tried vainly to illuminate their tepid reunion, he soon began to look like some ghostly reincarnation.

'I'm not here for a holiday, Creasey. I'm thinking of it as deportation, but without the surfing or the bikinis. I don't know what you've been told, neither do I expect you to tell me, but the sooner we can sort this, the better, agreed?'

Creasey nodded, reflecting on his earlier conversation with Chief Inspector Worthington. He said nothing.

'So what have you got?' Fletcher asked.

Creasey took him to the incident room. Irene and Lonsdale followed, trailed by a lascivious Simpson, who kept far enough behind, the better to observe Irene's legs.

The room was busier than they'd expected. Also, they quickly realised that the room was divided into two. Two sets of information boards and two teams of officers. Fletcher looked at Creasey.

'We've two concurrent investigations going on, Inspector. This lot are a branch of the North Manchester team working in conjunction with the West Yorkshire Ripper squad.'

Fletcher snorted in disbelief.

'Fat chance,' he said. 'In your dreams, Creasey.'

One or two of the officers gave him a stern look, but he stared them out. If they didn't know him, they'd surely been told about him. Creasey ignored this and pointed at the other team. Smaller board space, fewer officers.

'This lot are working on cases which don't fit the Ripper profile. Linda Eckersley belongs to them.'

'What profile?' asked Fletcher.

Creasey glanced across at the Ripper team. One or two were looking at him meaningfully.

'You'd better ask them,' he said.

Fletcher spoke above the buzz of conversation.

'So who's in charge of the Ripper squad?'

A face he'd not wanted to see ever again appeared from behind one of the screens.

'Bloody hell. DI Sutton! Well, there's your evidence.'

Sutton came slowly towards him. The room went quiet. You'd have to be from another planet to be unaware of the impending clash of male testosterone.

'Evidence of what, Inspector?' said Sutton. 'I don't remember you ever bothering to spend your time looking for evidence.'

'Not when the answer is staring you in your face. Nor did I ever get round to planting any when I couldn't add two and two and get even.'

By now Sutton was within smacking distance. Fletcher hadn't moved. The tension was electric. Irene thought things were beginning to look up. Lonsdale recalled what PC Burke told him in detail of the violent damage Fletcher had inflicted on the girl's punter.

Fletcher waited for the next response, but Sutton had run out of repartee. He'd told himself he wasn't going to let this happen, but the sight of Fletcher's arrogant face and the way he immediately undermined him made his blood seethe.

A voice from the doorway hushed the already silent crowd.

'Ah, gentlemen. I'm glad to see you've managed to rekindle the warm relationship you enjoyed in your previous encounters.'

Everyone glanced at the chief inspector and immediately clocked back in. Conversations were awkwardly rewound and play buttons pressed.

'DI Fletcher. My office, now.'

Fletcher followed him out. Simpson clapped his hands and laughed. 'Just like the old days.'

Sutton glared at him, but turned back to his team, none of whom met his eyes.

A bear stood quietly at Irene's shoulder. 'You'll be DC Garner, I presume. I'm DS Lockwood. It's alright, I've worked with DI Fletcher before. I've been assigned to work with you on the Eckersley case. Follow me.'

Irene introduced Lonsdale and they followed the huge sergeant over to the information boards. As the saying goes, she thought – 'light on his feet for a big man'.

Upstairs in his office, Chief Inspector Worthington was offering Fletcher a seat. Fletcher noted that the carpet was nowhere near as thick as the one in Chief Inspector Aske's office.

'You've not changed, Fletcher. Can't have been in there two minutes and you're back in the ring.'

'Old dog – daft puppy. Recipe for a lot of yapping and the odd nip, sir. Nothing fatal.'

'Yes. Well. Let me try and teach you the odd trick or two.'

'I'm all floppy ears, sir.'

Worthington gave him one of his withering looks and Fletcher held up both hands. A truce was agreed.

'It may be a surprise to you, but I know your chief inspector very well. Roger Aske was the best DI on my force in Middlesbrough and that's not the prettiest patch in the world.' Fletcher knew no comment was needed regarding this assertion.

'He got his current job because of my strong recommendation. I've heard nothing to make me think I've advised anyone wrongly.'

'No complaints from me,' said Fletcher.

'Surprisingly enough the feeling is mutual.'

Fletcher raised his eyebrows.

'Apparently, he considers you a breath of fresh air up there. Lots of old stagers stuck in the fifties, according to him.'

'Local plods doing a grand day's work. "Home again, home again jiggedy jig." I sometimes think the world has ended and no-one had told me. The office is deserted at six every day.'

'So anyway, apart from a general shake-up, you also decided to take on the local top dog?'

'It was personal, sir.'

'It always is with you, Fletcher.'

'No. This was different. It affected a certain lady's daughter. I feel responsible, for once in my life.'

'I'm well aware of the reasons for your behaviour and you're well aware of the correct procedure in such cases. It's for your own protection as much as the villain's.'

'Ah. So he *is* a bad guy then?'

Worthington gave him another look. Fletcher mimed zipping his mouth.

'As DI Sutton was pointing out in his rather clumsy manner, we need the evidence.'

Fletcher's eyes widened.

'I'll be brief.'

Fletcher suppressed a smile. No-one was a better briefer than Chief Inspector Worthington.

'To put it simply, there does seem to be a connection between a string of the recent murders, rapes and abductions of known prostitutes, including Linda Eckersley. When you get back downstairs – with your tail between your legs – DS Lockwood will show you what we've got. We have reason to believe that many of these women were taken from places frequented by truckers and in particular men who work for your 'friend up north'. We have one very frightened young woman in a safe house who is willing to testify against one of his truckers. Unfortunately that's not enough. One woman's testimony against a man like that will go nowhere against the sort of legal team his boss could assemble. She also remembers little of the actual rape and only scraps of details which don't make sense to her, but they do to us.'

'So . . .' Fletcher had an inkling of where this might be heading.

'Don't jump the gun, Inspector. DI Aske and I have a plan. The need to get you out of the picture suggested it. Your new sidekick – as usual – happens to have certain qualities which helped develop that plan.'

'I think I get your drift. I dare say she'll go for it. She's brave, a bit tasty with her arresting techniques and ambitious.'

'As I said – she has many of the qualities needed for the job.'

'So where do I fit in?'

'She needs some protection.'

'But people know me down here.'

'Don't flatter yourself. You were only here for less than a year and a lot of that time you were suspended or on leave. You've got a worse reputation with your colleagues than the criminal fraternity. '

'Must be doing something right then?' Fletcher laughed, saw Worthington's face and re-zipped.

'In any case, you're not going to be up close. DC Garner can only get near these guys if they can't see anyone around her. We're going to take off your leather coat, get you a woolly jumper, a baseball cap and put you in a truck.'

'What? I can't drive one of them.'

'No, but DC Lonsdale can. He got his HGV licence before he even joined the force. He's got his advanced driver qualifications since.'

'Light under a bushel, eh?'

'We don't all sing out loud, Fletcher. Some of us like to keep a little back.'

Fletcher nodded sagely, trying to think of some skill he had that he'd not yet disclosed. He couldn't think of anything, other than dancing to ska. He didn't think this was the best moment to demonstrate it.

Five minutes later Fletcher was back downstairs, listening to DS Colin Lockwood tell him what he knew. He couldn't do 'tail between legs', so had blanked Sutton completely. It was hard, but gave him some limited satisfaction. It still hadn't fully dawned on either Irene or Lonsdale where all this information was taking them.

Fletcher had a quick word with Lockwood, to say that he'd prefer to explain the thickening of the plot to them in the pub. Lockwood did his big-bear shrug and agreed.

*　*　*　*

Fletcher took the two of them to the Eagle and Child. It made him think of Courtney, but Simpson had told him he was inside. Some drugs deal gone wrong. Courtney had been badly beaten up but hadn't talked, so was doing a six-year stretch in Strangeways. He'd asked Simpson to arrange a visit.

There was another person who Fletcher wanted to see, but that was personal. The fewer people who knew about that the better. Particularly Laura. She and Grace had come down with him and they were all staying at Laura's sister's house in Todmorden. It had begun to feel like a bad idea, but they'd thought it might be good for Grace to be on home ground for a while.

Laura's sister, Jessica, was not Fletcher's favourite woman. She considered herself a cut above and had made it clear that she considered her sister was worth someone better than him.

Fletcher ordered their drinks and found a quiet corner. It was late afternoon and the pub was empty. He reckoned he'd got an hour before the 'stop-off before home' crowd piled in. He took a sip of the Boddingtons and pulled a face. Gnat's piss compared to the Jennings. The looks on Irene and Lonsdale's faces confirmed his opinion.

'So, you two. The sooner we carry out Mr Worthington's little plan, the sooner we'll be back in the Fox supping Farmer Jennings Spotty Chickens.'

They grinned at him.

'Now a clever lady like yourself has probably worked out her role already by now,' he said, looking into Irene's hazel eyes. She stared him out.

'I think I get it. My promotion review is in two weeks time. If I can turn myself into an inviting little morsel for a certain friend of ours, it'll be a shoo-in . . . or otherwise . . .'

'As I said before – the perceptive and deductive powers of a real detective.'

Lonsdale was currently adopting the role of northern farmer's lad dunderhead. 'What do you mean "morsel"?' he asked.

'Alan,' she said, with a ladylike reproachful look.

'No, I'm sorry. I don't get it.'

Fletcher and Irene exchanged looks which said 'shall you tell him or shall I?' He gave her the slightest of nods.

'I'll tell you straight, farm boy, and then you'll know.'

Lonsdale pulled a face. He hated being called that, even if it had been true up until five years ago.

'What these senior officers have dreamed up in their perverted little minds is a scenario in which I dress like a tart and offer myself up as a trucker's delight. Except I'm only for sale to a particular buyer. You dig.'

Lonsdale stared at her in disbelief. He opened his mouth and closed it again.

'But the really big surprise is you – Mr HGV "keep it under my hat" advanced driver . . . Mr T, huh?' laughed Fletcher.

Lonsdale reprised his goldfish impression. It was Irene's turn to follow him round the bowl, but with bigger and better made-up eyes. Lonsdale spluttered and nearly choked on his beer.

'What d'you mean?' he demanded.

'Well, it's your own fault,' replied Fletcher. 'My mum always said keeping secrets would get you into trouble.'

'But . . .'

'No buts, you're the driver, I'm the muscle and Irene's the honey trap. What else do you need to know?'

'But . . .'

'When? Don't know. We wait for Colin. Any other questions? . . . No? Right, Jim Clark, it's your round and me and Irene don't want any more of this Boddingtons' piss, so halves of best and a double Bushmills. Okay?'

It wasn't okay, but Lonsdale was in deep. The poor sap still thought this gave him another chance with Irene. He knew he could do the driving – he'd started on tractors when he was twelve. He couldn't think of a nastier piece of work than Fletcher to be his 'muscle'. So, he went to the bar.

On his return he was surprised to find the two of them sitting in silence. He wasn't to know. Fletcher had told her she didn't have to do this. She'd told him she did. End of conversation. They only had one more round and then went their separate ways: Irene to see a 'friend' of hers in Bolton; Lonsdale back to the police flat, a take-away and a late night TV extravaganza, and Fletcher to a little pub in Bacup – his own little secret.

CHAPTER 11

1977

Fern had spent all night outside the shed in her sleeping bag. It reminded her of the many nights she'd spent under the stars, although in the clearing you could only see a small circle of the sky between the treetops. She recognised Vega shining brightly overhead. She didn't sleep much. She knew the last injection would probably keep the woman quiet until the morning. She'd searched her handbag and discovered her name. Eileen Stanhope. There were few other clues to where she lived or her connection to the man and the young girl. Fern had guessed they were husband, wife and daughter, but knew only too well the variety of other possible combinations. She'd cut off the woman's blonde hair and left her untied on the floor. The old mirror was within easy reach.

Fern had avoided examining her feelings or wondering why she'd left Eileen untied. She knew it was something to do with the visceral excitement she'd experienced when she captured her, but her alertness to any sounds of reawakening kept her from analysing that excitement. She just knew this was how she wanted it. The dragon was awake and stirring.

As the star faded into the light of dawn, she heard the first sounds of movement. Fern slipped out of her bag and went to stand behind a nearby tree. The rustling inside the shed was interrupted by a loud scream of anger, followed by the shattering of glass. Seconds later the door burst open and the woman appeared in the doorway. She didn't see Fern, but waded out through the nettles, stinging her legs in the process. As she bent down and cursed, Fern stepped into view. The woman looked up, a startled expression on her face, which was rapidly replaced with a fleeting recognition and then blazing anger. She reached up to her head. The remaining spikes were dark; her blonde identity was lying all over the shed floor.

'Did you do this?' she asked in a hoarse whisper.

Fern nodded.

'I'm going to kill you,' said the woman.

Fern's face was blank.

Eileen Stanhope didn't know how she was going to do what she'd promised, but something told her it wasn't going to be easy. Her head was spinning. She knew she was probably going to be sick. This monster standing before her held all the cards. Eileen had no idea where they were. She hated the woods. Full of insects and small furry animals. She shuddered. She had no weapon and this creature seemed very sure of herself. She hadn't moved or said anything since she'd appeared out of nowhere.

Eileen looked around. Her eyes alighted on a wooden pole leaning against the shed. She looked back at Fern, who just stared at her. Taking a breath, Eileen took two unsteady steps to her right and grabbed the pole. She held it in both hands and looked back at the woman . . . who reached out towards the nearest tree and produced a stick of similar length and thickness. She held it lightly in one hand.

170

Eileen reconsidered her position. Whatever was going on here, the creature had planned it. The shed, the haircutting, the pole and the stick. All planned. Eileen had never fought anyone with a stick before, other than an occasional high tackle in hockey. She lowered one end to the floor and offered diplomacy.

'What's this all about? I don't know you. I don't think you know me? So why the theatricals?'

Fern said nothing and didn't move, just continued to stare. The light was increasing all the time. Eileen could see that the woman was dressed in a dark-green coat and jeans. Her blonde hair was cut short and she obviously didn't care much about her appearance. Eileen struggled to make sense of her situation. A stronger flicker of recognition came to her.

'You were in the pub, weren't you? I remember now. You were reading a book.'

Still no response.

'You were outside when I . . . with that young bloke . . .'

Her memory was coming back. Her eyes opened wide.

'You watched us fucking . . . You're weird . . . perverted!' Her voice began to rise.

Fern's face shifted imperceptibly harder. Her eyes darkened. Her pupils dilated.

'What do you want?' screamed Eileen. She lifted the pole from the ground.

Fern spoke quietly. 'You're a vicious bully. I'm going to give you a taste of your own medicine.'

Eileen's eyes widened in disbelief. 'You're what?'

'You heard. You don't know where you are. It would take days to find your way out of this forest. You're only chance is to fight for your life.'

Eileen looked at her in terror. She gripped the pole until her knuckles hurt. Her eyes searched the trees that disappeared into darkness in every direction. She glanced behind her at the shed. She considered retreating but she knew there was only one door. She couldn't see it as anything other than a prison. She looked back at Fern. She hadn't moved, but Eileen could see that there was tension in her body – a tightening of muscles. She'd never been this frightened in her entire life. Instead of trying to reason with the creature, she decided to run. The one bit of hockey training which helped her was to feint to the left and run to the right. It gave her just a few seconds start.

Unfortunately, her advantage soon evaporated. Years of easy living counted for little against heightened animal instinct. Fern went with the feint but easily caught up. Eileen managed four steps before the stick tripped her up. She staggered and dodged the next blow as it thwacked against a tree. The venom of it whistling past her head forced a rush of adrenalin through her terror-struck limbs. She regained her balance and swung her own weapon at her enemy. The pole splintered across the trunk of a tree, but caught Fern a glancing blow on the side of her head and she spun away clutching her temple. Blood flowed from between her fingers. She staggered and fell, dropping the stick as she tumbled.

Eileen controlled her astonishment and leapt on top of her fallen opponent as she lay dazed on the ground. She forced Fern onto her back and slapped her hard across the face. Blood splattered everywhere. Eileen punched her adversary in the face and more blood started to come from her mouth. Eyes blazing, Eileen grabbed Fern around the throat and began to throttle her. She was going to win. She was going to kill the bitch. She took one hand away and punched her hard again, heard the crunch of breaking bone. Fern cried out, but Eileen was filled with blood lust. She leaned forward and put both hands round her victim's neck again and began to strangle her with all her strength. Fern's face was covered with blood, her eyes beginning to bulge.

At the last second, Eileen saw the hand coming up towards her head but was unable to prevent it reaching her face. She screamed as a handful of nettles was rubbed against her eyes, mouth and cheeks. Her hands released their grip as she fought to push away the stinging pain. Fern's other hand came up and punched her on the side of her head and she fell to one side.

The tables were turned. Fern forced Eileen onto her back and pushed the nettles into her screaming mouth. She choked. Fern's strong hands gripped her throat. She couldn't get her breath. Fern's blood was flooding down into her eyes. She gasped and choked and croaked.

And died.

Fern remained still for a long time with her hands around the woman's throat. The bleeding slowed. The pain in her nose increased. The stinging had made her hands numb. Finally, convinced the woman was dead, she collapsed on top of her.

She must have lost consciousness for a moment. When she came to, she was lying face to face on the dead woman. Eileen's dead-fish eyes looked past her at the trees.

Fern climbed slowly to her feet. She turned away from the blood-soaked horror on the ground and staggered to the shed.

She found her rucksack and pulled out her first aid box. She knew her nose was broken and there would be bruises on her neck. She felt the bump on the side of her head and looked at it in the small mirror. The bleeding had stopped, but her hair was matted and sticking out like a crown of thorns. She allowed her training to take over and did what she could. She had a bucket of clean water behind the shed and washed herself. She knew she needed help and figured out where she was going to head for. She knew she couldn't do anything about the woman. She'd have to leave her to the creatures of the forest for a while.

She made her way out of the wood and got into her car. She drove to the old man's house. He would take care of her. No questions asked. He was a Robinson.

*   *   *   *

It was two days before Fern was able to make her way back to the clearing. Eileen Stanhope had almost certainly spent a lot of time and money on her appearance whilst she was alive. Dead, she looked like any other half-eaten corpse, but Fern had been brought up in the countryside. She remembered seeing her first fly-blown sheep when she was four or five. It was the stench which she'd found most difficult to endure, but when you know what to do, it doesn't last for long.

She lifted the turf and dug the hole. The body left a trail of innards as she dragged it across the pine needles, but she knew they'd be devoured soon enough. The forest dwellers wasted nothing.

It took her less than an hour to complete the business. The rose she'd dug up the previous night stood erect in its new position. It hadn't travelled far and the compost she kept in the shed would aid Eileen's contribution to its re-establishment and growth.

Fern phoned through to work and explained she'd had a bit of an accident out on the fells, but she'd be back for Wednesday. As it happened, her boss took one look at her and told her to come back when she wouldn't frighten the customers. The only lasting physical effect she carried from the battle was a boxer's nose and a thin scar above her left eyebrow . . . but inside there was a different story.

* * * *

Louisa had come in disguise. She still turned every male head as she walked in, but none of them would be able to recognise the much-featured local socialite. Fletcher doubted whether they used the term in Rochdale, but was certain it was not in the vocabulary of the regulars at the Britannia Inn, Bacup. He'd been surprised the first time she'd agreed to meet him there over a year ago. For her to suggest it a second time told him she enjoyed the game.

The trademark Bacall hairstyle was hidden under a blue headscarf. She'd selected a spy-thriller white mackintosh, but had failed to disguise the shapely calves and high heels. Bacup men were probably legs and bottom watchers anyway. Fletcher gave them all a 'jealous boyfriend' glare and they went back to their pints. He was enjoying a Golden Best, but she only wanted an orange juice.

'I've moved on since the D-notice case, Louisa. I'm afraid the current investigations are far more sordid. Sex and violence.'

'More your field of study anyway, I would have thought, Michael.'

'Not this one. He's a particularly nasty combination of "nouveau riche" with a penchant for young girls.'

'Nabakov without the panache?' she asked.

'I wouldn't know. I prefer the more experienced woman myself.'

'Can't fault you there, Michael. You certainly need taking in hand.'

They tired of this banter and each took a sip of their drink.

'So how can I help?' she asked.

'Caroline Soulby,' he answered.

'I've told you all I know. I haven't seen her since last December and that was only by chance. As I said, she's not a friend. I imagine she has far more enemies than friends. She's an unpleasant woman who has a serious problem with men.'

'How do you mean?'

'She doesn't like them.'

Fletcher waited.

'In fact, she goes out of her way to humiliate them. Always has done.'

'Any idea why?'

'Father was a vicious bastard. Mother was an alcoholic.'

'Usual upper-class upbringing then?'

She shook her head at him.

'So why would she disappear?'

'Probably to cause poor Charles distress. Gone off with some young thing to Italy or somewhere more exotic. I expect he'll realise soon enough when the bank statements arrive.'

'Well, it can't be that exotic. She's not left the country. Her passport was in her room.'

'Michael, darling, there are plenty of people who can come and go as they please. She could be on a yacht or a private jet.'

'Um. I can never get my head round how rich people break the law so thoughtlessly and so frequently.'

Another shake of the head. This time the movement caused the headscarf to slip down over her glossy hair. A few eyes strayed her way. She had her back to the bar, but even so she quickly replaced it with a practised manoeuvre. She finished her drink and stood up to go.

'I'll ask around, Michael. That's the best I can do. Now I must go.'

He nodded and watched her slink out of the bar. One or two men looked across at him and nodded in appreciation. He sat there for a while and remembered his previous meetings with her. Eventually he sighed and set off back to Laura.

*　*　*　*

He'd not intended the next encounter, but as he drove down the valley into Todmorden, his thoughts had turned to Courtney and, inevitably as he got nearer, his girlfriend Cassie. Fletcher had ended up staying with her the previous year, when everything had gone pear-shaped once again. He'd been suspended. Head-butting a fellow officer wasn't considered acceptable behaviour up north, even if the idle tosser deserved it. He'd little time for the West Yorkshire police as it was, but they just couldn't handle what was going on. He'd ended up fighting the madman on his own. He and Sadie had saved a lot of people's lives. Both of them had received commendations and neither of them or anyone else could say a word about it. So idiots like DI Sutton were still making a cock-up of everything they touched.

Fletcher realised he was driving too fast. The anger was revving him up. He used this as an excuse to go and see Cassie. She lived up the hill off the Bacup Road so it was a simple diversion. As he parked on the verge, he looked up and saw that the light was on in her studio. He smiled to himself as he pictured the portrait she'd done of him. A man on fire!

He knocked on the door and went in. The walls had changed colour. Blue and grey had been replaced by yellow and orange.

He shouted up the stairs and, without expecting a reply, he went up. Her studio door was open and she had her back to him as he entered. Like the walls, the black, white and blue stripes in her long hair had been replaced by much shorter orange and yellow spikes. He'd learnt not to be surprised by the changes in her appearance and wouldn't dream of making a comment.

'Still burning up inside, Fletcher?' she said, without turning round.

'I'm afraid so,' he replied.

He looked at the walls. They were still covered with flying people. Not angels: just ordinary people, real people, but flying – with their clothes on. And there he was, flying through the air. The visible parts of his body were burning inside. His clothes were singed at the edges. Flames licked at his hair. His green and blue eyes shone like jewels.

She was facing him, her own deep-blue eyes boring into him. She slowly cleaned the brush in her hand.

'Have you eaten?' she asked.

He shook his head. They went downstairs. Fletcher knew that his dinner at Jessica's was heading towards the dog, but he could only hope the ugly thing choked on it. He sat at the scrubbed oak table and watched Cassie as she prepared a meal you'd never see on Jessica's dining table. Fletcher couldn't ever see himself becoming a vegetarian, but if anyone was to convince him it was Cassie. He hadn't realised he was so hungry.

They didn't speak much. They never did. It wasn't like him, but he found it strangely restful. She didn't ask him what he was doing, where he was going or what he was thinking. While she was preparing the meal she completely ignored him, even though she must have known he watched her every move.

He'd lived in her house for several weeks but they'd never had sex, just one night in her bed. She'd held him until he'd stopped shaking and the adrenalin factory had clocked off. They hadn't spoken much. He hadn't told her about the train or the viaduct or the madman. She knew Quirke; he was on her wall, flying with everyone else. Unlike the others, he had really flown, briefly – like Icarus. It was an image Fletcher would never forget.

They ate in silence.

'I'm going to see Courtney tomorrow,' he said.

'I know,' she replied.

'Is there anything you want me to give him or tell him.'

She shook her cockatoo head. He could tell nothing from her face.

'Your daughter's in trouble,' she said.

He looked at her in astonishment.

'Grace? Laura's daughter?' she added.

'Yes . . . but how do you know . . . ?'

'I've seen her with Chas Harvey. That's not good.'

'Is he the . . . ?'

She nodded. 'He's got his claws into her. You need to get her away from here.'

Fletcher looked at her sadly. 'We thought she might be better with her old friends.'

Cassie shook her head. 'You can't go back. It's one of the immutable laws of physics. Time's arrow.'

Fletcher stared at her. She nodded again.

'Take her back. Catch the man who hurt her and put him away. Love her. She will be fine. She's of the earth. One of Gaia's children. She needs to feel the ground beneath her feet. Flying from fear won't help her. She must face it and put it behind her.'

He listened without really understanding. Not sure he believed in her way of seeing the world. But he knew he trusted her . . . and couldn't have told anyone why.

'You're late,' she said. 'Your woman needs you.'

She gave him one last look and left the room. He heard her going up the stairs. He got to his feet and went to the door. His instinct told him she was watching him. He turned to see her sitting on the top step.

'I see a dark place overgrown with thorns. You must run from the flames again, Fletcher . . . the numbers are a lie.'

She stood up and disappeared from sight. He slowly closed the door and walked out into the orange glow of the street lights. He looked up at the studio. No face at the window. He got into his car and drove through the town, his mind whirling with images.

* * * *

His woman was not happy. Laura had never got on with her sister. She'd only come back to Todmorden for Grace's sake and that wasn't working, either. She'd thought her daughter would pick up with her old friends, but she'd gone out and found the worst possible playmates. They'd already had one enormous row about Grace staying out late.

Laura knew the pub, she knew the landlord. He'd been to prison twice for drug-related crimes. It was obvious what was going on but, like a lot of Todmorden pub landlords, he got the warning long before the police arrived, by which time the drug crowd had moved elsewhere. Fletcher had tried his best, but the local police were helpless. Being at her sister's only made it worse. They'd argued the first night. Fletcher had left them to it and made himself scarce ever since. She'd rung the station to see where he was, but no-one knew.

She saw his car pull up on the drive. He'd missed dinner. Jessica had declared that she had standards: dinner was at seven thirty and anyone rude enough to be late didn't deserve feeding anyway. As Laura watched through the window, she could see him sitting in the car staring out across the valley. What was he up to?

He got out of the car and slowly made his way up the steps.

Later in bed she asked him. 'What are you doing down here, Mick?'

'Trying to catch the bastard who abuses young girls like Grace.'

She sighed. 'I don't know what to do with her, Mick.' Her eyes filled up. He put his arms round her.

'Listen. I can't tell you the detail, but we're setting a trap. Hopefully he'll be behind bars within a week or so.'

'But that's not going to stop Grace destroying her life, is it?'

Fletcher had no answer for her. He'd tried talking to Grace but the relationship had gone sour. She'd made it clear.

'You're not my dad. I haven't got a dad. So keep away from me.'

He'd no answer to that. All he could do was to try to nail the perverted bastard who'd made her feel like that. He knew that the honey-trap was probably the only way they'd stand a chance of catching him red-handed, but he didn't like it. Irene fancied her chances but Fletcher didn't like the odds.

He'd had a long day, sleep overtook him.

Laura cried herself to sleep.

*   *   *   *

There was no comfort at breakfast time. Grace had stayed out late. Laura and Jessica argued about bringing up children. All of

181

Jessica's three had gone off to university; but as they'd all gone as far away as possible, Fletcher imagined the motivation was more to do with escaping from their mother rather than furthering their academic ambitions. Fletcher gave Laura a hug and promised to meet her for lunch.

Simpson had fixed up a visit to Strangeways to see Courtney at ten thirty. Fletcher had told Simpson to tell the other two he'd see them at two thirty. He'd decided to go on the train, because he liked the journey; it gave him time to think. Time to people watch. He remembered not recognising Sadie Swift the day she arrived in Rochdale. Seeing her on the train and not being able to place the face. Irene had a long way to go before she'd emulate her.

He took a taxi from Victoria Station and presented himself at the prison gates for ten twenty. Five minutes later Courtney sauntered into the visitors' room and slouched down in the chair opposite.

'Hey, man. It's good to see your ugly face.'

'Courtney. What you doing getting caught?'

The black man leaned forward and beckoned Fletcher close. 'Getting put in here's da least of my trubals, man.'

Fletcher leaned towards him.

'I ain't telling you notink, whitey.'

'I ain't asking you anything, you black bastard. Least, not about what you're in here for.'

'So what d'ya want to know?'

'What d'you know about the girls who work the truckers?'

'Dey gets in da cabs and shags 'em. What else is der to know!'

'It's not what, but who I'm after. A guy called Castle?'

Courtney laughed and leaned back. 'D'you play chess, whitey?'

Fletcher nodded.

Courtney winked at him. 'D'you know what "castling" means?'

'Yeh. The king and the castle swap places.'

'Why?'

'So that the King can . . .'

Fletcher smiled. Courtney beamed. Fletcher stood up and beckoned to the guard.

'Take this black bastard back to his cell and make sure he gets a thorough beating, officer,' said Fletcher.

The prison officer was surly and could only manage a sneer. 'If only . . .' he muttered as he followed Courtney out of the room.

Fletcher stepped out into the rain and looked for a taxi. There were none to be seen. He walked all the way back to the station. On the train he considered what Courtney had told him. Did he mean that Len Castle was the king, or was he protecting someone higher up the food chain? He sat in his damp clothes and wondered about Grace.

His daydreaming came to an abrupt end when he arrived at the station. He wasn't due to meet Laura for another half hour, so thought he'd drop in to see what was going on. He wasn't pleased to hear that Irene and Lonsdale had already set off for Birch Services. They'd had a tip-off about some of Len Castle's drivers arranging a get-together. One of the girls who was a snout for Creasey had told him she'd been invited to 'audition' for a special event that night. Irene got to hear about it and persuaded Lonsdale to take her.

Fletcher cursed Creasey and commandeered a car from the pool. Ten minutes later he was cruising round the lorry park.

He spotted Lonsdale's truck, parked up and wandered over. Lonsdale was looking the other way as Fletcher climbed up and got in the cab.

'Where is she?'

'Over there,' replied Lonsdale, who was both scared and relieved to see Fletcher.

'It's alright; I know it wasn't your idea.'

'She told me to wait here. If she gets in the truck, I'm to follow them.'

They both watched the figures gathered near a lorry bearing the Castle logo. There were two men and four women. Well . . . girls. Irene was by far the oldest. The conversation seemed relaxed. One of the men had his arm round one of the younger women.

As the two policemen watched, they saw Irene move towards the other man and reach out blatantly to fondle his crotch. The man put his hand round her neck and pulled her towards him. He reached up, grabbed her hair and kissed her. Two of the girls walked away, and Irene and the younger woman climbed up into the cab. Another man was already in the driver's seat. The truck's engine chugged into life and it moved slowly towards the exit. The two other men walked towards another truck with the Castle logo.

Lonsdale switched on his engine, looked at the dashboard and cursed. Before Fletcher could ask him what the problem was, he'd opened the cab door and leapt down. Fletcher yelled after him; Lonsdale shouted back. Fletcher couldn't hear, so opened his door and got down.

As he came round the front of the truck he saw the problem. Lonsdale was kicking one of the back wheels. A screwdriver was embedded in the tyre wall. The tyre was flat. Lonsdale looked at him.

'Bastards are onto us.'

Fletcher turned and ran towards his car. 'Get in touch with

Creasey. Tell him to get some unmarked cars to follow that truck. If they're on to us, they're going to know about Irene.'

He got into the car. Got out again. Ran round the car checking the tyres. All okay. No – wait a minute – what was that on the ground? He bent down and looked under the car. Bastards had cut his brake pipes; there was fluid leaking all over the floor. He leant into the car to reach for the radio. It had gone. Ripped out. He ran back to Lonsdale. He was nowhere to be seen. Fletcher cursed and went looking for a phone booth.

Having yanked a phone out of some old fellow's hand whilst shoving his warrant card up his left nostril, he rang Simpson.

'Simpson. The bastards have got Irene. Get the traffic police on the line and tell them to stop any Castle lorry travelling north on the M61 or M6.'

He gave Simpson the registration number and then hared off to find a car. As he reached the car park, he saw Lonsdale. He was leaning against a wall, blood pouring through his fingers.

'What the bloody hell have you been doing?' demanded Fletcher.

'I was trying to catch those other two blokes.'

'And they didn't like the look of your nose?'

'There were two of them, sir. One of them's not going to win any beauty contests either.'

'So where are they now?'

'I didn't see, sir. Knocked out cold.'

'Right. Go into the service station and get some help. I'm looking for a car.'

'I'm not staying here,' yelled Lonsdale and followed him as he strode into the car park. Fletcher saw a young chap getting out of a new Mercedes. He walked over and produced his card.

'I'm commandeering your car, sir. We need to pursue some criminals who've kidnapped two young women. Please hand over your keys.'

Before the man could take in what Fletcher was saying, his keys were torn from his fingers and the two men jumped into his car. His brain kicked into gear too late and, in his frantic attempts to hang on to his new toy, they nearly ran him over with it. He watched in despair and disbelief as his pride and joy was driven savagely out of the car park and hurtled towards the exit. He sat on a wall and wept.

Fletcher cut across to the outside lane and flashed his lights at the cars in his way. Fortunately it was mid-afternoon; otherwise this manoeuvre would have been impossible. Death Valley would be solid in less than two hours, but Fletcher managed to bully everyone out of his way. He turned on to the M61 and sped north. The car lived up to its reputation. As they roared past the first junction, Lonsdale could see the speedometer hovering over a hundred miles an hour. His hands gripped the seat. He wished he was driving. He knew he could drive at that speed, but he wasn't sure about Fletcher, even if he wasn't angry . . . and Fletcher was very angry indeed.

What they didn't realise was that, as they flew over the junction, the lorry they were chasing was parked under the motorway bridge. Behind it was a white Ford Sierra. In the back seat sat Irene and the younger girl. The driver looked through his mirror at the two frightened faces and smiled. Next to him sat Freddy Flusco, who was also smiling. The two women looked at the gun in his hand. They both knew he would use it and that he'd shoot to hurt, not kill.

'Now then, ladies,' he was saying. 'We'll all calm down. The excitement is over for now. We've got a couple of hours to drive and I don't want you to get all tense, so I'd be a lot happier if you'd not try to get out or make a fuss. Is that okay with you?'

They both nodded.

'Off you go Geordie. Nice and smooth, if you please. We don't want to upset the traffic officers, do we?'

The car moved back onto the road and Geordie took the slip road up onto the motorway. By now they were some way behind the rescue party, but that was as they'd planned it.

The lorry followed them, but travelled slowly. It was stopped and searched twenty minutes later and the driver taken into custody. He pleaded innocence and asked to speak to his boss. Mr Castle's solicitor arrived at the police station within the hour and the man was released without further ado.

The car carrying the two women continued northwards. Irene saw Fletcher standing by a blue Mercedes a few miles north of the Blackpool turn. She glared at him, but he paid no notice. She started to make a plan. She reckoned she'd got an hour and a half at most.

CHAPTER 12

Seeing Fletcher as they flashed past almost made Irene smile; he looked really cross. Poor old Lonsdale would be getting it in the neck and it was all her fault. However, that wasn't going to get her and Tania out this mess.

She'd met the Polish girl the previous night and liked her straight away. Tania was tall and thin, too thin, Irene suspected. Her naturally white-blonde hair, tied back tightly in a long ponytail, drew the punters. Coupled with the long legs and a tight skirt, she could name her price. She'd told Irene that most of her money went back home to her family. Her father had got on the wrong side of the state police and had disappeared. The family had been thrown out of their flat and was relying on equally poor relatives to put them up. Irene could tell the truth from a sob story.

They'd talked long into the night. Irene spoke a little Polish as her grandparents had arrived in England during the war, not sure whether they were more fearful of the Germans or the Russians. She remembered her *babcha* telling her terrifying fairy stories when she was little. She'd had the presence of mind to check on a few Polish words, which might come in useful in an emergency – like 'run' and 'look out'. Neither of these were much use in a car, but at some point they'd have to stop and get out. Irene knew this would be their only chance.

It came earlier than she expected. She had a good idea where they were going. Len Castle had a huge modern house near Askham that she'd driven past a couple of times. High walls, electric gates and dogs. Big dogs. Irene fancied her chances with a couple of puffed-up would-be gangsters like Flusco and Geordie. She knew their style: lots of bravado when they faced a couple of defenceless girls, but they'd cut and run in a real fight. But she didn't like dogs.

'Take the Shap exit, Geordie,' said Freddie, as they drove up the long hill. Geordie gave him a puzzled look.

'I fancy a bit of the action before the others get stuck in. Chances are we'll be on guard duty anyway,' Freddie explained, leering at Tania.

Geordie did as he was told. As he drove onto the slip road running down to the A6, Freddie told him to pull in. The car came to a stop in a small lay-by with a couple of straggly trees. Freddie got out and opened the door on Irene's side.

'Out you get and no funny business.' He stood back and pointed the gun at her.

She showed him a lot of leg as she got out, but he wasn't distracted. As she stood up, he moved quickly towards her, pushing her back against the car. Holding her by the throat, he punched her hard in the stomach. She opened her mouth to gasp, but found the gun barrel up against her lips.

'Open wide, Irene,' he said.

Her eyes widened with fear and realisation.

'Oh, yeah, copper. You didn't really think we wouldn't recognise you, did you? Although I have to admit, you make a very convincing tart. Go on. Suck it and see.'

He forced the gun barrel into her mouth and laughed. She preferred sucking to having her teeth smashed in.

'Dekker and a few other guys have a score to settle with you. You're in for a right workout. Although I don't suppose you'll remember very much by the time they've finished – assuming you live to tell the tale. Now get in the front seat while I have a little fun with Tania. I like a bit of foreign.' He laughed.

A few seconds later, they drove on. Freddie had arranged the passenger side mirror so she could see what he was doing. The gun was pointing at her from behind his grinning face.

'You can watch, if you like Irene,' he laughed.

She looked forward. She could hear what was happening without having to look. She glanced at Geordie. He was one of those male drivers who thought one hand on the wheel was enough. His left hand was groping his crotch. He was half watching the road and half checking out the action on the back seat. Irene decided this was the best chance she was going to get.

A quick glance in the mirror told her that although Tania was still wearing her seat belt, Freddie hadn't bothered. He obviously thought that it would interfere with his exploration of Tania's body. Irene had instinctively put on hers and Geordie hadn't unbuckled since he left the underpass.

She weighed up the odds. They weren't good and she didn't have long. They'd already gone through Shap village and were now heading towards the Askham turn off the Penrith road. Six or seven miles to go. As she pondered her move, she adjusted her feet and felt something hard under the seat. She reached down and her hand touched the cold hard shape of a bottle.

'What you doing, copper?' said Freddie.

'You've broken my shoe, you bastard,' she replied.

'See what I mean, Geordie. That's no way for a police officer to speak to a member of the public. You won't need your shoes where you're going.' He groaned with pleasure. Tania was doing her best to keep him occupied.

Irene's fingers found the neck of the bottle. She grasped it hard; it was now or never. She looked ahead. They were dropping down to a bend. Geordie was letting the slope do the work, his hand still in his crotch.

With one swift movement, she pulled the bottle out from the floor and smashed it against Geordie's head. As she let go of the bottle neck, glass flying everywhere, she reached down and pressed the release button on his seatbelt. Despite the blow, Geordie's driving instincts told him to brake and change down, but his arm became entangled in his seatbelt as it slithered across his belly.

Irene ducked down as she heard the blast of a gunshot. The windscreen shattered. The car skidded and crashed through a fence into a field. The force of the blow catapulted Geordie towards the windscreen, but his half-undone seatbelt did its job. He ended up crushed into the steering column with the belt round his neck. Freddie would have crunched into the back of Geordie's seat, but instead his head was forced through the gap above. His face was streaming with blood.

The car swerved to a halt, steam bursting out of the bonnet. Irene shouted at Tania, not in Polish, but Tania didn't need telling. The two of them scrambled out of the car and ran. They'd only got a few yards when a voice called after them.

'You fucking whores! I'm gonna kill you!'

Irene crouched down and turned to look. Tania kept running, zigzagging her way to the nearest trees. Freddie was leaning over the car and aiming his gun, his face black with blood. He fired and the car exploded.

Irene flattened herself on the ground. There were more explosions. The radio came on and the Rolling Stones bellowed out 'She's so cold' for all they were worth. As Irene watched she saw a figure stagger away from the inferno. Freddie Flusco was enveloped in flames. Three more steps and he collapsed.

Irene felt a hand tugging at her shoulder. It was Tania; she'd come back for her. The two of them watched as the flames continued to find new life in the car's interior. A car's headlights swept along the road; it was getting dark.

Irene realised she was shaking. Tania helped her to the side of the road. A car stopped and ten minutes later they were in casualty.

Irene passed out.

* * * *

1977

Her boss meant well, but time off wasn't what Fern needed. With nothing to occupy her hands and concentration, she was prey to a confused and increasingly deranged conscience. It wasn't that she'd now killed four people. They hadn't been good people; they'd deserved punishment for the injustices and cruelty they'd meted out to others more vulnerable than themselves. She knew she could claim self-defence against the man Helen Courtney had sent to kill her. She could justify the same defence for killing Helen herself. She'd only meant to humiliate her, but the woman had come at her like a wild animal. But the other two . . . ? She didn't like to think of why she'd done it and how it had felt. She'd not seen or heard anything about either of them since.

She couldn't settle to anything. She tidied the flat. It wasn't big so it didn't take long. She traded in the car, after giving it a really good clean. She couldn't read anything for long and didn't have a television, didn't like any of the films on offer. Newcastle had a very lively nightlife but she felt like an outsider. Too old for that.

She walked the beaches and sat looking out to sea for hours on end. Not thinking of sailing away, just staring. The different moods of the sea calmed her. Whatever the conditions, storm-driven or lapping gently, the repetition of the waves hypnotised her. But this was during the daytime. At night she was assailed by the emptiness of her flat and the nightmares that invaded her sleep. Sleep! If only!

Sometimes the stories were tangled. She didn't know whether it was worse to see the right face in the right nightmare or not. It was as if the four of them were playing horrible games with her. She'd wake sweating with adrenalin. She must have fought each one a hundred times. There was no rest.

A voice inside her head asked whether another one would give her some release. She furiously rejected this idea. She only realised she was talking to herself – or rather arguing with herself – one day when she was on the Metro. She wasn't going anywhere in particular, just planning to get off in town, walk about and then go home again. A woman sitting across the aisle said something to her. She looked at her in bewilderment.

'Are you alright?' the woman said again.

'Sorry?' Fern blurted out.

'You seem upset. You're angry with someone.'

'Angry?'

'Yes. You were telling someone that you weren't going to put up with it anymore.'

Fern looked at the woman. She was small. Fair hair with an untidy fringe. Open face. Pale yellowy-green eyes. Lovely smile. Nice blue dress.

'It's alright. I talk to myself all the time. Only one I can get any sense out of,' said the woman. 'My name's Anna. I live round the corner from you. I've seen you on the beach as well.'

Fern didn't know whether to be afraid or friendly. The woman spoke quietly. She seemed kind.

'Are you going anywhere special?'

Fern shook her head.

'Me neither. I thought I'd take a look round Fenwick's, have a cup of coffee at that new place off Eaton Square. Do you want to join me? I could do with a bit of company. What's your name?'

Fern couldn't think of any reason to refuse this offer and blurted out the name she'd invented for the hairdresser – 'Rose White' – and so began a relationship which was to change her life.

A week later she'd moved into a room in Anna's house. Anna had three teenage children, two girls and a boy. No-one mentioned their father, so Fern didn't ask.

It was the happiest family Fern had ever experienced. The house was a warren of untidy rooms with clutter everywhere. All the corridors and staircases were filled with the oddest collection of pictures and objects. Anna collected stuff. Fern eventually gave up trying to construct some order from this chaos and relaxed into it. The house was full of laughter, children and animals. Other people's children seemed to spend more time at Anna's than in their own homes. There wasn't a television, but Radio 4 muttered on all the time. Cooking and eating were both at unpredictable times, but frequently a group activity. Bedtime was optional, as far as Fern could work out.

Anna taught the piano. Pupils arrived at all times of the day: children and adults; polite little boys and working men with big fat fingers; old ladies who liked a chat, and girls who chewed gum. Anna would listen and offer advice. She never scolded or got annoyed whatever the noise they made. Cats sat everywhere. Cats slept everywhere. The two dogs were a delight. Fern recalled the dogs from her childhood. They were mostly sheepdogs – working dogs – and some of them could be nasty. These two were just happy to be alive. Stan was a crossbred Gordon setter, mad as a hatter, who would chase his own tail and snap at passing flies. Issy was a thoroughbred Saluki, who ran with a flowing grace. She was a gift from one of Anna's many lovers. Fern took them on the beach, where they dashed into the sea after sticks and stones. Sometimes children would accompany her, but often it was just the three of them.

In the space of a couple of months, Fern made more friends than she'd ever had in her life. She was reborn. She slept without nightmares; they receded like half-remembered fairy tales. And she cut everyone's hair. She'd gone back to the previous job, but soon she had enough regulars to hand in her notice. Anna designated one of the many sheds clustered round her tumbledown garden as Fern's workspace. The eldest daughter, Clio, and her friend, were keen to help and within a few days she had a newly-equipped, brightly-coloured salon of her own. Clio wanted to learn, so on Saturdays she had a willing assistant. Everything in the garden was rosy.

Fern hadn't thought about the clearing for what seemed like forever, until one day she felt a pang of remorse. Not for the three victims lying in their shallow graves but for her mother. She'd always visited her grave after each event. She couldn't say why. Forgiveness or an apology? Or something else? Once the thought was planted it grew quickly. She explained to Anna that she needed to go and see an elderly relative and visit her mother's grave. Anna smiled and said of course she must go.

Fern got the train to Penrith and the bus out to Shap. She walked to her mother's grave carrying a single white rose. The graveyard was empty. The day was windy but bright, clouds scudding across the high fells. Fern stood and named them all. She walked to the pub in Bampton and booked herself in for the night.

The following day she got a lift up to the head of Haweswater and did the round. Harter Fell onto High Street, Kidsty Pike and down to her childhood village. The reservoir was full, right up to the old bridge. She sat and gazed into the water, remembering the church and the pub, the houses and the dusty lanes. She cried for her drowned past. She'd never done that before, and she felt a burden lift. She didn't go to the clearing. She went home to Anna. She felt absolved and free. She was sure she would never kill again.

* * * *

Fletcher was furious. A couple of traffic police had caught up with him north of Lancaster and flagged him down. If they were going to do him for speeding that would be it. He'd have to resign. He was so angry, he knew he'd hit the first person who crossed him. Lonsdale knew it as well. He kept as quiet as possible and hoped he wasn't going to die.

Someone must have warned the traffic guys because as soon as the two cars had pulled up on the hard shoulder, one of them jumped out and ran back to the 'borrowed' Mercedes. Fletcher was out of the car and ready to kill. The traffic cop put up his hand and said the only thing Fletcher wanted to hear.

'The women are okay, Inspector, both in casualty, but no serious injuries – just shock. Somehow or other they managed to get out when the car crashed. Both the other occupants died at the scene. DS Simpson said we were to escort you to the site and on to the hospital.'

Fletcher leant against the car and looked at the darkening sky.

'Irene Garner. You are the luckiest, most infuriating chancer I've ever met.'

'Can't disagree with you there, sir. Apparently the car's completely burnt out. The two bodies are unidentifiable. Forensics are there, but it'll be sometime before they can tell us who they were.'

Lonsdale had wound down his window as soon as it seemed safe, so got the gist of what the officer was saying. Fletcher and the traffic cop got back in their cars and set off to the crash site. With its lights flashing and horn blaring, the police car cut a swathe through the early evening traffic. Even so, Lonsdale felt a lot safer than he had done. At least now they were doing less than a hundred.

They arrived at the crash site within the hour, got out of their cars and surveyed the carnage. The SOCOs had put up a barrage of lighting, which lit the devastation caused by the last few minutes of the vehicle's life. The fence was scattered like broken matchsticks. The grass was churned up where the car had swerved to a standstill. The wreckage was slumped in the middle of the lights like a dead carcass. Fletcher couldn't tell what make it had been or its colour. Now it was a blackened shell. The mortuary assistants had removed one of the bodies which had been found a few yards from the car, but the firemen were still trying to cut the other guy loose. He was welded to the steering wheel. Fletcher caught a glimpse of his skull; the hair and flesh had been burnt away. He shook his head at the horror from which somehow Irene and the other girl had escaped. Lonsdale couldn't look and walked back towards the road.

Fletcher saw Dr Sykes beyond the car and made his way round to where she was talking to a senior fire officer.

'Good evening, Inspector,' she said with a grimace.

'I assume you've nothing to tell me,' he replied.

'Two bodies, probably male, burned beyond recognition. How your colleague and the other woman got out of this we just can't believe.'

The fire officer nodded his agreement.

'Nothing on the car either, I suspect?' asked Fletcher.

'Not yet, Inspector,' said the fire officer. 'But it'll be easier to identify than the two victims. We haven't got round to imprinting numbers on our bones yet.'

'More's the pity,' said Fletcher. He stood and looked at the men struggling with the second body.

'I think you're going to need an acetylene torch for the postmortem, Doctor,' he said and walked off.

He'd only gone a few yards when he trod on something that was both hard and squelchy. He bent down and picked up a gun. He looked round. Useless pillocks! Fancy missing this. But then he realised why. He smelt his hand. Cowshit. The gun had fallen into a cowpat. It was all over his shoe and his hand. Something soft dropped back onto the grass. He bent and fumbled for it, realised what it was and winced. He took out an evidence bag from his coat pocket, dropped the stinking gun in and folded it over. He took out another bag and delicately placed the smaller object inside whilst fighting the urge to throw up.

He looked back at the rest of them. He knew he should hand both things in straight away and give them a bollocking, but a vicious idea had come into his head. He grinned, a wicked grin. He wiped his hand on the grass and dragged his shoe all the way back to the car. As he crossed the field, the last sound he heard was the whining of a metal blade cutting through metal . . . and bone presumably. What a way to go. Well at least they'd save on the gas at the crematorium.

Lonsdale was waiting beside the car. He'd been sick. Fletcher clapped him on the shoulder.

'Don't feel bad son. At least you still find it revolting; better than becoming accustomed to it, eh?'

They got back in the car and followed the traffic cops to the hospital. None of them commented on the Inspector's newly-acquired aftershave.

Irene was sitting up in bed reading a magazine. She looked up as Fletcher knocked and walked in. She waved at Lonsdale as he stood outside.

'Nurse says I've got five minutes,' Fletcher said. 'Only one of us at a time; so make it quick and then you can give poor old soppy face a kiss.'

Irene pulled a face. 'He's not soppy. He's okay. Leave him be,' she said, with a sparkle in her eyes. She winked at Lonsdale through the window. He blushed and looked away.

'Come on. Spit it out.'

'Nothing to it, really. I waited till Freddie was otherwise engaged, whacked Geordie across the head with the empty whisky bottle, dodged the bullets – the car stopped, the girls got out and ran, the boys got burnt to a cinder.'

Fletcher shook his head and grinned. 'You're one cool cookie, Irene Garner.'

'Never been so scared in all my life. I'm just glad Tania got out as well. She's a star.'

'So who are Freddie and Geordie? Apart from barbecued.'

'Freddie Flusco and Geordie Bluwit. Two of Len Castle's local lads. Although he'll swear blind he hardly knew them. They've both done time. GBH, assault, pub brawls – typical Geordie lads on a good night out. I'm sure they'll be missed.'

'And where was tonight's party going to be?'

'I'm pretty certain it was going to be at the big house, but unfortunately I thought the odds might not have been so favourable behind those electric gates.'

Fletcher beckoned to Lonsdale.

'I'll be off. I might pop in to see how the party's going without you. I'll bring you a canapé, if there's any left. Be good and do as you're told.'

Fletcher smiled and waved Lonsdale in, not waiting to witness his embarrassment. He went back to the two traffic cops and used their radio. He knew he was probably wasting his and everyone else's time, but he wanted the bastard to know they were on to him.

Half an hour later, he was getting out of the traffic car as four other police vehicles pulled up outside the gates of 'The Castle'. DS Strickland got out of one of the cars and stumped over towards him.

'You know this will be a waste of time, don't you, Inspector?' he said.

'Not so, Sergeant,' said Fletcher. 'I like a party as much as the next rich bastard. And I've got him a present.'

Strickland gave him a dubious look. 'You're not going to cause any trouble are you, sir?'

'Oh, I am, Sergeant. But don't worry. I shall be ever so polite.'

Without another word, he walked over and pressed the bell on the gatepost above the speaker, but instead of waiting to respond to the speaker grille he went to stand by the middle of the gates. The other police officers watched with puzzled expressions as he ignored the scratchy voice coming from the speaker. A light came on, dazzling them all. The scratchy voice got louder. Fletcher continued to stand at the centre of the gates.

Dogs could be heard howling in the distance. The assembled squad began to fidget as they heard the barking getting nearer. Soon they could hear the pounding of the beasts as they hurtled towards them. One or two of the officers backed towards the safety of their cars. The dogs suddenly sprang from the darkness and attacked the gate in a ferocious cacophony of barking and snarling. As Irene had told him, they were big dogs, South African lion dogs, trained to kill men as well as animals. Four of them. He'd seen one before, but four made a terrifying spectacle. In their frustration they snapped and snarled at each other. Fletcher could feel the fear in the men around him. He knew Strickland wanted to speak, but instead he put the small object that had been hidden in his hand to his lips.

The police officers heard nothing, but the dogs did. They hated it. The snarling and barking turned to whining and whimpering. They shook their great heads and lunged at each other. One of them sank his teeth into another one's neck. The victim responded in kind. The other two turned tail and ran. The dogfight turned into a bloodbath. One of them screamed and limped off into the darkness. The other stood for a minute and stared at Fletcher, its head cocked to one side. It gave its head one last shake and barked at him. Fletcher's cheeks filled and he blew as hard as he could.

The dog yelped and backed away before galloping off after its companions. Fletcher's colleagues watched in amazement. He put the small object back in his pocket and waited in silence, staring into the blackness of the thick foliage. The dogs could be heard howling in the distance.

They waited. A man walked out of the gloom, dressed in the uniform of a security officer. He approached the gates and stood facing the man in the leather coat.

'Are you the one with the whistle?' he said.

'Detective Inspector Fletcher to you, sonny. Tell Mr Castle to make sure those South African mutts are securely corralled or I'll be forced to contact the chief constable and ask for an armed response unit to assist us with our enquiries. You can also ask him to make sure he has the requisite paperwork and licences for those dogs available for inspection, as I understand they're only allowed in this country under very specific conditions. Finally, you can tell him that I'd be glad to accept his invitation to tonight's social event. Unfortunately my fellow officers have forgotten their white ties, so I'll be on my own.'

The security officer looked at Fletcher sullenly. 'Are you serious?'

'Never more so, my old china.' He turned to Strickland. 'Sergeant. Will you get Mr Findlay on the phone right away, please.'

Before Strickland could move, the radio phone in the security guard's hand crackled into life. He put it to his ear and listened. 'Yes, sir . . . of course, sir . . . immediately, sir.'

He took the radio from his ear and, giving Fletcher a sneer, walked to the side and pressed a button. Nothing happened for a few seconds but then, with a whirr and a click, the gates began to swing back up the hill. Fletcher stood and watched. Without looking back he spoke to Strickland.

'As they say in the movies, Sergeant. If I'm not out within the hour, send in the marines.'

He set off up the path. The security guard watched him go, pressed the button to close the gates and followed him into the darkness. The lights went out. The officers looked at each other and let out a collective sigh.

* * * *

Fletcher was as scared of big dogs as the rest of the world, but he'd been given the high-pitched whistle by an old dog handler. He was only a young constable at the time and they'd been sent to raid an illegal dog-fight. It hadn't been nice. They'd arrived after the first fight and the loser lay dying on the floor. The second dog had just been put in the ring. The audience trying to escape wasn't the big problem, it was the two dogs, who'd been starved and beaten, who were the main risk. Once their trainers had scarpered, they were let loose. The old guy didn't like to shoot them – which was what normally happened – so he'd acquired these whistles which completely disorientated them. Well, sufficiently for him to catch them with the neck wires. It was still terrifying, but the dogs didn't attack anyone and one of them was saved. The other two had to be put down. Fletcher had persuaded the old fellow to let him have one of the whistles. He hadn't known whether they worked on lion dogs, but now he did.

He followed the little fairy lights up to the main door. Framed in the doorway was the unmistakeable thick-set figure of Len Castle. As he approached the man reached out a hand to welcome him. Fletcher ignored it and walked right up to him.

'Are we going to stand out here in the dark, so the hired help can hear, or shall we go in and have a little brandy?' he said, giving the genial smile a returning grin.

'Welcome to my home, Inspector. You didn't need to upset my pets. Why didn't you give me a call?'

'Because I like surprises. Don't you?'

Fletcher walked past him and went into the house. Castle snarled at the guard and followed him inside.

His uninvited guest had shown himself into the main room, which was a vast open space with a central fireplace. It reminded Fletcher of those drawings in history books about Saxons. Maybe that's how Len Castle saw himself – a latter-day warrior enjoying the spoils of war, rape and pillage. Fletcher walked over to a large armchair and plonked himself down.

'Would you like a drink, Inspector?' Castle asked.

'A large Armagnac, if you've got it,' said Fletcher trying desperately to analyse which style of decoration the man had tried to capture in this huge space. In the end he decided it was a melange of Dynasty and Gothic with a strong element of hunting lodge. The soft pastel furnishing did clash with the hundred animal heads glowering from every wall, but when you're so rich . . .

A fairy appeared from a doorway. She didn't have wings, but the rest of the outfit was straight out of Walt Disney's *Cinderella*. Castle asked for the Armagnac and a whisky for himself. The fairy disappeared.

'Did you kill them all yourself?' asked Fletcher, looking at the incongruous crossed-eyes of a zebra above his host's head.

'Many of them. Why? Are you a hunter, Inspector?'

'Only women.'

Castle smiled. 'A difficult quarry in my experience.'

'Maybe you're using the wrong approach.'

'You have a bit of a reputation in the field I understand,' said Castle with a smirk.

The fairy reappeared and fluttered over to them with the drinks. Even her eyelids fluttered as she handed Fletcher the largest balloon glass he'd ever seen. The honey-coloured liquid barely covered the bottom.

'Well, I've had a few interesting encounters, but I'd be reluctant to claim any total conquests.'

'Modesty becomes you, Inspector.'

'Not at all. Not one of my virtues I'm afraid.'

'Vastly overrated in my opinion.'

Fletcher took a sip of his drink and felt foolish; it was like drinking out of a goldfish bowl.

'As I was saying, I suspect your approach is the problem.'

'I'd appreciate your advice,' said Castle, walking over to the roaring fire.

'Well. Firstly, you should do the job yourself instead of expecting minions to successfully pull off the catch.'

Castle picked up an outsize poker and began to prod the already massive flames into further excess. He said nothing.

'Secondly, the selection of potential prey should be done with care. Some are more aggressive than you might expect.'

Castle looked into the flames.

'Finally, it's a sign of psychological immaturity to prefer little girls. In fact, it's sick.'

The haulage contractor turned to face his guest. The genial smile had gone. So much fairy dust.

'You're pushing your luck, you southern bastard. Finish your drink and piss off. You've no evidence. You've invaded my property without a warrant. You've tortured my pets. We'll see how long you last once you've left this property. Now get out!' He stood with the poker clenched in his fist.

Fletcher finished his drink and put it down on a small table made from an elephant's foot. He stood up and reached inside his coat.

'I'm on my way, squire,' he said, with a sly grin. 'But first I'll show you something.'

He pulled the plastic bag containing the gun out of his pocket and held it up for Castle to see.

'Here's a piece of evidence, sir: the gun which was found in the possession of one of your associates, a Mr Frederick Flusco.'

Castle glared at him.

'I know you'll deny all knowledge of him or his activities, but as a memento of your relationship I thought you'd appreciate this little gift.'

Fletcher walked over to Castle and went up close. Castle raised the poker threateningly. From another pocket Fletcher produced a smaller object wrapped in tissue paper and held it out. Without taking his eyes off Fletcher, Castle put the poker down within easy reach and accepted the gift. Fletcher watched as the man unwrapped the paper and waited until he looked down to see what he'd been given. At the same moment as the light of recognition lit his eyes, Fletcher punched him hard in the face. He staggered back towards the fire. Fletcher followed Castle and pushed his head against the huge metal hood. Blood gurgled from his mouth, but it was the heat of the metal that took his breath away. Despite this, Fletcher's face was up close and his eyes blazed.

'That was my daughter Dekker was fucking for your perverted pleasure, you fat bastard!'

Castle struggled to escape the heat – his cheek was burning. Fletcher stepped back and released his hold, but simultaneously kicked the fat man's knee. Castle yelped and stumbled to the floor. Fletcher kicked him in the guts and crouched down beside him as he gasped for breath.

'This is just for starters. I've contacted a few friends – and I don't mean police officers – who like nothing better than playing dodgems with HGVs. You'll be lucky to have a single vehicle on the road within the week.'

Castle glared at him and his hand reached for the poker, but Fletcher was too quick for him. He flipped it into the fire and stood up. Castle looked up at him, his face glistening in the heat, his cheek red and beginning to blister.

'You're finished, Fletcher,' he breathed, his chest heaving beneath his sweat-drenched shirt.

'Leaner and hungrier men have tried and failed, fat man – so I won't hold my breath, but here's a little reminder of what you're up against. My young sergeant, who's probably half your weight, half your age, has put two of your thugs in hospital and another two in the crematorium – and I haven't taught her a thing yet . . . and don't forget the women who've witnessed all that mayhem. What are they telling their mates – never mind their punters?'

Castle's face was set in a grim stare.

'You're the one who's washed up, Len. You're like my spit in that goldfish bowl. A big fat carp in a teacup – out of your league, mate – in fact you're fucking castled, checked and mated.'

He took one last look and walked to the door, where he paused *Columbo* style, and delivered his coup de grâce.

'Oh, by the way, I nearly forgot. I took the liberty of inviting Linda Eckersley's father and her two brothers to accompany me this evening

– but they said they'd be along later – with a few mates – make a night of it. I told them the way – they'll be here soon, I'm sure.'

He gave the sullen host a little wave and a smile.

'I'll see myself out.'

He didn't look back and walked quickly down the path. He knew this was the most dangerous bit. Castle might order the release of the dogs and close the gates and he'd be dog meat, but there was no sign of either the dogs or the security guard before he reached the gates. They were open. He went through and got into the car.

The other officers stubbed out their fags and hurried to their own vehicles. He was half a mile away before they caught up with him. He was still whistling when they got back to the station.

The whistling ended abruptly when Laura finally tracked him down. In all the excitement, Fletcher had completely forgotten his promise to take her for lunch. He picked up the phone with considerable trepidation.

'Hello. Laura. It's me,' he said.

The voice at the other end of the line was unrecognisable.

'What did you say? Is that you, Laura?' he asked.

He listened carefully. His face became very serious. 'Of course, darling. I'm on my way.'

He handed the phone back and sat down.

'What is it, sir?' asked Lonsdale.

Fletcher looked at him as though he'd never seen him before. 'It's Grace. She's taken an overdose. She's in a coma.' He stood up. 'I've got to get back there straight away.'

'Of course, sir, I'll drive you,' said Lonsdale.

In the event, Fletcher got a lift with the two traffic cops who'd stayed to have something to eat before they set off back to

Rochdale. They pulled out all the stops: lights, sirens, all the way to Halifax General.

He got out of the car, thanked them and rushed into the hospital. He spent the next two nights there with Laura and Grace. Nothing else mattered.

CHAPTER 13

After Dave Ransome's revelation and Rivka's odd response to it, Octavia didn't feel like going in on the Saturday, so she wasn't there when the team came up against the next problem. She'd excused herself by saying her arm was aching quite badly and she needed a rest.

Martin came round to her cottage on the Saturday afternoon to see how she was doing.

She opened the door to find him bending his tall frame to meet her eyes with a concerned expression on his face. She smiled and invited him in. Five minutes later they were sitting at her kitchen table having a cup of coffee and some cakes. She'd had to admit that they were Mrs Hesket's, not her own culinary masterworks.

'So, how's the arm?' asked Martin.

'It's fine, thanks. The rest has done it good.'

Their eyes met. Martin may be a bit of an oddball, but he was surprisingly sensitive to other people's troubles sometimes.

'Is there anything else?' he asked.

She hesitated and prevaricated. 'No. Not really. How did you get on today?'

'Well. I think Rivka and Sylvia have completed their

cataloguing, although there was a rather sharp disagreement between Lex and Sylvia this afternoon. Lex was convinced there were two Rossettis upstairs, but when they went to look, there was only one. Rivka agreed with Lex, but Sylvia was adamant that there was only one. It got a bit difficult for a few moments. I missed your diplomatic skills actually.'

'I'm not sure I would have been much use. I . . . I find Sylvia a bit . . . difficult myself,' stuttered Octavia.

Martin gave her a puzzled look. 'Well. It was she who resolved it, saying she might have got it wrong. But we couldn't find it anywhere.'

'So what had Lex got on her list?'

'The missing Rossetti? A "Red Pandora". Apparently there's more than one already in existence.'

Octavia remembered it instantly. She could have taken Martin straight to the point where it hung on the long top corridor. She knew at that moment Sylvia had somehow or other taken it. Stolen it! She looked at Martin. She needed to be sure. She'd talk to Rivka and Lex first; there was nothing to be gained by making allegations now.

Martin left soon afterwards and Octavia returned to her kitchen. As she washed the pots, she thought about the Rossettis. They were about halfway along the corridor, side by side. One was the 'Red Pandora' and the other was a sad image of Persephone. In the paintings they were facing towards each other. Octavia could see why Sylvia would want the Pandora. It was red, the same red as in the painting she so resembled on the main staircase. And the character was how Sylvia probably saw herself: someone who had control of fate – a femme fatale. Octavia shivered at the memory of when she first saw the picture.

She spent the rest of the weekend in a turmoil of indecision. After all, what could she say? She determined that the only thing she could do was to get there early on Monday morning and check for herself.

That was what she did. Once again it was a fine spring morning, not a cloud in the sky. The dew lingering on twig ends and the catkins were like beads of angels' tears. She had persuaded Tom to drive her to the house; he'd been up since before dawn. They didn't say much, but he gave her a hurried boyish kiss as she was about to get out of the truck.

'What are you after Tom Harper?' she asked.

He grinned back at her. 'What time do you want me to come and fetch you?'

'How about five o'clock,' she said.

'Five on the dot.' He gave a big smile and roared off.

She watched him go and shook her head.

'Men,' she murmured.

She walked up the steps and opened the door. She knew Dave Ransome would be here already. Martin had told her that he'd had to give him a key. The man couldn't sleep. He was determined to search every nook and cranny to find some hidden cache of political secrets. Octavia called his name and Dave appeared from the library.

'Well, Lady Octavia. Hail the returning warrior to the field of battle. We missed your aristocratic wit in the last foray.'

She had learnt to enjoy this outmoded conceit. He could play all day. But she needed to get upstairs.

'Yes, David. Martin came to tell me about the difference of opinion.'

Ransome laughed. 'Is that how he described it? I'd say more

of a catfight, myself. Epées at dawn. Sylvia has a fine temper: eyes flashing, hair swirling, positively Victorian hysterics, darling.'

Octavia frowned. 'So how did Lex deal with it?'

'How do you think? Cold as ice, stood her ground, argued her case, never raised her voice – but inside she was a seething snow leopard. Best entertainment I've seen for a long time.'

'But Sylvia backed off in the end?'

'Flounced off, you mean. An exit worthy of Carmen. "With one backward vengeful glare she was gone!"' declared Ransome, with a flamenco stamping of feet and hand high above his head. He burst out laughing. Octavia had to giggle at his histrionics.

'And how was Rivka handling all this?'

Ransome became serious. 'She turned into stone, Octavia; watched the display without a word, disappeared upstairs afterwards, and I didn't see her again. She could still be up there for all I know.'

'So she was upset?'

'Not sure. Difficult to tell. More embarrassed, I think. I don't think she can handle such extreme emotional behaviour. Martin neither.'

They stood together in the centre of the great hall. The sun streamed through the high windows, spotlighting the painting on the staircase. Ransome followed her gaze.

'It's uncanny isn't it?' he said.

She nodded and set off towards it. 'Creepy if you ask me,' she replied as she climbed the stairs.

Ransome watched her all the way to the top and until she disappeared towards the long corridor. He sighed and set off back to the library.

Upstairs, Octavia walked resolutely to the place where she knew she'd seen the painting. As she approached she could see that there were two frames hanging on the wall. She passed the dark-blue Persephone and stood before what she remembered to be the 'Red Pandora'. Instead she found herself staring back. It was a mirror, same sort of frame, same size. What sleight of hand could have achieved this?

She looked further along the corridor. Everything else seemed to be as she remembered it. She went back and looked at the mirror. She stepped forward and lifted it away from the wall. Behind it she could clearly see the outline of a slightly smaller frame. She let the mirror rest back, stood back and considered herself in it. She saw a tall woman with a swirl of dark infuriating curly hair. More Gorgon than Pandora, she thought. A slight sound sent a frisson of fear through her body. She made herself look towards the source of the noise.

At the far end of the corridor stood the thin figure of Rivka Weill; she looked venomous, her dark eyes blazing with anger.

As she walked towards her, Octavia felt a little concerned. She'd not seen the older woman like this before.

'Sylvia has taken it,' Rivka said, as she came near. 'I don't know how or why or when, but I'm sure.' She didn't look at the mirror, but looked severely at Octavia. 'I think the mirror was downstairs somewhere. I can't remember where. You've looked behind it. You've seen the marks. You know it's true.'

Octavia nodded. It felt like Rivka was holding her responsible.

'Why would she do such a thing?' the older woman asked.

Octavia shook her head. 'It must be worth a fortune,' she offered.

Rivka shook her head slowly. 'No. It's something else, some other motive. I'm afraid of her. I haven't been so afraid since the war. I think I'll have to go.'

Octavia didn't know what to say. She reached out and held Rivka's arm. It was so bony, the numbers still visible on her forearm. This woman had endured such horrors and was afraid. What could they do?

The moment was interrupted by the sound of voices downstairs, including Sylvia's unmistakeable finishing-school intonation followed by her high-pitched laughter. The look on Rivka's face was disconcerting. She was like a trapped bird, unsure of any means of escape.

Octavia took her by the hand and they quickly made their way towards the other end of the corridor, where they knew there was another staircase which led to the ground floor and outside. They didn't stop until they'd scuttled across to an outbuilding which had been recovered from the briars. It looked like it had been part of the stables. They stepped inside into the darkness and paused for breath.

Octavia peered through the gap in the doorframe. There was no-one in sight. She still held Rivka's hand in hers and turned to look at her. Their eyes met. Suddenly, to Octavia's surprise, Rivka laughed. A girlish laugh, her eyes shining in the gloom of the stable.

'You must think I'm a silly old fool,' she said. 'Here I am. Persuading you to run away from a stuck-up, stupid harridan, when I've hidden from the Nazis and survived a concentration camp. I'm sorry.'

'No. Don't be sorry. She frightens me as well.'

'We can't let her get away with this, can we?' Rivka said.

Octavia nodded. 'No. But we need proof. We'll have to be clever. Good detectives.'

The two of them made a pact to look out for each other and

to confound the wicked witch. Newly resolved, they walked back to the house.

Inside they found the rest of the team gathered round the large table in the main kitchen. Ransome was regaling them with some story, which had just finished, and they were all doubled up with laughter. Octavia and Rivka stood in the doorway. Martin invited them in.

'We wondered where the two of you had got to. Dave had said you were both here. What have you been up to? Come and have a cup of tea.'

They joined the table, both of them making sure that they gave Sylvia a determined look. She smiled sweetly at them in turn.

'So,' said Martin. 'The tower. Any minute now the locksmith I told you about will arrive and we'll be in.' He beamed at his assembled team. They looked at him expectantly.

Ransome was the first to speak. 'Well, Martin. Shall we play a little guessing game before we find out what's really in there?'

They all laughed. Martin frowned and then realised he was being teased. He played along.

'Alright, Dave, your game. You get first stab.'

'No problem. I've got a wish and a guess. A stack of seriously incriminating letters between Lord Asquith and Bismarck, which plot the destruction of the Franco–Russian alliance.' Everyone smiled at his high hopes. 'But actually I think we'll find a rotting corpse or two. How else can it have been locked from the inside?'

They gave him a melodramatic gasp for that suggestion. Ransome laughed.

'Right. I get to choose the next guesser. Octavia. What's your worst nightmare?'

Octavia looked startled and immediately put away what was in her mind. 'Er . . . I've no idea. Er . . . perhaps a body or two .

216

. . but how about some unseen love letters from Rossetti to Jane Morris?'

This produced another gaggle of 'oohs and 'aahs', although Rivka could only manage a cool smile. Octavia chose Martin next. He suggested a store of jewellery and more fine art. He chose Rivka.

She hesitated and finally whispered: 'Nichts . . . nothing.' She held the moment before making them all jump with a cackling laugh. They enjoyed that; she'd really tricked them. She didn't look at Sylvia. She chose Lex, who shook her head.

'How about a dragon that's been asleep for a thousand years, which we'll awaken and release into the world, where it'll wreak mass destruction?'

She also got a lot of 'oohs' and 'aahs'. She looked towards Sylvia, who gave her a cold smile.

'I don't really play party games,' she said, giving Ransome a haughty stare. 'But I think Rivka might be half right. I think it will look like there's nothing, but then we'll discover some amazing secret.'

That silenced everyone, not least because it was said with such authority, as if she knew what they were going to find. Octavia wasn't the only one who shivered. The awkwardness was broken by a polite cough. At the door to the kitchen stood a small, thin man with a sharp face; he was carrying a brown leather bag.

'The door was open. I could hear you talking, so I made my way here,' he explained. 'I'm Sam Whittle, the locksmith.'

Martin was on his feet and shaking his hand. He introduced the team, explaining they'd been playing a childish guessing game while they waited for him to arrive. The little man gave them a rueful look.

'Ay. Well. There's plenty of tales about this place and there's many would say we're asking for trouble opening doors that's been closed these three-score years.'

Octavia grinned to herself at his old-fashioned speech. She'd not heard anyone say 'three-score years' since her grandmother passed away, but the seriousness of his manner quietened them all.

To be truthful, the tower had intrigued them from the beginning with its odd reconstruction. Ransome and Octavia had instantly agreed that it was a genuine fifteenth century pele tower, built to protect the local landowner from the marauding Border reivers who had roamed the area, cattle rustling and perpetrating other nefarious deeds for over four centuries. It had always been a lawless place at the edge of imperial and subsequent royal power. They'd also agreed that it had been the starting point for the late nineteenth-century neo-Gothic additions which surrounded it on three sides. What had confused and puzzled them was that the only entrance they could find was on the first floor at the end of the long corridor. Despite all their investigations, there was no ground floor door to be found apart from a solidly shut metal plate about five feet off the ground. Their best guess was that this was a coal bunker but it had resisted all attempts to prise it open.

Octavia had spent some time creating a series of architectural possibilities within the three-floor square tower – of which the ground floor must only be accessible from the first floor. In an earlier time, the solution would have been that the ground floor was a dungeon or grain store, but neither of those medieval uses fitted with the dating of the later renovations. She had proposed, therefore, that the ground floor would be some kind of storage space – adapted to receive coal or wood for a stove perhaps; the second floor a living room or study or work room, and the third floor sleeping quarters. Whether this was for the Duke or his wife or for servants was impossible to say, although

Octavia's educated guess was the Duchessa. There was something about its squat security that indicated a need for protection.

All this was going through her mind as she went with the others and the locksmith to the door at the end of the corridor. They stood in an expectant group like nervous fathers awaiting their first-born child. Mr Whittle, on the other hand, went about his business in a calm and meticulous manner. He spent some time studying the door from a couple of feet away before examining the large hinges and the edges. Finally he reached into his bag and produced a narrow tool with which he explored the key-hole. After only a few seconds, he sighed and stood back. His audience held its breath.

'As I thought,' he said. 'The key is still in the lock. I may have to tackle the hinges.'

'Is that a major problem, Mr Whittle?' asked Martin.

'Not as such. But it'll take a lot longer and the door may get damaged.'

The team shuffled their feet and waited to see what he'd do next. He bent down and searched through his bag, before producing what looked more like a surgeon's tool than a locksmith's. It reminded Ransome of the gruesome weapons used by torturers to extract teeth and nails from unwilling prisoners.

They watched as Whittle pulled up a chair and stared into the keyhole. He carefully inserted the pincers and slowly began to turn them this way and that. Octavia thought this was unlikely to work. If the key had been in that lock for over sixty years, it was almost certainly rusted solid. She glanced across at Rivka. The look on her face was extraordinary. Her dark eyes were fixed on the lock as though she was trying to open it through sheer will power. The sinews in her neck were knotted with concentration and effort.

To everyone's astonishment, there was an audible click of metal shifting against metal. They stood transfixed as the little man slowly stood up and looked at the door. With his right hand he grasped the handle and turned it. Another sound of smooth greased metal disengaging and the door was open. He pushed it away and it swung back without a sound. There was no atmospheric yawning screech – just the faintest sigh of escaping air, as though a vacuum had been eased open. He stood back and turned to his hushed audience.

'That's unbelievable. It's been locked for sixty years yet it's better than brand new.'

They all stared at his disbelieving face and at the darkened room behind. They weren't expecting to see much light. Octavia had pointed out that there were only four small and two slightly larger windows in the entire building – and from the ground you could see that they were all boarded in.

The team looked at each other. Lex produced a torch, which she now shone into the space. As they all craned their necks to see what was lit up, Mr Whittle backed away. Lex ventured forward and the others followed.

Their expectations were confounded. Here was a dining room with a long table of dark wood, gleaming with polish. Six chairs perfectly spaced. Glasses and cutlery and plates and napkins perfectly laid out. Lex's torchlight glinted on the silver and glass. As she shone it this way and that, they could see cupboards and side tables, paintings on the panelled walls, a chandelier smaller than the one in the great hall glittering above the table. In an alcove there was a huge sideboard bearing large bowls and dishes. At the opposite side was a large stove with a metal chimney up the wall.

Ransome stepped across, pulled back some bolts and opened

a shutter. Daylight flooded in, blinding them all with its sudden brightness. He and Lex opened the other two shutters and unfastened the window catches. It felt like the room had begun to breathe again. The furniture and tableware dimmed in the light, becoming tarnished and dulled. An early bluebottle buzzed lazily in through the window, but quickly left through another. They could hear the sounds from outside: birds singing, cattle bellowing, lambs calling, a tractor passing along the lane.

Rivka had found another door and they peered in after her. It was a small kitchen. They saw a sink and a small range with a chimney up to the ceiling, a table and pans hanging from shelves.

Ransome called from across the room.

'I'm afraid I was right. Here's the maid, I guess. Not a pretty sight.'

Despite his warning, they all took a peep inside the small side room. No window, just enough space for a bed and a sink; a crucifix on the wall – a sad little room, which had become a coffin. The desiccated body of a woman lay on the bed. Considering the length of time she'd laid there, they could see her hair was still dark and long, as though she'd combed it one last time before lying down to sleep. The skin on her face was like tautly-drawn paper, revealing cheekbones and jaw. Her eyes had gone – only dark, empty sockets remained.

Each one who looked came away saddened. It wasn't gruesome, but to see that frail skeletal body with its empty eyes was piercing. Rivka was the only one who ventured inside. She approached the bed and knelt beside it. Her fingers touched the faded tresses and they heard her whispering a few words. Not English, Octavia suspected, but ancient Hebrew. After all she'd been through she surely knew about dignity.

They reassembled in the main room.

'More Marie Celeste than horror movie,' said Ransome.

No-one disagreed with him. Lex spoke from the far side of the room. She was holding open another door. Through it, her torch lit up a staircase going upwards. They followed her in single file, Sylvia bringing up the rear.

At the top of the stairs was another door. Lex found a key in the lock. She turned it; it worked as well as the one downstairs. Another room in total darkness. Her torch lit up a bed in the centre of the floor, covered with a red silken sheen of cloth.

Again Ransome went to open the shutters and windows. Again the blinding light, followed by the sigh of air entering a long-closed place. The sounds of the spring day outside to remind them this wasn't a dream. But this room was different. There was only the bed and a dressing table at its foot rather than against the wall, on which were laid out brushes and bottles and small jars. The walls were the same dark panelling as the other room, but Octavia realised that this had been used to make an octagonal interior. The eight walls were bare, gleaming wood. They stared at this emptiness wondering what to make of it. Three of the panels held the windows. These were the ones which were flat against the outside walls.

On an impulse, Octavia approached one of the corner sections and, seeing the dull gleam of an inlaid pair of brass handles, pulled them open.

The effect was electrifying. The two panels swung back either side to reveal two full-length mirrors. She could see the rest of them standing behind her but more astonishing still was that as the panels swung back against the walls they revealed another two mirrors on their backs. As she let go they kept unfolding until, with a gentle click, they engaged with clips at either edge. They stood looking at themselves in four shining mirrors.

As they recovered their composure, Lex and Ransome simultaneously worked out the conceit of it. They each approached the other two corners and repeated the trick. The room was filled with the reflected light of twelve mirrors. The team gazed about in wonder.

Before anyone else could work it out, Rivka crossed to the one wall without a window or mirrors. She found a brass handle. It pulled back to cover the whole of the doorway they'd come through. Another four mirrors and a fifth were revealed, covering half of the final wall. Studying this she figured out the final piece. The right-hand side of the panelling slid silently behind the nearby mirror, revealing the other half of the biggest mirror anyone had ever seen. Eight feet square at least. The entire room was walled with mirrors. They were all lost for words.

They discovered that the three corners held a toilet, a shower room and a wardrobe full of exquisite – female – Edwardian clothing and shoes. For the next hour they wandered to and fro in awe of the riches they'd uncovered. Martin found his jewellery in the drawers of the dressing table. Ransome was once again disappointed with the lack of documents. Octavia found no passionate letters. Sylvia seemed to have guessed it the best, but even she seemed shocked by the extraordinariness of the hidden secret.

It was Octavia who voiced what they were all thinking.

'This is a special place. It's somewhere to be alone: a rich woman's hideaway. Just her and her maid. But who? Eleonora? Or his first wife, Ursula? And why so many, many mirrors. What terrible vanity . . . '

Octavia glanced at Rivka to find her already looking at her. A dark enigmatic gaze; Octavia looked away.

It was only when they'd reconvened back in the house kitchen that they realised that Mr Whittle had gone. No note or bill. Martin promised he would track him down and reward him handsomely. They put together some lunch and sat around in twos and threes; only Sylvia sat alone deep in thought. Octavia, Lex and Ransome were trying to figure out where the entrance to the ground floor must be located.

Octavia went back upstairs and took measurements. She drew the two rooms. When she went down again, she, Lex and Ransome compared the spaces. They leapt to their feet and ran up the stairs, all the way to the top. The others trailed up after them to find the three puzzle solvers in the shower room, searching every corner for something to move or press back. They were baffled until Rivka laughed and told them to get out of the way. They reluctantly gave way and watched as she stood clear of the basin and pulled out the drain cover. She reached inside and they saw her hand turn a hidden handle. The bottom of the basin slid soundlessly back underneath the floor to reveal a black hole.

All of them jostled like schoolchildren to look. Inside the hole was a metal ladder which descended to a stone floor. Lex shone her torch down. As the thinnest and most agile, she was elected to go first. She disappeared out of sight, the sound of her boots on the metal rungs getting quieter and quieter.

They waited impatiently. When Martin shouted down to see if she was alright, there was no reply. They looked at each other.

Lex was gone for what seemed a long time. Ransome went to get another torch. When he returned he shone it down. There was nothing to see. They waited another minute before Martin said he'd follow her down. Ransome reminded him that he was claustrophobic. He was saved by a shout from below.

'It's alright. I'm okay. Coming back up now.'

Seconds later Lex reappeared out of the hole. She was covered in cobwebs and dirt, her face was black but her eyes shone with excitement. They helped her out and she was silent for a moment until she got her breath back.

'It goes down below the ground floor. There's an underground tunnel down there and a door at ground level I think, although it was locked. I followed the tunnel for a few yards or so, before it split into two at right angles to each other. Both went off as far as my torch would shine. The batteries are going. So I came back. I need a drink!' she gasped.

Everyone went back to the kitchen. Lex sat with Octavia and they tried to figure out which way the two tunnels went. One seemed to be back under the house, whilst the other headed off under the garden. Lex said they'd need caving gear and long-lasting lamps. Martin agreed to go and find Mr Whittle and see if he could get into the door at the bottom of the shaft.

In all the excitement they'd not realised that Sylvia was no longer with them. She'd said nothing to anyone. Martin said he'd ring her PA, see if she'd contacted her. Octavia said she'd ring her father.

They were exhausted and decided to call it a day. Ransome suggested going to the pub. Octavia rang home; her father hadn't seen Sylvia since breakfast and her clothes and suitcases were still in her room. She rang Tom's mother and told her where Tom could find her.

Martin arrived at the pub having failed to find either Mr Whittle or Sylvia. The house seemed to delight in presenting them with one mystery after another.

Tom eventually arrived and Octavia put her tongue out at Ransome, who had given her a quizzical look. As they talked, Rivka confessed that it was her concentration camp experience which had told her immediately where the tunnel entrance would be. Martin only stayed for one drink saying he'd got some paperwork to catch up on; Lex went for her evening run – which left the four of them. It was after Tom had agreed to have just one more drink that Ransome suddenly slapped his forehead.

'Of course! It's as clear as day! It's Snow White!'

The others looked at him in bewilderment.

'What is?' Tom asked.

'Snow White!' repeated Ransome.

'What?'

'Listen,' said Ransome, producing pen and paper from his jacket pocket. 'What is the family called?'

'De Blanche,' said Octavia. 'French for white . . . is that it?'

'Remember the love letters? What was the woman's name?'

'Eleonora di Nerezza,' said Rivka.

'A stranger from the darkness,' translated Octavia, with a solemn face.

'So . . .?' demanded a sardonic Tom.

'Don't you see?' said Ransome urgently. 'She's the wicked stepmother. She's not the mother of Edward de Blanche's daughter – Rose Marie. They were only married in 1912. The first letters between them are dated 1911. The girl was born on 29th of February 1896. She'd have been sixteen when her father remarried.'

'I get it,' said Tom, less sceptically, 'so the room with all the mirrors belongs to this Eleonora.'

'And the Singer Sargent is her. The woman in red,' added Octavia.

They looked at each other in disbelief. Ransome burst out laughing.

'Who's going to tell Martin – or Lex – that we're uncovering a fairy tale?'

'But that's what they were all obsessed with,' said Octavia.

'Who?' asked Tom.

'The Pre-Raphaelite brotherhood. Myths and legends. Fairy stories. Chivalric romance. Ladies imprisoned in dark towers. Rossetti. Burne-Jones. Morris. All of them.'

She looked across at Rivka, who nodded, but her face was blank.

'So . . . what happened in the end?' asked Tom.

'It depends which version you choose,' replied Ransome. 'Do you want the older, darker version which finishes with the disappearance of the stepdaughter or Walt Disney's seven dwarves and the happy ending?'

'Well. We've not been able to find death certificates for either the daughter or the stepmother. That's why we've been able to use the father's will and gain possession,' said Octavia.

They sat in silence for a few minutes trying to take it in.

'I expect the stepmother went back to Italy,' Ransome continued, 'although I'm surprised she didn't take some of the artwork with her. She didn't even take the jewellery. Not so wicked after all?'

'But did she kill the daughter?' asked Tom.

They spent another hour debating the possibilities, but in the end Tom insisted on taking Octavia home. He needed to be up at five o'clock.

Octavia had a restless night. She couldn't get Sylvia's face out of her head. One minute she was smiling at her in the kitchen, the

227

next she was imperiously looking down at her from the picture. Where had the woman gone? Was there some connection with the family?

By the time she fell into a deep sleep, Tom was already milking the cows.

CHAPTER 14

Every winter Anna booked an old croft in the Borders north of Kelso. Apart from the room above the kitchen – which everyone accepted would be Anna's – it was long and low with tiny bedrooms off a single dark, cold corridor at the end of which was an icebox with a bath in it, but the main room was cosy with the old range fired up. Wood was provided, and the landlady always had the range roaring away before they arrived.

The excitement of arriving was heightened by the knowledge that the croft lay on the other side of a fast-flowing river. The only way to reach it was to stagger across a swaying footbridge which dangled over a tumbling waterfall, the brown and white water rushing headlong between the jagged rocks. It had been built by Royal Engineers some time ago to provide access to an ancient *broch* high on the hill behind the croft. The first job was to get all the week's supplies across the bridge. As Anna couldn't go anywhere without inviting everyone, there were always plenty of hands to help and soon the first arrivals would be ensconced in front of the fire eating scones and drinking tea. People would come and go, just like in Whitley Bay.

Fern loved it. Sometimes it snowed, so everyone put on their warmest clothes and went for walks and sledged and had huge snowball fights. There was no television here and so the evenings were spent singing and telling stories.

It was her second visit, in December 1978, when Fern was persuaded to tell her story. She was very reluctant; it was a dangerous disclosure to make, even if it was only a story, but eventually with Anna's gentle, slightly mischievous coaxing, she told her mother's tale.

'Once upon a time there was a huge, gloomy Gothic house with one dark tower buried deep in the deep, dark woods.' She told them of the wicked stepmother and the beautiful stepdaughter. How the stepmother ill-treated the girl for years; told lies to her father and turned him against her. How she pinched her and threatened her. How she made her cut off her long golden hair. How she ill-treated her friends and the servants. How the stepmother spent all her time in the tower in a room full of mirrors. How she had bribed the gamekeeper to kill her stepdaughter.

Her audience was spellbound. Of course, they all knew the story, but this was different. It was as if this storyteller had been there herself. Fourteen pairs of eyes wide with anticipation . . .

Fern's voice became softer and softer, until she whispered hoarsely: 'And as the girl went deeper and deeper into the forest . . . she heard in the distance . . . the unmistakeable sound . . . of . . . the howling of wolves . . .'

An ancient fear filled the silence of the room. The fire flickered and, one after another, the occupants let out their breath.

Afterwards everyone said it was the scariest story they'd ever heard. In turmoil, Fern excused herself and went outside. Anna found her down near the bridge, looking up at the stars. Anna put her arm round the taller woman's waist and held her close. No words were spoken, but at that moment Fern knew that if she could tell anyone what she'd done it was Anna. She didn't tell her, but there was comfort in knowing it was possible.

It was soon after they got back home that Anna invited her into her bed. Fern had not expected that. She knew that Anna was as promiscuous with her body as she was with her kindness. She knew this included men and women, young and old. She also knew the same as everyone else, her children included, that if Anna's bedroom door was shut, she wasn't available. She'd reappear with a contented look on her face. The man or woman would eventually come down. Sometimes they just left and were never seen again; sometimes they stayed for a few days, even weeks, but not for too long. Anna made people happy, but she didn't need to keep them.

Fern had thought that their friendship was different. She wasn't sure what this would do to them, so she'd not gone that night. Anna just smiled and said it was fine – she would wait.

Two nights later, Fern stood at her open door. Anna lifted her eyes from her book and beckoned her in. Fern closed the door behind her and stood, uncertainly. Anna got up and came towards her, led her to the bed and undressed her.

Fern had never made love with a woman before. In the morning, she felt sheepish, but no-one said a word and everyone smiled at her as though nothing had changed. She ate breakfast and went to her hairdressing salon. She floated through the day and found herself at the doorway the following night. It lasted for two months.

It was the happiest time of her life. She'd loved her mother and her mother had been kind, but there was always an uncertainty there, a faraway look in her eyes if she ever paused in her work. Fern knew that her mother had never opened her heart – that there were secrets which she took to her grave. It was different with Anna. It wasn't only the sex, which was both gentle and lusty. It was the fact that she had found someone to talk to, who smiled at her for nothing. The dragon began to fade and become a distant memory – like a fairytale.

Their love survived even when, one morning a few days after her birthday, Anna held her close and told her she'd met a young man. Fern was dismayed, but had known all along that it would happen. Since then, she'd been back in Anna's bed many times and occasionally Anna had slipped into hers. She realised that this is how it was to be and accepted it. Jealousy wasn't permitted in Anna's world; she had enough love for everyone.

It was the third visit to the winter croft, early December last year, when Fern's carefully reconstructed life fell apart. They'd been there for four days. It was a Saturday and Fern had taken the dogs for a long walk. She'd followed the course of the river, which entailed some scrambling and the odd foot-fall in the freezing water.

Eventually she came to a point where the valley side was too steep to continue. Overhanging cliffs reared up on both sides, so she backtracked to where she could scramble up. The dogs were, as usual, breathlessly ferreting about, wet through, but still full of energy. Stan was in the lead. Fern could hear them climbing effortlessly ahead of her.

It was only as the tremendous noise from the thrashing, snow-fed river receded below that she heard the gunshots. She redoubled her efforts and reached the top of the climb. Spread out across the hillside was a line of beaters moving from left to right. Out of the steep-sided valley there were fewer trees; it was mainly heather and dead bracken. Fern called the two dogs. Issy appeared almost instantly from the bracken, wagging her feathery tail. She stood next to Fern and sniffed the air. Fern couldn't see the guns, but knew they must be over to her right, probably behind a straggly line of trees marking a smaller tributary making its way to the river. She whistled for Stan again.

She saw him high up the hillside, chasing something. He was running full pelt, turning this way and that. A single shot cracked the cold morning air. Fern saw Stan's body leap into the air. She knew straight away he was dead. She began shouting and clambering her way through the bracken, tears streaming from her eyes and blinding her as she ran, falling a dozen times. She could see the line of beaters had broken rank and five or six of them were heading to the same place as her. Two of them were there before her.

Her heart was beating like thunder. She burst over a small rise and saw Stan's broken body; the shot had catapulted him into a gorse bush. She staggered towards him, keening with grief, and knelt before him in the wet moss. He must have died instantly. Most of his beautiful head was smashed beyond recognition. One unblemished amber eye stared at her accusingly. She reached out and stroked the softness of his still-juddering leg and wept uncontrollably.

Issy nuzzled up to her and sniffed at Stan's shattered body. One of the beaters crouched beside her.

'I'm really sorry, miss, but you are on private property.'

Fern looked at him with fierce eyes. 'How would I know that?'

'There's fences with notices, lassie,' said the older man quietly.

'I came up from the river. I saw no fence or notice.'

The two men looked at each other, but didn't speak.

Fern leant towards Stan and put her arms gently round his warm body. He was not a small dog, but thin and leggy. She lifted

233

him from the bush and held him in her arms, rubbing her face in his blood-covered fur. She gave the men one last glare and set off back towards the croft.

Other people appeared, including some of the shooters. She heard a man speaking to the two beaters but she continued walking away. The man called after her in an upper-class voice. She ignored him and continued to stagger through the bracken. She fell, picked herself up and gathered Stan up into her arms again. The man caught up with her and stood beside her.

'Listen. I'm really sorry about your dog. Where are you going with him?'

Fern looked at him. He was dressed in green waterproofs and a checked flat cap. Issy growled at him. She dropped to her knees.

'Look. We've got a Land Rover over there.' He pointed to the trees. 'Please let me help you. We can carry him there and I can drive you back to wherever you're staying.'

She wiped her face. 'Was it you?'

He didn't understand at first and then shook his head.

'Who was it?'

'Look. I'm really sorry about the dog, but you're on private land, my land. I imagine whoever it was who shot your dog must have thought it was a deer or a fox. None of us would want to shoot a dog.'

'It's not my dog,' she said and burst into fresh floods of tears. 'It's my friend Anna's; we're staying at the croft by the footbridge.'

He nodded. 'I know Anna. She's been coming for years. The croft belongs to my sister,' he said.

Fern continued to weep, kneeling in the wet bracken holding Stan in her arms. The man called over to the watching beaters and three of them came and helped Fern carry Stan to the Land Rover.

Standing nearby was the group of other shooters, both men and women. They watched as Fern carried the dead dog to the vehicle and gently laid Stan in the back. Issy jumped up and lay next to him, whimpering and licking him. Fern turned to the watching people.

'Which one of you killed my dog?'

Most of them looked at their feet or away, but a woman stepped forward with a gun under her arm and jutted her chin out at Fern.

'It was me,' she said haughtily. 'You're lucky I didn't shoot you as well. You damn fool. This is private property and you have no right to be here.'

The man who'd come to help Fern moved towards the woman. 'Come along, Caroline. There's no need for that. The poor woman didn't know she was trespassing. She came up from the river.'

He turned to Fern. 'I'll take you back,' he said, indicating the passenger seat with his arm.

Fern ignored him and stared fiercely at the woman. 'What's your name?'

The woman looked at the man and the others behind her, none of whom met her eyes.

'Why? What do you think you're going to do? Report me to the police? You'll get no sympathy from them I can assure you. If I were Philip, I'd have you arrested for trespassing and have your other mutt put down.'

Philip strode across to the woman. 'Caroline. Shut up. You're a bloody selfish, cruel bitch. You've shot this woman's dog for God's sake. You can pack your things and leave. We've all had enough of your unpleasantness.'

He turned on his heel and walked back to Fern. She was staring at the woman. Everyone heard what she said in a low, dark voice.

'This is not finished. I'll find you and you'll pay.'

The woman snorted and stalked off. People stared after her, some shuffled away, while Fern went to sit with the dogs on the back of the Land Rover. She continued to follow the woman with leaden eyes as the vehicle bumped up the track and over the hill.

Back at the croft, Philip followed her across the bridge. He went ahead, found Anna and explained what had happened. Eventually he left, and Anna came down to where Fern was sitting at the edge of the river, Stan in her arms, crooning a lullaby to him that she'd learned as a child. The rest of Anna's friends and family watched as she knelt beside the weeping, singing woman and comforted her.

They went home the next day, but not before Fern had found out the woman's name. Caroline Soulby.

* * * *

By the time Fletcher had arrived at the hospital, the doctors had decided what to do. Once they were convinced Grace had only taken a handful of paracetamol less than five hours before she arrived at the emergency unit, they put her on an intravenous drip and told her mother she should recover and there would be no permanent damage. This hadn't convinced Laura; Fletcher found her holding Grace's limp hand, whilst the tears streamed down her face. He knelt down and put his arms round her but that only increased the sobbing to fever pitch. She held onto him till it hurt. He tried soothing words and stroking her hair, but she was inconsolable and unable to speak.

Fletcher wondered how long this would have continued if Grace's eyelids hadn't suddenly fluttered open. She struggled to comprehend what was happening before realising it was her mother who was making all that noise. Grace tried to reach out and touch her, only to find her arm was tethered to a tube and a metal hat stand. So she squeezed the hand that held hers. Her mother's head rose up and she let out a cry of joy.

'Oh, Grace, my darling! My baby,' she cried.

Even in her current state of incomprehension and semi-consciousness, Grace found this outpouring of mother love too hard to take.

'Mum, please. I'm okay. Where am I?' she asked, trying to look round the room.

'You're in hospital, Grace,' said Fletcher. 'You took too many pills and passed out. You're going to be alright.'

Laura was wiping her face with a sodden handkerchief.

Fletcher pressed the button above the bed, as he'd been told to do if there was any change in Grace's condition. Grace followed his action with suspicion, still unsure what was going on. A nurse appeared at the door. She came in and smiled at Grace.

'Well, hello. Good to see you. How's the headache?'

She spoke in a strong Scottish accent, whilst looking at the dials on the machines and holding Grace's wrist.

'I haven't got a headache,' Grace grumbled.

'Ay. Well you will have, lassie,' said the nurse with another beaming smile, but this disappeared as she gave Grace a stern look. 'I know what you're thinking, but you've to do as you're told in here. No trying to get out of bed. No eating or drinking. Understand?'

Grace wasn't used to such abruptness, but nodded meekly.

'Now,' the nurse continued. 'I'm going to send your mum and dad away for a wee while, so that you can rest. The doctor will be here in a minute and after that you're going to sleep. No arguments, alright?'

Grace looked at her mum and then at Fletcher. They could tell she wanted to contradict this harridan, but the drugs won in the end. She looked back at the nurse and nodded her agreement.

'We won't be far away,' said Laura, as she stood up and kissed her daughter. Fletcher squeezed her hand and the two of them backed out of the room. Grace gave the nurse one more look and closed her eyes.

Outside in the corridor, Laura fell into his arms and wept. The nurse came out and ushered them down to the end of the corridor, telling Fletcher to take his wife to the canteen and get a strong cup of tea down her. He did as he was told.

Grace was declared well enough to go home three days later. She'd had to spend an hour with a psychiatrist, but physically she was strong enough to be discharged on the Tuesday evening. By then, Fletcher and Laura had gone through some long and tearful heart-searching hours. They'd been called in to see the psychiatrist after she'd spoken to Grace and were horrified to hear the doctor's assessment. She was blunt.

'First, a few questions,' she'd said.

They'd nodded, afraid to hear what she'd got to say.

'No. I'll tell you some facts for a start,' she said, seeing their response. 'Your daughter loves you both dearly. She feels she's let you both down and is terribly ashamed.'

She paused and looked at Fletcher's frown.

'I know you're not her real father,' she said. 'But you're going to have to do your best. She needs you to be.'

She turned to Laura. 'You've got a hard task, Mrs Walshaw. You need to be firm and forgiving. Tough and loving.'

Laura nodded and smiled, fighting back the tears, whilst Fletcher heard Cassie's prescient words in his head.

'Keep your tears in check. She needs to know you're strong,' said the doctor with a stern look, which then softened. 'She'll be fine. Just don't give up on her.'

She stood up and showed them the door. They shook her hand, thanked her and walked back to the ward. Grace was sitting on her bed, fully dressed with a little pile of clothes by her side. She smiled ruefully at them and they had a group hug.

In the car, Laura turned and looked at her.

'I've had my instructions. I've not to cry. We both love you so much. So don't get me going.' She burst into tears of joy.

They all laughed and set off home . . . and home was not Aunty Jessica's.

*   *   *   *

Fletcher had received numerous phone calls from Chief Inspector Aske, who kept him up to date with the surprising developments following Fletcher's visit to the haulage contractor.

Unaware of Fletcher's behaviour, Aske had thought he'd better try to calm the situation with a personal visit to Castle on the Sunday morning. He was astonished to find that the bird had flown.

He'd taken DS Strickland with him, but the house was empty. They pressed the call button on the intercom, but received no response. Aske pushed at the gate without much hope of them being open but they swung back. The two of them set off up the drive. Strickland was apprehensive, having seen the ferocity of the dogs last night. He wished he'd got a whistle like Fletcher's, but it was unnecessary. As they approached the house they could see the high-fenced kennels and the four bodies lying on the floor. There were no signs of injuries, so they assumed the dogs had been doped or poisoned. They didn't go in, but left the compound closed just in case.

Aske and Strickland knocked at the locked door. Receiving no reply, the chief inspector invited the sergeant to gain entry through a side window. No alarms sounded, although they both knew this might not prevent the arrival of a team of security men or, indeed, their own colleagues.

They wandered round the house. No sign of anyone. No signs of any urgency in attempting to get away. There were suitcases in a cupboard, no clothes lying around. In fact it didn't even feel abandoned – just empty. Everything was in its place: television, expensive hi-fi system, money in a drawer, furniture and lots of valuables untouched. It was strange tramping the deep-pile carpets, soundlessly looking for anything, something, which would indicate what had happened.

There were two cars in the garage. Neither of them knew how many cars Castle owned. He was certainly rich enough to have more than two. Aske rang the station and ordered a full search team to come out and do a more thorough job.

The team arrived and searched the house from attic to cellar. It took most of the day. They searched the grounds. There was nothing out of the ordinary other than the four dead dogs, and the vet quickly agreed that they'd been poisoned. He took away some uneaten scraps of meat and confirmed his initial assessment within the hour. Aske was at a loss. He phoned the chief constable who could shed no light on the matter and went back to the golf course.

Aske phoned Fletcher and told him. Fletcher was as surprised as he was.

'Have you checked all the airports and ferries?' he suggested.

'It's underway now, but if he left as soon as you came away, he's had a good twelve hours start on us.'

Neither of them could think of anything else they could do. Aske enquired about Grace. Fletcher told him he didn't know when he could come back to work. Aske told him to take all the time off he needed.

Irene rang three times to ask after Grace. She also had news of Derek Wray.

'He's done a runner too, sir. Disappeared without trace, but he did at least pack a bag. Difficult to tell how urgent it was, his flat was always a tip at the best of times. No passport though. My bet is they're all in Spain.'

Fletcher couldn't disagree but, even with all the trouble with Grace, he was a little disappointed that the case seemed to have dried up. Still, it meant he could try to live up to the psychiatrist's instructions. He realised he'd no idea how to be a father. He loved Grace to bits, but couldn't for the life of him think what else he could do for her.

She seemed calm at home. Fletcher and Laura had both been pleased when some of her old friends came round. They'd sat in the kitchen listening for the sound of teenagers upstairs. At first it was eerily quiet but after a few minutes, to their relief, the familiar beat of their music began. They grinned at each other when the music was overridden by an outburst of girlish laughter. They hugged each other tight and Laura allowed herself a brief weep. Later they were more than happy to agree to a sleepover. Things seemed to be returning to normal.

Fletcher rang the station on Thursday morning. Nothing had happened and there was no sign of Castle or Wray. The security firm said they'd been told they were no longer needed late on the Saturday night and the men on duty had been told to leave. The dogs were still alive when they left. There were no reports of either of the men leaving the country in any legal way. Interpol and the Spanish Consulate had been alerted but, as the only possible crime Castle could be arrested for was the destruction of his own pets, these requests were received with polite disinterest.

The only other matter was a call from a Ms Cunninghame – a personal matter. Fletcher said he was going for a paper and found a phone box.

'Michael,' said the familiar voice.

'You rang, ma'am?' he said.

She ignored the taunt and asked after Grace. He told her. She offered her sympathy and said she thought he'd make an excellent father. He laughed.

'No. I mean it,' she added. 'Hopeless as a husband, but fiercely protective as a father. Anyone who's ever met you would know that.'

He was so taken aback he couldn't think of anything to say.

'Anyway, the reason I rang was to tell you what I've found out about Caroline Soulby.'

'What? You know where she is?'

'No . . . and don't interrupt, Michael. I was talking to Elizabeth Campbell the other day, about the wedding arrangements actually.' She waited to hear if he was going to be rude at this point. He was silent.

'You won't remember, but it's at her place the picture was taken.'

'The one with you wearing that silly hat?'

'Michael. Don't try to offer comments about things you couldn't possibly understand.'

'Yes, ma'am,' he replied meekly.

'And stop using that submissive tone with me. It's childish.'

He snorted. She ignored him and continued. 'Well, apparently, after John and I had come away, Caroline shot someone's dog. Philip was furious. They've not spoken since. She was very offhand with the dog's owner and Philip had had enough.'

'Philip?'

'Campbell, you idiot. He owns a huge estate near Kelso. Caroline was a guest and she shot some trespasser's dog.'

'And?'

'Well. This woman – I don't know her name – apparently vowed to avenge this dog. Everyone there heard her say to Caroline that she would find her and she would pay. Elizabeth says it was quite scary the way the woman looked at Caroline . . . so she might be a suspect.'

'I see,' said Fletcher, wondering what was going on with all these dead dogs.

'So do you want Philip's number?'

'Yes, please.'

She told him the number; he wrote it on the margin of the newspaper. 'Is that it?' he asked.

'I'm afraid so, Michael. I have thought of relenting and inviting you, Laura and Grace to the wedding, but I couldn't trust you . . . so it's your own fault.'

'It's alright, Louisa. I couldn't afford the kilt.'

She sighed in exasperation and cut the connection. He walked slowly back to the house. He had an image of himself in a kilt jigging about in his head. As he closed the door he heard Laura on the phone.

'Hang on, he's here now.'

She handed him the phone. He listened . . . for a long time.

'How many? . . . Five ?! . . . Good grief . . . alright, I'm on my way.'

He put the phone down quietly. Laura stared at him.

'What is it?' she asked.

'Some National Trust people think they've found five bodies at an abandoned place called Blanchard House. Down towards Haweswater. I'll have to go.'

'Five?' asked Laura in amazement.

'Apparently. Each one sprouting a white rose.'

Laura looked to see if he was joking. He shook his head.

'Where's Grace?' he asked.

'Upstairs.'

He made his way up to her room. As he knocked on the door he didn't know what he was going to say. A few seconds later she opened it and looked at him. Her brown eyes were serious. She invited him in. He sat on the bed and looked at her, while she stood by the window looking out, with her back to him.

'I've got to go back to work, Grace.'

She turned and smiled at him. She'd done something to her hair; it was less severe.

'I knew you would. It's alright. I'll look after Mum. I'm going back to college next week, so I've a lot of catching up to do. I'm not going to let you down again.'

For the first time in his life he felt like crying. She crossed the room as he stood up and hugged him.

'Be careful,' she said.

He nodded and smiled. 'You too.'

He walked back downstairs, kissed Laura and set off for the station.

'So that's what it's like to be a father,' he said to himself. Anyone watching would have seen his pace quicken and a big irrepressible grin spread across his face.

* * * *

It took Fern a month to find Caroline Soulby. She could have asked Philip Campbell in the Land Rover. He was so angry and apologised constantly all the way back to the croft; he probably would have told her there and then. Fern was more concerned about how she was going to tell Anna. In the end she couldn't face her and stayed by the bridge with Stan and Issy.

Of course, Anna wasn't angry with her. She was more concerned with the living. She talked to Fern about Stan running free on the beach, in the house when he was a puppy, causing mayhem wherever he went. How big his feet were right from the beginning. How he barked and barked at flies and beetles and anything that moved.

They went back to Whitley Bay. Issy was sad and moped about, but gradually her energy returned. Fern couldn't cope with it. She sat in the salon, refusing to accept customers and shaking her head when one of the kids asked her to come for a walk. People would see her shaking her head as though she'd got something in her ear. She had started to talk to herself again. Anna tried talking to her, but Fern wouldn't even look at her.

Almost to the minute a week later, something clicked. The dragon was back and filled Fern's head with its fierce hissing, its red eyes tearing her apart, stoking the fires of revenge.

Anna came downstairs to find her in the hallway sitting on the bottom step. Her bag and a rucksack were by the door. She stood up as Anna reached her and mumbled a little speech she'd prepared. Anna tried to hold her, touch her, talk to her, but Fern pulled away and went to the door. Before Anna could stop her, she picked up the bags, opened the door and stepped out onto the street. She didn't look back. It was the last Anna saw of her.

She found a note in the salon, read it and wept.

Dearest Anna,

You are the best thing that ever happened to me and I destroyed it.

I know you forgive me, but I can't forgive myself.

(Here something was furiously crossed out.)

I will always love you.

I am so, so sorry,

Rose.

Anna kept it in her drawer. Everyone in the house was sad, including Issy.

*   *   *   *

Fern found Caroline – well at least she knew where to look for her. Quite by chance in her salon she'd got an old copy of the *Cumbria* magazine. She flipped it open and was startled to see Stan's killer in a photograph. She was standing, glass in hand, with three other rich, overdressed young women. Fern couldn't believe it. There was that haughty smirk, the long dark hair in ringlets down the side of her face, staring arrogantly at the camera. Fern greedily read the details below. There was her name and more helpfully 'recently married to Charles Soulby, the celebrated Cumbrian historian'. A quick visit to the library and she found their address and phone number. She ransacked Anna's disorderly map collection until she found the Penrith map, which was now in the pocket of her rucksack.

Fern hired a car in Newcastle and drove to the house. She parked the car behind the old ruin and went to the clearing. She stood and looked at the roses. The grass and weeds had got a hold, but she could soon sort that out. She made her preparations and drove back to Penrith. Parking the car in a side street, she went to a hairdresser's off the High Street. Inside, the woman styling a young girl's hair did a double take and nearly cut the girl's ear off.

'Fern Robinson, I thought I'd seen a ghost!'

They embraced and an hour later sat drinking in The Fox. Joan Fulbright was the daughter of Fern's mother's friend. They'd spent their teenage years together until Fern went away to nursing college. They'd written a few times, but lost touch. Fern managed to sustain an easy-going conversation and Joan readily agreed to put her up until she found a job and a flat.

Later that night, Fern was in a small guest room at Joan's house. Joan had separated from her husband a couple of years previously, but she'd managed to hang on to the house. After a few days Joan agreed to take her on part-time in her salon. Fern was happy to do the early shift and finish at lunchtime. That allowed Joan to sleep off the previous night's drinking and put on a better front than she had been doing.

During the following days and weeks, Fern spent her afternoons and evenings tracking down her enemy and planning the kill. It was easy to find the Soulby's house. Fern discovered a hiding place across from the gates, which she could approach through a small wood, leaving her car on a little National Park car park. From there she watched the comings and goings. The most regular visitor was an older woman, who was probably a cleaning lady. She arrived on foot, so Fern assumed she came up from the nearby village. This was confirmed one day when she saw the woman coming out of a small house near the village post office.

Fern quickly realised she'd have been wasting her time watching in the mornings. Caroline was a late riser. She came and went in her own car or someone else's. They were mostly women friends, but there was a younger man. He waited further down the lane out of sight. Caroline would come out the gate, generally in the evening and often after dark, and totter her way down to his little green sports car.

Her movements gave Fern the spark of an idea. She followed the young man one night after he'd dropped Caroline off. He drove through Penrith and out the other side for a few miles before sweeping through the wide gates of a manor house.

At the local pub back in Eamont Bridge she innocently asked after him, saying he reminded her of a school friend. The landlady gave her a crafty look.

'I think you're wasting your time there, girl. He's a bit out of your league.'

Fern laughed but got the woman to tell her where he went drinking. She went the following night. He was already there with a group of friends; they were loud and full of themselves. At about seven the young man waved goodbye and swaggered out of the bar.

She went up for another drink and heard one of his friends grumbling.

'Lucky bastard. Shagging Caroline Soulby. What I'd do for a bit of that.'

His friends were less than complimentary about his chances, pointing out his complete lack of money, looks or charm. It was this that crystallised Fern's plan.

The next day she asked Joan to give her a new look and Joan obliged. Fern suggested a different colour. She'd let her fair hair grow longer at Anna's, but Joan quickly converted her into someone completely different. Fern emerged with a short, black, spiky cut that made her look ten years younger, Joan said. Fern went and bought some new clothes – short and black and shiny like her hair. Black boots and startling make-up completed the makeover. She went back to the pub. The young man's friends were there, including the young lad she'd targeted.

He was a bit slow on the uptake, but eventually she got him outside and gave him a taste of what she could deliver if he'd do her a favour. It was so easy. All he had to do was introduce her to his rich friend and his dreams would come true. She'd encouraged his agreement by hinting that his friend wasn't going to get anything like the same deal – in fact the opposite. He believed her, hook, line and sinker.

When the young man arrived, his friend pointed across at the striking-looking woman. The young man couldn't resist, but made a pathetic attempt at playing hard to get and delayed his move until she called his bluff. Fern downed her drink, gave him an arrogant sneer and set off towards the door. He caught her up outside, jumping round in front of her and blocking her path. She stopped and stood her ground. She desperately wanted to kick him in the balls as he leant against the doorway into the car park.

'Hey. Spike. I thought you wanted to talk to me?' he said, in a mock innocent voice.

'My name is Ursula, you prick,' she replied.

'Ooh. I am sorry, *pardonnez-moi*.'

'My boss said you were a complete tosser'

She went to go past him.

'Your boss? Lucky man! Do your duties include a daily service?'

'She's a woman, you chauvinist pig!'

Even though it was all part of her trap, she was enjoying herself.

'Wow. Give me some of that.' He laughed.

It was her turn to laugh.

'Look little boy. Try to understand that most women wouldn't touch you with a condom on a stick. You're an arrogant, jumped-up little twerp with far too much money. Give it a rest and listen to me.'

'I think you might have the wrong person,' was all he could say, with a touch of a pout appearing on his bottom lip. God, how much she wanted to punch him.

Controlling herself, she got him by the throat, pushed him up against the wall and grabbed him by the balls. He squealed like a piglet.

'Answer this question correctly and I'll not crush the life out of your pathetic little dick.'

He gasped for breath as she strengthened her grip on his windpipe.

'Are you calling on Caroline Soulby tonight?'

He nodded as furiously as her stranglehold would allow. She let him go and he crumpled to the floor. She gave him a little kick to keep him concentrating, before stamping her foot on his knee. He gurgled a yelp.

'Second question. Where are your car keys?'

He struggled to get them from his pocket. She snatched them up and smashed her fist into his face. He put his hands over his head and began to whimper.

'Third question. Are you going back to your boyfriends and telling them about your new conquest? What a great shag I was?'

He shook his head and ducked an expected slap.

'I didn't hear what you said?' she asked.

He looked up at her from between his fingers. 'No,' he yelled.

She kicked him hard three times and bent down to make it clear. 'If I find out you told anyone about this, I'll kill you. You understand?'

He shivered and nodded, blood dribbling from his nose.

She dragged him to his feet and frogmarched him to his car. Opening the boot she pushed him in, got in the driving seat and roared out of the car park. Five minutes later she stopped, dragged him out and pushed him over the fence and down towards the river bank. In the twilight, he'd have little idea where he was, but she knew with a bit of luck it would take him some time to scramble back up the steep banking and find his way home . . . or he might fall into the river and drown. Either way she didn't care. She repeatedly crashed the gears as she careered back through the town.

A few minutes later she did a noisy U-turn outside the Soulby's house and pulled up in his usual place. A quick parp on the horn, then she waited, watching through the mirror. Sure enough, her victim appeared on the pavement, clicking her way down on her four-inch heels.

'What the hell time d'you call this . . .' yelled Caroline, as she opened the passenger door and bent down to get into the car.

Fern had seen that this wasn't an easy manoeuvre for a half-drunk woman who was nearly six feet tall in her ridiculous heels. She'd got out of her side as Caroline bent down and was round the front of the car in a flash. She grabbed the doubled-over woman by her long curls and dragged her backwards, letting Caroline's weight carry her onto the banking by the side of the pavement.

Before Caroline could even begin to understand what was happening, Fern slapped her fiercely across the head and dragged her by her hair on her hands and knees to the back of the car. She'd released the boot from inside, so it was simply a matter of lifting the lid and pushing the gasping woman inside. There wasn't much room, but Fern didn't care how much she hurt her as she forced the lid down until she heard the reassuring click. The woman's cries for help and angry curses were lost in the roar of the engine as the car set off on its evening tour.

Fern took the car down a valley it had never frequented before, until it came to a halt behind the ruined, tumbledown farmhouse. She got out of the car and listened to the struggling woman. She waited until Caroline's energy was sapped and quickly opened the lid. Before Caroline could attempt to get out, Fern punched her hard in the face. The woman slumped and gurgled again, her chin on her chest.

Fern picked up the syringe from the wall where she'd placed it ready and stabbed it into the woman's arm. The drug worked its magic and Fern was able to resurrect her fireman's training. She carried Caroline up the little track by the old ruin, across the road and through the secret entrance, along the overgrown path and round the clearing, into the shed and onto the old chair. Ropes and chains tightly fixed. All those expensively curled tresses lopped off and her head shaved. Fern gave her one final, gentle slap and set off to get rid of the car and establish an alibi. She drove carefully back down through the lanes and up onto the A6.

Ten minutes later she left the car in the Eamont Bridge pub car park, jogged back to where she'd left her own vehicle and went home to Joan. She persuaded her friend to come to the pub and forced her to join in the quiz. Joan got noisy and drunk, so Fern apologised to everyone, took her home and put her to bed.

She didn't sleep and left the house just after six. She drove down the motorway and came off at Shap. By half past she was waiting outside the shed door for the woman to fight her way out of her ropes and chains. But this was not going to be a fair fight. Fern was going to give her as much chance as she gave Stan, although her choice of weapon would cause a more horrific death. She needed Caroline to know what was happening and who was doing it.

Then she would die.

CHAPTER 15

Tuesday morning it was raining. Lex had acquired a load of caving equipment, although there were only two people who were likely to be using it. Martin got claustrophobic in a pub; Rivka didn't even want to talk about it, and Ransome 'thought it beneath him' – they groaned at his terrible pun. Sylvia gave Lex a look of utter disbelief that she could even think she'd go underground in clothes like that – especially the day after she'd had her hair done.

Sylvia had reappeared shortly after they all arrived and breezily explained that she'd had to go and see a friend the previous afternoon. There was no apology or sense of causing anyone any concern. Octavia gave Martin such a look that he bit his tongue as he was about to demand an explanation. They were all momentarily transfixed by the new hairstyle. The long dark tresses had gone, cut back to a short, elegant bob which gleamed with hairspray. She'd also changed her outfit. Only a woman with Sylvia's chutzpah could have considered a trouser suit in pale blue and a hat to match as appropriate to wear to work. She looked stunning, but totally out of place – and, thought Octavia, nothing like the woman in the painting.

Sylvia went to work on Ransome in the library, trying to wheedle information out of him that she thought he was keeping to himself. He was enjoying the smell of expensive perfume and the attention of a beautiful woman. He knew he had nothing to tell her, but was adept at hinting that he had.

Octavia and Lex donned the caving waterproofs and boots, followed by hard hats and headlamps. Lex had brought her caving hammer, two-way radio and a climbing rope. They went up to the top floor with Rivka and Martin, then Lex led the way down the metal ladder. At the bottom she called to Octavia to come down.

Octavia waved at the solemn couple watching from the room of mirrors. They'd closed most of them up, finding it too much to bear. Rivka and Martin waved back.

Octavia reached the bottom and Lex immediately moved forward. They'd agreed to explore the tunnel which led back under the house first, reasoning that it probably came out inside somewhere. They weren't disappointed, but their journey did cause some embarrassment – and a lot of amusement. The tunnel travelled for only a few yards before dividing into two. They took the one to the left, which they suspected went back under the house. Sure enough, a few yards further on there was a steep flight of steps cut into the rock, leading to a short tunnel which ended in a blank wall.

When they reached it they found an old wooden door to their left. In the top panel was a small piece of wood. Lex fingered it and found it would move to one side, revealing a small hole. A spy-hole. She looked through and gasped, then turned to Octavia and put her fingers to her lips. Intrigued, Octavia put her eye to the hole. She was looking into the library and she immediately saw what had made Lex gasp. Sylvia had Ransome up against one of the bookcases and was forcing herself upon him, kissing him and stroking his hair. To be fair, Ransome was trying his hardest to resist, but was visibly weakening; especially when, while Octavia watched, she saw Sylvia reach her hand between their wriggling bodies.

Octavia jerked back her head and suppressed an outburst of hysterical giggling. Lex had another quick look, but then they both had to retreat back down the steps. The two of them leant against the walls and laughed till they cried. Eventually they were able to return to the parting of the ways and try the other tunnel.

This was a completely different story. It went on and on, at one point getting very narrow and at another dropping down and rising up again. They stopped for a rest. They were both quite tall and the constant stooping was beginning to hurt their backs.

'How far do you think we've come?' asked Octavia, as Lex looked at her watch.

Lex made a rapid calculation. 'I'd say about nine hundred yards.'

'We must be nearly outside the walls.'

Lex nodded and shone her torch down the tunnel. It disappeared into the distance.

'Not yet,' she said.

They continued on. After another steep descent and a longer, easier ascent, they reached the end. They looked up. Another metal ladder rose up about twenty feet. Lex carefully climbed up, afraid the ladder might no longer be safe, but it proved solid.

At the top she found a wooden trapdoor. At first it wouldn't move but eventually, with a lot of grunting, she was able to force it up and back. She disappeared from Octavia's view.

Octavia waited. She couldn't hear a thing. She looked back along the tunnel. She wasn't frightened of being underground, but she knew that without a torch she wouldn't be comfortable. She felt a slight breeze from above and when she looked up, Lex reappeared.

'It's okay. Come up,' she shouted.

Octavia climbed up and found herself in a room with the windows boarded up. Lex had found a door and forced it open. A quick look outside was sufficient to confirm this was an outbuilding next to the outer wall. Standing outside they couldn't see the house because of the trees, but beyond the walls they could see the distant fells and the dilapidated roof of an old farmhouse. They were disorientated, but Lex used her compass and said that they must have come out on the northern boundary. When she checked her map, she was able to show Octavia the farmhouse. They were roughly halfway between two of the marked entrances.

'So why's it come out here?' asked Octavia.

Lex shook her head and looked towards the wall. 'You'd expect it to be near a way out, wouldn't you?'

They walked towards the wall. Although the undergrowth was very overgrown, Octavia found a way through. At first she didn't see it but, after doing a double take, she called out to Lex who was hacking her way through to her left.

'Lex, it's here. I've found the entrance.'

She'd followed the faint path to where the wall overlapped. From even a few yards away you wouldn't notice it. Within the gap there was a doorway in the outer wall. It was locked.

Lex came through behind her. They stood and looked at the lock and then at each other. This was a surprise. The lock was not that old.

'That's strange,' said Octavia.

Lex nodded. Putting down her bag, she expertly climbed the door, reached up to the top of the wall and yelped. She dropped down to the ground and grasped her right hand with her left. Blood was seeping through her fingers.

'Quick. In the bag. First aid,' she said, calmly.

Octavia found a bandage, wincing as she saw the cut on Lex's palm. Lex crouched down and drew deep breaths. Octavia waited, full of concern.

'It's okay. Stupid of me. I don't think it's as bad as it looks,' said Lex.

'We'd better go back and get it seen to nevertheless,' said Octavia.

Lex nodded. 'Let's see if we can get through without going back down to the tunnel,' she suggested.

Octavia agreed. They left the hidden door and followed the way through to the cottage.

Walking round the other side they both saw the path heading off into the woods. Lex's raised eyebrows confirmed Octavia's impressions: this path had been used recently. There were the occasional broken stems of plants and the odd footprint in the soft pine-needled mud.

They followed the path into the dark forest. It had stopped raining, but here the ground was hardly wet. Even though it was nearly midday, there was little light. The path twisted and turned. Octavia knew that it would not be so easy at night when it would be pitch black. Lex tutted as she tried to keep track of their direction with her compass but gave up in the end.

They seem to have walked much further than they'd come through the tunnel. Just when they were both wondering whether this had been a good idea, the trees gave way to a clearing.

Octavia knew instantly that this was the same clearing her father had described in his childhood adventure. The hairs on the back of her neck stood up and she stopped. Lex had already come to a halt. They stood there in the deathly silence of this unexpected amphitheatre, enclosed within its dark-green curtains. Neither of them had ever seen anything like it in their lives. The clearing wasn't large, perhaps as big as the entrance hall of the house, which in an odd way it resembled. The trees rose thirty or forty feet all around like the walls of the house, but without any windows. High above, they could see white clouds slowly moving overhead.

But it was what was in the clearing which stopped them in their tracks. Here in the middle of a Lakeland pine forest was a rose garden. In the centre was a large, well-established bush already coming into bud. Two or three of the buds had opened, revealing pure white flowers. Evenly spaced around it at the points of the compass were four more bushes, three of them of medium size and a small one with only one main twig. The buds on all of them showed white at the edges. The bushes were surrounded by a neatly-trimmed, slightly patchy lawn. It had been recently cut.

It took some time for the two of them to take in the strange landscape. Lex was the first to speak. 'Weird,' was all she said.

Octavia cleared her throat. 'It's how my father described it . . .' she began.

Lex looked at her with a frown. 'What do you mean?' she asked.

'I didn't tell any of you. To be honest I'd forgotten about it.'

'You mean after your father and his friend left the house, they found this?'

'Yes . . . but it's different.'

'How different?'

'When they saw it . . . it was over forty years ago . . . there was only one rose . . .' She pointed at the largest bush. 'In the middle . . .'

Lex's eyes widened. She looked at the roses and back at Octavia. 'Can a rose live that long?' she asked.

'I don't know,' replied Octavia.

They stared for a while longer before walking round the perimeter. Like Octavia's father and his friend before them, they felt unable to walk across the middle. At the other side they found the track again and, with one last look back, followed it on into the forest. Soon they came to a garden shed, overgrown with ivy and briars. A clump of fierce-looking nettles guarded the door. There were cracks in the windows and some of the roof tiles were looking the worse for wear.

'My father said they'd got from the shed to the house by climbing along a wall.'

Octavia and Lex made their way round to the far side and there was the wall. Beyond they could see the tower and, a few paces further on, they reached the edge of the trees. As they stepped out onto the churned-up garden, the sun broke through the clouds and lit up the entire building. The red sandstone glowed in the light for a few seconds before the gloom returned. The clouds recovered their complete dominance and the two women clambered their way across the mud and stumps, keeping close to the new metal fence. Martin had hired a firm to clear all the briars but they'd found the going very tough. There was still much to do.

They arrived at the front steps covered in mud up to their knees, both of them looking like they'd come out of the jungle after a long and arduous trek. They hesitated to step into the opulent hallway in this condition, so Octavia opened the door and hallooed into the echoing space. A cheery response came back and soon they were surrounded by the rest of the team.

'We were beginning to worry,' said Martin.

'What did you find?' asked Rivka.

'You two need a shower,' said Sylvia, with her fingers to her nose.

Ransome said nothing. He didn't know whether to smile or look sheepish. He frowned as Lex and Octavia both gave him knowing looks and burst out laughing.

They both had to agree with Sylvia and decided that the story would have to wait until after lunch. Octavia took Lex back to her cottage for a quick shower and a change of clothes, before joining the others at the Bampton Arms.

Back at the house, they gathered in the kitchen and listened to the underground adventure. Lex and Octavia had agreed to keep what they'd seen in the library to themselves, but both of them noticed that Sylvia and Ransome gave each other a stern look when they explained the first tunnel's destination. Octavia took over the telling of the second tunnel's revelations.

The rest of the team immediately wanted to go and see. Donning wellingtons and raincoats, they trooped along to the clearing. It was just as well they were wearing their waterproofs as the rain began to come down with a vengeance. It was torrential by the time they reached the roses and Sylvia, for one, was quite happy to take a quick look and head off back. The day descended into anti-climax. The rain had obviously set in for the day, so it was agreed they would leave it until the following morning.

Octavia was the last to leave the clearing. She was both captivated and disturbed by its stillness and a sense of something she couldn't quite place. It was only as she came to the edge of the trees and saw the tower that she remembered what her father had said.

'Not just silent and empty, but like a vacuum, devoid of any life.'

*   *   *   *

Fern had not slept for twenty-four hours. She'd not eaten much, just some pie and peas at the pub after the quiz match. She'd not had much alcohol either, just made sure that Joan was drunk. She felt a slight pang of guilt at using her teenage friend like this; Joan had enough of a drink problem as it was, but Fern's thirst for revenge overrode such thoughts.

She sat on the trunk of a fallen pine. When she arrived just before dawn there were no sounds from the shed. She loved the utter peace this place gave her. She watched the quiet creatures scuttling and crawling about her feet. A less knowledgeable or less observant person might have thought these woods were empty of life, but she knew they teemed with a restless energy and the endless battle for survival.

It was just as the light began to make shapes out of the darkness that she heard the first stirrings of her enemy. A choking cough. A whimper. Some groaning – a bit of sobbing.

Silence. Now the struggling had begun. Her victim's animal instinct for survival had begun to surface.

Fern could hear the rustling of chains, the unspoken curses and the skin-scraping wrestling with rough hemp. After a while the noises stopped. She was listening. Fern held her breath.

'I know you're there,' said an arrogant voice.

Fern breathed out quietly.

'You're not going to get away with this.'

Fern smiled to herself. She thought they'd all used that phrase.

'There will be people looking for me already. The police will hunt you down. Like an animal.'

Fern nearly laughed at this. If only the woman knew. She stayed silent and waited for the next stage.

'I suppose you want money. You won't get a penny from my

husband, you know. He'll be glad to be rid of me. Poor sap will be able to sleep peacefully at night. Won't have to worry about the next beating he's going to get. Mind you, it's what he wants more than anything else, actually. Sad little man.'

Fern laughed inside again. If only the woman knew what was going to happen. Still, that was a different take on the money angle: subtle – telling your kidnapper that there's money there without actually offering it; clever – but utterly hopeless. Fern sighed; such people always thought they could buy themselves out of trouble. Generally, of course, they could. They'd no idea about how to cope when they couldn't pay someone off.

She waited. The light had increased so that she could make out the detail on the side of the shed walls.

'I was brought up in South Africa, you know. I'm used to waiting and insects and all that. I'm not scared, but you should be. I've killed enough animals in my time. One more won't make much difference to me.'

Fern had had enough. She stood up and walked to the shed door, opened it and placed herself in the doorway. She knew this would only allow her victim to see a silhouette. She didn't expect Caroline Soulby to recognise her anyway, but Fern knew she'd find this unnerving.

'I'm going to release the chains and ropes and bring you out. If you resist, I'll use my knife. Not to kill you, but to maim you. Do you understand?' She held up the butcher's knife so that the woman could see its shape and size.

There was no response other than a sharp intake of breath. Fern crossed to where Caroline was sitting and slapped her hard across the face. She showed her the mirror. The woman's face curdled with anger.

'You jealous bitch,' she shouted. 'I am going to kill you . . . you . . . you bloody savage.'

Fern slapped her again – harder. Caroline's eyes brimmed with revenge and then alternated between outrage and fear. Fern cut the ropes and unfastened the chains. She backed out of the shed, watching as the woman rubbed her wrist and staggered to her feet. She was still wearing one of her high heels so, as she stood up, she overbalanced and fell forward towards the door.

Fern backed away again and watched as the woman crawled and scrabbled to her feet, removing the useless shoe in the process. They stood facing each other. Caroline screwed up her eyes as she tried to place the face before her. Fern watched with a curious smile playing on her lips.

'It's alright. I've changed my appearance. You might remember a tear-stained peasant grovelling at your feet, carrying a dead dog.'

Slowly, Caroline Soulby's befuddled memory ground into recognition.

'You!' she said.

Fern nodded.

'Is all this because of that stupid dog?'

Fern controlled her immediate impulse. She didn't want it all over in one quick swipe of the knife.

'Whatever else he was, Stan was not stupid. Over-enthusiastic, highly-strung, given to chasing his own tail, but not stupid . . . whereas you, Caroline . . .'

The woman gazed in astonishment and snorted her contempt. 'So what are you going to do now? Kill me?'

Fern stared at her long and hard. 'Yes.'

Caroline snorted again. 'You're mad.'

'Clinically? No. I don't think I'd get away with the "disturbed mind" defence. I've spent too long planning this moment . . . and . . . you're not the first, so . . .'

For the first time Caroline faltered. Then she said, 'Look, I honestly didn't realise it was a dog. I thought it was a deer. That was what we'd been promised, damn it. I thought it was a deer. I was wrong. I'm sorry . . .'

Fern let Caroline's voice tail away. Then she spoke. 'Maybe at the time, if you'd said that . . . I might have forgiven you . . . but if I remember correctly you said you'd have shot me as well and have my other dog put down, if you'd had the chance.'

Caroline stared at her.

'But it's too late. My mind's made up. You're going to die.'

Caroline took a step forward and held out her hand. 'Look, what I said about my husband was a joke. Of course he'll pay. Anything you ask. He's very rich. He's worth millions. He doesn't care about it – just his bloody books.'

Fern backed away. She knew that the offer of recompense was a lie and that the step forward was a calculated move towards an attack. She deemed it the moment to reveal her true intent. She whistled: a sing-song note, more coaxing than a command. Caroline frowned and peered into the gloom.

Nothing happened for a few seconds, but Fern could hear his approach. Shortly afterwards, Caroline's heightened senses picked up the same soft sounds. She tried to locate it, figure out its direction, but she got it wrong. He came into the light from the opposite direction. Caroline turned, her spine already rigid with fear. She knew before she saw him what it was going to be.

In the shadow of the trees beside Fern stood a shape; its outline had been drawn thousands of times throughout the history of man, from the first moments they'd started to hunt together.

The sharp ears, the long snout, the fur raised rigid on its back. Two legs fast; four legs faster – both hunting the same prey, using their different skills to combine into a ferocious killing machine.

Caroline nearly fainted with fear. At first she thought it really was a wolf, but the remaining rational part of her said it was merely an Alsatian. He was young but Fern had worked with him every day. He would defend her to the death. She had slept with him, eaten with him and run the fells with him. She'd found him the day after she arrived at Joan's, two weeks before Christmas when she'd gone to see her Robinson relatives. She'd spotted the puppy as she pulled up in the muddy farmyard. She told them she'd lost her previous dog. How much was he? They wouldn't accept any money. She walked away with him that day. They were soon inseparable.

Now the dog stood waiting. He hadn't growled, merely looked at the dishevelled woman with his head cocked to one side. He glanced at Fern. The woman began to back away. The dog sensed her fear and growled deep in his throat. He sniffed the air. It was full of fear. He looked again at Fern. The fear wasn't coming from her; she was exuding a totally different smell. The dog looked back at the woman. She was on her knees, crying.

Fern waited. Neither she nor the dog moved towards the woman.

'You have a choice,' said Fern quietly.

The woman groaned in terror.

'I can "put you down" as you so quaintly put it. I have stronger drugs than the one I gave you earlier. You won't feel any pain, but I'll watch you die and then bury you, where no-one will ever find you.'

The woman began to whimper.

'Alternatively you can run. Any direction you like. We'll give you a start. The end will probably be the same but you'll have a slim chance of survival. You could get lucky. You may make it to the edge of the forest. You could find someone who'll save you, but it's very unlikely. The dog will go for your throat. It takes seconds. You'll pass out with the shock. You'll either die from a heart attack or you'll bleed to death, although I'll be merciful. I'll shorten that time the moment I catch up with you.'

The woman lay on the floor and curled up into the foetal position. Fern blanked her out with the abiding image of Stan's amber eye and his juddering leg. She waited. The woman lay there a long time until she stopped crying. Eventually she sat up slowly.

'Please don't do this,' she implored.

Fern didn't listen to the outpouring of apologies; she closed her ears to them. The dog sat on its haunches, occasionally cocking its head or looking at Fern. When the whining voice stopped, Fern spoke.

'I didn't listen to any of that. It's between you and your conscience, nothing to do with me. We'll leave you now. You need time to prepare. If you decide to run, he'll tell me. If not, I'll return later and offer you the same chance. There are no alternatives.'

When Caroline looked up again, they'd gone. She couldn't hear them, but she knew they'd hear her. She hugged herself. It had started to rain. She staggered back into the shed and tried to think of a way out.

Later that afternoon, Fern returned. She saw that the shed door was shut. She smiled. The woman had chosen the only possible defence but it was hopeless. Fern stood outside.

'Very good, Caroline, make me or the dog come in to get you. You've probably found something to make into a weapon of sorts. An old garden fork tied to the end of a stick. Very resourceful and brave, but it doesn't alter the choice. The other thing which made man and dog so powerful was fire. No-one will even see the smoke, but you'll come out coughing. I was brought up in the countryside, Caroline. I know how to make smoke without fire. You can choke to death or you can run. The only easy death is to be "put down".'

She waited. She'd judged her enemy well. The door burst open and Caroline hurtled out of the shed. As Fern had guessed, she'd made a spear. She swung it back and forth, finding nothing but thin air. Then she stopped. There was no-one. No madwoman. No dog. Maybe it was only a trick. She backed round the side of the shed. She saw a path. She walked towards it . . . and ran . . . and kept running.

She didn't hear the dog until the last few seconds as the chasing animal launched himself into his final leap. Dogs – and wolves – rely on the speed and the weight of this leap to bring their quarry down. The ripping out of the prey's throat is the secondary intent, but it comes only a moment later. Bigger animals than humans, like deer or bison, might withstand the initial blow, but even they would stand little chance if the fangs sank deep into their throat. Caroline was dead before she hit the ground. Her primordial fear and the strength of the attack were too much for her heart. The dog had only a second before the whistle stopped him. He'd hardly broken the skin. Caroline's neck was broken and her heart had stopped. Her body was still in spasm as Fern arrived.

Fern buried her that night. She'd taken a cutting from the main rose bush last year and it had flourished in the darkness of the forest. She didn't understand how, but they did.

The two shadows slipped through the door in the wall and were soon ascending Long Stile in time for the sun coming up over Wild Boar Fell. They spent the whole day on the fells, running and playing in the bright sunshine. Stan would have loved it.

* * * *

The day after Octavia and Lex discovered the clearing, the rain continued its deluge until well after lunch. Even as the sun came out, the land between the trees and house had turned into a giant mudbath.

The team had little to do. All the artwork had been thoroughly catalogued. Rivka and Lex were busy tidying up the extensive records so they could send them off to headquarters, where an army of experts from different fields was being assembled to begin the process of verification. Provenance was going to be hard to prove. Both Rivka and Sylvia said they knew of few references to any of the paintings – even the 'Red Pandora'.

In any case, it was difficult to work in a house without any lights. Ironically this house had been one of the first in the late nineteenth century to enjoy electricity via a state of the art hydraulic system, but in the intervening sixty years the wires had corroded, the hydraulics were flooded and needed a complete overhaul. Martin was very excited by this and had already brought numerous engineers and technical historians to look at the arrangements. They were less excited, explaining that it would cost millions to restore, but he was not put off. There was also gas-lighting on the upper floors, but again this was defunct and even Martin couldn't get excited about it.

He had quickly organised the installation of three generators and arc lamps were dotted about in crucial places. However, once it was dark it became difficult to see anything in detail. There had been one or two near accidents with wires trailing everywhere, and so Martin had declared that daylight hours would have to suffice.

They'd not got much done during the morning. Rivka's eyes were hurting and Ransome was getting more and more irritated.

They agreed at about half past ten to take the rest of the day off.

Octavia went back to her cottage and made a half-hearted attempt to tidy up. By lunchtime she'd had enough and rang Tom. He'd had a tough morning in the rain, but had just got out of the shower and declared it would brighten up in the afternoon. Octavia was less than convinced as she looked out of her window at the solid grey mass of clouds from which heavy rain continued to pour. She accepted his invitation to lunch at the pub in Askham.

He called for her in his old US Army jeep, of which he was inordinately proud, having reconstructed it almost single-handedly from pieces of scrap metal. They had a pleasant lunch during which Tom brought her up to date on many of the school friends she'd lost touch with.

As he had forecast, the sun made a watery appearance about two o'clock and by three the clouds had disappeared. He suggested going for a drive as he didn't need to see to the cattle until six. Octavia's eyes twinkled mischievously.

'Do you want to go to a secret place? A place nearby, where you've never been?'

He frowned and looked to see if she was teasing him.

'We'll need a twelve-foot ladder and some old blankets,' she added. He was intrigued, but she wouldn't tell him any more.

His father's farm was on the way, so it wasn't long before they'd picked up the breaking-and-entering equipment – along with Tom's dog, Grey. She'd been a working sheepdog for over nine years, but had now been relegated to family pet. Tom's father thought it overly sentimental, but Grey had been Tom's constant companion since he was a teenager, so he would hear nothing against her. She squirmed with excitement behind the back seat mesh as they set off.

Tom knew every square inch of the valleys going up to Haweswater, including the countryside around Blanchard House, but he was surprised to be directed up the turning to Aika Hill. He knew the farms up there, but had forgotten the road also ran round the back of the Blanchard estate. He was even more astonished to find himself parking in the entrance to the ruined farm which probably still belonged to the Robinsons. He followed Octavia across the road and watched as she scrabbled about behind some bushes.

'Over here,' she shouted from a few yards further on.

He strode over, wondering what on earth she was doing. Forcing his large frame through the holly trees he stared at the estate wall. Where had the infuriating woman gone? Suddenly, she popped out three yards away. He fought his way to where she'd disappeared once again and found her in a little hidden corner where the two walls overlapped. Behind her in the inner wall was an old door.

'Lex and I found it yesterday,' she announced with pride. 'We followed a secret tunnel from the tower to a small cottage the other side of the wall. The door's locked and it's not the original. Someone has used this way in recently.'

He couldn't take it in. He walked over to the door and inspected the lock.

'You're right,' he agreed.

'So don't just stand there, you gurner!' she yelled. 'Go and get the ladder and the blankets. There's glass embedded in the top. Lex got a nasty cut trying to climb over.'

Against his better judgement, Tom collected the ladder and the blankets, put them in place and climbed over. As he lowered himself down the other side, his foot slipped on a loose stone and he tumbled the rest of the way to the ground.

'Are you okay?' yelled Octavia.

'Just a broken neck and serious head injuries,' he replied laconically.

Octavia fidgeted in exasperation. She started to climb the ladder, when suddenly the door opened and Tom stood smiling in the gap. She was so astonished she nearly fell off the ladder.

'How did you do that?' she demanded.

He held up a key for her to see. 'It was in a hole in the wall. I must have dislodged the rock which was hiding it.'

He stepped back and performed a mock bow.

'Would my lady care to enter?'

She glared at him and stomped through. Grey was going wild in the back of the jeep, so Tom went and let her out. She was across the road in a flash, her nose to the ground. Just as quickly she shot back past the jeep and down into the old farmhouse entrance. Tom gave Octavia a puzzled look and called the dog back. A few seconds later she came bounding over, gave Tom's trouser leg a lick and set off into the woods. He called her back. He frowned when she didn't come immediately and called again. This time she came, but the hackles on her back were rigid. Surprised, he bent down and stroked her head. She looked back down the track, which he hadn't noticed until that moment. He looked at Octavia who had watched all this with growing apprehension.

'What's the matter?' he asked.

'I'm not sure . . . Grey seems as unnerved as I was . . . am.'

Tom laughed. 'Hey. You can't bring me this far and leave me dangling.'

She grinned at the ambiguity. 'It's along that track. It goes all the way to the house. Well, to the edge of the trees. Thereafter we'd need to be in one of your bigger tractors. It's like the Somme.'

He frowned. Grey was sniffing everything. The hackles had stiffened again. 'Come on, let's go,' he said.

He let Grey go and she raced ahead. The two of them followed into the gloom. The dog came back and forth to check they were still following, until Octavia thought they must be getting near. Grey reappeared and wound herself round Tom's legs. She whimpered and barked. He silenced her but frowned at Octavia. They walked the last few yards to the clearing. Even though she'd seen it before, Octavia was still awestruck by its cathedral-like quality . . . or as Lex had succinctly put it . . . its weirdness.

Tom was speechless. Grey whined at his feet, wanting to go. Tom reached down to quieten her. She licked his hand and lay still, but her ears were cocked and tilting this way and that as she tried to pick up some sound in the deafening emptiness.

'What is this place?' he asked.

'I don't know,' said Octavia. 'Botanically I can't see how it's possible. In the winter there must be hardly any light in here.'

'Someone must be tending it.'

'It must be so,' she said softly.

'But why?' he asked.

She had no answer to that. They stood in silent contemplation. Grey's nostrils were driving her haywire.

'There's something else,' said Octavia.

Tom looked at her. She coughed. 'My father came here. Over forty years ago – with your uncle Billy.'

Tom stared in astonishment.

'It was a dare. They got into the house but lost their nerve, so they followed this track and found this clearing.'

'You mean it was like this forty years ago?'

'No. Forty years ago there was only one small rose in the middle.' She pointed at the six-foot bush. 'I think that's it.'

Tom stared at the thick, flourishing bush with its many buds promising a bounty of blossoms. He stared at the other roses.

'So how did the others get here?'

'Well, they're not suckers from the first one. They must have been planted . . . and cared for. They're much younger. Less than ten years old. It's difficult to say, I'm not an expert.'

Grey could bear it no longer; she rose from beside Tom's feet and crept round the outside. They watched as the dog approached the smallest rose, as though she was gathering in a particularly difficult and aggressive tup she'd cornered. Tom hadn't seen her do this for over a year. They watched spellbound. Without looking back at them, the dog crept lower and lower. She reached the edge of the small rose and sniffed the ground. She growled and glanced back at Tom. Suddenly, without warning, she began to dig. Furiously. They stared, eyes wide open. Before Tom could stop her, Grey began backing away with something between her teeth. It looked like blue material. Octavia's hand went to her mouth. Tom gasped.

'Down,' he commanded. 'Down! Grey!'

The dog hesitated. They could see years of training fighting with canine instinct. She let go. The white hand flopped onto the green grass. Octavia's scream was silent. Tom held her close. They were both white faced as Grey slunk back to them.

It was a whole minute before Tom could venture over. He'd seen plenty of dead animals before and one or two people, including once on the fells when they'd found a climber who'd fallen a couple of hundred feet . . . but this was different. Frightening.

He crouched by the open grave. He realised that it couldn't be very deep. Grey had hardly scratched the surface, maybe a foot at most. There was a smell, but not like he'd experienced with dead sheep when the build-up of trapped air had ruptured the intestines. So that had already happened. The hand seemed undamaged. So . . . maybe only a week or so.

He felt Octavia approach. She was half covering her face, but had to look. He stood up and pulled her away. The two of them walked back to where the track came through the trees. After one final glance they made their way back to the cottage and the door in the wall. They locked the door after them. Tom thought it best to put the ladder back on his jeep and, without saying a word, he set off home. Octavia didn't speak until they pulled up in the farmyard.

'She's not been there long, has she?'

'Maybe a week or two,' said Tom.

Neither of them had questioned the gender of the hand. They had both been able to see the nail polish and the rings . . . it was such a slender hand.

Inside the kitchen, Tom quickly explained what they'd found to his mother and father, before picking up the phone. Tom's father shook his head and looked at Octavia sitting at his kitchen table.

'Ah telt yer father. It's a wicked spot. Thar'll be mair budies afor thaas finished, lass.'

Tom's mother hushed him and put her arm round Octavia, who was still shaking.

Tom spoke quietly to the police, agreed to meet them at the main gates of the house and show them what they'd found. He came back to the table and put his arms round Octavia. His mother put the kettle on.

It was going to be a long night.

CHAPTER 16

Fletcher didn't get the phone call until the following morning because there had been little progress made the previous evening. As the police arrived it began to rain again. The scene of crime people were soaked just getting to the clearing.

Chief Inspector Aske squelched through the pine needles to find Jane Sykes inside a waterproof tent examining a body. She looked up as he shouldered his way in. There wasn't much room, because although she was tall and thin, he was much bigger and far heavier.

'Bloody hell, Jane! What a night.'

'As my dad would say – it might rain later . . .'

Aske was now used to the Cumbrian penchant for laconic understatement – particularly about the rain, so he ignored it.

'What have we got?'

'Female: mid-thirties, fully clothed, broken neck but no other signs of injury, although there are bruise marks on her wrists and ankles suggesting she was tied up before she died, but not when she died. Difficult to tell until I get her on the slab, but I don't think it was an accident.'

'When?'

'That's the main puzzle, Chief Inspector. This close to the surface and in these conditions, I'd normally expect a body post rigor to be more . . . decomposed. Plenty of micro-organisms about – as well as larger beasties. But she seems strangely untouched. It's possible, I suppose, that she was kept in a freezer for a few days before being buried, but that still doesn't make sense.' She frowned to herself and stood up.

Outside the tent, she agreed to do the autopsy as soon as possible and splashed off across the clearing. Aske turned to DS Strickland and asked him about the couple who'd found the body.

Ten minutes later he was drinking tea in Mary Harper's kitchen, listening to Octavia's tale. It took some time but it held the chief inspector's attention, because what he heard beggared belief. The worst thing was that, if the young woman's suspicions were correct, the four other roses marked four more bodies. He explained to them that he'd called off the team, because of the rain and the dark; if there were four more bodies, they weren't going anywhere before tomorrow morning and he'd been reliably informed the rain would have abated by then. He'd left six despondent officers at the scene, having assured them they'd be relieved in a couple of hours.

So when Fletcher arrived the next morning, he and DC Garner found the team sweating in their overalls as the sun beamed down onto a harrowing scene. They'd arrived at eight. By eleven it was confirmed that there were four more bodies interred in the clearing.

Jane Sykes was in a state of utter bewilderment. The evidence defied scientific explanation. The three other outer graves contained bodies which had decomposed a little, but were still recognisable people. They were all females in their mid-thirties.

Two looked like they'd been strangled and had red blotches all over their faces, which the pathologist couldn't yet explain. The third had been nearly decapitated by a sharp-edged implement.

But it was the body under the largest tree that caused her the most trouble. This woman was only a teenager. Her body was desiccated, but decomposition seemed to have been arrested somehow. The only thing she could think of was some kind of mummification – but in this soil? Impossible! And, disconcertingly, this one had been shot by a shotgun at point-blank range. The shredded clothes on the front of her body were still blackened. Much of the ribcage had been destroyed in the explosion and the innards burnt and shrivelled. However, it was the clothes which completely disorientated her. She was no historian, but they looked to her as if they were straight out of a Dickens novel. The girl was dressed in a thick woven skirt, woollen stockings, well-worn shoes, white cotton blouse and a white servant's hat. And yet, despite all this, the most striking difference between her and the other four bodies was that she still had a full head of reddish, fair hair. The other four all had shaven heads. Bizarre.

Fletcher listened to her increasingly exasperated descriptions with the detached air of someone waiting his turn to make a point. In fact, he was listening very carefully. When she finally paused for breath, he waited to see if there was more. She shook her head in disbelief.

'I'm going to need expert help with this,' she said.

'Have you anyone in mind?' he asked.

She shook her head again. 'I'll try a few people I know, but this is inexplicable.'

Fletcher had lifted the sheet off one of the bodies. It was one of the women who had been strangled. He stared dispassionately at her for a while.

'Could that be a nettle rash?' he asked.

'Your guess is as good as mine, Inspector,' she replied.

He looked around. There wasn't a nettle in sight. He sighed.

'Well. Let's get them all back to your lab and you can get started. Have you got anywhere with the first one?'

She nodded.

'I did it this morning before I came out here. As I said to the chief inspector last night, cause of death was a broken neck, although my internal inspection indicates that she probably died of shock. There are marks on her knees where she seems to have crawled through the dirt . . . her hands too. There are also two marks on her throat. We could be dealing with werewolves, Inspector.'

He looked to see if she'd regained her sense of humour. She wasn't smiling.

'I can't give you a time of death. I need to see the results from some tests. I should know later today.'

She said her goodbyes and departed, leaving a large team picking over every inch of the clearing. Throughout all this Irene had said nothing.

'Cat got your tongue, Detective?' he asked.

She stared at him blankly. 'Can't make any sense of it, sir. It seems so . . . so . . .'

'Ritualistic?' offered Fletcher.

'Um, yeh,' she replied.

Fletcher walked back to the track. 'Let's go and talk to the couple who found them.'

They'd been told they'd find them in the big house. They'd also been told to go the long way round unless they'd got knee-high boots. Fletcher didn't share his image of Irene in knee-high boots with her; it didn't seem very respectful in the presence of so many dead women.

They drove round from the side gate and up the drive to the main house. It was at its most impressive this morning in the spring sunshine. Water dripped from every gutter and corner, so that it looked like an enormous fountain. Inside, the great hall stopped them in their tracks; Fletcher was immediately struck by the painting of the woman in red and its resemblance to a similar picture on a similar staircase in Rochdale. Only that was of Louisa – all blue and white – with her long blonde hair. As he stood and stared, Irene nudged him back to the present. A tall, angular man was approaching with outstretched hand.

'Good morning,' he said. 'I'm Martin Winter, director of the local National Trust. Octavia and Tom are through in the kitchen with the rest of the team. Please join us.'

He led them through to the biggest kitchen Fletcher had ever seen. Six pairs of eyes met his as he entered. Fletcher was rarely shy, but the intensity of their looks momentarily disconcerted him. He allowed Martin to introduce them all and he and Irene accepted their offer of coffee and cakes.

Martin quickly filled them in with what they'd found so far. Fletcher was impressed: it was a summary of which his old chief inspector, Frank Worthington, would have been proud. Fletcher had a well-honed facility to listen to what was being said and watch other people's responses at the same time. He felt a considerable tension in the room. There were lots of looks and glances as their director gave his report.

Fletcher's eyes lingered on a dark-haired woman introduced as Sylvia, an art expert from London. She met his gaze with a look of amusement, before giving him a vivacious smile. Startled, he looked back at Martin, but when he chanced another glance she was still looking at him. Martin told them about how they'd got permission to gain entry, the amazing collection of paintings and artefacts, the tunnels and the different rooms in the tower. He showed the police officers the carefully drawn diagrams and architectural drawings. When he finished, Fletcher waited to see if anyone else had anything to add. They didn't. He looked at the young woman who'd found the bodies.

'Miss Hutton, is there somewhere we can go for you to tell me exactly what you found yesterday?'

Octavia looked across at Tom. 'I wasn't alone, Inspector.'

'I know,' he said with a smile. 'Just procedure, miss. Sometimes it's useful to hear different versions of the same event. We all see and remember things differently. My colleague will take a statement from your . . . friend.'

This produced a lot of smiles and a general relaxation in the room.

Octavia took the inspector to one of the drawing rooms, while Tom went off into the dining room with Irene. When they'd gone, Ransome couldn't resist a comment.

'All a bit Cluedoesque,' he said. Sylvia giggled. The others sighed.

As Fletcher hadn't told them to stay in the kitchen all of them, except Sylvia, wandered off to find something to do. Ransome had given her a smile, but she seemed distracted and didn't notice. He went back into the library.

He'd now searched the room twice from wall to wall and floor to ceiling. They'd found the lever, which opened the secret door into the tunnel, hidden behind a false line of books. He went and sat at the desk and tried to look at the room with new eyes. Suddenly he had an idea. Absurd, but it proved inspirational.

He went to the centre of the room and lay on the floor. From this angle he could see under all the tables and chairs. He'd already felt under all the table edges and the back of the writing desk to no avail, but from here he spied the tiny catch under a side table, on which stood a large vase and other smaller receptacles. He jumped up, quickly removed the vases and boxes and felt underneath for the catch. It was a simple flat hook. After he'd released it, he felt the edge of the table and found the hardly visible dividing line. Carefully he got his fingernails into the gap and lifted up the top, which was folded over onto the bottom half. Both surfaces were revealed to be frames which left a gap a couple of inches smaller than the size of the table. Inside this was a space nearly an inch thick, which was more than enough to hide the large collection of drawings and other papers hidden there.

Ransome wanted to shriek 'Eureka!', but his thirst for secret knowledge got the better of him. Delicately, he fingered through the brown-tinged papers. He knew instantly there weren't going to be any letters but was fascinated by what he did find.

The largest papers were at the bottom; they were maps and diagrams of the house and gardens. He quickly realised these weren't designs, but representations of the actual buildings, including dotted lines marking the paths of the two tunnels. The other papers were genealogical. He traced with his fingers the history of the de Blanche family – all the way back to Charlemagne, of course! Above them lay his wife, Ursula's, line back through the Red Douglas to Macbeth and beyond. There was nothing of the di Nerezza here. That was most intriguing. He wanted the papers for himself, but knew he couldn't keep them. He put down the table top and backed away. He was just in time because the door opened and Martin peered into the room.

'Time for lunch, David.'

Ransome obediently followed him out. They'd decided to have lunch in today as they knew the police would want to talk to them all, so they all reassembled in the kitchen and awaited the release from questioning of the two lovebirds. Tom and Octavia appeared almost immediately, but had little to tell the others that they didn't already know.

Fletcher and Irene had refused the invitation to lunch and were standing outside, leaning on the balustrade. They quickly ascertained that neither of the two witnesses had anything different to say other than what they'd told Aske the previous night. Martin had told them he'd be happy to guide them round the house, although Lex would have to show them the tunnels. Fletcher thought that could wait. He was more interested in finding out about the victims. His instinct told him that these National Trust people had nothing to do with the bodies. He and Irene set off to the hospital.

Ransome waited until the detectives had gone; he didn't think his find was of any use to the police. As the team got up to go about their various tasks, he coughed and said in a sonorous voice: 'I've made a little discovery that you might all find of interest.'

They turned wearily to look at him, expecting some joke or other. He set off across the room.

'Oh, well if you're not bothered, I'll not bore you with the details.'

He stood at the door. They gave in and followed him. He had his second moment of glory as they gathered in the library and were suitably astonished when he lifted the table top. They goggled at the drawing and diagrams. Taking them to the large drawing room, they spread them out on the big table and examined them. Martin was full of praise for Ransome's dogged research. This would make their eventual presentation complete.

Rivka and Lex went off to put the finishing touches to their catalogue. Martin had to make some phone calls and said he'd see them all in the morning. Sylvia said she wanted to take one last look at the paintings and disappeared upstairs. Ransome and Octavia continued to pore over the documents. Tom had already gone to feed the cattle. He and Octavia had had a little tiff when she'd said no to the pub that evening. She was worn out and wanted an early night. He'd gone off in a huff.

Eventually Ransome said he needed to go and check some of his books at home, leaving Octavia studying the diagram of the house. She found a vertical section of the tower and remembered they'd still not managed to find a way into the ground floor from above. It was time to take a look.

Picking up one of the many torches that were lying about, she went up the stairs and along the long corridor past the mirror which remained in its place where the 'Red Pandora' had been. She opened the door which led into the tower and walked round the dining table, thinking that there must be an entrance down to the cellar below from here. She looked in the kitchen, opened the cupboards and pushed and prodded at the wooden panelling. Nothing.

Octavia went back into the main room and crossed to the servant's room. The skeleton had been removed the same day they had found it. As far as she knew, they'd found nothing exceptional. It was the body of a woman about forty years old and there were no obvious signs of any violence. The autopsy report suggested it could have been an illness or perhaps poison that killed her, but it was too long ago to be sure. They were doing further tests. In the room there was the bed, the crucifix and the mirror, nothing else. No-one had wanted to spend time in this small room, even after the body had been removed. Octavia sat on the bed and tried to imagine such a death.

As she gazed absentmindedly around, she noticed that the floor behind the door was a darker colour – almost black. She pushed the door shut and looked at the panelling behind it. Why hadn't they seen it before? She reached out, pushed up the little latch and the panelling swung away from her. She shone the torch down the stairs and laughed to herself. Where else would you have the access to the coal hole? She took a couple of steps down the wooden stairs.

She heard rather than saw the figure behind her, but it was too late. A hand came towards her and pushed her hard. She stumbled and fell to the bottom, banging her head on a beam at the foot of the stairs. For a brief second she could see a thin figure silhouetted at the top of the steps, but then it all went dark.

*　　*　　*　　*

Fern had watched the coming and going from the edge of the trees. She'd arrived in the morning, innocent of what had occurred. She became suspicious when she passed two police vehicles so she decided to park in the village and walk, leaving the dog on the back seat.

Like Tom, this was the world of her childhood. She was older than he was but not much had changed in her lifetime, never mind his. She soon realised that her usual route was no longer a secret. The entrance was crawling with police and other people. But she knew other ways in; it wasn't the only secret entrance. She reflected on how paranoid a family she was descended from that they should have so many escape routes, but that it was common in the Borders.

She scaled the wall where an old oak provided a simple climb. She didn't need to work out the way to the clearing; she could hear the racket they were making, destroying her quiet place. A part of her

285

was angry, but mostly she was driven by a cold, animal cunning. She approached the site unseen and unheard. Watching from the trees, she saw they had found her victims. They'd even dug up the old rose bush.

She bit back a sob, made her way round to the house and approached in the lee of a high wall. Even though she'd never been in the house, she felt drawn to it now. She fought back her mother's stern warning never to even think of going inside. At a side door she tried the handle; it was locked. She remembered where she'd found the second key to the secret door in the outer wall. She stood back and assessed the doorway in front of her. Unerringly she felt along the ridge at the top. The key fell from its perch and clattered on the stone doorstep. She froze. No-one came.

In seconds she was inside, in a scullery. She could hear voices through the door. Peering through the keyhole she saw a group of people sitting at a large table, eating and talking. She crept out, locked the door behind her and moved swiftly back into the safety of the trees. She reckoned on returning at night and going in that way, but her plan changed when she got close to the shed. She could hear three or four of them standing outside.

'. . . but the floor is covered with hair. Look! Black, blonde, all mixed up!' said a man's voice.

'So, this is where she must have kept them before she killed them,' said another.

'Look, there's the nettles Fletcher was asking about,' said the first voice.

'Come on,' said a third.

She heard them making their noisy way along the track. She ran parallel on the pine-needles a few yards away. When they stopped at the clearing to report their findings, she carried on. It was when she got back to the cottage that she overheard the vital information. She listened intently and smiled to herself.

Five minutes later she was over the wall and running back to her car. Now she knew how to get in. She didn't know why, but tonight she'd be in the tower.

* * * *

In the bright lights of the pathology lab, Fletcher stood and listened to Jane Sykes.

'It's impossible,' she was saying, over and over again.

He'd listened to her explain, although not really understood, that the state of the bodies was against all scientific reason, especially if the one under the big tree had been dead for more than sixty years.

'There shouldn't be an ounce of flesh on her,' said the pathologist as she paced the room. 'Just powdered bones and a ring. That's all. Like the corpse in the tower, but even less. That was entombed, but it was in a worse state than this one. '

She held up the simple gold ring she'd taken from the girl's right hand.

Fletcher asked about the first woman.

'If this was an ordinary case I'd say she'd been dead just over a week, but given the state of the other bodies, it could be two or three months!' She threw up her hands in exasperation.

Irene's face brightened. 'How about Caroline Soulby?'

The other two looked at her in astonishment.

'Well,' said Sykes. 'That's easy enough. Ask her husband for her dentist's name and we can see about that in a matter of minutes.'

And so it was that the first identification was made. By four o'clock

Fletcher was back at the station ringing Kelso. The first call had been to Philip Campbell who gave him Anna's number. She confirmed that the woman she knew as Rose White had left her house last December, but she had no idea where she had gone. She was cagier about how Rose had behaved after the shooting of the dog. Fletcher didn't push it. He had enough intuitive nous to know he was on the right track.

He spoke to a Detective Inspector Nixon in Newcastle, who said he'd check missing persons for thirty-something women in the last few years. He faxed over four likely records. Eileen Stanhope's fingerprints fitted the taller of the two strangled women. The Morpeth police had arrested and questioned both her husband and a young man who'd confessed to having a sexual encounter with her. They'd had difficulty in believing his story about being beaten up by the woman and coming round to find her gone, but in the absence of a body, they'd had to release them both.

Fletcher felt he was on a roll now but then the trail dried up. They photographed and fingerprinted the other three corpses and sent out a nationwide request. Chief Inspector Aske arranged to go on television to appeal for information. All they could do was wait.

Fletcher went home and paced the garden. He was missing something. What was the connection between these women and Blanchard House? He resolved to go back the following day and see if the National Trust people could shed any light on it.

* * * *

Fern didn't wait long. As soon as it was dark she drove out to the village. She knew there would be a guard, perhaps even dogs. She was wrong about the dogs. She climbed over by the oak tree and made her way to the cottage. The three policemen outside were sitting around a small campfire, talking in quiet voices. She could hear from their accents that they were local.

It was easy to climb through one of the open windows and find the trapdoor she'd heard them talking about that afternoon. She lifted the door and found the top of the ladder.

She descended into the darkness, pulling the door down as she went. It was only when she'd found the stone floor and travelled a few yards along the tunnel that she put on her torch. She hurried along until she came to the fork. Unsure about which way to go, she turned right and found the door with the peephole.

The library was in darkness. Fern turned out her torch and opened the door. She could make out the shapes of the furniture from the dim light coming through the window. She made her way to the door and listened for any sound. The house seemed empty.

She stepped into the great entrance hall and shone her torch here and there. She stopped as it lit up the picture on the stairs. She walked up to it and looked at it closely. She shivered; the long dark hair, the red dress and the arrogance of the face – she knew exactly who this was. She wanted to rip the painting apart, but instead she went back down and into the tunnel.

She turned right at the junction, found the ladder and climbed up until she could see the handle in the roof above her head; she turned it round and pushed up. She climbed out, took three steps into the room and shone the torch round at the gleaming dark wood. A sixth sense told her to run but she didn't; she couldn't move. As she stood rooted to the spot, a door on her left slowly opened, warm air drifted towards her and a voice echoed round the room.

'I knew you would come.'

* * * *

Fletcher was watching the television. Well, his eyes were pointed at it but if you'd asked him to close them and tell you what he'd been watching . . .

Suddenly he stood up and cursed. Laura and Grace both jumped.

'I've got to go out,' he said. 'I won't be long.'

He went to the door, came back and kissed them both. He went out to the car, came back, picked up the phone and rang the station. He asked if they had a number for the woman called Rivka Weill. They had; she was still staying at George Hutton's house. He rang the number. Octavia's father answered. He hadn't seen Rivka – or Sylvia Urquhart – since breakfast time.

Fletcher rang the station again and told them to get Irene to meet him at the big house. He went back out to the car and drove off at speed.

When he got to the house, Irene hadn't arrived. He climbed out of the car and shouted for the guards. They came quickly to the gate and opened it. Fletcher wound down the window.

'That was fast, sir,' said one of the guards.

'What d'you mean?' asked Fletcher.

'We only radioed the station a minute or two ago.'

'What for?'

The officer pointed down the drive. 'We saw lights in the house. Jenkins and Binks have gone to look.'

Fletcher was about to drive on, but reversed and asked: 'Were all the occupants checked out when they left?'

'Everyone apart from Miss Hutton and the Urquhart woman,' the officer replied.

Fletcher drove to the house. The two guards had only just arrived. Jenkins was struggling with the lock.

'I can't get in, it must be locked from inside,' he was saying.

Fletcher shouted: 'Break it down.'

The two officers looked at him. 'You're joking, sir. It's nearly six inches thick.'

Fletcher cursed again. 'Follow me. No! Binks, go and get back-up. Armed unit. Fire brigade, the bloody lot!'

Binks stared at him open-mouthed.

Fletcher yelled at him. 'Do it, you bloody idiot. Now!'

Binks turned and ran. Fletcher signalled to Jenkins and they clambered over to the nearest window. Jenkins gave him a bunk up and Fletcher broke the window with a brick he'd picked up on the way. He smashed out as much of the glass as he could before climbing through, yelping as he caught his ankle on a stray spike. Jenkins heard him falling onto the floor and cursing for all his worth. He could hear Fletcher trying the lock but there was no key. Jenkins shouted that he'd get a ladder. He heard Fletcher say something about the tower, but nothing else. He set off back to the main gate.

Inside, Fletcher tied his handkerchief round his ankle and limped towards the library. He found the secret door and pulled the lever. Nothing happened; it was also locked from the other side. He cursed in desperation. How was he going to get in?

He thought about the other tunnel and went back to the main door. He found one of the generators and switched it on. The hall was flooded with light. He looked up at the woman in red. She'd gone! There was just a broken, empty frame leaning against the wall. He limped up past the forlorn frame and down the long corridor, knowing full well that the door would be locked – from the inside. It was.

He stumped back down to the hall, spied a tool box on the floor in the corner and found a hammer. Going back to the window, he used the hammer to knock out all the glass. He took off his coat and put it over the bottom of the frame, climbed through the window and jumped down onto a bush to break his fall. As he got unsteadily to his feet, Jenkins and Binks arrived with a ladder.

'It's no use,' he called to them. 'All the doors are locked. Get into the car.'

They got in; he reversed and roared down the drive. At the entrance he skidded to the right and round to the hidden entrance. They piled out of the car and headed for the gate in the wall. It was locked. Fletcher couldn't believe it; it was like the Keystone Cops. They'd left the ladder by the front door.

Fletcher yelled at the guards on the other side. There was no reply and Fletcher feared the worst. He sent Jenkins back to get another ladder and instructed Binks to help him climb the wall. Between them he got to the top. He knew about the glass so asked Binks to give him his jacket. Taking a deep breath, he jumped down the other side. He rolled into a puddle and got to his feet. Not two yards away a constable lay dead on the grass, the blood already drying on his head. Fletcher cursed in frustration. How could they have let this happen?

'How many guards should there be?' he shouted to Binks.

'Three!' was the answer.

'Oh God.'

He found the second one leaning against the wall. Another head wound – also dead.

To his left he heard a sound. He ducked down and listened. It was a groan. He crept towards the sound and found the third guard, still alive despite the blood running down his face. Fletcher pushed him upright against the wall. His eyes fluttered open.

'It's alright,' said Fletcher. 'The ambulance is on its way. Just stay where you are, lad.'

The young man blinked his understanding.

'How many of them?' asked Fletcher.

The policeman frowned. 'Only one I think. Only saw one. It was quick. Out of nowhere.'

'You'll be alright.'

He stood up and called to Binks. 'Get over here as soon as you can. Get the medics here. Three men down. I'm going into the tunnel.'

He didn't wait for a reply but opened the door and lifted the trapdoor. He didn't have a torch, but knew there were only two tunnels: one to the tower, the other to the library. He wished he could remember which one went which way.

At the bottom of the ladder it was pitch black. He set off as best he could, trying to keep his head down and not lose his footing. Both proved impossible. He ended up at the junction with a gashed head and dodgy ankles.

He stood and listened but could hear nothing. He chose the right-hand fork but he knew soon enough that he was wrong. He bumped into the end wall. He felt for the doorway, pulled back the peephole. The small amount of light filtering through from the hall was enough for him to see that the door had been wedged shut with a stout piece of wood. He tugged at it and it fell on his foot. He winced with pain. He used the piece of wood to hold the door open and set off back to the junction.

Again he stopped and listened. Not a sound. He followed the darkness until he bumped into the wall and banged his head on the ladder. He could feel the blood dribbling down by his ear. He wiped it aside and felt again for the ladder. Instead he found another piece of panelling. Was this another door? He found a handle . . . and a key. They'd not said anything about a door here; it must lead into the cellar.

He opened it carefully. The room was as dark as the tunnel,

although as his eyes adjusted he could see a faint light at the far side of the room, which was sufficient to give him a second's warning as a figure staggered towards him.

The body hit him in the midriff. He nearly fell backwards but clung on as the wildcat clawed at his legs. As he struggled to gain some purchase, the animal released him and backed off. Suddenly a torch light dazzled them both. Fortunately it soon began to fade and they were able to identify each other. Fletcher shielded his eyes and saw the young woman holding the wavering torch; Octavia saw a bloodstained detective, whose name she couldn't remember. They both collapsed on the floor with relief. Neither could manage to speak, which probably saved their lives.

The torch had expired seconds after they'd recognised each other. A grating sound came from above and a bright light shone down the shaft. There was sufficient light for them to see each other, eyes wide and fingers on lips. The grating noise sounded again and the light was extinguished. Octavia and Fletcher huddled towards each other and had a whispered conversation.

'What are you doing in here?' he asked.

She shuddered. 'I was locked in.'

'Who by?'

'I'm not sure.'

'Was it the woman with the funny smile?' he asked.

'You mean Sylvia?'

'Dark hair?'

'I doubt it,' she shivered, and shone her torch towards the bottom of the stairs. Sylvia's body lay huddled on the floor.

'Oh,' said Fletcher. 'I see.'

He limped over. The woman's left eye stared at him, but her right eye was just a blood-encrusted hole.

'Good grief,' he thought, 'it's a bloody massacre!'

They heard footsteps cross the room above. They stopped and listened. The sounds stopped.

'What are we going to do?' asked Octavia.

'You're going to get out through the tunnel. Go the long way. There should be lots of policemen there by now.'

'What are you going to do?'

'I'm going to see who's upstairs.'

Octavia thought about this. 'Have you been in the top room?'

'No. Is there something I should know?'

'Don't you remember – we told you? It's completely surrounded by mirrors.'

'Mirrors?'

'That's right.'

'Why?'

'Not sure.'

They stopped and listened again. Nothing.

'Off you go,' Fletcher said. 'I'll wait until you're well on your way.'

Octavia didn't like the idea, but she didn't fancy going upstairs either. She insisted on giving the torch to Fletcher, then crawled out of the door and set off. When she reached the split in the tunnel, she whispered back to him. Fletcher gave her a quick on and off with the torch. He gave her two minutes to get further along the tunnel, before stepping onto the ladder once more.

He climbed to the top and bumped his head gently on the lid. He felt the wheel which he figured must shift the lid to one side. It was at this point he realised he could hear something.

He wished he could open the lid, but he'd heard the noise it made. He grasped the wheel and tried to ease it a fraction. It shifted a bit. He inched it slowly open – sufficient to hear the voice. It was a woman, speaking so quietly that he could hardly make out what she was saying. He listened.

'. . . long time, but now it's over.'

There was a hush.

If he put his head sideways, he could see through the crack. Octavia was right; he could see dozens of reflections of a small woman with her hair scraped back. It was the one called Rivka, with the numbers tattooed on her arm. He pictured her birdlike figure perched on the edge of the group. Watchful dark eyes . . . her bare arms, hands unmoving on her lap. Cassie's warning!

There was a gun in Rivka's hands, which she was pointing at another figure. The reflected image showed a tall woman with short spiky hair. He didn't recognise her at all. He worked out that Rivka must be facing away from him so that if he could move quickly, he might surprise her and stop what looked and sounded like a final solution.

Gathering all his strength he turned the wheel and pushed up as quickly as he could. A shot rang out. He felt rather than heard it ricocheting off the metal lid. He ducked and nearly fell down the shaft.

There was a loud shriek and the sound of breaking glass. He risked a quick look through the gap. The room was full of crazy shapes and angles. There were shards of mirror everywhere, a face reflected in them, contorted with rage. There was more shattering of glass, followed by the whole building shaking as there was louder noise and the splintering of wood and falling stone. The building was collapsing!

Fletcher scrambled down the ladder and hit the stone floor as another crash shook the building. He couldn't stay here. He edged back along the tunnel and found his way to the junction. The door to the library was still wedged open, light filtering into the tunnel. He made his way towards the light.

The sound of the first explosion nearly deafened him. He fell to the floor with his hands over his ears. He sensed the heat as it came down the shaft. He staggered to his feet and was close to the door as the fireball came towards him. At the last second he leapt through the doorway as the flames burst into the room.

Ahead of him he saw a figure running. In the light of the flames he saw it was the woman from upstairs – not Rivka – the other one with the black spiky hair. He scrambled across the floor, through the doorway into the great hall. The flames followed him, eating anything combustible as they travelled. Out in the open space of the hall they billowed up and became smoke.

Fletcher crawled and slid across the floor until he reached the broken window. With one last surge of energy, he clambered up and flung himself out into the open.

Another explosion shook the building. The flames followed the same route, but now they blew out all the windows. Fletcher was on his feet and staggering down the drive. The third explosion blew him flat into the mud. He gathered himself and took one quick look back at the building. It was consumed with fire; flames were leaping from every window and doorway. There were further explosions as huge beams fell from the upper floors.

He limped towards the gates. From the gateway a monstrous vehicle appeared and came charging towards him. He leapt to one side into the mud and uprooted briars. His head hit a stump and everything went black.

CHAPTER 17

Fletcher's leg hurt. He grunted, turned over and reached for Laura. She wasn't there. The bed was cold. And wet. He opened his eyes. The room was full of light . . . and smoke. The house must be on fire. He called out and struggled to get out of bed, except he wasn't in bed. He was on the floor. Not the carpet, but mud. He was outside. Why was he outside? He leant up on one elbow and looked at the fire. Slowly it came back to him.

He got to his feet.

Two figures came hurrying out of the smoke – and then he fainted.

The next time he woke up, he was in an ambulance. He could hear the radio. A woman in green smiled at him. He thought about Cassie.

He tried to remember what had happened. Various disconnected images flickered across his mind . . . a woman with black spiky hair . . . a constable staring at him with blank eyes . . . grappling in the dark with that young woman . . . a contorted face in a broken mirror . . . black numbers on a bare arm . . . someone running through the hall. He let the darkness take him into its arms.

*   *   *   *

Chief Inspector Aske had never seen anything like it; it was a scene from hell. He was roused from his bed at about midnight. A car took him to Blanchard House where he found the entire building in flames. He caught sight of it just after the car raced through Helton. The sky was filled with an orange glow.

The car pulled up at the main gate. Police vehicles were slewed here and there; figures ran around, silhouetted against the glare of the fire. Up near the house he could make out three fire engines, but their efforts seemed puny against the enormity of the blaze. An ambulance skidded and swerved towards him through the mud, before getting onto the road and speeding away with its blue lights flashing. He didn't recognise a single person. Those that came close had blackened faces and staring eyes.

Suddenly a voice called his name, but he couldn't tell who or where it was coming from. He realised that the noise of the fire was almost as disorientating as the sight of it.

A hand gripped his elbow. He swung round. The blackened face in front of him said that he was DS Strickland, but he hardly recognised him. Aske allowed himself to be shepherded back to one of the police cars and tried to take in what the sergeant was telling him.

'We received a call about eleven thirty, sir, from Constable Binks who was on guard duty here. He asked for back-up, fire and ambulance. The emergency teams reacted quickly, but by the time they got here the house was beyond help. We've been trying to check who might have been in there. That ambulance which just went through was taking DI Fletcher to hospital.'

'Fletcher? Is he alright?' asked the chief inspector, recovering some of his authority.

'Not sure, sir. He was found lying in the mud beside the drive.

He's covered in blood and didn't seem to know where he was, kept blacking out, sir.'

'What was he doing here?'

'No idea, sir. Binks said he'd arrived without warning and told them to get back-up, but that was before the explosions happened.'

'Explosions?'

'Apparently, sir.'

Aske looked up to the fire. Part of the roof caved in, sending flames and sparks high into the night sky.

'There's something else, sir,' said Strickland, tentatively. Aske turned to look at him. The sergeant was looking towards the fire. Aske waited, knowing it wasn't going to be good.

'Two constables shot dead, sir. One injured.'

'Who?'

'Crosby and Forsyth, sir.'

'My God! Why . . . when?'

'Not certain, sir. According to Binks and Jenkins, DI Fletcher was trying to get inside the building but all the doors were locked. He wanted to get into the tower, but all those doors were locked too . . . from the inside. So they went round to the hidden entrance. That was locked too. Crosby, Forsyth and MacDonald were on guard there. DI Fletcher got over the wall, found them and told Binks to get help, before setting off alone into the tunnel. That was the last anyone saw of him before he was found in the mud.'

'Right. So what have you done?'

'Called everyone, sir, but I think we might be too late. If there's anyone in there . . .'

They both looked up at the inferno, which seemed determined to consume the whole edifice.

A fire officer arrived and gave Aske an update on their efforts.

He said the SFO thought that all they could do was contain the fire to the building. It was collapsing in on itself and they couldn't risk sending anyone in. Aske stood and watched, feeling helpless in the face of such terrifying destruction. Was it deliberate? But why? And why was Fletcher so determined to get inside? What had he discovered?

Another officer came running up, recognised the chief inspector and saluted. He pointed up the lane. 'We've found one of the National Trust people, sir.'

Aske walked towards a couple of officers who were helping a young woman along the road. Her clothes were torn and dishevelled, her knees and hands blackened, her hair a mess, her face tearstained and filthy. They helped her into a car and it set off for the hospital.

'Where did you find her?' he asked.

'Wandering about near that clearing, sir.'

'What did she say?'

The two officers looked at each other.

'She was singing, sir.'

'Singing?'

They nodded. Aske looked back at the house. How many others, he wondered?

* * * *

Back at the station, they managed to contact Martin, who rang the rest of team. He'd got through to Lex and a grumpy Ransome, but not Rivka or Sylvia. George Hutton said he hadn't seen either of them since the previous morning. The only other person unaccounted for was Irene. She'd disappeared, last seen in The Fox talking to someone on the phone.

By dawn the fire was under control. The majority of the main building had been razed to the ground. Only the old pele tower seemed to have survived intact. The fire officers said it was still too dangerous to try and gain entrance, especially as there had been explosions. They'd sent for the local bomb disposal team, which was on its way.

Constable Jenkins stood looking towards the smouldering building. Binks came and stood beside him.

'Funny thing is, that's where I think the fire started,' Jenkins muttered.

'What d'you mean?' asked Binks.

'The explosions. They came from the tower. Yet it's the only bit left standing.'

The two of them continued to stare. They were so tired they hadn't the energy to do anything else.

*　*　*　*

Laura had arrived at the hospital to find Fletcher propped up in bed with a bandage on his head. The doctor told her that he would be fine. He'd got a number of superficial head wounds, mild concussion, a badly gashed leg and cuts and bruises everywhere. He needed to rest but was too wound up. After she'd been in they would give him a sleeping pill.

'Hello, Mick,' she said, kissing him on the lips.

He opened his eyes and managed a weak smile. 'What's happened?' he asked.

She shook her head. 'I don't know. People are saying the whole place has burned to the ground. You were lucky to get out. What were you doing in there?'

'Trying to stop . . .' He sighed and frowned. 'I don't really know . . . just something Cassie said to me . . .'

'Cassie? You mean in Todmorden?'

He nodded. His eyes closed. She held his hand. He didn't need the sleeping pill.

* * * *

Chiara di Nerezza watched from a dark corner of her mother's *camera di chiari* – her 'room of light'. Fern Robinson stood in the centre of the room. Slowly, one by one, the mirrors opened. The light hanging from the ceiling seemed to burn brighter and brighter. Each mirror reflected her across to another, so that she was bedazzled by a blinding kaleidoscope of herself. She couldn't even hide her eyes. She became dizzy with the brightness and the room began to sway.

A slim silhouette moved slowly towards her. A hand reached out and stroked her face. Fern shuddered. The voice spoke again.

'This was my mother's special room. Your grandfather made her go away because of your mother's lies. Now you must pay for her jealous treachery. I promise you a slow death – your life slipping away as the smoke and flames envelop you in their suffocating embrace . . .'

The susurration of this soft voice made Fern's eyelids heavy, but a warning hiss came from deep inside. She needed to get out. She forced her eyelids open. The woman's face was close to hers. She was smiling, a hideous grin hanging beneath two engorged, shining eyes. She backed away and spoke again.

'It's been a long time, but now it's over.'

Fern watched as the woman's hands came up in front of her.

She had a gun and she was pointing it at Fern. The moment hung in the multitude of reflected faces. There was a hush as if there was a gap in time. No sound. No movement. Nothing. *Nichts*.

A grating sound came from behind the woman who, startled, turned and fired the gun.

From deep inside Fern the dragon roared. She lashed out at the woman who was only two steps away. She aimed at her face but caught her hard on the shoulder, spinning her thin body away. The older woman tried to keep her feet but instead tumbled face forward into one of the mirrors with such force that the mirror cracked and splintered.

For a couple of seconds there was no sound or movement.

Fern was transfixed as she stared at her own disjointed face reflected in the multiple segments of the glass.

But then there was a gasp of pain . . . Fern stared in horror as the woman pulled away from the mirror to reveal the blood bubbling from the slivers of glass embedded in her face and chest. Her hand dropped to one side and the gun clattered to the floor.

Fern backed away, unable to take her eyes off the blood streaming down the arms of the figure now reflected in the same mirror, who slowly dropped to her knees – a myriad eyes burning with hatred.

A scarlet hand slowly reached out for the gun.

Fern scrambled her way to the door in the mirrors, opened it and tumbled down the stairs. She found herself in a dining room. It was incredibly hot. To one side there was a stove. Its door was open and the fire was roaring in the chimney.

Fern heard another two shots and a huge crash from above. Heavy thuds on the floor followed by the clashing of glass. The mirrors! Clanging like broken bells. The floor above sagged and gave way. A gap appeared and the whole ceiling began to cave in, bringing the chimney with it belching smoke and flames. The beams and floorboards were followed by an enormous kaleidoscope of broken glass, flashing lights and reflected images.

Fern's terrified eyes fixed on the red and black figure flailing and falling towards her, only to be arrested in mid-flight as it was impaled on a giant shard of angular glass.

Two dark eyes glistened for a second in the firelight before the lights were extinguished.

More mirrors came down, showering Fern in a hail of light. She covered her eyes and staggered back against the wall. Her frantic fingers found a door handle. There was a key in the lock. She turned it and found herself on a long corridor. She ran along it, without noticing that all the paintings had disappeared from their frames. She stumbled down the stairs, crossed the great hall and burst into another, bigger dining room. Turning briefly, she thought she saw a bent figure falling forwards as the flames burst into the room – she didn't stop. Beyond was the kitchen, the one she'd seen through the keyhole. She opened the door and ran out into the night.

She headed for the clearing, before remembering that it was no longer her special place. She changed direction and headed for the oak tree. Behind her there was an enormous explosion. She was propelled forward by the blast.

She turned at the sound of the third explosion. The whole house had burst into flames. She could feel the heat on her face. She turned and ran. She didn't stop until she got to her car. The dog licked her neck.

She drove through Rosgill and onto the motorway. She went south, not stopping till dawn. She parked on a promenade and watched the sea. Later, she got out and walked the length of the beach. The dog tried to play but soon realised that wasn't going to happen. He trailed back and forth along the shoreline.

At the end of the beach where the cliffs began, Fern sat on a large stone and stared out to sea. She thought of Anna . . . and cried.

*   *   *   *

It was late the following day before the bomb disposal unit declared the site safe. Chief Inspector Aske had set up investigation rooms in three large caravans near the front gates. The sun had spent the day trying to dry out the mud, but away from the duckboards he'd requisitioned it was still a quagmire.

He was sitting in one of the caravans when the captain in charge of the bomb squad came to see him. Aske wasn't that old himself, but this young man looked like he'd just left school. He introduced himself as Captain Vaizey and asked if he could have a quiet word. Aske nodded to the two other officers in the room and they took their work elsewhere, shutting the door behind them.

Vaizey was looking out of the window at the smouldering ruins. Aske went and stood next to him. The soldier seemed reluctant to talk, but eventually he said, 'Terrible shame.' He had a soft voice with a slight trace of a Highland accent.

Aske frowned and waited.

'Your officers told us that there were two or three explosions. One of them said he was certain they came from the tower.'

Aske knew this. Jenkins had been adamant, even though the tower still stood resolutely squat beside the rest of the demolished building. The captain seemed to be struggling to find the right words.

'From what we can make out, someone had lit a fire in an old stove. Maybe the chimney caught fire. I doubt it had been used since the house was closed up.'

He turned and faced the chief inspector.

'However the fire started, the wooden interior of the tower must have been rotten anyway. The beams would have helped fuel the flames once there was enough heat. But then there was only one way for the flames to escape. One open door caused the through draft and after that . . . the rest of the building was at its mercy.'

He paused for the chief inspector to take this in.

'I understand that the National Trust people say that the rooms in the tower were furnished in a rather unusual way.'

Aske nodded. He'd seen some of the photographs. Again the captain paused, looking the policeman in the eye.

'There's nothing left now. No wood panelling. No mirrors. No floors. Nothing. It's just an empty shell. The tunnels were also scorched and the longer one has collapsed, so we've filled it in – at both ends. It's too dangerous to leave open.'

He waited to see that the policeman had understood.

'We searched what was left of the house. Obviously, there's been an enormous conflagration . . . but again there was no evidence of any explosive device. You'll have to talk to the fire officers to see what they think, but I've already had a chat. They're as baffled as we are. It's as if a fireball swept through the building igniting everything in its path. Once the place was on fire – it was old, lots of wood, furniture and material, it wouldn't have stood a chance.'

Aske stared at him in disbelief. The captain looked back at the tower.

'I know it's hard to believe. I haven't told the National Trust people. No-one else has been inside yet. I'm not sure how they're going to cope with it. Nevertheless there's nothing to see . . . apart from the body.'

'What body?'

The captain frowned. 'I assumed you knew.'

Aske shook his head. This was starting to annoy him. 'What body?' he repeated.

'Barely recognisable. Your forensics team is there now.'

Aske swore under his breath. 'Where did you find her?'

'In the tower underneath what was left of a large mahogany table – otherwise I don't think there'd be anything left of her.'

Aske walked to the door. 'Let's go and see, shall we?'

Five minutes later, Aske was standing looking down at the charred body lying on the cold floor of the tower. Above him the old walls rose to the roof three storeys high. Light streamed in through narrow, windowless gaps. The building had a silent quality about it that was surprisingly peaceful. There were a few smouldering beams, but otherwise the place was gutted. The walls were not local stone but a powdery, white colour.

The hushed tones of the forensic team echoed softly in the space. The pathologist, Jane Sykes, got up from where she was kneeling and came over to them.

'I don't know what you're going to say to the press, Chief Inspector, and as for the coroner's report . . . well . . .?'

'What's your verdict here?'

'Female. Pelvic bones too large for a man. I found a ring on what was once a finger. Might help with identification, but there won't be any fingerprints.'

Aske nodded and she went back to the body. He looked up at the roof high above. He couldn't get his head round what was happening.

Vaizey shuffled his feet and replaced his cap. 'I'll send you my report tomorrow at the latest, Chief Inspector.'

Aske shook his hand and watched him walk briskly away.

A few minutes later he found himself walking towards the outbuilding. On the way, he passed the clearing. It was completely surrounded by metal fencing. His men had dug up and sifted every square millimetre in a radius of about thirty feet. The rain had turned it into a huddle of huge molehills.

He walked round the outside and continued on towards the wall. Here, an army of officers slowly crept and carefully fingered every blade of grass and examined every tree trunk. A few of them nodded in his direction as they saw him arrive.

He walked into the cottage and went to where the trapdoor was propped against the wall and looked down at the rubble-filled hole. He slowly walked back to the caravans.

Standing outside waiting were three of the National Trust team: the director, a tall thin woman and a fat man who looked like a schoolteacher. They eyed him suspiciously as he approached. They'd been told repeatedly that they'd have to wait until he gave them permission to go and look at what was left of the house.

He walked up to them. 'I'm sorry to keep you waiting,' he said. 'Come inside, please.'

As he expected, they didn't believe him. He had to take them and show them. A mortuary van passed them as they reached the end of the drive.

They stood and looked in astonishment at what was left of the building. They looked at each other and at the chief inspector. There were no words to explain or help their incomprehension. In the end, they walked despondently back down the drive, got into Lex's van and drove back to their office.

Later, they went to see Octavia. She wouldn't believe them either. It was only when she was taken to the house two days later that she saw the extent of the damage for herself. Even then it was hard to believe.

She wasn't the only one. It was nearly three days later that they discovered that Sylvia had become suspicious of Rivka. She'd taken the 'Red Pandora' to have it checked. It was a fake.

Sylvia's husband had identified the ring on the remains pulled out of the fire. It turned out that even Guilio had been deceived. The real Rivka Weill had died with her family in a concentration camp.

No-one was able to come up with any convincing explanation for why the bodies hadn't decomposed. Except suddenly the bodies did just that! To add to Jane Sykes's consternation, they all deteriorated to what they should have looked like – in her freezers! Impossible! Two of the women had become unidentifiable. The Dickens character became, as the pathologist had said she ought to be, a pile of dust.

All of Octavia's photographs had faded as well, so that they looked like Victorian sepia prints, which slowly disintegrated whatever they tried to do to preserve them.

*　*　*　*

A week later, Fletcher and Irene were sitting on the floor of the tower with their backs against the white stone wall. The rest of the site had been cleared. Work had started on sifting through the building to see if anything could be recovered which might confirm what the National Trust team said they'd found. All their records had been in the house: the photographs and Octavia's drawings; Lex's meticulous catalogues; Ransome's papers and letters; all of Rivka's paintings, and Sylvia's Italian sculpture . . . all gone as if they'd never existed.

For a few minutes neither of them spoke. The white light shimmering from the walls was restful. They'd had an eventful few days. Both of them had left hospital on the same afternoon. Fletcher still had a bandage on his leg to keep the stitches clean and he'd have a scar over his left eye, the green one. Irene's arm was in a sling. Her wrist was still bruised.

'So . . . where did you find Dekker Wray?' he asked.

'He was at Trisha's – soft cow!' she snorted.

'And you broke his other arm?'

'Uhuh,' she nodded.

'Was this before or after he told you where Len Castle is holed up in Spain?'

She looked at him. 'Afterwards. Of course.'

He sighed. 'You're bad. You remind me of me.'

'Is that a compliment?'

'Absolutely.'

She looked at him and frowned. 'Did you really give Castle Freddie's severed finger?'

Fletcher grinned and looked away. Irene shook her head.

They sat in silence for another few minutes.

'So the woman in the tower. The dead one?' asked Irene.

'Sylvia Urquhart?'

'She's not the one you saw in the mirrors?'

'No. That was the other one.'

'The German woman? Weill?'

'Yes, except now they don't think she was German – or a Jew.'

'What?'

'According to the fat teacher bloke, she was Chiara Di Nerezza, the daughter of the de Blanche chap's second wife, who'd gone back to Italy just before the war. This daughter, Chiara, was born in 1928.'

Irene frowned. She'd always hated history lessons. Her teachers had always been bald blokes with bad breath, who leered at pretty girls like Nancy Potter. 'So this Chiara grew up in Italy and came here after the war.'

'Yes.'

'Changed her name and her story and waited thirty years to get into her mother's house . . . to get the paintings back – even had those numbers tattooed on her arm?'

'Probably. Although Ransome can't prove that.'

Irene laughed. 'It's not going to stop him making a fortune from the book he's writing.'

He nodded.

'And she killed the two policemen and Sylvia?'

'According to the forensic experts, it was the same gun – what was left of it. Small calibre pre-war Beretta.'

'Still no trace of her?'

'No. Disappeared in a puff of smoke!'

Fletcher got to his feet and limped towards the door. 'Come on, let's go and have some lunch. I'm starving.'

Irene reached out with her good arm and he went back and pulled her up.

As they walked back down the drive, Fletcher suddenly doubled back and went towards the clearing. The fence had been removed and the ground had been levelled. In the middle was the large rose bush. Octavia Hutton had persuaded her father to use his influence to get it put back. It was covered in white roses.

Fletcher and Irene stood for a few minutes like people in a graveyard. 'I don't think we'll ever find her either.'

'Rose White? If that's her real name?'

'If we had the manpower I'd keep someone here all the time. I'm sure she'll keep coming back.'

'And she'll keep killing?'

'Probably. The profilers think she has no reason to stop. The sort of women she kills are always out there – if we accept Ransome's theory. Both Caroline Soulby and Eileen Stanhope were classic wicked stepmothers – although I'm more inclined to think that the killing of the dog is a more rational motive. The other two still haven't been identified. They just needed to be unlucky enough to put themselves in her sights. She might have to change where and how she kills and buries them, but the motive will still be there.'

'What about the Dickens character?'

'Well – according to Ransome – she was probably the Duke's daughter, Rose-Marie.'

Irene frowned. 'And so our "Rose White" is carrying out some sort of belated revenge?'

Fletcher shook his head. 'It's only a theory . . . a fairytale . . . I'm just glad there weren't any dwarves . . .'

Irene looked to see if he was smiling. He wasn't.

They made their way back down to the main gates. Fletcher took one glance back as he opened the car door. For a second he thought he saw a face at one of the windows. Impossible. There was no floor. He squinted in the sun.

Just an empty black rectangle in the glimmering white stone.

* * * *

Fern watched the two detectives walk back to the car. When they'd gone, she went to stand in the clearing. She didn't know why they'd put the rose bush back. She stood for a while in the sunshine. They'd cut down a lot of the trees in their search for evidence, so it could hardly be called a clearing now.

Back near the ruins of the house her grandmother's roses were stubbornly resurrecting themselves again, their white blooms dotting the green foliage. Soon there would be nothing but roses. A sea of white. The notice at the main gate declared that the grounds would be left to return to nature. There was no reference to the history of the family or the terrible events that had occurred. She knew what they'd called her – 'The Snow White Killer'.

They'd found out who two of the victims were and made some connections. Ransome had guessed who the young woman under the first rose bush must have been. He was wrong. He thought it was her mother, Rose-Marie, who'd been murdered and so it hadn't occurred to him that she could have had a daughter.

She thought sadly about how Fern Rigg's story would never be told. How she'd given her life to save her friend. Only Fern Robinson could honour her memory.

She plucked a rose from the bush and put it in her rucksack. Without another glance, she set off through the wood to the hidden gateway, already overgrown and without a gate. An hour later she was sitting on Castle Crag looking towards the drowned village with the dog panting at her side. It was a fine day for her customary walk.

She looked up at the fells. She would take the rose to her mother's grave. She thought back to that first night, when they'd gone to the clearing and she'd heard her mother's story.

High above her an eagle croaked. She stood up and began to climb. The dog raced ahead.

She'd called him Rigg.

IN MEMORY OF FERN RIGG

This was the story my mother, Rose-Marie de Blanche, who was known since she was sixteen as Ursula Robinson, told me on my sixteenth birthday – February 29th 1952.

The second time I came to Blanchard House was my sixteenth birthday, February 29th 1912. I'd been born here, but my mother died soon afterwards and my father took us away. I spent my childhood in the chateaux and palazzos of France and Italy. My father was often absent. He tried to explain it once. He said he was a diplomat. It didn't sound very exciting to me. People talking all the time and it didn't seem to stop any fighting.

But then he met my stepmother, Eleonora di Nerezza. At first I liked her. She was beautiful and funny and full of life. We went to balls and parties all the time. It was like living in a whirlwind. The wedding lasted for days, but my father spoilt it all by bringing us back here. I don't know why he did it, but it was a disaster.

Fern Rigg, the only friend I had in the end, told me how it all began. The day had come: February 29th 1912. The servants were in a heady state of excited anticipation. We were due to arrive in time for lunch. We'd come by train all the way from York to Penrith and Mr Cartwright had been sent to fetch us in the carriage.

There'd been a final panic earlier in the morning when Fern, one of the kitchen girls, had dropped a tray of glasses in the entrance hall. Annie Robinson, the housekeeper, had scolded her angrily and told her the cost would be deducted from her wages. No-one had the slightest idea how many weeks or months that might take. But just as Fern and a couple of the other girls were clearing up the glass, Annie's hand went to her mouth. She was looking up at the large painting of my father's first wife, Ursula.

Fern often stopped to admire it. She was the most beautiful woman she had ever seen. Although she had similar long auburn hair, she knew in comparison her own face was plain. She stopped her brushing to see what Mrs Robinson was cross about now. She was both astonished and upset by what she told them to do.

'We've got to take it down. Immediately!' cried the housekeeper.

It took four of the footmen to get it off the wall and take it up to my father's room, where it was re-hung. Fern was in tears. She'd never see it again. But all this did was get her into more trouble. Even though it was also her birthday that day; sixteen and only the fourth real birthday she'd ever had.

At exactly midday, our coach pulled up outside the main entrance and the servants stood two-deep in lines down the steps and along the walls at either side. Mr Colden, the butler, approached the carriage and opened the door.

My father, who was still a tall and elegant man, leaned out of the door and stepped down onto the carefully raked gravel. He was forty years old, but looked older. His dark hair was already going grey. He stood looking up at the building, which he'd not seen for fifteen years. He turned and held out his hand for me.

Fern gasped as I stepped out of the carriage. I was the image of my mother; my red-gold hair was hanging loose over a dazzling white dress. I took a few steps beyond my father and looked at the house with a serious, but curious face. I'd no memory of my mother but knew that this was where we were briefly together. I saw that it was as magnificent as my father had always said it was.

I looked at the servants. It was the first time I set eyes on Fern Rigg, who looked older than me but had the same colour hair, tied up under her white cap. I gave her a faint smile. But then everyone heard my stepmother's sharp, strongly accented voice.

'Is anyone going to help me from this spine-breaking excuse for a carriage?'

My father turned and offered his hand into the darkness of the interior. The servants held their breath. A high-laced black boot encasing the slimmest of ankles was placed on the carriage step. A whiter hand than his appeared. He grasped it and she stepped out onto the gravel. She adjusted her hat, before standing to her full height. She was tall. Black, luminescent curls tumbled around her dark face. Her crimson dress accentuated the slimness of her waist and the swell of her breasts.

She looked around and flapped away an impudent fly. She lifted her face to let everyone see her beauty. Few of them could hold her gaze except for Fern, who continued to stare at her. My stepmother gave her the haughtiest of looks.

As she raked the line-up with a final arrogant glare, everyone saw her catch the eye of Thomas Skirgill. She gave him the gift of her smile. She whispered a curt question to Colden. He glanced at Fern and replied. She made her sinuous way up the steps and into the great hall. Without hesitation she went up to the first floor and along the long corridor to see that her precise instructions had been obeyed.

And so it began.

Fern was the first to feel the woman's hatred. She was told to report to her private chambers in the old tower. The Duchessa had her own maid, a terrified mouse of a woman called Franca, who couldn't speak any English and who was always covered in bruises, black eyes and burns on her arms and hands.

No matter what Fern did, it was wrong. The Duchessa hit her, threw things at her — vases, cups, books — anything she had to hand. But worst of all, she insisted that at first she hid her hair under a ridiculous hat and then had it cut off. She said she'd seen lice crawling in Fern's hair and insisted her head must be shaved.

But it got worse. She argued with other servants and had many of them dismissed. My father did little to stop her. He could refuse her nothing and, in any case, he was away for weeks on end. They were all at her mercy. The only person who stood up to her was Annie Robinson, but even she was dismissed in the end.

It was the roses. At first the Duchessa didn't pay much attention to the gardens. She said it was too cold for her to go outside but, as summer came and the roses blossomed, she discovered that they were her predecessor's pride and joy. The gardeners who had tended Ursula De Blanche's gardens had been re-employed and worked hard to re-create the wondrous landscape she had designed. But Eleonora decided she could not abide them. She said they were ugly and scratched her delicate skin. So whilst my father was away, she ordered the roses to be destroyed, dug up and burnt. The gardeners protested. She dismissed them all. Annie went to try and reason with her but returned downstairs with a deep cut across her cheek. She gathered her belongings and walked out.

It ended one dark night in February 1914.

I had waited in vain for the rain to stop. The house had resentfully settled under a malignant sky, huddling its bulk into the mass of trees. The lights had been on since midday, making the gloom less solid. People and furniture were indistinct outlines emerging from soft yellow walls.

Dinner was conducted as if we were on deck in a foggy sea. Servants moved like sailors in a dream. The main course was fish. I didn't eat it. My father gave me a sad look. I looked away, but not towards the other end of the table. Eleonora would be watching me. I knew without having to look. My father stood, bowed towards my stepmother and was gone.

I stared at my white plate. I heard the rustling of material, felt the air crackle and caught the scent of almonds as the silken figure crossed behind me. No fingers catching in my hair. No whispered taunt.

Later I crept down the stairs. Each one had its own creak. Annie had told me it was the trees calling to their children in the woods outside. Through the kitchen, turn the old key and pull back the heavy bolts. The wet air wrapped itself around me in an eager embrace. The trees reared up before me, but the sodden leaves did not betray me. The tower's window lit my way.

The outer wall was more than a mile away. My coat grew heavy. I could feel the dampness creeping into my dress. The light faded and the darkness pressed around me. I felt the rough bark of a nearby fir. Four steps and I found another. Raindrops dropped from the dense canopy above me. I could feel the pine needles pricking my ankles. I swam from tree to tree, deeper into the dripping forest.

Suddenly there was a familiar but unexpected smell. A scratch of sulphur. A lantern blossomed. I tripped and the light was split in two by the trunk of a tree. I clawed my way up its trunk and crushed myself into its crinkled bark. I couldn't breathe. The light grew brighter, swaying back and forth, nearer and nearer.

A voice called my name. It was Thomas. The pieces fell into place. Every gesture and glance became clear. His smiles were lies. I edged my face towards the light. Through the fronds of a branch I could see him — the lamp held high in his left hand, the gun in his right. He was going to kill me.

From behind him came another creature, hurtling out of the trees. It knocked him down. The light was thrown to one side. The two creatures struggled and the gun exploded. They were still. Thomas pushed the dead weight from his chest and struggled to his feet, staring at the body. His hand went to his face. An inhuman moan escaped his lips. I saw. It was Fern Rigg. I understood.

The lantern spluttered and died. I slipped away into the comfort of the night.

I was lost high on the fells when Isaac Harper found me the next morning. It was one of those soul-destroying days when the whole land from valley bottom to fell top was smothered in cold, wet mist which clung to your clothes and skin. You couldn't see further than your next step. No sense of direction or up or down. Only someone like Isaac, who'd spent his life on the fells hunting for lost sheep and lambs, could possibly know where he was. He found me cold and swooning by the side of one of the many little streams which were full this time of year. I was so light he was able to put me over his shoulder and carry me down to the village. His wife had died three years ago, so he took me to the Robinsons.

My father instigated a huge search, involving the local constabulary and all his employees and tenants. They searched for weeks. Eventually they came to Mardale. They insisted on looking in everyone's house – even in the church. The last house nearest the lake belonged to the Robinsons. Annie Robinson had returned to her village after she'd been dismissed.

I begged her not to let them find me. Now she stood with arms crossed outside her door whilst the constables searched her house. Beside her stood her children, including a 'boy' with a cap pulled well down over his face. I looked at the ground. One of the constables snatched off my cap. My head was shaven. No sign of my red-golden locks.

'Head lice,' barked Annie Robinson.

The constable kicked away the cap and walked back to his sergeant. They left the village and continued their search.

As spring turned to summer, my father gave up the search. No-one saw the Duchessa leave but a few weeks later he dismissed all the servants, locked up the house and the gates and rode off to war. He never returned.

I never forgave myself for the heartache I caused him – but I couldn't go back while she was there. She would have killed me.

Instead I became a Robinson, with my mother's first name, running wild on the fells with the fierce black horses. I had a daughter and I called her Fern – in memory of my friend.

And every year on this day I come to prune the rose bush which marks my friend's grave.

Fern Rigg was buried where she was found by the gardeners — too afraid to tell a soul. They planted one rose. My mother's favourite.

Boule de Neige.

About the Author

Rick Lee was born in North Yorkshire in 1948, went to study History in London in the late 60's, but spent most of his time going to Jimi Hendrix and Cream concerts, whilst squatting in a series of elegant but condemned Edwardian mansions.

He became a drama teacher in 1974 and later studied for a MEd in Education through Drama with Dorothy Heathcote. He worked in a variety of secondary schools, colleges, special needs departments and residential homes - including a 4 year spell as Senior Advisory Teacher with Leicestershire LEA – after which he returned up north to be a Head of an Expressive Arts Department in Barrow-in-Furness, followed by 5 years working for the Barrow Educational Action Zone and as an education consultant. As well as classroom drama, he was also writing and directing plays with students including several successful Edinburgh Fringe productions.

He has an MA in Writing Studies from Lancaster University and written many short stories and has already published two volumes of poems. His involvement in outdoor education, taking city kids into the wilds of Snowdonia, the Lake District and the mountains and islands of Scotland, have provided the backdrop for his London cop's adventures.

He moved to France in 2006 to enjoy retirement – although serious bouts of DIY and gardening have kept him busy!

He began writing the Mick Fletcher suspense thrillers two years ago and has not been able to stop since!

Lightning Source UK Ltd.
Milton Keynes UK
UKOW031355120412

190576UK00001B/16/P